"This thrilling [Kay H...

—*Library Journal*

"Well paced. . . . [Kay] . . . keeps the plot whizzing along. . . . [She's] gutsy." —*Publishers Weekly*

Rosarito Beach

"If you haven't read M. A. Lawson, start right now with *Rosarito Beach*! I loved this riveting thriller, which launches a new star in crime fiction, the tough-minded and tough-talking DEA agent Kay Hamilton."

—*New York Times* bestselling author Lisa Scottoline

"*Rosarito Beach* grabs you by the throat ten seconds after you've settled into your easy chair for a read. The writing's lyrical, the plot is breathtaking, and the characters, the good ones and bad, are utterly compelling and, most important, thoroughly believable. And then there's Agent Hamilton. I fell for her on the first page." —*New York Times* bestselling author Jeffery Deaver

"I love tough guys, even when they're gals, and Glock-toting, fast-thinking, wisecracking DEA agent Kay Hamilton is one of the toughest going."

—*New York Times* bestselling author Stephen Hunter

"M. A. Lawson hits his stride in a big way with *Rosarito Beach*, featuring the impressive debut of DEA agent Kay Hamilton. . . . This is T. Jefferson Parker's brilliant Charlie Hood series on steroids with just enough Elmore Leonard thrown in for good measure. Flat-out great." —*The Providence Journal*

continued . . .

"[Lawson] brings his considerable talents to bear in *Rosarito Beach*, a novel that goes beyond edgy to explosive and introduces a character whose future exploits promise further excitement."
—*Richmond Times-Dispatch*

"It's no surprise if this new series hooks you. . . . Kay impresses both by her recognition of the reality of her job and her courage in trying anyway. . . . [Lawson's] trademark caustic humor and dialogue zing on almost every page."
—*The Cleveland Plain Dealer*

"A highly promising debut."
—*The Seattle Times*

"[A] great start to a promising new series, with a gripping story line and a gutsy, likable heroine. Readers who enjoy fast-paced thrillers and detective novels with a female protagonist who's fully developed, vulnerable, and intriguing will gobble this one up and ask for more."
—*Library Journal* (starred review)

"An intense, action-packed, edge-of-the-seat thriller. Lawson turns a sharp and penetrating eye on the front lines of the war on drugs. Kay Hamilton is an original, provocative protagonist with great panache. Kudos to this innovative, thoroughly enjoyable launch of what promises to be a grand new series."
—Open Letters Monthly

"With this new character and proposed series, [Lawson] shows his breadth of talent. I will read anything he writes—his prose is so smooth, his plotting so engaging, and his pacing so near perfect."
—*Deadly Pleasures*

OTHER BOOKS BY M. A. LAWSON

Rosarito Beach

(WRITING AS MIKE LAWSON)

The Inside Ring
The Second Perimeter
House Rules
House Secrets
House Justice
House Divided
House Blood
House Odds
House Reckoning

VIKING
BAY

A Kay Hamilton Novel

M. A. LAWSON

A SIGNET BOOK

SIGNET
Published by New American Library,
an imprint of Penguin Random House LLC
375 Hudson Street, New York, New York 10014

This book is a publication of New American Library. Previously published in a Blue Rider Press edition.

First Signet Printing, November 2015

For more information about Penguin Random House, visit penguin.com.

ISBN 978-0-451-47254-0

Printed in the United States of America
10 9 8 7 6 5 4 3 2 1

Penguin
Random
House

For the Sheppard sisters: Gail, Linda, and Joanne—but especially Arlyn, who once sent me an e-mail that said, "When will I get a book dedicated to MEEEE???" So here it is, Arlyn.

PROLOGUE

It began with a text message.

Alpha texted Bravo and the burner phone in Bravo's pocket vibrated. Bravo looked at the message: TRANSFER COMPLETE.

Bravo punched numbers into the same phone, calling Charlie. He let the receiving phone ring twice, then disconnected the call. No words were necessary.

The man designated as Charlie removed his phone from a leg pocket in his cargo pants, punched in five digits, and hit CALL—and a transformer at a substation half a kilometer away disintegrated, sending bolts of white light a hundred feet into the sky. Witnesses later said that lightning—on a clear, cloudless night—had struck the transformer.

Delta didn't need a text message or a call to tell him to perform his task: the power going out in the compound *was* his signal. He put on night-vision goggles and slipped into the house. He caught the old man just as he was coming out of his bedroom to investigate the power outage, and Delta slit his throat as if the old man were a newborn lamb. He dragged the body into a closet and left the house.

Delta called Bravo's phone and it vibrated twice. Again no words were needed to tell Bravo that Delta had completed his mission.

Bravo didn't use the burner phone for his next call. He used his personal phone, because it didn't matter if his next call could be traced. He dialed a number and spoke for less than ten seconds. Then he counted slowly to sixty—sixty seconds should be plenty of time. If he was wrong, a man Bravo needed to live was going to die. At the count of sixty, he reached into his pocket and, without looking, punched the # key five times.

The package erupted inside the house. Stainless-steel ball bearings and roofing nails spread outward faster than the speed of sound, and an odorless flammable gel inside the package ignited. The people in the room, some sitting no more than two feet from the bomb, were ripped asunder in an instant. Their flesh was burning seconds after that.

Bravo was confident that no one had survived; nothing made of flesh and bone could have survived.

Bravo was wrong.

PART I

1

"We need a woman," Callahan said.

As always, Callahan looked like an unmade bed: hair sticking up in tufts like small whitecaps on a gray ocean, a wrinkled blue suit, an unpressed white shirt. His ash-stained tie hung at half-mast, and his battered black loafers hadn't seen polish since the day he bought them. He was also one of the unhealthiest-looking individuals that Anna Mercer had ever known: overweight, pale because he rarely ventured out into the sun, bloodshot eyes from the booze he'd consumed the night before. He had high blood pressure, high cholesterol, was probably diabetic, and should have been on a transplant list for a new liver. He was the only person Mercer knew with an IQ of more than 140 who still smoked; she doubted that he'd last much beyond sixty-five, and he was sixty now.

She couldn't believe they'd once been lovers.

"She needs to be close to Ara's age," Callahan said, "and she can't come across as a corporate lackey. We need someone like what's-her-name, Ara's roommate at NYU."

"Carolyn Harris," Mercer said.

"Yeah, Harris. She needs to be like Harris. Aggressive, funny, physical. Sexually, ah . . ."

"Loose?" Mercer said.

"I was thinking *adventurous*, not loose. Ara wouldn't find a slut attractive. And blond. Blond would be good. Harris was blond. I want her to make a subconscious connection."

"I guess I could dye my hair," Mercer said, primping her short, dark hair.

"Nah, you're way too old."

"Well, screw you, Thomas. That was a mean thing to say. I'm only forty-five. And I was joking."

"Yeah, sorry. But she needs to be younger than you. Closer to thirty."

He wasn't sorry; he was tactless.

What had attracted her to Callahan in the first place was his mind; he hadn't really looked all that much different fifteen years ago when they'd been lovers. His cynicism, his quickness, his insights, his wit—and the fact that he'd been going places and could take her with him—was what had made him attractive. The funny thing was, other women had always found him attractive, too. He'd been married four times, wife number four dropped abruptly by the wayside a few years ago. Mercer couldn't remember whether he'd been married to wife two or three at the time they were sleeping together.

"If Harris was available, I'd actually try to recruit her," Callahan said. "But since she's not, we need someone like her, somebody Ara will instantly relate to."

As Carolyn Harris had died in a car accident a year before, Mercer saw no point in reminding Callahan that Harris had been a protest-marching liberal who would never have gone along with Callahan's plan.

"So, you got anybody in mind?" Callahan asked. "We need to get moving on this. Ara will be in New York in less than a month."

The original plan had not been to approach Ara Khan in New York, but when Callahan found out she was coming to the United States he decided to change the plan.

"Actually, I do," Mercer said. "And I suspect you know who it is and you've already decided she's the one, even though she hasn't completed her training. Why are we even having this conversation?"

"Maybe I just enjoy your company," Callahan said.

He was such a bullshitter—but it was almost impossible not to like him.

2

Bowman struck faster than a rattlesnake and his right hand darted out and grabbed Kay's sweatshirt, his big hand clutching the material between her breasts. As he jerked her off balance, she slashed downward with her right hand to break his grip, but all that did was hurt her hand; hitting Bowman's forearm was like hitting a baseball bat.

Bowman quickly shifted his grip and started to turn to his left, the move a precursor to his tossing her over his shoulder—again—and as she began to counter the move, she realized, too late, the move was a feint. Bowman's right leg snaked behind her left calf and he simply smacked his hand into her chest, knocking her down, and then he belly-flopped onto her, knocking the wind out of her. His forearm—the baseball bat—slammed across her throat and started to crush her larynx.

"Stop!" Simmons said.

Simmons was a tough little nut in his fifties, about five foot six, built like a pint-sized version of Superman. He was an ex–Marine master sergeant and in charge of the hand-to-hand combat course. For some reason, he'd matched Kay up with Bowman, who was six foot four—eight inches taller than she was—and weighed two hundred thirty pounds, almost exactly a hundred pounds more than she did. On top of that, Kay sensed that Bowman liked to knock women around—his way of demonstrating that they shouldn't be on the same playing field with the boys—and he was just beating the shit out of her. She already had a mouse developing under her left eye when he "accidentally" hit her with his elbow, and she knew tomorrow there would be a bruise the size of Bowman's big paw in the center of her chest.

"Hamilton," Simmons said, "how many times do I have to tell you? You can't let him get ahold of you first. You gotta be quicker than him."

Kay just shook her head; she didn't bother to say that she wasn't *intentionally* letting Bowman maul her.

"Okay, let's try it again. This time, Hamilton, circle to his left. He's right-handed. And when he reaches for you—"

"Yeah, I got it," Kay said, but she was thinking that this whole thing was total bullshit. It was only in movies that women beat up men who outweighed them by a hundred pounds. For that matter, that was why they had weight divisions in boxing, because, in general, big guys beat little guys. If a monster like Bowman had attacked her on the street—out in the real world—she would have pulled out a gun and shot him or hit him with anything that would dent his thick skull. Or she'd kick him in the nuts—a move not permitted in this particular course.

Bowman came toward her again, and Kay circled to his left as Simmons had told her. Then, when Bowman's back was to Simmons so Simmons couldn't see his face, Bowman made a smooching gesture with his lips.

And Kay kicked him in the nuts. As hard as she could.

Bowman fell to the mat, grasping his crotch, and Simmons started screaming at her. Well, fuck them both.

"Are you okay, Bowman?" Simmons asked.

"I think she crushed my testicle," Bowman said. At least that's what Kay thought he said. It was hard to understand him with his teeth all clenched.

Simmons turned to one of the other students—there were only four people in the class, and Kay was the only woman—and said, "Connors, go get the medic. And Hamilton, you get your ass to my office and wait for me there."

Simmons's office, just down the hall from the gymnasium, looked like a high school coach's office, and not a coach who taught at one of the better schools. There was a battered metal desk, a wooden chair behind the desk that swiveled and could be tilted back, and a couple of straight-backed chairs in front of the desk. On the walls were charts showing photos of men in various judo and karate positions. In one corner was a set of weights for doing curls, which explained Simmons's hard little arms. Kay shut the door and noticed a small mirror on the back of the door.

She looked into the mirror and touched the blooming mouse under her eye. It wasn't too bad and could be covered with makeup. She was lucky her eye wasn't swollen shut. She was also lucky Bowman hadn't broken her nose. She'd had her nose broken once before and it had really hurt.

She didn't know what she was going to say to Simmons. She knew he was going to chew her out, but she also knew that's all he was going to do. They weren't going to fire her for kicking Bowman; she was more valuable than Bowman to the Group.

Bowman was muscle, pure and simple. He was good with his fists, okay with a pistol—although he wasn't any better than Kay with a pistol—but he was exceptional with a rifle. She wondered if Callahan was grooming Bowman to be his designated sniper. Bowman, however, didn't have her language skills; in fact, he had an accent like the guys who hawked the beer at Fenway and was barely understandable in English. Kay could speak Spanish like a native, and in a few months would be passable in Farsi. Bowman was also slow when it came to the technical stuff—alarms, computers, listening devices, GPS systems—anything with a microchip—and Kay outscored him in those classes.

The door opened and Simmons stepped into the room

and slammed the door shut behind him. "Hamilton," he said, "I don't know what I'm gonna do with you."

Kay almost smiled. She remembered her last boss saying the same thing to her—right before she was fired.

Three and a half months earlier, Kay had been an agent with the Drug Enforcement Administration. She'd enjoyed the work and had been a good agent; she made a name for herself in Miami after she killed a major player there named Marco Alvarez and three of his men. Marco was the one who broke her nose when he tried to beat her to death after he found out she was an undercover cop who'd penetrated his organization.

After Miami, she was transferred to San Diego, placed in a vacant supervisor's spot, and put in charge of her own team—and she immediately set her sights on the brother of Caesar Olivera. Caesar was the leader of the most powerful drug cartel in Mexico, and his little brother, a moron named Tito, ran his North American operations. Kay eventually arrested Tito for murdering another San Diego drug dealer—a murder she could have prevented had she chosen to. Unfortunately, it didn't end there.

Caesar Olivera kidnapped Kay's daughter, Jessica, and forced Kay to break his brother out of jail in return for her daughter. By the time it was all over, Tito Olivera died in a car accident, Kay killed Caesar Olivera and one of his top guys down in Mexico, and a colonel in the Policía Federal died assisting her. Then the United States Coast Guard virtually committed an act of war by sailing into Mexican territorial waters and killing more of Caesar's people to help Kay and Jessica escape.

Kay could have been prosecuted for breaking Tito Olivera out of jail, but the DEA wanted to keep what she had done in Mexico under wraps as much as possible and didn't want the publicity that would accompany a trial. On the other hand, the DEA at that point didn't want Kay Hamilton anymore, either.

Kay had made the mistake of not informing anyone in her chain of command that Caesar had kidnapped her daughter, and she didn't get permission to go into Mexico on her own to save her. She'd already had a reputation for being insubordinate and playing loose with the rules before she killed Caesar, and killing Caesar the way she did was the last straw: The DEA fired her.

Ironically, the person who fired her was the best friend she had in the DEA, a woman named Barb Reynolds, who was a deputy director back in D.C. and who had been Kay's mentor. After Barb fired her, she took Kay out for a drink. While Kay was sulking, wondering what she was going to do for a living and how she was going to support her daughter, Barb told her that she might be able to get Kay into a certain organization in Washington who valued her talents.

"Do they know what I did in Mexico?" Kay had asked, and Barb had responded by smiling and saying,

"As far as this particular organization is concerned, Mexico was your job interview. Believe me, they want you."

When Kay had asked if the unnamed organization was the CIA, Barb had said, "Not exactly."

Not exactly turned out to be one hell of an understatement.

Simmons chewed her out as expected, essentially giving her a lecture on fair play and sportsmanship as if she and Bowman were a couple of five-year-olds on a T-ball team. Kay pretended to be contrite and Simmons pretended to believe her. After Simmons finished, Kay showered and had just exited the gym when her phone rang. It was Anna Mercer, Callahan's deputy.

"Drop whatever you're doing and come to my office," Mercer said.

"I'm down at the gym in Alexandria," Kay said. "I just finished with that stupid hand-to-hand combat course you're making me take."

"Yeah, well, drive fast."

3

A week after she was fired from the DEA, Kay received a phone call.

"Kay, my name is Anna Mercer," the caller said. "Barb Reynolds suggested we hire you, so we need to meet and talk." Before Kay could ask who *we* was, Mercer said, "I'll be flying in from D.C. tomorrow. Meet me in the bar at the Sheraton on Harbor Island at four p.m." Kay didn't like Mercer's dictatorial style, but as her employment prospects weren't all that promising, she agreed.

Kay arrived at the Sheraton promptly at four, dressed casually in form-fitting white slacks, a yellow tank top, and sandals. It was June, eighty-five degrees outside, and she hadn't felt like putting on anything more formal. She looked into the bar and saw only one person there, a woman sitting alone at a table with a view of San Diego Bay. The woman raised her hand when she saw Kay; she obviously knew what Kay looked like, even though they'd never met.

Mercer was in her forties, pretty and trim. She had short dark hair and smart brown eyes. She was also dressed very well for a person Kay assumed was a civil servant. Kay didn't know the brand name of Mercer's white linen suit, but she was pretty sure she couldn't afford it. She did know the brand of Mercer's shoes—she was a bit of a shoe freak—and she definitely couldn't afford them.

A waitress arrived as soon as Kay took a seat across from Mercer and asked if Kay wanted a drink. Mercer was drinking what appeared to be a Manhattan, the maraschino cherry bobbing in the whiskey.

Kay wondered if it would be appropriate to drink at what was essentially a job interview and decided: Why not? It wasn't too early in the day for a cocktail. Plus they wanted her badly enough to fly someone out from Washington to meet with her. "I'll have a Stoli martini with a twist," she told the waitress.

While waiting for her drink to arrive, Kay made an attempt at small talk, asking if Mercer had been to San Diego before—she had—and if she'd had a pleasant flight—"The usual hassle" was Mercer's response. Mercer made no attempt to be friendly or put her at ease, and Kay was glad when her drink was served so they could get down to business.

"So. You have a job for me," Kay said.

"Maybe," Mercer said. "There are a few things that need to be done before we finalize anything."

"Like what?"

"We need to complete background checks on you equivalent to those required for a top secret security clearance."

Kay knew that for a top secret clearance, the government looked at an individual's work history, tax returns, financial solvency, and travel abroad. They looked at every document they could get their grubby little hands on. Federal agents also interviewed people who knew the person and tried to get them to spill dirty secrets; they talked to past employers, neighbors, and ex-spouses. What Kay didn't understand was what Mercer meant when she said the background checks would be *equivalent* to those required for a top secret clearance. It was either a top secret clearance or it wasn't.

"Then a doctor here in San Diego will give you a very thorough physical."

"I had a physical just a year ago. There's nothing wrong with me," Kay said.

"Things can change in a year," Mercer said. "I should know. And we can't afford to waste a lot of money training you and find out later that you have some incurable disease."

Now, that was cold.

"Following the physical, you'll fly out to D.C. and meet with a psychiatrist we use."

"You think I might be nuts?" Kay said. She smiled when she said this, but she was actually offended that her prospective employer questioned her mental health.

"No, we don't think you're nuts exactly, but the type of people we employ tend to have issues—we probably wouldn't hire them if they didn't—and we consider an in-depth psychological profile a prudent precaution."

"I don't have any *issues*," Kay said, no longer smiling.

"Sure you do. You have authority issues. Control issues. Trust issues. You're conflicted about your daughter. You like sex, but you appear to have no desire to have a normal relationship, get married, and have more kids."

Kay wondered whom Mercer had talked to and started to protest, but Mercer held up a hand, silencing her. "Hey, we're okay with all those things. But we need to make sure you don't have some deep-seated psychosis or phobia that we're not aware of, the type that could affect your work. By the way, you may be hypnotized as part of the evaluation. Do you have a problem with that?"

"Yeah, maybe," Kay said. "It all depends on the job I'll be doing and my pay grade." Although Kay didn't have any big secrets she was hiding, she didn't like the idea of someone hypnotizing her and probing into the dark corners of her mind. But what she really didn't like was Mercer's attitude, acting as if Kay was so desperate that she'd do anything to land a job.

As if Kay hadn't spoken, Mercer said, "In addition to the psych eval and the physical, you'll also be polygraphed. That's just to make sure we haven't missed something in our background checks. The flutter testing is nothing to get alarmed about unless you're a Chinese spy."

The polygraph testing didn't bother Kay or surprise her; top secret government programs often included periodic lie-detector tests.

"So what agency will I be working for?" Kay asked.

"You won't be working for an agency. You won't be employed by the federal government."

"Whoa!" Kay said. She'd assumed that she'd be working for the feds based on what her friend, Barb Reynolds, had said—or implied—and working for the feds was important for two mundane reasons: The government had a good health insurance program—which mattered now that her daughter was living with her—and a good retirement program in which she already had ten years invested.

"You were a GS-13, weren't you, when you worked for the DEA?" Mercer said.

"Yeah. Well, a temporary 13. They fired me before they made me permanent."

"Your starting salary will be twice as much as a GS-13 makes."

"Really?" Kay said. That was good news.

"Yes. We know the cost of living in the D.C. area is high and that you'll have to pay full price for health insurance for yourself and your daughter. But the main reason we're willing to pay so much is because of the risks you may be asked to take."

"Like what?"

Mercer shook her head. "Sorry. Before I can tell you more you need to complete the physical, meet with the psychiatrist, and get polygraphed. Then you'll be required to sign a nondisclosure agreement that legally prevents you from ever discussing your employer and what you did for him. A really smart lawyer prepared the nondisclosure agreement, and if you violate it, we'll sue you and ruin you financially and maybe even throw you in jail. Or maybe we'll just kill you in the interest of national security."

Mercer smiled slightly when she spoke of killing Kay, like that old joke you always hear in the movies where the CIA agent says: *I'd tell you, but then I'd have to kill you.* At least Kay assumed it was a joke. She also wondered what her job had to do with national security if she wouldn't be working for the government.

"Look," Kay said. "I can't agree to any of this without having a better understanding of what I'll be doing."

"Why not?" Mercer said. "Your last employer fired you and isn't about to give you a good recommendation, so the likelihood of you getting a decent job in law enforcement is almost zero. We, on the other hand, are impressed by what you did in both Miami and San Diego, including your little adventure down in Mexico with the Olivera cartel. We're offering you a job at twice your previous salary doing things that are compatible with your prior experience. What have you got to lose?"

Before Kay could say anything, Mercer opened her purse and pulled out a cashier's check. She noticed that Mercer's purse, like her suit and shoes, was top-of-the-line—leather softer than a baby's bottom—and she had the unwanted image of a newborn calf being sacrificed to become a handbag. Mercer handed her the check and said, "That's to compensate you for your time while you're completing the physical and the psych eval."

The check was for ten thousand dollars. Wow. Like Mercer had said: What did she have to lose?

She later found out that the answer to that question was: her life.

The next two weeks passed quickly as Kay was cracked open like a clamshell and rudely poked at both mentally and physically.

She had no problems with the physical. She was, in fact, surprised that she didn't have high cholesterol or high blood sugar or some other biological indicator that she should change her eating habits. She really paid no attention to her diet and when her daughter wasn't around, tended to feed primarily off junk foods. The only reason she still wore a size 6 dress was that she exercised fanatically.

Her relationship with her daughter turned out to be the thing that most interested the psychiatrist—and Kay hadn't expected that. She thought the shrink would be more concerned about affairs she'd had with a couple of married men and with Marco Alvarez, the drug lord she'd killed in Miami. She'd slept with Marco for almost a year to build a case against him, and she'd expected the doctor to explore the moral issues associated with her using sex to put a man behind bars. But he didn't, and actually passed over that phase of her life rather quickly.

What the psychiatrist was most curious about was how she and her daughter got along, if she felt guilty about her, if she resented her, if she understood her own feelings for the girl. Why the shrink cared about all this shit, Kay didn't have a clue; she didn't see how her feelings toward her daughter had anything to do with her job. In the end, the doc must have concluded that she wasn't a total psycho—or a completely unfit mother—and gave her a clean bill of health.

Anna Mercer called Kay two days later and asked how soon she could move to D.C.

"I don't know," Kay said. "I have to sell my house in San Diego and . . ."

"We'll take care of selling your house and moving your furniture."

"And I'll need to find a place in D.C."

"We have a real estate agent here that will do that for you. Just give her a price range and she'll find something that will make you happy."

"But the big thing," Kay said, "is I have to find a good school for my daughter, and I know that's going to be a hassle."

Kay had had a hard time getting Jessica into a decent private school in San Diego until she strong-armed a snooty Catholic school principal. She told the principal that if she didn't enroll Jessica, DEA Agent Kay Hamilton was going to make her overpriced parochial school the new front line in the war on drugs. Kay said this knowing that half the brats who went there snorted, swallowed, or smoked some banned substance. After that, the principal had had a change of heart.

"Pick any school you want in the D.C. area," Mercer said. "We'll make sure your daughter is accepted."

"You can actually do that?" Kay said.

"Yes."

Now, *that* impressed Kay.

"Be at this address next Wednesday at one p.m.," Mercer said, and rattled off a number on K Street. "You'll sign the nondisclosure agreement at that time, and then I'll introduce you to Callahan."

"Who's Callahan?" Kay asked.

Mercer hung up.

4

The following Wednesday, Kay entered a twelve-story office building on K Street and proceeded to room 711. On the wall outside the door was a small brass plaque that read THE CALLAHAN GROUP. Higher up on the wall was a security camera looking down at her. She tried to open the door, but it was locked. Then she heard a click, and the door opened the next time she turned the knob.

She found herself standing inside a small reception area, and sitting behind the only desk in the room was a large black man—extremely large.

"I'm Kay Hamilton," she said. "I have an appointment with Ms. Mercer."

The man nodded, as if he'd been expecting her, and said, "I need to wand you before you go in."

"Wand me?"

"For weapons and eavesdropping devices."

"Okay," Kay said, wondering what in the hell these people did that required such precautions.

The receptionist stood up—although it was hard to think of a guy who was six foot six and built like the

Incredible Hulk as a receptionist. Holstered on his belt was a Dirty Harry .44 Magnum with a seven-inch barrel and a walnut grip. *Whoa*. He passed a standard metal detector over Kay, then some other device the size of a pack of cigarettes with an antenna sticking out of it. Apparently satisfied that she was neither packing heat nor wired for sound, he picked up the phone and said, "Anna, Kay Hamilton is here."

A moment later, Anna Mercer opened the door behind the receptionist's desk and waved Kay toward her. As she passed through the door, Kay noticed a keypad next to it for entering a cybercode.

Mercer's office was beautifully decorated, but windowless and not very large. She had a glass-topped table she used for a desk, and Kay thought it might be an antique because the legs were gilded and elaborately carved. On the floor was a thick Oriental carpet that looked expensive and on the table was a Tiffany-style lamp, a laptop, a normal phone, and a second phone that Kay recognized as a Stu III encrypted phone. In one corner was a Gardall safe with a large combination lock. Above the safe was an oil painting depicting a canal in Venice that looked as if it had been painted by some famous old-time artist; Kay didn't know anything about art.

Next to Mercer's desk, resting regally in a wicker basket, was a large, snow-white Persian cat with aquamarine eyes. Mercer noticed Kay looking at the animal and said, "That's Scarlett. She's not in a good mood this morning."

Kay didn't know what to say in response to that. She was also surprised that a seemingly no-nonsense person like Mercer would bring a pet to work.

Like the last time Kay had seen Mercer, the woman was dressed in a gorgeous suit—this one hunter green with matching high heels, which Kay loved. If she ever got to know Mercer better, she was going to ask where she shopped. Mercer pointed Kay to one of the two chairs in front of her desk and pushed a manila folder toward her.

"That's your nondisclosure agreement. Read it if you want, but if you don't like something in it, too bad. We're not going to change a word. Sign it on the last page."

"I haven't agreed that I'm going to work for you yet," Kay said.

"The nondisclosure agreement covers everything you've done in connection with the Callahan Group since the day we met in San Diego. You need to sign it before we proceed any further."

Kay opened the folder and saw a twelve-page document written in incomprehensible legal gibberish. She flipped through the pages—she didn't bother to read every word—and signed it. She figured: What the hell. If she ever felt like disclosing something, a piece of paper wasn't going to stop her.

"Okay," Mercer said. "It's time for you to meet Callahan."

* * *

Kay followed Mercer down a long, narrow corridor. She noticed another surveillance camera as they were walking. They passed several closed doors—Kay didn't hear anyone behind the doors—until they came to an office at the end of the hall. There was another camera above this door. Mercer rapped, the door lock clicked, and Mercer pushed open the door.

The man behind the desk was gray-haired and overweight, and the first word that came to mind when Kay saw him was *rumpled*. He was wearing a blue shirt that had never been introduced to an iron and a baggy gray suit that Kay suspected came from some outfit like the Men's Wearhouse—and not from the part of the store where they kept the high-end clothes. He had bright blue eyes and a heavy, pale face. Unlike Mercer, he smiled at her and seemed friendly. He reminded Kay of a well-known actor who had died the year before of a drug overdose, but Kay couldn't recall the actor's name.

There was a conventional wooden desk in the office instead of an elegant table like Mercer had, and the desk bore marks of repeated abuse. Kay could see what looked like cigarette burns on one edge of the desk and rings where hot drinks had been placed without using a coaster. Like Mercer, he had a laptop and an encrypted phone, but his desk, instead of being neat and organized like Mercer's, was covered by small mountains of paper.

A greasy McDonald's bag sat on the keyboard of the laptop, and Kay could smell not only French fries but also cigarette smoke. But that couldn't be, she thought; no one smoked inside office buildings anymore.

Instead of individual visitor's chairs, there was a brown leather couch in front of Callahan's desk. (Kay later learned that Callahan often ended up sleeping on the couch—and sometimes passed out on the couch.) Today's editions of the *Washington Post,* the *Wall Street Journal,* and the *New York Times* were spread out all over the couch.

"Hey, sit down," Callahan said. "Push that shit onto the floor."

Kay gathered up the papers, made an attempt to fold them neatly, and then, when she couldn't figure out where to put them, dropped them on the floor near one end of the couch. She and Mercer sat down.

Callahan didn't say anything for a moment as his blue eyes took her in. "Wow," he said. "You're a knockout."

Mercer turned to Kay and said, "Fortunately—for Callahan, that is—the nondisclosure agreement you just signed prevents you from suing him for sexual harassment."

The name of the actor suddenly popped into Kay's head. Philip Seymour Hoffman—that's who Callahan reminded her of.

Ignoring Mercer's jab, Callahan said, "Okay. I'm Thomas Callahan and I have the controlling interest in a limited partnership known as the Callahan Group. All my partners are silent; in fact, I don't really have any partners. If you were to go online, you'd find our Web site, www.Callahan.Group.com, and it would tell you we specialize in helping U.S. companies do business abroad. The Web site says we know how to deal with such things as taxes on income earned overseas—meaning we tell companies how to avoid paying Uncle Sugar his fair share. It says we have special relationships with the right people in foreign governments—which means we know who to bribe if you want to operate in Dubai. If you want to set up a factory in Thailand and spew god-awful shit into the river that flows through downtown Bangkok, we know how to bend the environmental rules. And there actually are a few people who work for me who do that sort of stuff, and we always have about a dozen legitimate clients. If you were able to get your hands on the Callahan Group's tax returns, you'd see that we are an enormously successful company for a business our size."

"So what do you really do?" Kay asked. "I'm pretty sure you're not hiring me to be a tax consultant."

Callahan smiled. "When George W. Bush was president, I worked for his national security advisor and I'm sitting in my office late one night, this shitty little shoe box over in the EOB. I remember I was eating a pizza that was left over from the day before and a guy whose name I can't tell you comes in, closes the door, and explains to me that the president wants me to set up a special type of organization.

"You see, Bush decided after he invaded Iraq that he

wanted an option. He wanted an organization he could turn to for things that needed to be done but that he didn't necessarily want the federal government doing. And what he really wanted was an organization that, if it fucked up, he could say: *Hey, I got nothing to do with those guys.* He could have turned to the private sector, but he realized, being a good capitalist himself, that the private sector is profit motivated and what we do is not about making a profit. Plus, W wanted to be able to control this group, and no matter what kind of contract you write, the private sector will do whatever its little black heart desires when it comes to money.

"The president also had other concerns, which I think were totally justified. Government organizations, even ones like the CIA, are run by bureaucrats who are always worried that they'll end up taking the fall if they get caught doing something illegal on the president's behalf. So lots of times these bureaucrats balk when the boss gives 'em an order that's just a little bit in the gray zone. And after Powell stood up in the UN and swore on a stack of Bibles that Saddam had weapons he didn't actually have, the intelligence community became *really* risk averse. It was like they became afraid to do anything unless they were a hundred percent positive something couldn't go wrong, which rarely happens in intelligence work."

"They were willing to take some risks when they went after bin Laden," Kay said.

Callahan had the kind of eyes that seemed to literally

twinkle, the kind of eyes Santa Claus was supposed to have. They twinkled when Callahan said, "It might surprise you to learn that the night Obama gave the order to invade Pakistan, he had some information other folks in the Situation Room didn't have."

Kay had enough sense not to ask: *What information?*

"Anyway," Callahan said, "Congress is also a problem when it comes to covert ops. The various oversight committees want to know what's going on, they want to be involved in decisions even though they're not qualified to decide anything, and the bastards control the purse strings. I mean, Congress is just a gigantic pain in the ass."

But Kay was thinking: *Covert ops.* Now, this was starting to get interesting.

"So that night," Callahan said, "the president's guy said the boss wanted me to set up an organization that he could call upon from time to time when he needed something done. In other words, like I already said, he wanted an *option*, and that's what the Callahan Group is. It's not a federal agency and it's not really a private-sector company; it just looks like one." Callahan smiled. "You know what I said when he finished talking?"

Kay shook her head.

"I said I want to hear this directly from the president. Well, the president's pal said there wasn't any way in hell that was going to happen. So I refused. A couple days pass, and I get called to the Oval Office. That was the first time I was ever in the room by myself, and the president's not wearing any shoes, putting into one of those office putting cups. He smacks a ball, misses the cup by about ten inches; then he turns to me and says: 'You had a discussion with a close friend of mine the other night, and my friend tells me that you wanted some assurance that I approved of what he said. Let me just say that I don't disapprove.'"

Kay said, "What?"

"Exactly," Callahan said. "Complete gobbledygook. And you know what a lousy speaker Bush was, and I could tell that he'd memorized what he'd just said, but if push ever came to shove, he could testify that he'd never ordered me to do anything. But I was okay with that. I was satisfied that he was personally giving me the go-ahead and that's the best I was going to get."

"Why did the president pick you?" Kay asked.

"Because of my background. I'm ex-CIA and I spent time over at the Pentagon and on the National Security Council. Also, I was never in the limelight; nobody in the media knew who I was. So if I quit my White House job and set up a company that looks like a typical K Street operation, there wouldn't even be a ripple in the news. Anyway, that was the last time I talked to the president, and I've never received a direct order from the president, not the last one or the current one."

"You're saying Obama's aware of your existence?"

"Of course. He has to be. I'm guessing that when he moved into the White House, Bush briefed him on the Callahan Group and he decided not to upset the apple cart. All I know is that Bush's guy was replaced by Obama's guy. Like I said: I don't talk to the president and the president can testify to that without committing perjury.

"What happens instead is I'll bump into the president's guy in a bar or while he's taking a stroll around the Mall, and he'll update me on things that are bothering his boss. Then a *suggestion* might be made, but an order is never, ever given. Then I'm left to my own devices.

"There is only one link between me and the United States government, that link being money. I have a young guy, you may meet him sometime in the future, and he's my money guy. He's ex–Goldman Sachs, ex–Treasury Department, ex-OMB, and he's bright as a shiny new button."

Kay didn't know what the OMB was; she'd look it up later.

"His job is to move money from the U.S. Treasury to the Callahan Group without leaving a trail, and for the last decade or so that hasn't really been too hard because we've spent about four trillion dollars on two wars and *nobody* knows where all the money ended up. I mean, when we left Iraq we were literally shipping home crates filled with cash, millions of dollars that we *didn't* spend on bribes and rewards. Nobody has any idea how much cash was there in the first place and where it all went."

Callahan winked. "But if my money guy is ever caught, I imagine he and I—and maybe Anna—would find ourselves in a little hot water."

"Not me," Mercer said.

"Well, maybe not you," Callahan admitted to Mercer. "So do you understand?" he asked Kay.

Kay was wondering if by *a little hot water* Callahan was saying he'd go to jail. Instead of asking that question, she instead said, "Yeah, I understand. But how about giving me a couple examples of the sort of things you've done in the past?"

"Sorry, I can't do that," Callahan said. "In one respect, we're very much like a typical intelligence organization and everything's strictly need to know."

Kay shook her head. "Mr. Callahan, I'm not even going to pretend that I understand the limits of the president's powers and what he is or isn't supposed to tell Congress. And I definitely don't understand how money gets moved internally to the government or from the government to the private sector. But what I do know is that I'm not going to go to jail working for you."

"Hey, you're not gonna go to jail. We're not criminals. We're acting in the nation's best interest as determined by its chief executive."

"Like I said, I want an example of the kind of things you do so I can decide if I want to work for you."

Callahan's lips compressed into a stubborn line. Kay figured he was probably trying to decide if he should fire her before he'd even really hired her.

"Okay, I'll tell you what I'm going to do," Callahan said. "I'm going to give you a hypothetical that's pretty close to something we actually did so you'll understand."

"Thomas," Mercer said, a warning tone in her voice.

Callahan waved a hand at Mercer, a gesture that Kay interpreted as: *Don't worry about it.*

"Let me think for a minute," Callahan said, and as he was thinking, he pulled a cigarette out of his shirt pocket, ignited it, then said to Kay, "I hope smoke doesn't bother you."

"Well, actually . . ."

"Tough shit." He gazed up at the ceiling as he continued to contemplate, puffing on his cigarette, spewing toxins into the air.

"There's a company," Callahan said, "in, let's say Germany, a country which happens to be a U.S. ally. This company makes a gizmo that's used, peripherally, in the enrichment of plutonium. It's actually an instrument that measures atomic shit and it has various applications in laboratory testing, commercial power plants, et cetera. Anyway, the German company is allowed to sell the gizmo to other countries, like the British or the French, but not to places like Iran or North Korea, and the number of gizmos sold is carefully tracked.

"But this German company is run by a greedy prick and he starts selling the gizmo to Iran for ten times the market price in a very clever under-the-table way so he doesn't get caught. How do we know this? Because the CIA has a spy in Iran. But we have a problem. If we tell the Germans to arrest the greedy prick, the Iranians might figure out who our spy is, and we can't afford to lose this spy. The spy is much more important to us than the Iranians having the gizmo.

"The CIA could, of course, do something like you see in movies and bump off the German, making it look like an accident. But the CIA doesn't usually, or at least not very often, knock off our allies' citizens because if they got caught we'd have a real mess on our hands. So the president's guy met with me and *suggested* I do something."

"And you bumped off the German?" Kay said.

"Oh, hell, no. We don't do things like that." Callahan said this like he was astounded Kay would make such an accusation—but the twinkle was back in his eyes. "What we did—hypothetically—was put the German out of business. This company was suddenly *besieged* with problems. Union hassles, material shortages, lawsuits, sabotage, accounting disasters. We *destroyed* this fucking company. Could the CIA have done the same thing? Sure. But keep in mind that this was a legitimate enterprise that employed three hundred taxpaying, beer-drinking Germans, and if the CIA got caught . . . Well, like I already told you, there would have been hell to pay. On the other hand, an international company like the Callahan Group was just doing what private companies do: annihilating another company. You understand?"

"Yeah."

"And do you approve?"

"Yeah. I guess."

"Whew! What a relief. I'll be sure to let the president know."

Ignoring Callahan's sarcasm, Kay said, "But if that's the sort of thing you do all the time, I don't see why you're hiring me. I don't know anything about business or taking over companies or anything like that."

"Well," Callahan said, "that's not exactly the kind of thing we do all the time."

5

After Hamilton left his office, Callahan lit another cigarette and thought about Hamilton and her reaction to what he'd just told her about how the Callahan Group had been formed—and what he'd just told her was total bullshit.

As for Hamilton . . . He'd seen her photograph before they hired her, but the photo didn't really do her justice. The woman had a body that could stop traffic and she was incredibly . . . hell, *sexy* was the only word he could think of. Not all beautiful women are sexy, and Hamilton wasn't as beautiful as some women he'd known—but she just oozed sex appeal. A man would have to be either dead or gay for her not to turn his crank. And like he'd been told before he hired her, she came across as bright and cynical and not the type that he or anybody else was likely to intimidate.

Which was pretty much the same conclusion the Group's psychiatrist had come to. He basically said that Hamilton wasn't a team player and not really suited for work in a conventional law-enforcement or military unit.

She would excel at special ops, undercover, something where she could be out there on her own. She would be loyal to people, not organizations. She'd follow orders, but only if she agreed with the orders. The shrink's bottom line was basically the same thing Callahan decided two minutes after he met her: She'd be a good operative but tough to control—which made Callahan wonder why they even bothered with the shrink.

Her reaction to the origination of the Callahan Group was no different from the way other employees had reacted when he told them the same story. Hamilton had been surprised, of course, but she appeared to believe him, and he suspected the reason why was that people had so little faith in politicians these days. That is, they were willing to believe that a president really would set up an off-the-books organization to do nefarious things and avoid congressional oversight. Anybody old enough to remember the Watergate "plumbers" would have no problem believing this. The other reason people bought the story were the little details: like he'd been eating pizza the night the president's guy came to see him, or how W had been in his stocking feet playing with his putter.

The story about how the Callahan Group had destroyed a German company selling nuclear hardware to the Iranians was completely true and had actually happened. There had been nothing hypothetical about Callahan's example.

The part about intelligence agencies being extremely risk averse was also true, and it was true that there were advantages in using a private-sector company to do certain things the U.S. government wanted done. True, too, was the fact that the Callahan Group had provided some information that made Obama's decision to go after bin Laden in Abbottabad a little less risky, but the information was never provided directly to the president.

It was also true that Callahan had a bright young man who moved money from the U.S. Treasury to Callahan's accounts, but the money wasn't in any way pilfered from the government's coffers. It came instead from funding sources that were classified as secret, difficult to identify, known to very few people, and *arguably* legal—but which would prove problematic if Congress or the GAO ever asked the right questions. And, as he'd said, the tremendous amounts of cash poorly accounted for during the Iraq and Afghanistan wars had greatly increased the amount of money Callahan had to spend.

So Callahan had told Hamilton many things that were true, and one reason for this was some advice his mother had once given him. "Thomas," his mom had said, "you should tell the truth as often as you can, because that way it's easier to keep track of all the lies you tell." His mother had been an interesting woman.

What was completely untrue was that George W. Bush, or anyone on his staff, had authorized the formation of the Callahan Group. Neither Bush nor Obama had any idea the Group existed. *The president's guy*, whom Callahan frequently referred to, did not exist. The complete truth about the Callahan Group was known only to Thomas Callahan and three other people, and none of those people worked at the White House.

6

Following her initial meeting with Callahan, Kay and her sixteen-year-old daughter, Jessica, moved to D.C. They arrived on the first of July, and the weather that entire month was hot, humid, and miserable. Jessica particularly didn't like the humidity and she missed the beaches of San Diego, but July was good as it gave them time to settle into their new apartment on Connecticut Avenue near the National Zoo and get Jessica enrolled in school.

Kay didn't really want to live in an apartment, although the place she was renting was nice enough and convenient to Jessica's school. In Miami and San Diego, she'd bought houses that needed some work, then spent her free time fixing the places up so she could turn a profit when she sold them. She not only enjoyed the money she made, she also enjoyed doing the home-improvement projects; they were like a hobby for her and, thanks to her dad—who'd been a cop and a terrific father—she knew how to use a few tools. The only reason she decided to get an apartment was that she wasn't certain she'd be staying with the Callahan Group, and until she was sure, she was going to wait before investing in a house.

Kay decided that in many ways she liked what the Callahan Group did. That is, she liked the idea of a covert organization that dealt with national security issues but wasn't hobbled by the bureaucracy of the federal government. She also liked the salary. What she found particularly enticing was the training they were going to give her, especially the language training. That was something that would look good on a résumé if she had to look for another job. So she'd stick with Callahan at least until she completed her training and see, as time passed, if working for him would land her in "hot water." A little hot water she could tolerate; becoming an inmate in a federal penitentiary was a totally different story.

Regarding the school Jessica chose to attend, it was basically an egghead factory—a Juilliard for math and science wizards, as opposed to musicians and dancers. Jessica had decided that she wanted to be a doctor, and the school would give her a leg up on getting into medical school. And, as Mercer had told her, Kay had no problems getting Jessica admitted. The Callahan Group had some *serious* clout.

In mid-August, Jessica began school and Kay started what was supposed to be nine months of training. For the first three months, three days a week, six hours a day, she would attend language classes. They wanted her to learn Farsi first, then Arabic. She guessed the priority was placed on Farsi because of Iran. The other days of the week—which would include some Saturdays and evening sessions as well—the curriculum would include classes on Mideastern cultures; there would be surveillance and surveillance-avoidance training conducted at the FBI's training facility in Quantico. There was one forty-hour course that would be taught over at Fort Meade in Maryland where the NSA's headquarters were, and here she'd be given an introduction to listening devices, alarm systems, and computer security. These classes weren't intended to make her an expert in any of these subjects but to simply acquaint her with the state of the art so she'd know the technologies available to her and those she'd be up against.

In the spring would come the fun stuff, and Kay was really looking forward to it: scuba training down at the navy's dive school in Panama City, Florida, and jump school and survival training at Fort Benning, taught by the army. The jump school would focus on low-altitude night drops—and Kay could hardly wait.

Kay was surprised to learn that although she wouldn't be enrolled under her own name, she would just be another student attending classes with a variety of people from the military services, government agencies, law-enforcement organizations, and private companies. Some of the other students might even be from countries that were supposedly—or currently—U.S. allies. The language classes, for example, would be held at Georgetown University in D.C. and the Mideastern cultural classes at George Mason University in Arlington, and in these classes, Kay was told, she would most likely meet people from the State Department, the FBI, and the CIA.

The only classes she took where she was not a student in some standard program were the classes related to killing people: demolitions, firearms training, knife fighting, and the stupid hand-to-hand combat course. Kay had tried to get out of attending the hand-to-hand and firearms courses, saying that she'd already had similar training when she was at the DEA, but Mercer refused to give her a pass.

The killing classes were taught by the Callahan Group's own instructors, and the only people in these classes were Callahan employees. As near as she could tell, the Class of 2014 included only three other people and they were told not to socialize with one another. She had no idea how many people the Callahan Group employed; she did get the impression that they had employees in several places around the globe. One thing she was sure of, based on her training alone, was that the Callahan Group did a whole lot more than hostile takeovers of foreign companies.

She was only forty-five days into the training program the day she kicked Bowman in the balls and Anna Mercer called her.

* * *

Kay stepped into the outer office and the colossus who acted as the receptionist said, "Hello, Kay. I'll tell Anna you're here, but just head on down to her office. By the way, my name's Henry." This time Henry didn't wand her to see if she was wired or armed; apparently, she was now a trusted member of the club.

Kay learned later that Henry was an interesting fellow: an ex-Marine with enough medals to cover even his big chest. He got the medals in Iraq, where he hardly got a scratch; then he went to work for Callahan and his right leg was blown off below the knee. Kay never did learn what he'd been doing when he lost the leg because she didn't have *need to know*—the mantra of classification.

Kay proceeded toward Mercer's office, but Mercer stepped into the hallway before Kay reached her door. She was cuddling her fat white Persian cat, Scarlett, in her arms. "We're meeting in the conference room," Mercer said.

Kay thought that was rather rude: No *how are you doing, how are the classes going, is everything okay with your daughter?*

The conference room contained a typical boardroom table with seats for ten, and at one end was a flat-screen TV mounted on a rolling stand. Along one wall was a sink, a microwave, and a small refrigerator. There were two people already in the room, a man and a woman.

The woman was younger than Mercer and older than Kay, maybe forty. She was slender and dressed in a dark blue pantsuit and a plain white blouse; her clothes didn't come close to matching Mercer's in terms of style or expense. She wore no makeup, no jewelry, and had wire-rimmed glasses with fairly thick lenses. Her long, dark hair was tied in a sloppy ponytail, a few unruly strands falling onto her forehead. Kay thought she might have been pretty—even sexy—if she applied a little lip gloss and ditched the glasses.

The man sitting next to the woman was in his late thirties or early forties, and Kay's initial reaction was: *Wow!* The guy was absurdly good-looking: perfect straight nose, little crinkly smile lines radiating from blue-gray eyes, a strong chin, and lips God had engineered for kissing. He had sandy brown hair and a slim yet muscular build. He was wearing a blue suit that Kay guessed cost about five grand and a shirt that was a perfect color for his eyes.

"Kay, say hello to Sylvia Sorenson and Eli Dolan," Mercer said. "Sylvia's one of our lawyers and specializes in international law. She may not look like it, but Sylvia's a wolverine. That story Callahan told you about the hypothetical German company that we destroyed with lawsuits and financial sabotage? Well, Sylvia was behind the lawsuits. Hypothetically."

Sylvia blushed at the compliment. She looked to Kay more like a field mouse than a wolverine—but you can never tell.

"Eli's our money guy," Mercer said, and Kay remembered Callahan telling her about the Group's money guy: Goldman Sachs, Treasury Department, OMB; she still didn't know what OMB stood for, because she'd forgotten to look it up.

"Not only is Eli cute as a button," Mercer continued, "he's also richer than God from old family money and all the people he fleeced in investment banking. I've been throwing myself at him for years, but he keeps spurning me. I think he's gay."

Kay was pretty sure, judging by the way he was looking at her, that Eli Dolan wasn't gay.

"Guys," Mercer said to Eli and Sylvia, "this is Kay Hamilton, one of our newbies. She looks good now, Eli, but we know she was fat as a child and will most likely get fat again when she gets older. And her boobs are fake."

Sylvia looked away, embarrassed by Mercer's bawdy comment, but Eli laughed. Kay felt like punching Mercer in the face.

Kay had come right from the gym, and she was dressed casually as she was through with classes for the day. She was wearing jeans that were tight and low on her hips, and a designer sweatshirt that tended to leave one shoulder bare and exposed her flat midriff. Her long blond hair was still a bit damp from her shower and hung in tangled tresses down to her shoulders, since she hadn't taken the time to comb it out. Thank

God she had taken the time to apply a little makeup and her lipstick.

Dolan stood and reached out to shake Kay's hand. "Nice to meet you," he said. He was a perfect height, too: six foot three, which Kay liked, since she was a tall girl at five-eight. She could wear high heels when she went out with him.

Then she thought: *Stop it! You don't know anything about the guy.*

As Mercer was placing Scarlett in a basket identical to the one in her office, Callahan flung open the door to the conference room, holding a cup of coffee in one hand, and dropped heavily into the seat at the head of the table. He was dressed exactly as Kay had seen him the first time she met him: rumpled gray suit, wrinkled shirt, loosened tie.

"Kay, have you met Eli and Sylvia?" Callahan asked.

"Yes."

"And I'm assuming Anna's already introduced you to Scarlett."

"Uh, yeah," Kay said, but she was thinking: *What is it with the fucking cat?*

"Okay, then let's get started," Callahan said. "Now, I'm bringing you in on something even before you've completed your training, because you're the only person I currently have that fits the bill for the job. It's not a hard job—basically, all you have to do is be yourself—but it's something you might be involved in for years. This is a really long-range operation, and it's complicated."

Callahan picked up a remote that Kay hadn't noticed lying on the table next to his right hand. He hit a button on the remote and the following appeared in the center of the TV screen:

7

"Lithium," Callahan said, "is a soft white metal and its atomic number is three. It's the lightest metal in existence, and it's highly reactive because . . ." Callahan stopped when he saw the look on Kay's face, and said, "Yeah, you're right. Who gives a shit?"

He tapped the remote three or four times, skipping past PowerPoint pages that had more information on the atomic properties of lithium. He stopped when a map of Afghanistan appeared on the screen. The map showed the country's thirty-four provinces in different colors.

Callahan zoomed in on a province in the eastern part of the country, south of Kabul. "This is Ghazni Province," he said. "It's an absolute shithole of a place, made more so by the fact that the Taliban are constantly killing whoever in Ghazni pisses them off. But in 2007, a U.S. Geological Survey discovered the mother lode of lithium in some dry salt lakes in Ghazni. In fact, an internal Pentagon report said that Ghazni could be the Saudi Arabia of lithium."

Kay wondered how Callahan had gotten his hands on an internal Pentagon report, but didn't ask.

"You see," Callahan said, "lithium is used in a number of applications—glass, ceramics, optics—but the big one is batteries. And these days, with everybody trying to build electric cars, batteries are a big deal. But there's another application for lithium that's even more interesting. It's an element that's used in nuclear fusion; it's a neutron absorber. Do you know the difference between nuclear fission and nuclear fusion?"

Kay wondered if he was intentionally trying to make her feel stupid. She was an ex-cop, not a fucking physicist. "I know fission is when you do things like split atoms and fusion is when you, ah, fuse 'em together." She could feel her face turning red and avoided looking at Eli Dolan.

"Exactly," Callahan said, sounding pleased as Punch that she knew anything at all. "In fission, we split uranium and plutonium atoms, and when you split 'em, they give off heat, or energy, which is a good thing. What's bad is you're left with a lot of radioactive garbage, and basically all we can do today is stick the garbage someplace like Yucca Mountain and wait ten thousand years for it to stop being radioactive.

"But fusion is different. Fusion is the holy grail of energy. In fusion, instead of using uranium we use water—actually, something called *heavy* water—and if you can jam these water atoms together they give off energy, too, but you don't end up with the nasty, long-lasting radioactive shit you get from fission. Up until now, however, the boffins haven't figured out how to make fusion work in an economically viable way. Well, it appears DARPA knows something. You know what DARPA is?"

"Sort of," Kay said, "I know it's a government research-and-development outfit."

"That's right," Callahan said. "DARPA is the Defense Advanced Research Projects Agency, and they're theoretically responsible for developing new technologies for use by the military. Some of the brightest nerds in the country work there, and they're always looking into the future, trying to come up with things that sound like science fiction. If we ever have time travel, the guys from DARPA will be the ones who take the first ride back to the Middle Ages. Anyway, it appears DARPA knows something about nuclear fusion that nobody else knows, and they whispered into the president's ear that it might be a good idea for the government to stock up on lithium."

Callahan pulled a cigarette out of his pocket, then looked around the conference room, growing more annoyed the longer he looked. "Where's my ashtray?" he asked Mercer.

"I have no idea," Mercer said.

"Liar," Callahan said. He got up, walked over to a sink in the conference room, and partially filled a paper cup with water, intending to use the cup as an ashtray. He sat back down and started patting all his pockets. "Goddamnit," he muttered. "I don't suppose any of you has a book of matches," he said.

No one answered him except for Sylvia, who said, "Sorry."

"God, you're a bunch of Puritans," Callahan said. "You all make me sick."

He put the cigarette back in his pocket and, turning to Kay, he said, "Today, about half the world's known supply of lithium is in Bolivia, in a place called Salar de Uyuni. It's not easy to get the stuff out of Bolivia, however, as that part of the world is a tough place to mine and South Americans, in general, are pretty wise to our act when it comes to filching their natural resources. Well, these dry lakes in Ghazni Province are thought to contain as much lithium as there is in Bolivia, and if it weren't for the politics of Afghanistan and the Taliban and the fact that the country has been in a continual state of war for half a century, it'd be a lot easier to mine there than Bolivia. You with me so far?"

Kay nodded but was irritated that he'd asked the question, like she was the slowest kid in the class. Then it occurred to her that in this particular class, she *was* the slowest.

Callahan tapped the remote again and a photograph of a bearded man in his fifties appeared on the screen. He had short black hair streaked with gray, an axe blade for a nose, and intense dark eyes. He was wearing a brown vest over a collarless white shirt.

"This is Sahid Mohammad Khan, the current governor of Ghazni Province. Like most provincial governors, he's a complete thug and he relies heavily on force, intimidation, and tribal connections. He's also corrupt, meaning he takes every opportunity he can to line his own pockets, but he's no more corrupt than the president of Afghanistan or the other governors. The good thing about him is, he hates the Taliban, which isn't surprising since they've tried to kill him a dozen times. He's not a big fan of the United States, either, but he's played us like a fish to get money for himself and his province. But the truly unique thing about Sahid Khan is his daughter, his attitude toward her, and his relationship with her."

Callahan tapped the remote again and a picture of a beautiful young woman in her twenties filled the screen. "This is Ara Khan."

Ara Khan had lustrous black hair, a model's cheekbones, and full lips. The most striking thing about her was her eyes, which were a stunning shade of jade green—and Kay was immediately reminded of that famous picture of the young Afghan girl that appeared on the cover of *National Geographic* magazine years ago. The girl on the cover of *National Geographic* had exactly the same color eyes.

"Sahid Khan dotes on his daughter; he doesn't have any sons and his wife is dead. No one can figure out why he hasn't married again. Anyway, Sahid sent Ara abroad to be educated during the war to protect her from the Taliban. Or maybe, considering the way she looks, to protect her from U.S. troops. She got the equivalent of a high school degree in France and her college education at NYU. She speaks French, English, Pashto, Dari, and Uzbek. Her university degree is in international studies.

In addition to being educated in a manner that's extremely unusual for an Afghan woman, Ara Khan is her father's principal advisor."

"How do you know that?" Kay asked.

Callahan winked at her. "Because the CIA has a spy in Khan's government. The same spy probably works for the Russians and the Chinese and the British and anyone else willing to pay his price. It's really easy to buy an Afghan spy, but you can never be sure who they're working for. At any rate, Sahid consults with Ara on all his major decisions and he includes her in his inner circle, which really pisses off his other guys.

"One last thing about Ara, then we'll take a break, because I need a smoke and I gotta take a leak. The person who I guess you'd say *discovered* Ara was Hillary Clinton, when Hillary was secretary of state. Hillary met her on one of her trips over there where she got together with a bunch of women to talk about women's shit, and when she got back she told people that Ara impressed the hell out of her. Okay, let's take a break."

Callahan left the conference room and Dolan walked over and opened the door to a small refrigerator. "Would anyone like something to drink?" he asked. "Coke, bottled water, fruit juice? There's also beer in here, but I imagine that's reserved for Callahan."

"Nothing for me," Sylvia said.

"I'll have a Diet Coke," Mercer said.

"Kay?" Dolan said.

"Uh, just water."

Dolan handed her a bottle of Perrier and Mercer a Coke. Kay opened the bottle, but before taking a drink, she said, "Do you live here in D.C.?"

"Part-time. My primary residence is in Manhattan, but I have a small place in Georgetown where I stay when I'm down here."

Mercer snorted. "He has a gorgeous town house. It's worth more than two million. And if he offers to show you his etchings, I'm going to throw up."

Mercer was really annoying Kay. She almost said: *Don't you have to go to the bathroom, too?*

"How about you?" Dolan asked. "Do you live here?"

"Yeah, we just moved here. We have a place on Connecticut."

"We?" Dolan said.

Before Kay could tell him that by *we* she meant her daughter and not a husband, Callahan came back into the room and they all resumed their seats at the table. She noticed Callahan had brought an ashtray with him.

"Okay," Callahan said. "One last picture, and then we'll get down to the mission."

The next photo that appeared on the screen was of a young woman in her early twenties. She had long blond hair and blue eyes, and she looked . . . Well, the best word Kay could think of was *mischievous.*

"Who does she look like, Hamilton?" Callahan asked.

"I don't know," Kay said. "Am I supposed to recognize her?"

"She looks like you," Callahan said.

Kay looked at the photo again. The woman sort of looked like Kay, but she actually looked more like Kay's daughter, if Jessica ever let her hair grow that long.

"Her name is Carolyn Harris," Callahan said, "and she was Ara Khan's roommate at NYU for four years and her best friend. Harris is dead now. She was killed in a car accident a year ago, and Ara flew back from Afghanistan to attend the funeral. The other thing about Harris is she not only looks like you, but your personalities are somewhat similar. Harris was a bit of a wild thing. She liked to party, and she introduced Ara to Western decadence and dope and a couple of men Ara slept with while she was over here."

"Callahan," Kay said, "I don't know what that psychiatrist told you, but I was never a *wild thing*. That's absurd, not to mention offensive. As for dope . . . I worked for the DEA, Christ's sake!"

"Hey, don't get your panties in a twist. I'm just saying Carolyn Harris knew how to have a good time and so do you."

Before Kay could object again, Callahan said, "Okay, now you have the background on all the players. So here's the job, and like I told you before, it's complicated. We want—the president wants—two things. First, we want to get a company we control in place as soon as possible to start mining the lithium in Ghazni Province. The idea is since we control the mining company, we'll be in a better position to control who gets the lithium.

"But to do what we want is going to be tough politically. Really tough. The guys currently in charge in Kabul are going to be hard to manage and they're going to try to shoehorn their way into any deal we make. On top of that, even if we are able to get the mining rights, it's still going to be hard to get the stuff out of the ground, because they don't have any real infrastructure over there and we'll probably be fighting the Taliban while we're going after it. We'll also be competing with the Chinese, the Japanese, and half a dozen American companies who also want the lithium for battery production, and they'll be trying to cut their own deals with the big boys in Kabul.

"So the politics are going to be a bitch, and in order to better ensure that things come out the way we want, the second thing we're going to do is support Sahid Khan to become the next president of Afghanistan. We know he'd like to be the top dog over there and his chances for being elected are going to increase dramatically because we're going to give him a substantial war chest to fund his campaign. This political war chest is also a great big bribe to get him to play ball."

"You want to put a guy you say is a corrupt thug in charge of the whole country?" Kay said.

"Hey, the guy *currently* in charge is a corrupt thug— but Sahid Khan will be *our* thug. The other thing is, Sahid Khan's not a religious nut and he's more likely to make Afghanistan into a secular country like Turkey, instead of a place like Iran that's run by a mullah."

Kay was thinking that the United States had been

down this path before—supporting handpicked dictators—and it often didn't turn out the way we wanted. Like Manuel Noriega and Saddam Hussein. Or, for that matter, supporting the Shah in Iran—which was maybe one reason there was now a mullah in charge of that country.

But before she could say anything else, Callahan said, "The main thing is, and the reason why you're here, is I believe the key to convincing Sahid to play along with us is his daughter. She's not only smart, but she's progressive and leans toward the West ideologically. If we can make her believe that what we want to do will be good for her country, I think she'll talk her old man into it.

"The other thing about Ara is we think that she has even more potential than her father in terms of politics. Afghanistan is a long way from having a female president or even a woman in a powerful position in their government, but if there's any woman who can get there, it's Ara Khan. She could be like that woman in Burma. . . ."

"Myanmar," Mercer corrected.

"Yeah, whatever. Anyway, we think she could be like that gal who was under house arrest there for a couple of decades and is now a major political force."

"Aung San Suu Kyi," Mercer said.

"Yeah, her," Callahan said, irritated by the interruption. "Kyi's smart, attractive, educated, progressive, democratic, all that stuff, and Ara Khan is the same type of person. What I'm saying is, if we can get Ara Khan into a leadership position in her country, it's not only good for her country, but she's a person the U.S. can work with."

Callahan's plan sounded way too complicated to Kay—there were too many moving parts—and she had no idea if what he was planning could be done. But all she said was, "I don't understand. How do I fit into all this?"

Callahan smiled at her. "You're the one who's going to convince Ara Khan to do what we want."

"What?" Kay said.

"We could approach this in a lot of different ways," Callahan said. "For example, we—meaning the U.S. government—could send over a delegation from the State Department to talk to Khan secretly about allowing some U.S. company to mine the lithium, and at the same time tell him how the U.S. will support him politically. But we know if we did this, the guys in Kabul would find out what was going on and screw things up, and nothing happens fast over there if the government's involved. Either ours or theirs. The other thing is, we don't think that Khan would trust us if we went straight at him, and we don't want to try to convince him using interpreters. So we're going to approach this in a different way. *You're* going to convince Ara, and then she's going to convince her dad."

Now Kay didn't know what to say. What Callahan wanted was a hell of a big order for anyone, but it was particularly a big order for someone with her background.

She didn't know anything about the politics of Afghanistan, mineral rights, mining, or the personalities of Ara Khan and her father. She couldn't imagine why Callahan would think she could do this. Callahan, however, didn't appear to notice any anxiety she might be feeling; he just kept talking.

"Ara's coming to New York in three weeks, and while she's here we want you to get next to her and talk to her. We want you to *pitch* her. You're going to sell her on what we want to do. We also want you to make a personal connection with her. What we'd really like, long term, is for you to become the new Carolyn Harris, her new American best friend, somebody she can trust and confide in."

"And I'm to establish this trusting relationship by pretending to be someone I'm not and lying to her?" Kay said.

"Don't be a smart-ass," Callahan said. "And you won't be pretending to be somebody you're not. You'll be representing the Callahan Group, which is partnering with a Swiss company to mine the lithium."

"A Swiss company?"

"Yeah, but that's a whole different story and I'm late for a call I gotta make. Eli can fill you in on the Swiss end later. What you need to do next is review the information we've compiled on Ara Khan. Anna will give it to you. Then you're going to start practicing your pitch with Eli, Sylvia, and Anna all coaching you.

You know, kind of like debate preps presidential candidates do."

Kay said, "I don't know if . . ."

"Hey, you'll do fine," Callahan said. He rose from the table, and Mercer scooped up Scarlett and followed him out of the conference room. As they were leaving, Kay heard Mercer say, "I don't think this is going to work, Thomas. She's . . ." Then the door shut and Kay didn't hear the rest of what Mercer said about her.

A moment after Callahan and Mercer left, Sylvia Sorensen stood and said, "Uh, I have to get back to work, too." She said this like she was apologizing. "It was nice to have met you, Kay, and I look forward to working with you."

"Yeah, me too," Kay said, but she was thinking that this was just awful. She'd loved being in the DEA, chasing bad guys. And with the DEA, the rules were pretty clear: They were drug dealers, she was a fed, her job was to arrest them, and if they tried to kill her, she could shoot back. The job had sometimes been dangerous but had usually been pretty straightforward, and Kay had really enjoyed it, at least most of the time.

But this thing with Ara Khan was a rats' nest involving an unpredictable foreign government, trying to dupe a woman into doing something that might not be in her country's best interest, and advancing the career of a crooked politician. Not only that, this wasn't a job that was going to be over with in a couple of months. If things went the way Callahan wanted, Kay could be holding Ara Khan's hand for years.

This sucked—and it wasn't at all what she had in mind when they hired her—and it sure as hell didn't match the training they'd been giving her.

Well, one thing didn't suck, and that was Eli Dolan. He was still sitting at the conference table, an amused look on his face, like he understood what she was feeling and found the situation funny.

"You wanna go get a drink and tell me about the Swiss end?" Kay asked him. She was curious about the Swiss end of the operation, but she was a lot more curious about Eli Dolan. She'd noticed he wasn't wearing a wedding ring.

8

Alpha knew it was time to make a decision. It was time to act.

Callahan's plan to go after the lithium in Ghazni Province didn't begin today, when he brought Hamilton into the operation. The plan had been set in motion more than eight months before. It had taken almost that long to get the Swiss company under Callahan's big thumb, and there had been a tremendous amount of research to do with regard to the law, lithium mining, the politics of Afghanistan, and the actors involved. And eight months ago, when Callahan began putting his plan together, Alpha began to plan. Alpha knew, even when the operation was in the preliminary stages, that at some point a very large amount of money was going to change hands.

Until now, however, it had been a theoretical exercise. But with Ara Khan arriving in New York in three weeks, it was either time to act or it was time to decide to never act. It was time to shit or get off the pot. And there was no time left for second-guessing the plan. There would only be six weeks to bring in the other players and for them to complete their tasks: the three weeks prior to Ara's arrival and then three weeks, maybe just a little more, after Ara left New York.

Alpha had identified the key person months ago: a twisted genius named Rodger Finley. Finley would have to be persuaded, but Alpha had no doubt that could be done. Alpha *knew* Finley. It wasn't just his personal circumstances that made Finley pliable; his enormous ego was really the key. If Finley couldn't be convinced, there were two other options, but Finley was the ideal choice. Alpha could fly up to New York tonight, talk to him, and be back in Washington early tomorrow. Callahan wouldn't even know Alpha had been gone.

In addition to Finley, three other men were needed, but only one would have to be recruited, the one who would become Alpha's Bravo. Bravo would recruit a Charlie and a Delta, and they would never know who Alpha was. Bravo was a bigger unknown than Finley, however. Alpha knew he was in desperate financial straits—but was he desperate enough? And where Finley's role would be bloodless, there would be blood all over Bravo's hands. The good news was that if Bravo couldn't be convinced, there were people he worked with who might be recruited. The bad news was that Bravo would have to be killed if he didn't agree to participate, and Bravo would be very hard to kill.

But convincing Finley and Bravo to help wasn't the biggest problem. The biggest problem—and the one Alpha had the least control over—was Kay Hamilton. If

Hamilton failed to sell Callahan's scheme to Ara Khan, then the whole deal would fall apart, no money would change hands, and Alpha would lose the best opportunity that had come along in years. And although Callahan may have been impressed with Hamilton, Alpha wasn't *that* impressed. Hamilton was bright enough, but she was basically a gunslinger. She was a weapon you pointed at a target. But what Callahan wanted Hamilton to do required diplomacy and finesse, and Alpha wasn't convinced a blunt instrument like Hamilton possessed finesse. Alpha would do everything possible to help Hamilton succeed, but would it be enough? There was no way to know.

So. Move forward today or never move at all? Alpha had no doubt the plan was feasible. The issue was really one of *courage*. Callahan would never stop looking for the person who betrayed him, and when Callahan found that person, there would be no arrest, no trial. There would be no mercy. There would be an execution.

9

Back in his office, Callahan made an encrypted call to a guy in Pakistan about something squirrelly going on over there. There was *always* something squirrelly going on over there. After that he made a few calls to people working the legitimate side of the Callahan Group to make sure the wheels were all turning properly, then poured himself a Scotch. As he sipped his drink, he thought briefly about what Mercer had said about Hamilton—how she didn't think Hamilton was the right person for the job—but he decided to stick with the plan. Hamilton was going to do just fine.

What he needed to do next was talk to Smee, something he hated to do, and something he'd been putting off for far too long. It couldn't be avoided any longer, however; he needed to let his partners—who thought they were his bosses—know where things stood with regard to Ara Khan and his decision to use Hamilton. And it was time to line up the money he'd need if things went as planned, and he needed a *lot* of money.

He called a number that went straight to voice mail.

No one ever answered the phone, and Callahan had no idea where the phone was located or if there even was a phone. Somehow Smee would be electronically alerted that a voice mail was waiting for him and he would call the same phone number Callahan had called, and retrieve the message. The message itself was one word, and in this case the word was *Cylinder*.

Cylinder was a code word designating one of several places where Callahan and Smee met, and Smee would be there in exactly one hour. Callahan didn't know for sure where Smee was located physically; all he knew was that in nine years Smee had never missed one of their rare meetings and was always on time. He had this impression of the man standing in a glass case like a fire axe just waiting for Callahan's call.

If Smee wanted to meet with Callahan the same procedure was used in reverse: Smee would call a phone number, leave a code word designating the meeting place, Callahan would be electronically notified, and he'd retrieve the message. Unlike Smee, however, Callahan wouldn't necessarily arrive at the meeting place in an hour because he might be busy. Sometimes he didn't arrive within an hour just because he didn't feel like jumping through his own asshole to meet with Smee. So when Smee wanted to meet with Callahan he'd designate the meeting place and wait for Callahan, and if Callahan didn't show up in an hour, he'd return to the meeting place every four hours until Callahan arrived.

Smee's name, of course, wasn't Smee. That's just what Callahan called him. Smee was a character in *Peter Pan*, Captain Hook's obsequious, sneaky lackey. Smee's real name was Peter J. Meece. Callahan occasionally called him *Pete*, as he knew that Smee hated to be called anything but *Peter*. In fact, he'd told Callahan once that he would really prefer that Callahan address him as *Mister* Meece—like that was ever gonna happen.

Smee/Meece was a walking tape recorder, an answering machine with feet. He had the ability to remember conversations verbatim, no matter how long those conversations might be or how long ago they had occurred. And that was Smee's only function, as near as Callahan could tell: to pass messages between Callahan and his partners.

The reason Smee was used as a conduit was simple: Callahan's partners refused to talk to Callahan on the phone, no matter what assurances were given that the phone calls were secure. Even though they routinely used encrypted communication systems during the normal course of their jobs, they were unwilling to take any chance whatsoever that a call to Callahan could be recorded or overheard. They never, of course, committed anything to writing, and all three of his partners considered e-mail the most insidious method of communication ever devised. They would talk to Callahan face-to-face, but only on rare occasions, and usually only when things had gone very badly. And thus the reason for Smee's annoying existence.

* * *

The meeting place designated as *Cylinder* was an apartment near Mount Vernon Square that the Callahan Group used occasionally as a safe house and as a place to put up visitors from out of town. It was swept on a routine basis to ensure it wasn't bugged, and Callahan had chosen it simply because it was close to his office and convenient for him. He didn't care if it was convenient for Smee.

Callahan arrived at the apartment first and, while waiting for Smee, poured himself another Scotch. Smee unlocked the door ten minutes later and walked into the apartment, although in Callahan's mind, Smee didn't walk—he slithered.

Smee was of an indeterminate age, maybe forty, maybe sixty, and blessed with a face so devoid of character and so nondescript as to render him virtually invisible. He was average in every way: medium height, neither fat nor slim, a nose that was neither short nor long, a chin that made no impression. His hair was the drabbest of browns. Callahan was convinced, even as many times as he'd met with the man, that he wouldn't be able to describe him to a police sketch artist.

"Would you like a drink, Smee?" Callahan asked. He only asked this question to annoy Smee, as he knew Smee didn't drink and didn't like that Callahan drank.

"No. Why did you want to meet?"

"I wanted to update your masters on the Lithium Op, as we're about to move on it."

Callahan then basically gave a briefing on the status of the operation as if he were talking to a blank wall. Smee just stood there. He didn't ask questions or ask for clarification. He didn't act surprised when Callahan said how much money he wanted. He simply recorded what Callahan said.

"That's it," Callahan said when he was done.

"I'll pass this on to Mr. Lincoln within the next two hours," Smee said, and left the apartment.

Lincoln, for some reason, was the primary spokesperson for Callahan's three partners. All three people had several things in common: They were all in their late fifties or early sixties, they were extraordinarily bright and extremely ruthless, and in spite of the power they had, they were not known to the general public.

If it ever became necessary to feed Callahan to the wolves, they wouldn't hesitate for even an instant.

10

When Kay got home that evening, she was a bit tipsy from the two martinis she'd had with Eli Dolan. She was also semi in love with Eli and fully in lust with him. She wanted to go to bed with Eli Dolan. She could still see his hands as they held his drink—beautiful, strong hands with long, tapered fingers—and she could imagine them touching her in all the places she liked to be touched.

The first thing she noticed when she opened her apartment door was the aroma coming from the kitchen. One of the many things Kay didn't have in common with her daughter was that Jessica could cook and she couldn't. Kay added boiling water to soup mixes, heated dishes in the microwave, and kept a list next to the phone with the number of every takeout place near their apartment. But Jessica not only liked to cook, she was good at it. She said all you had to do was follow the instructions in Betty Crocker, but Kay knew it was harder than that. Kay knew there was magic involved.

She walked into the kitchen and saw Jessica chopping up lettuce. There was a neat pile of diced tomatoes, mushrooms, red onions, and Kalamata olives on the cutting board, and next to the cutting board, a container of crumbled feta cheese.

Jessica was a pretty girl with a nice figure, although she wasn't as busty as Kay had been at her age. Like Kay, she had blond hair and blue eyes, but she was only five foot four and it seemed unlikely that she'd get much taller. She had no interest in fashion. In the summer, she preferred T-shirts and knee-length shorts; in the winter, jeans and sweatshirts. She always rejected Kay's offers to take her shopping and she rarely wore the things Kay bought her. Tonight she was wearing a white T-shirt with red letters that said *Don't Ask*. Kay had no idea what that meant; Jessica had a weird sense of humor.

"Hi there," Kay said. "What's for dinner?"

"Minestrone soup, a Greek salad, and big chunks of fresh French bread. It's international night at Chez Hamilton."

"God bless you," Kay said.

J essica.

Less than a year ago, when Kay was still employed by the DEA, she came home one day to find a sullen teenage girl sitting on her front porch. She had no idea who the kid could be, and when Kay asked who she was, the girl said, "I'm your daughter."

The biggest mistake Kay Hamilton ever made in her

life was getting pregnant when she was fifteen. Immediately after her daughter was born—an abortion had been out of the question because of her Catholic mother—Kay gave Jessica up for adoption to a cousin she barely knew and never saw the girl again or had any contact with her. Kay had not wanted to be a mother at the age of fifteen. For that matter, she didn't really want to be a mother at the age of thirty-one.

That day in San Diego, when she was reintroduced to a child she'd known for all of ten minutes the day she was born, Kay learned that Jessica's adoptive father had died of a heart attack when Jessica was only ten and that her adoptive mother, Kay's cousin, died of breast cancer when the girl was fifteen. Jessica had no other relatives, and she wanted Kay to become her legal guardian until she turned eighteen and could gain access to the money in her adoptive parents' will. She had been able to find Kay only because Kay's cousin told her who her biological mother was before she died.

It had not been a warm reunion. Jessica knew that Kay had wanted nothing to do with her after she was born—and Jessica wanted nothing to do with Kay now that she was fifteen. But Jessica was in a bind. If Kay didn't become her guardian and take her in, Jessica would go into the foster-care system, which she insisted she wasn't going to do. So Jessica emotionally blackmailed Kay, and Kay reluctantly became her guardian. Or, to put it another way, Kay reluctantly became her mother again. Then, a few months after Jessica moved in with her, Mexican drug czar Caesar Olivera kidnapped Jessica and Kay killed Caesar to free her daughter—after which Kay was fired by the DEA.

Kay didn't have a typical relationship with her daughter, or what she suspected a typical mother-daughter relationship was like. She genuinely liked the girl—there was nothing about her *not* to like—and they got along okay, but they had nothing in common.

For one thing, the girl was off-the-charts bright. Kay had never thought of herself as a dummy—she'd maintained a B average in school while being socially hyperactive—but her daughter, who was more than a bit of a nerd, got straight A's and had a big brain when it came to math and science. Kay figured the kid had about a thirty-point advantage on her when it came to their respective IQs—and this actually intimidated Kay.

Kay was also a physical person, and when she'd been Jessica's age she'd been into sports; Jessica couldn't care less about sports and tended toward snobbery when it came to jocks. Jessica listened to music, read, and bounced around on the Internet when she wasn't doing homework; Kay watched TV and did home-improvement projects and worked out. Politically, Kay considered herself a right-leaning independent; her daughter, who had been raised by a couple of liberal academics, was practically a communist.

Jessica was now sixteen years old and very mature for her age, much more mature than Kay had been at the same age. She didn't follow the crowd when it came to fashion or entertainment; she didn't spend every waking moment Facebooking, tweeting, and texting her friends. Kay suspected the main reason Jessica was so grown-up was that when her adoptive mother was dying of breast cancer, Jessica, only fourteen at the time, had been her primary caregiver.

Whatever the case, the kid was bright, motivated, and self-sufficient, and Kay had once told a friend that living with her daughter was like living with a really smart, independent cat—a cat who didn't want anything to do with its owner. After Kay risked her life and her career to free Jessica from Caesar Olivera in Mexico, they became closer, but they were still more like good friends—or maybe sisters—than mother and daughter. Jessica called her *Kay*, not *Mom*—and that suited them both.

And this is what had fascinated the Callahan Group's psychiatrist: how Kay had dealt emotionally with giving up Jessica for adoption; how she felt about becoming a full-time mother; why she had risked her life and career for a child she barely knew. Kay had told the shrink that she didn't feel guilty at all about giving Jessica up for adoption. At the time, when she was only fifteen herself, she thought that was the right thing to do. As for risking her life to save Jessica from the Olivera cartel . . . Well, that's what a mother would do, she'd said, realizing that sounded contradictory and illogical.

* * *

"**H**ow was school today?" Kay asked as they ate dinner. The minestrone soup was marvelous, better than anything that ever came out of a can.

"Okay," Jessica said. "Just the usual stuff, except a guy came over from GU to give a talk on stem-cell research. That was cool."

Cool?

"How was work?" Jessica asked.

This was another thing Kay didn't like about her job: She couldn't talk to her daughter about it. When Jessica first moved in with her in San Diego, they didn't talk all that much because Jessica didn't like or trust her. Kay would make the attempt, however, to engage her in conversation and she'd talk about DEA cases and how the legal system worked or didn't work. After she rescued Jessica from the Olivera cartel they talked more, but it still wasn't easy to talk to a person who thought stem-cell research was *cool*. Then they moved to Washington and Kay went to work for the Callahan Group and she couldn't say anything about her job.

She had told Jessica almost the truth: She said she worked for a private-sector company that was like a defense contractor, meaning it dealt with classified matters she couldn't legally talk about—and Jessica said she understood, and she probably did. It most likely bothered Kay more than it did Jessica that she couldn't talk about the job. She couldn't even tell her about the training she was taking.

Anna Mercer had told her: "You tell people you're going to jump school at Fort Benning, taking diver training with SEALs at Panama Beach, learning basic breaking and entering, and how to speak Farsi. . . . Well, it wouldn't take a genius to figure out that you're being trained for covert ops." So when Kay had to be gone for a few days, she again told Jessica a limited version of the truth: The company is sending me someplace for training, but I can't say more.

Because Jessica was so mature, Kay wasn't too worried about her when she had to go out of town. She also had her friend Barb Reynolds and the lady next door, who'd raised four kids, check in on Jessica when she was gone. All Barb and her neighbor ever said to Kay was: *God, I wish my kids had been like her when they were her age.* Kay had no idea how Jessica would have turned out if Kay had raised her as her own child, but she was damn sure she wouldn't have turned out so well.

There was one issue, however, that had become a major source of tension between them: Jessica had acquired a boyfriend since they moved to D.C. She met him the first week of school and there was some sort of instantaneous nerd electromagnetic attraction. He was a tall, gangly kid with a mop of dark red hair, and Kay had to admit that he was cute. He was also a brainiac like her daughter and would probably end up being the next Steve Jobs. The problem was that Kay suspected Jessica was sleeping with him, or soon would be. She'd discovered birth-control pills in Jessica's purse one day when she was short of cash and didn't have time to go to an ATM. She hadn't really been snooping.

Kay had a hard time talking to Jessica about sex because she didn't want to come across as a hypocrite. Kay liked sex, and even after she'd gotten pregnant and had Jessica, she'd continued to have sex during her teenage years. But in spite of her own experience—or maybe *because* of her own experience—she didn't want her daughter to have sex at the age of sixteen. She was terrified that Jessica might get pregnant the way she had.

Without admitting that she'd found the birth-control pills, she'd tried a couple of times to talk to Jessica about the inadvisability of having sex at her tender age. Hoping to scare her, she even told her, truthfully, that she'd been on birth-control pills when she got pregnant so Jessica wouldn't think that those damn pills were a hundred percent reliable. But her daughter basically blew her off when Kay broached the subject of an unwanted pregnancy; she didn't exactly say that she wasn't as stupid as Kay had been, but that was the implication.

But since her daughter *was* so smart, Kay decided to ask her a question she probably shouldn't ask.

"What do you know about nuclear fusion?" Kay said.

"Nuclear fusion? Why are you asking about that?" Jessica knew that Kay had no interest in science.

"Oh, it sort of came up at work today. I can't tell you exactly in what context, but I was just curious if you knew how close they are to making fusion work for providing energy."

"Who's they?" Jessica asked.

"You know, the eggheads, the scientists, the government. What I heard today is that nuclear fusion is the Holy Grail of energy, and I was just curious if anyone was actually building a power plant or something."

"Well, as far as I know, nobody's close. The other thing is, I doubt this country is really working all that hard to make it viable."

"Why do you say that?"

"Because there's no compelling need at this point. We've got tons of natural gas—more natural gas than Saudi Arabia has oil—and it looks like most of the effort is going into extracting the gas, no matter how dangerous fracking is to the environment."

Aw, jeez. The last thing Kay wanted to hear was a speech from her daughter about the evils of the government and large corporations when it came to the environment.

"And if the government is working on fusion," Jessica said, "it's probably looking at making a more effective fusion bomb."

"A fusion bomb?"

"Yeah. Most nuke bombs use fission and they're really dirty, meaning if you blow something up you have to live with all the side effects of radioactive contamination. But a fusion bomb . . . You could blow up Tehran today and start rebuilding the city tomorrow."

"Huh," Kay said.

"So if I had to bet," her liberal daughter said, "if this country's working on fusion at all, we're more interested in a military application than producing clean energy."

"Is lithium used in these fusion bombs?" Kay asked.

"Well, yeah. Lithium-6 deuteride is the fusion fuel in thermonuclear weapons."

Kay had no idea what lithium-6 deuteride was and she had no intention of asking. Instead she said, "How the hell do you know all this sh . . . stuff?"

Jessica shrugged. "You know. Chemistry and physics classes. Why are you asking about lithium?"

Kay figured she should stop talking about fusion and lithium. Not only shouldn't she be talking about those things, she didn't want her daughter going off on some rant about U.S. foreign policy. She got up to fetch a second helping of Jessica's minestrone soup, trying to think of a way to switch the subject to something else, when Jessica said, "Kay, there's something really important I need to talk to you about"—and Kay's first thought, because it had been on her mind so much lately, was: *Oh, God, please don't tell me that little son of a bitch knocked you up?*

"What is it, honey? You know you can tell me anything." Now nuclear fusion and the possibility that Callahan had lied to her were the last thing on her mind.

Jessica gave her a strange look, like: *Why on* earth *would you say something like that?*

"I had a meeting with Mr. Tanaka yesterday," Jessica said. "You know, my guidance counselor at school. You met him."

Kay remembered Tanaka, a tall, good-looking guy who seemed like he might be fun.

"Yeah, I remember him."

"Well, he said if I wanted to and if you agreed, I could probably skip my senior year and go to college. He graduated from Duke and has some pull with the school. In fact, he comes from a really rich family and they donate a lot to Duke; I don't know why he's teaching at a high school. Anyway, he said if I spent the rest of this year on a tailored curriculum, he's about ninety percent sure they'll admit me next year, and they'll give me some kind of partial scholarship. He knows I want to be a doctor, and these days it takes about twelve years with pre-med, med school, internship and residency programs, and he says I'm just wasting my time in high school. He said the sooner I can get through the pre-med stuff and into medical school, the better. And he's not doing this just for me; he's working with four other kids who want to go into medicine or medical research. The thing is, I'd be leaving home, of course, and Duke's pretty pricey even with a partial scholarship."

Kay was so relieved that Jessica wasn't pregnant, she almost blurted out: *Thank God!*

"Hey, if that's what you want," Kay said, "then I'm all for it. And as for the money, don't worry about it. I'm making a decent salary and we can take out a loan if we need to. Whatever. We can afford it, and you can't pass up Duke. It's one of the top schools in the country." Actually, the only thing Kay knew about Duke was that they produced great basketball teams. "But do you think it's the right thing to do from a social standpoint? You know, going to school with kids older than you, not having the whole, uh, high school experience."

"They'd be like *one* year older than me," Jessica said. "It's not like I'd be some ten-year-old savant on campus."

"Yeah, well, that's true." Plus, she was always bragging about how mature Jessica was, and now she was acting like if she skipped the senior prom she'd turn into an agoraphobic wacko.

Kay couldn't help it, but another thought occurred to her. If her daughter was in North Carolina, living in a dorm, Kay could go back to living by herself and she wouldn't have to worry about explaining things to Jessica when the Callahan Group sent her someplace like Afghanistan. Or when she wanted to invite a man, like Eli Dolan, over to spend the night. God, she was a lousy mother.

In an attempt to do the right thing, as opposed to the selfish thing, she said, "Okay. But I need to talk to Tanaka myself and make sure this really is the best thing for you."

"Sure," Jessica said. "I'll let him know and we'll set something up. You going to be around next week?"

"Yeah. At least I think so." She was fairly sure she'd be in town because she'd be prepping for Ara Khan's visit—unless they decided to do the prepping in New York, in which case she wouldn't be in town. She'd ask Mercer about that tomorrow.

"Would you mind taking care of the dishes?" Jessica asked.

"Hey, of course," Kay said. "You cooked."

"Thanks. Brian and I are going to a show."

Huh. She wondered if they were really going to a show. She wondered if that horny little bastard's parents were out of the house and they were planning to go to his place to fool around. But instead of saying what she was thinking, she said, "What are you going to see?"

"The new Woody Allen."

"Woody's a whiny little wimp," Kay said.

"He's a genius," Jessica said.

"Yeah, right, a genius who . . . Aw, forget it. You just make sure you're home at a decent hour. You got school tomorrow." Kay knew that was a totally unnecessary thing to say to her overachiever daughter. What she'd really wanted to say was: *You come right back after that show, young lady, because if that boy knocks you up, I'm going to shoot him.*

Kay cleaned up the kitchen, then unlocked her briefcase and pulled out the background material Anna Mercer had given her on Ara Khan.

The Callahan Group had done a lot of research on Ara, had looked at every record they could find, and talked to over thirty people who had known her. The picture that emerged during Ara's high school and college years was: normal girl, even normal Western girl.

Ara wasn't religious—she never attended a mosque while she was abroad, nor had anyone ever seen her praying—and she appeared to like the things that most young girls liked: fashion, movies, music, and boys. While attending high school in France, she'd been chaperoned by teachers at the school she attended but was able to travel extensively throughout Europe. She skied in the Alps every year, and when she went to the beaches on the Costa del Sol, she wore a bikini. Although she socialized with boys her own age, there was no evidence the Group could find that she'd ever had a lover while in France. Nor was there any evidence that she'd been particularly close to anyone, male or female, while in Europe.

Things changed in college, primarily due to her roommate at NYU—Carolyn Harris. Carolyn, as Callahan had said, was a bit of a wild thing. She partied a lot and dated a lot—meaning she slept around a lot—got drunk fairly often, occasionally did a little recreational dope, and in general seemed to go through life having a good time while managing to maintain a C average at NYU.

She introduced Ara to New York: shopping, after-hours clubs, booze, and men. Harris's wealthy Connecticut family also appeared to have adopted Ara, as she spent a lot of weekends and holidays at their estate in Connecticut. Carolyn Harris's mother told one of Callahan's investigators that she thought of Ara as a daughter and as a sister to Carolyn.

Ara, either due to her background or just plain common sense, was more restrained than Carolyn Harris. It appeared that quite often Ara was the one who managed to get Harris safely back to the dorm after Harris had imbibed too much. In college, Ara had sexual relationships with at least two men. She dated one of them—a now-married stockbroker in Boston—most of her sophomore year. The second man she dated for only four months but slept with him. Kay had no idea how Callahan's investigators had obtained this information. Also, unlike Harris, Ara was a serious student and had almost a straight-A average. She didn't join any campus organizations but frequently attended lectures on political topics when lecturers appeared in New York.

Kay had to admit that she was beginning to develop a grudging admiration for Ara's father, Sahid Khan. He may have been a corrupt thug, but in a country where women were often married off at the age of thirteen, where schools teaching girls were bombed by the Taliban, where women were expected to be completely subservient to men and hide their bodies in burkas, Sahid Khan had sent his daughter out into the world to become a sophisticated, highly educated young woman.

When Ara returned to Afghanistan at the age of twenty-four, things changed. Dramatically. She put aside the clothes she wore in college and dressed as most modern Afghan businesswomen do—in long modest dresses and with a scarf covering her hair. She didn't wear a burka or a veil. She immersed herself in her father's business of governing Ghazni Province and, as Callahan had told Kay, assumed the role of his chief advisor. She wasn't dating anyone, although a member of the French Embassy in Kabul—a young man from a good Parisian family who had known Ara in high school—would show up every so often for dinner at the Khans' house, but they were never allowed to be alone together. Kay felt sorry for Ara Khan. It sounded as if she was leading an incredibly drab, stressful existence for a young woman of twenty-six.

She wondered if Ara had any dreams of her own.

The final item in the file was a copy of a 2010 article from the *New York Times* written by a guy named James Risen. The article discussed the vast mineral deposits that existed in Afghanistan and the difficulties associated with extracting those minerals. According to Risen, the Taliban might very well attempt to gain control of the minerals or, because of the rampant corruption in the central government, a few well-connected oligarchs could gain control. The article noted that Afghanistan had mining laws that had never been tested and how "endless fights" could erupt between the central government in Kabul and the leaders in the mineral-rich provinces.

The thing Kay found most interesting in the article

was that the Chinese had been caught trying to bribe the Afghan minister of mines with thirty million dollars to gain control of copper mining. So it appeared that what Callahan was trying to do had been tried before— and there was a lot of dangerous competition.

11

Alpha knocked on Finley's apartment door in Brooklyn, not concerned that it was almost midnight. Finley would be awake; Finley was almost always awake.

Alpha had found Rodger Finley in a database at the Pentagon, did some preliminary research, and then hired an agency in New York to fill out his profile. He had double doctorates in math and computer science, the math degree alone making him a weirdo. In every high school algebra class there is maybe one kid in the entire class who thinks imaginary numbers make sense—and Finley would have been that kid.

People who get advanced degrees in mathematics used to seek employment primarily with universities so they could spend all day playing with numbers and no one would demand that the playing result in something useful. Some went to work for places like the NSA where they needed math wizards to break codes—code breaking was very math- and computer-intensive—and others went to work for high-tech companies. The companies would stick the geeks down in a basement lab just *hoping* they'd come up with something that would turn a profit.

All they could do was hope, because nobody could really communicate with them and they had a tendency to work on whatever interested them.

These days, however, the place where a lot of math freaks ended up was Wall Street. These people are known as *quants*—an unattractive abbreviation for "quantitative analysts"—although *quant* better captures the personality and often the appearance of those who bear the title. Wall Street firms use their quants to develop programs containing algorithms that can buy and sell stocks and commodities in nanoseconds. The Wall Street guys aren't smart enough to understand the algorithms—all they understand is that if you can buy and sell at the speed of light, you can make millions. Some people still remember May 6, 2010: the day the Dow dropped a thousand points because one of those algorithms had a little glitch in it.

And that's where Rodger Finley ended up—as a quant on Wall Street.

Fortunately—for Alpha, that is—Finley was arrested when he was seventeen; by then he was already a junior in college. He was arrested because he'd hacked his way into a DOD database, which was why they had a file on him at the Pentagon. Finley did it just because it seemed like a fun thing to do. His arrest didn't result in a conviction, however; it resulted instead in an immediate job offer from the NSA after he graduated. But then a silver-tongued recruiter lured Finley to Goldman Sachs.

Finley made a small fortune at Goldman Sachs—the

quants were well paid—but he didn't make anywhere near the salary of the big boys at the top. Then one day he stopped showing up for work. He'd become bored making money for Goldman Sachs. Goldman fired him after they hadn't seen him for a couple of months, and when they did, they pointed out the noncompete clause in a contract he hadn't bothered to read and which kept him from going to work for another Wall Street firm for two years.

Finley didn't seem to care that he was unemployed, however. The agency Alpha hired said he spent almost twenty-four hours a day in his apartment playing on his computers. He was a nut, but a talented nut.

Finley finally opened the door after Alpha banged on it with a fist for almost two minutes. Finley was six foot one and skinny, looking like he weighed maybe a hundred thirty pounds. His nose was barely long enough to provide a perch for heavy, black-framed glasses, and greasy dark hair hung down to his shoulders. When he'd worked for Goldman, Finley had always worn his hair short, but Alpha didn't think he'd changed his hairstyle; Finley was just too preoccupied with doing whatever people like him did to go to a barber. He was barefoot—his toenails needed to be severely clipped—and dressed in gray sweatpants and a black *Star Trek* T-shirt. The T-shirt said *Live Long and Prosper*.

Alpha considered the T-shirt a good omen: Living long and prospering was the plan.

"Who are you? What do you want? I'm busy," Finley said.

"I have a job for you, Rodger, one that pays very well."

"I don't need a job. Go away."

"Rodger, you were fired by Goldman Sachs almost two years ago and you haven't drawn a paycheck since then. You have nineteen thousand dollars left in your bank account and your rent and utilities add up to twenty-seven hundred dollars a month. I don't know what you pay for food."

"How do you know how much . . ."

"In six months, you're going to be completely broke."

Alpha could tell Finley was actually shocked to hear how little money he had left. All his bills were paid by automatic withdrawals from a checking account, and apparently Finley hadn't been paying any attention to how much money was going out. But instead of admitting that he was on his way to homelessness, he said, "Hey, if I need a job, I'll find one."

"But that's my point, Rodger: You don't need to find one. I'm willing to pay you two million dollars if you can do what I need you to do."

"Two million?"

"I'm glad to see that I've finally gotten your attention. But I'm not going to stand out here in the hall talking to you."

Finley hesitated. "Fine, come in, but I'm not prom-ising anything."

Finley's living room looked like a cross between a video arcade and a launch control room at NASA. There were three large-screen TVs and the controllers for various video games sat on the floor, cords and cables running in every direction. The floor looked like a snake convention. On tables around the room were computers and monitors and dozens of gadgets with blinking lights, and Alpha had no idea what half the equipment did. In the middle of all the clutter was a red La-Z-Boy recliner, more or less centered between the television sets.

Finley pulled over a chair on rollers that was near all the computers and gestured for Alpha to take a seat. He plopped down in the La-Z-Boy, sitting sideways, his skinny legs dangling over the arm of the chair.

"So what's the job?" he said.

Alpha told him—and then set the hook. "The problem, even as bright as you're supposed to be, is that I'm not sure you can do it. I'm not sure anyone can." Alpha knew that for Finley the challenge was more im-portant than the money.

"Is that right?" Finley said, displaying the ego and arrogance he was known for.

"Yes. And the computers involved have the best se-curity systems available today."

"I can do it," Finley said.

"Well, I doubt it. But if you can prove to me that you can, and if the operation is successful, your cut will be two million. Then you can sit in this loft for the next decade doing whatever it is you do."

"I can do it," Finley said again. His fingers were twitching now, as if he were already tapping on a keyboard.

"Anyway, that's the hard part of the job. After we have the money, I'm going to want you to route it to several bank accounts and no one must be able to trace it."

"That's easy, too," Finley said.

It turned out the job wasn't *that* easy. It took Finley almost three weeks, and during that time he slept no more than two hours a night. By the time he finished, he'd lost ten pounds he couldn't afford to lose, and the next time Alpha saw him he had this weird look in his eyes, like some wacko mystic in a state of religious ecstasy. But he succeeded.

Step one was complete.

12

Kay returned to the Callahan Group's K Street head-quarters the next day and began working with Anna Mercer, Sylvia Sorenson, and Eli Dolan on the pitch she'd be giving to Ara Khan.

Sylvia's role was to make sure that Kay had a basic understanding of Afghan law as it applied to mining and mineral rights. Kay didn't have to know all the legal ins and outs. She just had to know enough that if Ara said that what Callahan wanted to do couldn't be done legally, Kay would be able to say: *Well, I think it can be-cause* . . . Kay was also surprised that when Sylvia talked about the law, she didn't act like the shy introvert Kay had met in Callahan's conference room. She was very articulate and very sure of herself. She even snapped once at Eli when he disagreed with something she said.

The biggest surprise to Kay, however, was Anna Mercer. Sylvia was good with facts, and so was Eli. Eli was able to tell her how the mining operation would be accomplished, how much money could be made, and what would be needed in terms of infrastructure. But Mercer was better at *selling*: how to present information in the most compelling way, how to frame arguments in a manner that would be best suited to Ara Khan's personality. Mercer would pretend to be Ara and would toss out the kind of questions and objections she expected Ara to make, and then would coach Kay on how to respond. Mercer may not have been the most likable person Kay had ever known, but she was very bright.

While having martinis with Eli the night before, Kay had not only learned about the Swiss connection, she'd also learned more about the people she worked with. When she'd asked him about himself and his coworkers, he said he'd be happy to tell her everything that was already a matter of public record but couldn't say anything about what they had done for Callahan.

She found out that what Callahan had told her about his background the first time Kay met him was true. He'd graduated from Notre Dame's ROTC program and, thanks to some family connections and a lot of luck, ended up spending two years at the Pentagon as a lackey on the staff of an assistant secretary of defense. The assistant secretary took note of him, and after he moved to the CIA, and after Callahan completed his military obligation, Callahan joined him at Langley. Callahan then spent the next twenty years at the CIA, and while he was there, he was engaged in covert operations and mission planning and had the opportunity to mingle with various luminaries at the White House and the Pentagon. He quit the CIA, moving back to the Pentagon to work for the secretary of defense for a couple of years, then over to the White House as a deputy to the president's national security advisor, where he apparently impressed George W. Bush.

Sylvia's story was somewhat similar to Callahan's in that she also began her career in the military, in her case the navy. According to Eli, Sylvia had been raised in an Appalachian coal-mining hamlet and had been dirt poor—like barely-able-to-afford-shoes poor. She enlisted with the navy after graduating from high school and fortunately the navy recognized her intelligence, sent her to college, then law school. It took her ten years to become an officer and lawyer, and then she was obligated to give the navy ten more years of her life. "She was a JAG lawyer," Eli said, "and held the rank of commander. Callahan met her when she was stationed at the Pentagon."

"She doesn't seem like the type that would work for Callahan," Kay had said.

"Sylvia's incredibly bright," Eli said. "She doesn't have the personality to be a litigator, but no one knows the law like her and nobody can learn the law faster than her. And she's not a field agent—she hardly ever leaves the office on K Street—so working for Callahan in a lot of ways isn't much different than working for a law firm."

"Yeah, but *why* would she work for Callahan? Why didn't she just stay in the navy or sign on with a normal law firm?"

"She works for Callahan because he pays her extremely well. She's making three times as much as she was making as a navy commander and she probably knows she'd never make partner in a big firm. And she needs the money because of her mother. Her mom, who's been living with her for almost a decade, has had every disease known to man and it's cost Sylvia a bundle to pay for her medications and nurses to take care of her."

"What about Mercer?" Kay had asked.

Anna Mercer, Eli said, began her career in the State Department, then moved over to the CIA looking for adventure, and someplace along the way attached herself to Callahan's coattails. She followed along behind Callahan as his assistant when he moved over to the Pentagon, and then came with him when he formed the Callahan Group.

"Anna's a bit bitter, however," Dolan said.

"Why's that?" Kay had asked.

"Because she's figured out that she's never going to be anything more than Callahan's number two, and now that bothers her. She thought at some point someone would recognize that she was just as capable as Callahan, if not more so, and she'd be given a job where she wasn't a deputy to anyone. She's mentioned to me several times that if she'd stayed on at State when Hillary was there, she's positive that Hillary would have been impressed with her and, with Hillary's backing, she could have been the next secretary. Or something."

"And how about you?"

"My story's pretty typical, too," Eli said. "I got the usual Harvard MBA . . ."

He said this like every third person on the planet had one.

". . . hired on at Goldman, did quite well there, then when Hank Paulson and a bunch of other Goldman people went down to Treasury to help out after the financial meltdown, I tagged along. After Treasury, I spent a little time over at the OMB, and working there . . ."

Kay had finally looked up the OMB: It stood for the Office of Management and Budget. According to OMB's Web site its core mission was *to serve the President of the United States in implementing his vision across the Executive Branch*—whatever the hell that meant. As near as Kay could figure, the OMB helped the president develop a budget and then spend the money. She also learned that when Dolan said he spent "a little time over at OMB" he actually ran the organization for a year.

". . . I learned quite a bit more about how money gets moved around in Washington, which is what made me attractive to Callahan."

"How'd you meet him?" Kay asked.

"I can't get into that. All I can say is that he needed somebody like me for a specific job one time, told me about himself and what the Callahan Group does, and I agreed to help him." He hesitated before he added, "It almost makes me blush to say this, but I wanted to give back to my country. My family has been very fortunate, and so have I, and since I never enlisted in the military, I decided to join him. The other reason I signed on with him is, quite frankly, it sounded like fun—and it has been."

Fun? Maybe figuring out a way to get lithium out of a place like Afghanistan and putting a guy like Sahid Khan in a position of power so he could be controlled by the U.S. government was his idea of fun, but it certainly wasn't Kay's idea of fun. She remembered one time in Florida when she was part of a team sent into the Everglades to bust a guy with a meth lab protected by pit bulls and guarded by idiots with assault rifles—now, *that* had been fun. It was like the difference between a man who liked chess and a woman who liked . . . well, hockey.

She asked him one last question about himself, deep into her second martini: "Are you married? I mean, I can see you're not wearing a ring, but . . ."

Kay's last long-term relationship, which had gone on for over a year, had been with a married man—an assistant U.S. attorney in San Diego. In some ways, before Jessica moved in with her, she preferred affairs with married men, as they tended not to be particularly clingy and rarely wanted to marry her. Kay had been married once, for eight months when she was twenty-three, and had no desire to get married again. After Jessica started living with her, however, she didn't feel right about sleeping with some other woman's husband—she couldn't say why this was so, but that's the way it was—and she stopped seeing the assistant U.S. attorney.

The fact was, her sex life was in the toilet and it was a situation she needed to rectify. She didn't feel comfortable bringing men home for one-night stands—not with Jessica sleeping in the next room—and in the short time they'd been living in D.C., she hadn't met anyone that she thought would be anything more than a one-night stand.

Eli Dolan, however, might be a whole different story. He intrigued her. He was smart and funny and incredibly good-looking—and rich. He was a *catch*, as her late mother used to say.

In answer to her question about being married, Eli said, "No, I'm not married. I was married for about five years to a girl I met in college—my parents adored her—but we went our separate ways."

"Why?" Kay asked.

Dolan hesitated. "I guess, to be completely honest, after we'd been married for a while I found out she just wasn't that interesting to be with and I couldn't see myself spending the rest of my life with her."

Hmm. Kay didn't know how she felt about that answer.

After all the personal stuff was out of the way, he told her about the Swiss connection, and to hear Dolan tell the story, what he'd done was quite simple, although it didn't sound simple at all to Kay.

"We obviously need a mining company to get the lithium out of the ground, but like Callahan told you, we wanted to be able to control the company. Our objective is to stockpile lithium, not to turn a profit. We also didn't want to use a U.S. company, because of anti-American sentiment in Afghanistan. The company we finally decided to use is an old Swiss company called Glardon Mining. It has experience with international mining, mostly in Africa, and good engineers. But the main reason we selected Glardon was because it was vulnerable.

"The company was founded by a man named Gustav Glardon and has been around for seventy years. Gustav's son, Ernst, now runs it. Unfortunately for Glardon's employees, Ernst is an idiot who has run the business into the ground. Not only that, he's also an incompetent crook who's been embezzling from his own company. In the last six months, the Callahan Group acquired the controlling interest in Glardon and I've sat down with Ernst and explained to him that he's now working for me and if he doesn't do what I tell him, he'll spend several years in a Swiss prison.

"It was easy," Dolan concluded.

13

When Alpha called Bravo and said they needed to talk privately, Bravo knew Alpha's name, because they'd spoken before when the Callahan Group was investigating companies to provide security for the mining operation. Bravo was surprised, of course, by the meeting place, but agreed without complaint. Bravo needed the money too much to argue with a potential client, no matter how strange the client's demands might seem.

Meeting with Finley hadn't been dangerous. Finley's only weapon was his mind, and he wasn't physically impressive. Had it been necessary to dispatch Finley, Alpha had no doubt that would have been possible, even easy. Bravo was a different story. Bravo was a trained killer.

And where Finley had been motivated by arrogance and the technical challenge of the job, Bravo could only be swayed with money. And if Bravo had a conscience, which seemed unlikely, he might report Alpha to Callahan. A more likely possibility was that Bravo would demand a bigger slice of the pie and he might even think, considering his role in the operation, that he was in charge and Alpha was working for him instead of the other way around.

All Alpha knew for sure was that if Bravo didn't agree to cooperate, he'd have to be killed. Bravo couldn't leave the meeting place knowing Alpha's plan. But killing the man was not going to be easy. Alpha had no practical experience when it came to murder, whereas Bravo had a lifetime's worth of experience and there was no doubt, considering his profession, that he would come to the meeting armed. To make matters worse, if it became necessary to kill him, then it would also be necessary to deal with the logistics of committing a capital crime: making sure no evidence was left behind, that no witnesses existed, and figuring out what to do with the body.

It was with all these considerations in mind that Alpha chose the meeting place: a five-hundred-acre state forest near Strasburg, Virginia, with the ominous-sounding name of Devil's Backbone. The forest was about halfway between Bravo's company in West Virginia and Washington, D.C., and therefore convenient for both parties. The main reason Alpha selected the place, however, was that it was a research forest, not open to the general public, and one particular campsite was especially isolated. Devil's Backbone was, in other words, a good place to murder a man and dispose of his corpse.

* * *

Alpha arrived at the campsite an hour early; it wouldn't do for Bravo to get there first. The campsite was surrounded by trees, the small clearing for pitching a tent was overgrown with brush, and there was nothing else there but a fire pit covered with a rusty barbecue grate and a dilapidated, wooden picnic table. It didn't appear as if the site had been used in years, and it was unlikely that anyone would decide to use it today—or so Alpha hoped. When Bravo arrived, Alpha, as planned, was already sitting at the picnic table and the gun was in Alpha's lap, obscured by the top of the table.

Bravo was in excellent physical condition, and he moved with the grace of a large, powerful feline as he walked toward the table. He sat directly across from Alpha as expected. The gun in Alpha's lap was a Heckler & Koch P30 9mm pistol equipped with a silencer, and, if necessary, Alpha would fire under the table, never showing the gun. If the first shot didn't kill Bravo, the next one would.

Like with Finley, Alpha began with a discussion of Bravo's abysmal financial situation. He immediately became angry that his privacy had been invaded—although almost all the data was a matter of public record. Alpha knew what really angered him was that he was a proud man and humiliated by his circumstances.

Alpha's whole argument boiled down to that old

saying: *Which would you prefer? A bird in the hand or two in the bush?* It was really that simple. If Bravo's company was awarded the security contract, and if things went as Callahan planned, the company would eventually make a lot of money—the important words being *if* and *eventually*. The problem was that there was no guarantee that Callahan would succeed and *eventually* could be two or three years down the road.

Alpha pointed out that even if Callahan was successful, it was going to be a long time before the mining operation actually started—and during that time, Bravo's company would have nothing to protect and, therefore, no large amounts of money coming in. Furthermore, it was always possible that the boys in Kabul would manage to screw everything up and the security contract could be given to somebody else, in which case Bravo would be left out in the cold. The last thing Alpha told him was that the money from the security contract would go to his company—not him personally— and it would be visible to the gnomes at the IRS. The tax man would never see the money Alpha gave him.

So which did he prefer: the bird in hand or the two in the bush?

It actually didn't take him very long to make up his mind—no more than ten minutes. He was a man used to making decisions, and Alpha had been sure before sitting down with him that the bloodshed wouldn't bother him. He'd killed before and in large numbers. Killing, after all, had been his job. He was moved by the money; the amount Alpha was offering was simply too much for him to pass up.

After he made his decision, they began to talk about the details of how to execute the plan—and Alpha relaxed and put the gun back in a pocket. Bravo actually proved to be quite helpful; he was an experienced tactician, not merely a killer.

PART II

14

Kay wore a badge that allowed her to roam around the United Nations building without an escort. Ara Khan had arrived in New York the night before and Kay had been following her all day. She now watched as Ara left the UN building with three other Muslim women.

Ara had come to the United Nations to attend a symposium on women's issues: equal opportunity, infant mortality rates, birth control, AIDS, education for girls—all the usual things. Many of the attendees were from Muslim countries, and there were women from Pakistan, Iraq, Egypt, Indonesia, Saudi Arabia, and a host of African nations. Ara was one of two women representing Afghanistan. Kay didn't know if the purpose of the symposium was to simply sit around and bitch about the way things were, or if the intent was to get money from the richer nations to aid their efforts. She suspected the latter.

What Kay needed was a chance to get close to Ara and talk to her, but so far the opportunity hadn't presented itself. Ara had been in meetings and lectures all day, and when she left for lunch, she was accompanied by other people. It was now four p.m. and Kay watched in dismay as she and the other three women jumped into a cab. Kay waved down another cab and followed the group to the Hyatt near Grand Central, where many of the delegates were staying. She watched as Ara walked through the lobby with her friends, glancing once over at the packed lobby bar, and entered an elevator. When Ara had looked over at the bar, Kay got the impression that she wanted to join the noisy crowd in there.

When they'd been prepping her to talk to Ara, Mercer had emphasized that ideally Kay should find a way to approach Ara in a social setting, and somehow get her alone and establish some rapport with her. They didn't want her to go straight at Ara and bluntly lay out the Callahan Group's proposal.

"Why not?" Kay had asked.

"Because if you just walk up to her and say you want to meet with her, she'll ask why. And then you'd have to say you want to talk to her about the lithium reserves in Ghazni Province, and she'll most likely refuse. She won't talk to a stranger about something like that, and she'll suspect that you're trying to use her in some way. So you have to find a way to . . . I don't know, ease into it, to get her to like you first."

Kay found the idea of conning Ara into liking her distasteful. It wasn't as if she hadn't conned criminals before—she'd done that fairly often when she worked for the DEA—but Ara Khan wasn't a criminal. Sensing what she was thinking, Mercer had said, "Look. If you have some sort of moral objection to this assignment, you should resign. You're no longer in the black-and-white world of law enforcement, and if you can't handle the . . . the *ambiguities* of this kind of work, we'll find someone else."

Maybe Kay should have walked out the door right then, but she didn't. And by the way, she'd almost said, law enforcement wasn't all that black-and-white.

"I thought about staging a mugging," Mercer had said. "You know, a junkie tries to steal her purse and you save her. But that's just too Hollywood, and Ara would probably see right through it. She's not a dummy. But we need to devise some sort of scenario where you can get next to her."

In the end, Callahan told Mercer to quit trying to orchestrate the initial meeting and let Kay play it by ear. Mercer didn't like this at all; she was a control freak and she wanted a situation she could control, but Callahan said, "Look, it's a sales job, pure and simple. You walk into a showroom and the salesman approaches you, and if you don't like him, he couldn't sell you a Cadillac if he was selling them for a buck. But if you *like* the salesman, and even if you don't want a Cadillac, you'll listen to his pitch, and who knows, you might end up buying one. So Hamilton just needs to look for an opportunity to approach Ara, make Ara like her, then pitch her. And don't forget the amount of money we're offering; that'll get Ara's attention even if she doesn't like Hamilton or the pitch."

Kay took a seat in the lobby of the Hyatt, wondering whether Ara would venture out again that night. It was only five p.m. She was afraid, however, that if Ara did go out, it would be with her Muslim friends. Fortunately, she turned out to be wrong.

Twenty minutes later, Ara stepped out of the elevator. The Ara who had gone up in the elevator twenty minutes earlier had been wearing a flowing robe with a colorful scarf over her head. She'd looked like a Muslim woman. The Ara who exited the elevator was wearing a short, black leather jacket, tight-fitting blue jeans, and red high heels. Her long black hair flowed down to her shoulders. She looked like any other chic New Yorker who came from money and had excellent taste, except she was better-looking than most New Yorkers. There was something exotic about her.

Kay followed her out of the hotel, relieved that Ara didn't catch a cab. It was rush hour and it was going to be hard to get a cab to tail her. But it appeared as if all Ara wanted to do was stretch her legs and walk around the city where she'd gone to college, and it was a lovely October evening, more like summer than fall.

Kay watched as she went into one shoe store and spent ten minutes looking at the shoes—the expensive ones— but she didn't try anything on. She left the shoe store and

walked around Times Square for about ten minutes, ordered a hot dog from a street vendor, and ate it as she
walked, being careful not to spill relish onto her jacket.
Kay got the impression she enjoyed the hot dog more
than a multicourse dinner at some five-star establishment.

After she finished eating, she surprised Kay when she
took the stairs down to a subway station. She was familiar with the MetroCard ticket system and seemed
comfortable riding the crowded train. She exited the
train in lower Manhattan, and when she was back out on
the street she moved with a purpose, not dawdling along,
window-shopping, as she'd done earlier. She finally
entered a place called the Ulysses Folk House on Pearl
Street.

Ara walked past the bar and back toward the rest-
rooms, and Kay guessed she was going there to repair
her lipstick after eating the hot dog. As she waited for
Ara, Kay looked around. The Ulysses Folk House was
near the Financial District and appeared to be filled with
Wall Street types: young men and women, mostly men,
with expensive haircuts and expensive suits, drinking
martinis and bragging—and probably lying—about how
well they'd done that day gambling with other people's
money.

Ara came back from the restroom and took a seat at
the bar. Kay waited until Ara had a drink in front of
her, then took a bar stool one seat away from her. She
intentionally didn't take the seat next to her.

The bartender came over and asked what Kay wanted,

and she said, "Gee, I don't know." Turning to Ara, she said, "What's that you're having?" Ara's drink was a pale blue color served in a martini glass.

Ara said, "It's called a cool blue martini. It's made with blue curaçao and vodka or gin. I prefer vodka."

To the bartender Kay said, "One of those, just like hers with vodka." To Ara she said, "Thanks. Never hurts to try something new. By the way, I love your shoes." And she did.

"Thank you," Ara said. "They're Dolce and Gabbanas."

Kay knew that. She also knew she couldn't afford the seven hundred bucks they cost. "Well, I love them," she said. "Why did you decide to stop in here tonight?"

"I love to people-watch," Ara said. "I used to come here when I was in college. Did you ever read Tom Wolfe's *The Bonfire of the Vanities*?"

"No, I'm not much of a reader. But I saw the movie with Tom Hanks."

"Then you know what I mean. These are the people Wolfe was writing about, the ones who think they're the masters of the universe."

"Well, personally, I'd prefer a Mr. Universe type," Kay said. "You know, a guy with six-pack abs instead of a portfolio."

Ara laughed.

"And speaking of masters of the universe, I'll buy the next drink if that guy with the slicked-back hair and the suspenders who thinks he's Gordon Gekko . . ."

She'd seen that movie, too.

". . . doesn't walk over here in the next five minutes and hit on you. He's been looking at you ever since you sat down. No! Don't turn around. Use the mirror."

Ara looked at the Gekko wannabe in the mirror.

"He's kind of cute," she said.

"Yeah, he is, but his buddy's not so cute, and I'll bet they both walk over here and I get stuck with the buddy."

"Yes, the buddy, he's not so cute. But maybe he has a sense of humor." Then she laughed again, and Kay really liked her laugh. In fact, she couldn't help it, but she genuinely liked Ara Khan. She also felt sorry for her, living an almost cloistered existence in Afghanistan.

Sure enough, two minutes later, Gordon and his pal ambled over to the bar. Kay couldn't help but wonder what Ara might have done if Gordon had had any class. Maybe she would have taken the guy back to her hotel for a roll in the hay in a place far from the prying eyes of her father and his people. Fortunately, Gordon was very drunk, very crude, and very full of himself. He wasn't an Eli Dolan. Ara was polite to him but finally told him to take a hike, saying that she just wanted to sit with her friend and chat for a bit.

Now Kay was her friend.

"I guess this means I owe you a drink?" she said to Kay.

"Nah, we didn't spit on our hands and shake on the bet."

They sat there and chatted some more, Kay steering

the conversation toward Ara's college days in New York. Partially she did this to subtly remind Ara of her old roommate, Carolyn Harris. But her instincts were telling her it was time to get to the point. If she kept up the pretense any longer of just having bumped into Ara in a bar, Ara wouldn't trust her when she did reveal the real reason she was there. Ara gave her the opening she was looking for when she asked Kay, "And what about you? What do you do in New York?"

"I don't live here," Kay said. "I came to here to see you."

This made Ara sit back on her bar stool—increasing the distance between her and Kay—and a guarded look came into her eyes.

"Why?" she asked. "Have you been following me?"

Kay ignored the question. "Ara, I know you came to the UN to promote the kind of causes you believe in, the kind of causes that require money and political influence to make a difference. I work for a company that can help you."

"Really," Ara said, her skepticism evident.

Kay plunged ahead. "You may not know this, but you have a very valuable resource in your province—specifically, a very valuable mineral—and if you partner with my company, you can turn that resource to your advantage. I mean, to your country's advantage. I just want a few minutes to talk to you about this."

Kay realized immediately, in spite of all the hours she'd spent practicing with Eli and Anna, that she'd done a poor job of introducing the subject. She'd been too blunt and her delivery was stilted, and she doubted that Ara Khan was so naïve as to believe that any private company really cared about the people of Afghanistan. She now fully expected, after the way she'd botched the introduction, that Ara would tell *her* to take a hike. But she didn't. Instead Ara said, "Sure, I'd be happy to talk to you. Let's get a table. We'll order an appetizer to soak up some of the vodka."

Five minutes later, Kay realized that Callahan had been completely wrong about Ara Khan.

Ara Khan was well aware of the 2007 U.S. Geological Survey that had identified lithium reserves in the dry lakes of Ghazni Province. She was also well aware of its potential value, as well as the difficulties of extracting minerals from Afghanistan. But where Callahan had really been wrong was thinking that Ara Khan was some starry-eyed idealist who would balk at Callahan's proposal.

Ara Khan may have only been twenty-six years old, but she was a sophisticated young woman, completely immersed in the Machiavellian politics of Afghanistan. She'd spent the last two years, according to Callahan, helping her father govern his wild province and she wasn't the least bit naïve. She also knew, without having to be told, that the only way she and her father would profit from the lithium reserves in Ghazni was if they had some sort of outside help. It was apparent to Kay that Ara had been thinking about the lithium long before Callahan had come creeping along.

So Kay didn't have to sell Ara Khan on the deal at all; she just had to show that what Callahan wanted to do was feasible. She didn't have to convince or persuade Ara that it was in her country's best interest to accept Callahan's proposal, she just had to show that Callahan could really do what he was offering to do. When Kay brought up the fact that the Callahan Group was willing to support her father in a bid to become president of her country, Ara smiled. That wasn't something that had occurred to her or that she'd considered within the realm of possibility.

"We're obviously not doing this out of the goodness of our hearts," Kay said. "We know if your dad's the guy in charge, we'll have a better chance to accomplish what we want." Kay was relieved that she could now be honest with Ara; it was much easier for her to be herself and be honest than try to con her.

"That's very good," Ara said, "but I hope you realize that it will take a substantial, uh . . ."

Kay could see she was looking for the words to bring up the subject of money.

"He'll need a war chest," Kay said.

"Exactly," Ara said. "A very large one. A lot of people will have to be . . . persuaded. How much are we talking about?"

"Twenty-five million," Kay said. "We know it's going to be difficult to make this happen, but since the lithium is potentially worth billions, we're willing to make a substantial investment provided we have documents that spell out the details for the future. But we're not going to move on this unless the terms are clear and our investment is protected."

Kay had actually been astounded when Callahan said they were going to give Sahid Khan twenty-five million. Recalling the thirty million the *New York Times* said the Chinese paid the Afghan minister of mines in 2010, she wasn't surprised by the amount, but she was surprised that Callahan was willing to give him all the money up front. She was also surprised that Mercer agreed with her.

"If it was up to me," Mercer had said, "there's no way in hell we'd be giving a bandit like him that kind of money, but Callahan made the decision. He said he didn't want to get outbid by somebody, and although it won't cost two billion like an American presidential campaign, it's going to take quite a bit. Callahan said he didn't want to start out with some lowball amount and then have to add to it every couple of months when Khan needed to get something done. The main thing, however, is that Callahan can get the money—and it's not like it's *his* money—and in the grand scheme of things, considering the billions the U.S. has given to Afghanistan in foreign aid, twenty-five million is a drop in the bucket."

If Ara was shocked by the amount, however, she didn't show it. She simply nodded a couple of times as she considered the number. Kay also wondered if Ara was thinking at all about the issues she'd come to the United Nations to discuss; Callahan may also have underestimated the ardor she felt for those issues. Maybe the only thing Ara was thinking about was that she'd continue to be shod in Dolce & Gabbanas.

"Okay," Ara said. "Enough business for tonight. I'll be flying home in two days and I'll discuss all this with my father. If he thinks your proposal has merit, I'll contact you and we'll proceed from there. By the way, your company was smart to send someone like you to talk to me instead of some slick corporate bullshitter."

Before Kay could thank her for what had sounded like a compliment, Ara said, "Now, I didn't come to New York just to attend this conference. I also came to have some fun. I've been working my ass off the last few months, and I deserve some fun. There used to be a place a few blocks from here. I don't know if it's still there, but they used to have two guys that came from New Orleans after Katrina and they play dueling pianos and tell dirty jokes. Would you like to come with me?"

"Sure," Kay said.

Later that evening, Kay had another thought: Maybe Carolyn Harris hadn't led Ara astray; maybe it had been the other way around.

* * *

They had a great time that night. They drank too much; they laughed a lot. Handsome young men bought them drinks, caressed their egos, and tried to get them into bed. She also found out that Ara really was passionate about the causes being discussed at the UN. Maybe some of the money they were offering the Khans really would end up doing some good.

At one point, Kay could tell Ara was genuinely interested in a guy—a well-built stud who was a utility infielder for the Yankees but saw playing time only when Jeter was injured or needed a rest. Kay waited until they were alone in the restroom together before she said, "Hey, if you want to split with him you won't hurt my feelings, and I swear to God, I won't tell anybody. Really, Ara, you can trust me on that."

"I believe you, but I think not. I'm having a good time tonight, just the two of us. And I have his number. Let's move on to the next place."

The hangover Kay had the next day was of historic proportions, but she called Mercer and said, "Mission accomplished. It was easy."

"Easy?" Mercer said, sounding skeptical.

"Yeah. You and Callahan were completely wrong about Ara Khan. I didn't have to sell her on anything. She and her dad had just been waiting for someone like Callahan to come along. She said she'd call me after she's had a chance to talk things over with her old man. Then, after I told her what we wanted to do, we went out on the town together and had a blast."

"I know," Mercer said. "We had someone following you the whole night. He said the karaoke number you two did together was impressive but that Ara has a better voice than you."

"Well, I don't know about that," Kay said.

15

A week later, when Ara Khan hadn't called Kay back, Eli suggested to Callahan that Kay call her.

"No," Callahan said. "These things take time. What Ara's father is doing right now is trying to figure out if he can get a better deal from someone else. I don't think he'll find one."

Callahan turned out to be right. That night Ara called Kay.

"My father can see the merits in your proposal. He wants you to provide documents laying out a timeline for the mining operation, specific milestones that must be met, infrastructure upgrades that will be needed, profit projections, and how profits will be shared between the mining company and Afghanistan. My father didn't specifically ask for this, but I also want to understand how many local people will be employed and a document discussing the environmental impact of lithium mining on a large scale. Finally, you will provide a draft of the contract that defines our relationship. There will be nothing in these documents discussing your support of my father's political aspirations. How long do you think it will take to prepare these documents?"

"I don't know," Kay said.

"Well, find out and get back to me," Ara snapped.

Kay almost said: *Yes, ma'am*. "I'll do that," Kay said.

"Courier the documents to me when they're ready. Don't e-mail or fax them. If the preliminary documents appear satisfactory, we'll meet here in Afghanistan to finalize our arrangement. My father is unwilling to leave the province at this time. There are matters here that require our—I mean his—personal oversight."

Kay wondered if that meant that Sahid Khan was reluctant to travel because he needed to stay close to home to keep the people he governed in line.

"But there is a problem that needs to be resolved before we go any further."

"Oh, yeah? What's that?" Kay asked.

"Twenty-five million isn't going to be enough to facilitate what needs to be done."

"Is that right," Kay said. "So how much do you want?"

"Twice that amount." Before Kay could tell Ara that she was just a middleman and in no position to make a decision on the money, Ara said, "We're not trying to hold you up. You've simply underestimated what it's going to take to achieve your objective."

Kay thought that was probably bullshit. Ara and her old man probably *were* trying to hold them up.

"I'll convey all this to my boss," Kay said, "and call you tomorrow."

* * *

Kay immediately called Callahan and passed on what Ara had told her, and the next morning Callahan held a meeting with Kay, Eli Dolan, Sylvia Sorenson, and Anna Mercer in attendance.

"Eli, how long will it take you and Sylvia to provide the documents Ara wants?" Callahan said.

"They've been ready for a month," Eli said, "except for the environmental impact statement. I wasn't expecting that. And we can't give her a real environmental impact assessment, as those take months to prepare—analyzing waste streams, water tables, soil conditions, all sorts of things. But I think I can give her what she wants in terms of generic environmental concerns, with the caveat that an engineering firm will be hired to do a formal assessment later."

"Yeah, well, give her whatever you think will make her happy," Callahan said. "Kay, you call Ara back and tell her we'll give her everything she asked for by the end of this week and that she'll have a week to review the documents. I want to get moving on this. Eli, who besides Kay do you need at the meeting?"

"I don't see why I need to go at all," Kay said.

"You need to go because I want you to stay connected to Ara. So who else needs to be there, Eli?"

"We need somebody from Glardon Mining in case they want to get more into the nuts and bolts of the mining operation. I think I can handle everything else myself."

"Will you need me there?" Sylvia asked Eli. "I mean, in case there are legal issues they want to discuss. I'd prefer not to go—I mean, because of my mother—but if I have to . . ."

"No, you won't need to be there," Callahan said, answering for Eli. "The Khans aren't worried about the legal shit, because Sahid Khan plans to bribe his way through all the legal shit."

"But we're going to need security," Eli said. "I mean, if it's okay with you, Thomas, I'd just as soon come back from Afghanistan alive."

"I've already thought about that," Callahan said. "We'll use Cannon and Sterling."

"What are you talking about?" Kay said.

"For the initial meeting with Ara and her father," Callahan said, "we could send some of our own people with you to keep the Taliban from killing you while you're over there. But the Callahan Group is not in the security business, and when we actually begin mining operations we're going to need a heavy-duty, full-time security company. C and S Logistics is an outfit run by two ex–army colonels named Cannon and Sterling. They've been around for about ten years and they hire good people, all of them previously trained by Uncle. Our plan was to use them when we started mining and doing the infrastructure upgrades, but we might as well bring them in now so they can get the lay of the land. I'll call Cannon and tell him."

"But what about the money?" Mercer asked Callahan.

He'd only grunted when Kay told him that Ara wanted double what Callahan had initially offered.

"The money's not a problem," Callahan said.

"You're kidding," Kay said.

"The Pentagon's budget this year is about five hundred billion," Callahan said. "Fifty million is point zero one percent of that budget. The money's not a problem."

Kay wondered what the Pentagon's budget had to do with Callahan's calculations, but didn't ask.

"So," Callahan said, "Eli, you and Sylvia finish getting the documents together and courier them to Ara. Kay, you call Ara back, set a specific date for the meeting, and find out where she wants to meet. You can also tell her we'll give her the amount she wants, but if she asks for any more, tell her it might be cheaper for us to have her old man whacked and deal with his replacement."

"Are you serious?" Kay said.

"No. That was a joke. Sort of. Just make sure she understands that I'm not going to let her keep raising the ante."

Alpha couldn't believe it!

Alpha had been willing to risk everything for eighteen million as Finley was getting two and Bravo five. But now Callahan was planning to give the Khans *fifty* million instead of twenty-five, meaning that Alpha would walk away—if able to walk away—with over forty million dollars.

130 I M. A. LAWSON

This was like winning the lotto without even buying a ticket.

Alpha called Bravo and gave him an update, saying only that the plan was proceeding forward. There was no reason to tell Bravo that the prize had doubled, and there was no way that Bravo would be able to find out.

"As soon as I know where the meeting is, I'll let you know," Alpha said. "But you won't have much time. You're going to have to really scramble. You'll need to . . ."

"Don't tell me how to do my job," Bravo said.

And Alpha thought: *This arrogant son of a bitch is going to be a problem.*

O ther than a couple of phone calls to Ara Khan, Kay didn't really have anything to do in the two weeks before they left for Afghanistan. All the heavy lifting was being done by Eli and Sylvia. The only thing of note that she did during this period was go to bed with Eli Dolan.

One day, after another meeting to brief Callahan on how everything was proceeding, Eli asked Kay if she'd like to go out for a drink. The last time Kay had drinks with Eli, she'd gone home a bit tipsy—but she'd gone home. This time Eli Dolan charmed the pants off her— literally. Or to put it another way, Kay allowed those pants to be charmed off. She and Eli had two drinks on M Street, and when Dolan asked if she'd like to see his Georgetown town house, she'd called her daughter and said that Mommy had to pull an all-nighter for God and country.

Dolan was everything in bed that he was out of bed: attentive, unselfish, and adroit. She loved his slim body, and she hadn't had sex in so long, she was ravenous. Before they left for Afghanistan, Kay and Dolan managed to find time for a dozen encounters. Kay kept track of the number. Was she in love with Eli Dolan? She wasn't sure. All she knew was she felt more attracted to him than any man she'd met in a long time. She also wasn't sure what the future would bring.

She didn't know if she was going to stay with the Callahan Group—she wasn't enamored at all with her current assignment—and if she stayed, she knew having an affair with a coworker could really complicate things. She also didn't like that Eli preferred to live in New York, and although he claimed he was okay with her having a teenage daughter and was looking forward to meeting Jessica, Kay knew there was a big difference between being a lover and being a stepfather.

She finally decided she'd worry about the future later, and for now just enjoy having sex with him.

One thing she certainly didn't foresee was Eli Dolan trying to kill her.

16

Almost a month after Kay met with Ara Khan in New York, she, Eli Dolan, and two engineers from Glardon Mining flew to Kabul. They spent their first night at the Kabul Serena Hotel. Kay had been expecting a dump, but the place was more than adequate, except for a two-hour power outage, which the staff treated as normal. Dolan didn't come to her room that night; it had been an exhausting trip and they were leaving at dawn for Ghazni Province.

The following morning, Kay dressed in a loose-fitting black cotton *abaya*—a modest, long dress that buttoned up the front and covered her from chin to ankles. On her head was a black scarf to cover her blond hair, and she could wrap it around to hide her face. She didn't like wearing the scarf, but Eli insisted.

The security team from C&S Logistics was waiting in front of the hotel. They had arrived in Afghanistan six days earlier to reconnoiter the meeting place, arrange for transportation, and get whatever supplies they couldn't bring from the States.

The team consisted of ten men, including Steven

Cannon and Nathan Sterling, the founders and managing partners of C&S Logistics. Callahan had said that both men were retired army colonels, and Kay learned from Eli that they'd spent their combat time in Iraq and were not as familiar with Afghanistan, which was why both partners had come along on this trip. Sterling and six men would accompany Kay and Eli to the meeting, provide protection during the meeting, and remain with them until they left the country. Cannon would take two of his men and one of the mining engineers to the dry salt lakes; he wanted to examine the area near the lakes and begin developing a strategy for protecting the mining operation once the work started.

To Kay, Sterling and Cannon looked like bookends. Both men were over six feet tall, about sixty years old, and had close-cropped gray hair. They also appeared to be in excellent physical shape, flat-bellied and muscular. Kay could imagine them training with their men, refusing to give in to the fact that they were half their age, and bragging that they could still fit into the uniforms they wore as butter-bar lieutenants. Sterling had a big nose and a thin-lipped mouth. Cannon's features were rounder than Sterling's, and his hair was thinner, but the main thing that distinguished Cannon from Sterling was that Cannon wore glasses and Sterling didn't. Both men seemed on edge, their eyes constantly moving, looking for potential threats.

All the C&S men were dressed as working-class Muslim men would dress. They had on long shirts—gray, white, and brown in color—that reached their knees and loose, pajama-like pants. Kay learned that this style of dress was called *perahan tunban* and was worn by most Afghan men. Some of the men wore vests or jackets over the shirts, but Cannon and Sterling, maybe wanting to look like bosses, had rough woolen sport coats over their shirts. All the men were unshaven, and several had beards. A few wore brimless hats that looked like beanies, and others a floppy cloth hat called a *pakol*. The security team wanted to blend in with the locals as much as possible and not stand out as Americans. To stand out was to invite attention, which could mean trouble.

The group would travel as a convoy in four vehicles: two SUVs with tinted windows, a full-sized Ford sedan, and a Mazda pickup with a tarp covering whatever was in the bed of the truck. All the vehicles were a bit battered and several years old, but Cannon assured Eli that the vehicles were in excellent condition. A local man, hired as an interpreter, would ride in the lead vehicle.

Kay noticed that C&S's mercenaries were well armed, having a collection of M-16 and AK-47 assault rifles. She didn't know if the men had brought the rifles with them or obtained them when they arrived in Afghanistan. In a country that had been at war for half a century, weapons weren't hard to get. A number of the men had semiautomatic pistols in holsters covered by their jackets, and Kay was betting that hidden beneath the tarp covering the pickup's bed, in addition to sleeping bags and rations, were a few more lethal items, such as sniper rifles and maybe rocket-propelled grenades.

Kay disliked both Cannon and Sterling the moment she met them. When Eli introduced her, they treated her dismissively, like she was Eli's secretary—or maybe his punchboard. Cannon, in a distracted manner, said, "Yeah, nice to meet you," immediately followed by "You'll have to excuse me. I need to ask the interpreter something," and turned and walked away.

Sterling nodded to her, and without looking directly at her—he was focused on cars passing by on the street in front of the hotel—he said, "You need to stay in your vehicle during the trip and keep your face covered with that scarf."

Instead of responding to his curt command, Kay said, "I want a weapon." She figured that if everyone else considered it necessary to be armed to the teeth, she wanted to be armed, too.

Now Sterling looked at her. "You don't need one," he said. "My people will protect you, and I don't like civilians being armed." Then he said to Eli, "We need to get moving before the traffic gets heavy." As far as he was concerned, the discussion about her wanting a gun was over.

Had he been more polite, Kay might have been nice about the whole thing. She still would have gotten her way, but she would have been nice. Since he was an asshole, however, she said, "Hey! Let's get something straight. I'm not a civilian and I work for your employer—meaning you basically work for me. Second, I don't really give a shit about what you like or don't like. Now, I want a gun, because I have a lot more confidence in my ability to protect myself than I do in a bunch of guys I don't know."

Sterling's face reddened, but before he could respond and the situation could escalate, Eli said, "Nathan, give her a weapon."

Kay didn't really appreciate Eli coming to her defense, either. And the way he said *Give her a weapon,* it was like *Humor her.*

Sterling glared at her a moment longer, his jaw clenched, obviously controlling his anger. He wasn't used to women—or maybe anybody—talking to him the way she'd just done. He turned to one of his men and said, "Give her your sidearm."

Sterling's guy said, "Yes, sir," and handed Kay a matte-black .45 with a crosshatched grip.

She checked the magazine and dry-fired the weapon a couple of times, then said, "I'd prefer a .40 Glock, but I guess this'll do." Sterling walked away.

Kay lifted up the *abaya* she was wearing—she had jeans and a T-shirt on underneath the long dress—put the weapon in the front waistband of the jeans, and unbuttoned a couple of buttons on the *abaya* to make sure she could reach it in a hurry.

"I really don't think you're going to need that," Eli said.

She restrained herself from snapping at him and said, "It's better to have it and not need it than to not have it and need it."

"That sounds like an NRA bumper sticker. The next thing you'll tell me is gun control is using both hands." Then he smiled—and she forgave him.

The distance from Kabul to Ghazni is about ninety miles, and if they'd been on a highway in Kansas, the trip would have taken less than two hours. They weren't in Kansas. It took them four and a half hours thanks to traffic jams leaving Kabul, slow-moving construction workers repairing what looked to Kay like bomb craters in a couple of places, and two checkpoints manned by either policemen or soldiers. They negotiated the checkpoints without a problem by paying the expected bribes.

They made their way to Ghazni via the famed Kabul–Kandahar Highway—famed because the Taliban treated it like a shooting gallery and were constantly blowing up vehicles that used the road. The asphalt highway surface was like a patchwork quilt from repaired bomb craters. The road heading north to Kabul was filled with a seemingly endless line of trucks, tankers, buses, and overloaded cars moving at a glacial pace. Kay didn't know if the amount of traffic heading toward Kabul was normal or an anomaly. The road heading south, the direction they were headed, was busy, but traffic moved at a reasonable speed when it wasn't being stopped for one reason or another.

Young men stood in clumps at various places along the way, smoking, giving hostile looks to the passing traffic. Or maybe it was Kay's imagination that they seemed hostile. She noticed many of the young men—the teenagers—were dressed in jeans and sweatshirts emblazoned with the names of soccer teams as opposed to traditional Afghan menswear. She also noticed that some of the young men were armed—making no attempt to conceal their weapons—and she assumed they were all hanging around doing nothing but smoking because they were unemployed. She couldn't think of anything worse for the stability of a country than thousands of young, unemployed men with guns.

They seemed to pass a broken-down car or truck every couple of miles. The vehicle would have a flat tire or the hood would be up with steam billowing out of the radiator, and the driver would be gesturing wildly as he talked on his cell phone. The buildings they passed were surrounded by concrete walls and security fences, and were boxy and ugly; few bore signs in English that gave Kay any indication as to their function. The only thing worth looking at on the road to Ghazni was a mountain range in the distance with snow-covered peaks.

The landscape in some ways reminded her of a trip she'd once taken through New Mexico, passing through arid desert country with a view of the Sangre de Cristo Mountains. That is, the geography in this part of Afghanistan was similar to the part of New Mexico she'd been in, but the country just seemed . . . *tired*. It was as if the decades of constant warfare had exhausted not just the people but the land itself. Whatever the case, she found it depressing.

Before they reached the city of Ghazni, capital of Ghazni Province, the SUV containing Cannon, his two men, and one of the Glardon engineers peeled off from the rest of the convoy and headed in the direction of the dry salt lakes. The rest of the convoy drove another couple of miles, then took a right and proceeded down a dusty unpaved road. Half an hour later, at about ten in the morning, they stopped in front of a large white stucco house surrounded by an eight-foot concrete wall.

The interpreter went up to the gates, pressed a button, and spoke into a box. A moment later, the double gates opened electronically, the convoy pulled inside, and the gates shut automatically behind them. There was no grass or trees in front of the house—just hard-packed dirt—but the owner had planted spiky plants in a few places in a feeble attempt at landscaping.

Kay asked Eli, "Who owns this place? Ara's father?"

"No. It's owned by a local businessman who owes Ara's father. I imagine Ara wanted to hold the meeting here because it's outside Ghazni and enclosed, and hopefully a large group of Westerners won't be noticed.

Ara and her father will arrive after dark, and hopefully they won't be noticed, either."

"Why are you worried if they're noticed? The guy's the governor, and all we're doing is having a meeting."

"I'm worried because it's Afghanistan," Eli said. "I've told Ara to limit the number of people who know about this meeting, but people always talk too much. This means that anybody who opposes what we're proposing—Sahid Khan's local rivals, politicians in Kabul, and, of course, the Taliban—might desire to disrupt what we're trying to do. And in this country, disrupting something often means blowing it up."

A short old man in his seventies, maybe his eighties, came out to greet the Americans. He was dressed in a loose-fitting white shirt, baggy white pants, and a white *kufi*—a brimless, round cap. He smiled uncertainly, probably a tad uncomfortable with all the armed men standing in his front yard. He said something in Pashto, and Kay heard the word *Allah* a couple of times. Some sort of God-bless-you-welcome-to-my-home greeting, she assumed.

"Ask him if there's anyone else here, anyone inside the house," Sterling said to his interpreter.

The old man, in halting English, said he was the only one there, but Sterling wasn't the trusting sort. He sent four of his men into the house to make sure it was empty, and Kay could hear them shouting "Clear" as they went from room to room holding assault rifles. She thought that was a bit over the top. After Sterling's men concluded their sweep of the house, Kay and Eli went into the house while Nathan Sterling remained outside to deploy his men.

Kay was surprised by the interior of the house. In contrast to the concrete wall surrounding the place and the packed-dirt front yard, the interior had warm hardwood floors, Oriental rugs, leather furniture, and modern artwork on the walls. There was also a media room with six theater-type seats, an enormous flat-screen television set, and shelves packed with DVDs. She had no idea what a traditional Afghanistan home looked like, but she was pretty sure that most of them didn't look like this. Kay also couldn't help but wonder if the homeowner—and Sahid Khan—were connected to Afghanistan's best-known industry: opium production. From what Kay had seen, Ghazni was an impoverished area and she figured being its governor wouldn't pay that well—which made her curious about how Sahid had paid for his daughter's expensive education abroad.

The old man who had welcomed them to his employer's home introduced himself to Eli, saying his name was Yasir. He told Eli that if it pleased him, he would prepare lunch and provide them anything else they needed. While Yasir spoke to Eli, he made a point of not looking at Kay, who had removed her head covering the minute she stepped into the house. She'd always felt that if Muslim women ever wanted to be treated as equals, the first thing they should do was burn all the scarves and veils.

Yasir then showed Eli and Kay to their rooms; only Kay, Eli, the Glardon mining engineer, and Nathan Sterling would sleep inside the house that night after the meeting was concluded. Sterling's men would remain outside, hopefully awake, doing whatever security people were supposed to do.

17

The rest of the day passed slowly. Kay took a nap after lunch and, when she woke up, went looking for Eli.

As she was coming down the stairs, Nathan Sterling came into view. He seemed surprised to see her. "I was just checking on the old man," Sterling said. "He's in the kitchen making dinner."

"Okay," Kay said, but she was thinking the old man looked pretty harmless. On the other hand, being paranoid was a good quality for the guy in charge of her safety to have.

She found Eli in the media room, sitting in the dark.

"What are you doing?" she asked.

"Just sitting here. I was trying to find a movie to watch, but mostly all this guy has is porn."

"Maybe we can learn a few things," Kay said.

Eli barely smiled at her comment.

"Something bothering you?" Kay asked.

"I was just thinking about what we're trying to do with the Khans. It's going to be hard, and I wonder how many times I'm going to have to come back to this damn country to keep things on track."

Kay was surprised he was so tense. He'd seemed completely relaxed and confident in the meetings they'd held prior to coming here. But maybe he was like an athlete, putting on his game face before the game started. Kay sat down next to him and took his hand in hers.

"Maybe when we get back we can take a couple days off," she said. "You know, go to some place with a beach and where we don't have to bring our own bodyguards. And I think it's time for you to meet my daughter."

"Yeah, maybe," he said noncommittally. Then he rose from his seat and said, "I did find a copy of *The Godfather* here between *Debbie Does Dallas* and *Deep Throat*. I haven't seen the movie in years. Let's watch that."

It annoyed Kay, the way he'd changed the subject—particularly not responding to her comment about meeting Jessica—but again she chalked up his brusqueness to pregame jitters.

Eli relaxed once the movie started. When Clemenza said, *Leave the gun. Take the cannoli,* Eli laughed and said, "That's my favorite line in the movie."

"I thought your favorite line would be 'I made him an offer he couldn't refuse,'" Kay said.

"Nah, the guys I worked with at Goldman were saying that long before Vito Corleone came along."

Half an hour before it got dark, Kay heard vehicles pulling into the compound and looked outside. Two cars. The man driving the lead car stepped out; he was dressed in dark green military fatigues, a red beret on his head, a sidearm on his belt. Three identically dressed men stepped from the second car, and two of them were holding assault rifles. Kay assumed these were Khan's security people.

Khan's driver glared for a moment at Sterling's men, probably not liking the fact that there were so many of them, all holding weapons, then said something to the passengers in the car. Ara Khan emerged from the front passenger seat. Like Kay, she was wearing an *abaya*—a beautiful cerulean blue one—and a matching scarf that covered the top of her head but not her face. Sahid Khan and a bearded man in his sixties who was at least six inches taller than Khan exited the car next. Khan and the tall man were both wearing black business suits and white shirts, but no ties. Khan's head was bare, but the tall man was wearing a black *kufi*.

Kay left the house to greet the Khans. She was still wearing the black *abaya* she'd worn on the journey and had the scarf covering her hair. Eli had insisted she keep her head covered; Sahid Khan may have been fairly liberal when it came to his daughter, but Eli didn't know what his attitude was toward other women.

When she saw Kay, Ara smiled broadly. "It's so good to see you again," she said, and as they walked toward the house, Ara linked her arm through Kay's as if they were old friends. "When we finish our business this evening, we'll have to have a drink and talk. I did some research on you, whatever I could find online. You've had an interesting life."

"Did you ever call that Yankee?" Kay asked.

"Yankee?" Ara said.

"The ballplayer. You know, the stud you met in Fraunces Tavern there on Pearl Street."

"Oh, him," Ara said, and smiled.

"Well, did you call him?"

"Maybe," she said, and Kay laughed.

Kay really liked Ara Khan. The woman was smart, she was fun to be around, and she had a sense of humor. More important was the fact that even as young as she was, she was a woman of substance, one who had the ability, the grit—and yes, the trickiness—to navigate the treacherous political waters of Afghanistan. She was a person Kay would genuinely like to have for a friend regardless of how Callahan's plans worked out.

As Kay was leading the Khans into the house, she looked back once and saw Nathan Sterling talking to Khan's driver. She imagined Sterling was establishing whatever protocols were necessary when two groups of heavily armed men, who didn't trust each other, all gathered in the same place.

Inside the house, Kay introduced Eli and the Glardon mining engineer, whose name was Schmidt. Ara introduced her father and the tall man wearing the black *kufi*. He was Dr. Hamid Jalal, a professor of economics and international law. Jamal handed Kay and Eli his business card, probably so they could see how many different institutions of higher learning he'd attended and how many initials he had after his name.

Sahid Khan was shorter than Kay had expected, about five foot eight. He was broad-shouldered and stocky, and he hadn't shaved in three or four days. His black hair and beard were streaked with gray, and with his dark eyes and hooked beak he reminded her of a bird of prey. Kay's first impression was that he looked like the brutal thug she'd been told he was, but when he smiled at her as he was introduced, she could sense the charm in the man. He had a delightful smile and a mouth filled with white teeth that had been well maintained.

The group moved into the dining room, where the meeting would take place and where there was a glass-topped table large enough for everyone to sit comfortably. Kay, Dolan, and the Glardon engineer took seats on one side of the table, the Khans and the professor on the other. Kay was actually surprised by how few people were attending the meeting; if this meeting had taken place in the United States, each side would have bought six lawyers, four finance guys, and three VPs from headquarters. Eli opened a briefcase and took out a laptop and his copy of the contract, and Dr. Jalal did the same.

For the next two hours, Kay didn't say a word, and she wondered again why she had to be at the meeting. She was also surprised that the primary spokesperson for Sahid Khan was his daughter and not the professor. Ara began by saying that her father had a number of issues he wanted clarified—although Kay had the feeling it was really Ara who wanted the issues clarified. She said her father spoke English but he was more comfortable speaking Pashto, and she would translate as necessary. As the meeting went on, Kay got the impression that Sahid Khan was able to follow the discussion in English quite well and he spoke in Pashto to his daughter only when he didn't want Eli to know what he was saying.

As near as Kay could tell, Sahid Khan—or Ara Khan—had no major problems with the formal, written agreement that allowed Glardon to mine and export the lithium. Nor did they really have many questions about how the lithium would actually be taken from the ground, processed, and transported. They figured that Glardon had enough experience doing such things that they didn't really need to know the nitty-gritty technical details. Most of Ara's questions and concerns had to do with secrecy and speed. She wanted to make sure that as few people as possible inside Afghanistan knew they were planning to mine the lithium and Sahid Khan would decide who needed to know. They also wanted the mining equipment brought into the country without people knowing it was mining equipment. The main thing they wanted was a cover story for accomplishing the necessary infrastructure upgrades related to roads, facilities, and power. For example, they wanted to be able to say they were building some sort of manufacturing plant near the dry salt lakes that would employ local people and structures were being constructed for that reason. Then, when most things were in place, they wanted to move as quickly as possible to begin the mining operation and thus limit the time anyone would have to stop them.

After Ara ran out of questions, Eli said he'd like to talk about how Sahid Khan intended to handle the bureaucrats in Kabul. Without waiting for Ara to translate, Sahid shook his head and whispered something to Ara in Pashto.

"My father says he doesn't want to get into all that right now. He knows how to deal with the politicians in Kabul."

Kay could tell that Eli wasn't happy with this answer. He knew that it didn't matter what papers were signed in this room if Sahid Khan couldn't control or bribe the right people in Kabul. The situation was similar to the governor of Montana signing documents allowing the Chinese to come in and start mining natural gas in his state— something that would never happen unless the politicians in D. C. could be sold on the idea. But for whatever reason, Sahid Khan didn't want to talk about that right now—and Kay suspected she knew why.

Speaking in English for the first time, Khan said, "I think it's time to finalize this agreement before we move on to other issues."

What he meant was: *Show me the money.*

"I'm sorry," Eli said, "but I need to have a fuller understanding of how this agreement is going to be, uh, facilitated."

Sahid Khan just stared at Eli, and Eli stared back at him, and Kay was reminded of a drug deal where one guy brings the money and the other guy brings the dope. Somebody was going to have to move first, but neither guy trusted the other guy.

Ara Khan whispered in Pashto to her father. For a moment he didn't acknowledge her, then he said in English, "Okay, fine."

Ara had apparently convinced him to quit being so bullheaded and share a little of his strategy with Eli. Kay also couldn't help but think that Callahan had been completely correct when he said that Khan took his daughter's advice.

For the next hour, Sahid Khan spoke in Pashto, Ara translated, and the professor occasionally put in his two cents' worth. The discussion centered mostly around the legal and traditional relationship between the Afghanistan central government and the provincial governors, and how Khan would be meeting with—and bribing—certain people in Kabul. Eli seemed to know the people he was talking about, and judging by the way he nodded, he seemed to be agreeing with Khan's strategy. Kay, on the other hand, thought the political discussion sounded like a lot of nebulous bullshit and that everything Khan was planning was incredibly complicated, nuanced, and uncertain. The word *byzantine* came to mind. Finally, Khan said in English, "I think that's enough to give you an idea of how I will proceed."

Kay could tell Eli wasn't completely satisfied—as if he had a bunch of questions that he still wanted Khan to address—but he decided to allow Khan to have his way. He said, "Thank you for sharing that information with me. I think it's time to complete our agreement."

Eli opened the laptop that had been sitting on the table in front of him. It was already powered up and connected to the Internet. He tapped a few buttons and spun the computer around to face Sahid Khan.

"Please enter the password and routing information for your bank in the spaces indicated," Eli said.

Ara, not Sahid Khan, took the computer from Eli and from memory entered whatever numbers were needed to transfer fifty million dollars to Sahid Khan's bank. She started to swing the computer around so Eli could see the screen, but Eli said, "No. I'll come to your side of the table so you can see what I'm doing." He stood over Ara as he tapped a few more instructions into the computer, then hit the RETURN button with a bit of a flourish. "All done," he said.

"How do I know the money is in the bank?" Sahid Khan said in English.

"It's there," Eli said, "provided you entered the correct routing information. Call Bonhôte and Cie in the morning to verify if you wish. They've already gone home for the day in Neuchâtel. Obviously, if it's not there, the documents you're about to sign are null and void."

Khan nodded, then gestured for the documents

sitting in front of the professor. He slid them over, and Eli said, "Initial the paragraphs marked and sign on the last page."

As Sahid was signing the documents, Ara said softly to Kay, "What we've done here today is going to help a lot of my people. You can trust me on that."

Before Kay could respond, the power went out and the meeting room was plunged into blackness.

"Damn it," Eli muttered. "I hope this place has a generator."

"It does," Ara said. She didn't sound particularly concerned about the loss of power. Kay had noticed candles on a credenza behind the dining room table, and Ara must have noticed them, too. She said something to her father in Pashto, he handed her his cigarette lighter, and she stood to light the candles.

Eli's phone rang. He listened for a moment and hung up. "That was Sterling. His guys are having a hard time starting the generator and he wants to know if we've seen the old man, the servant." Eli picked up a candle. "I'll go see if he's someplace in the house."

After Eli left the dining room, Kay said, "Would anyone like a drink? Bottled water, fruit juice, whatever."

Sahid Khan, speaking in English, said, "I'll have a beer. Yunus usually has some in the refrigerator in the kitchen." He flashed a smile, which looked even brighter in the candlelight. "He keeps it for Western barbarians."

"I'll have a beer, too," the Glardon engineer said. "That is, if we're done for the day."

* * *

Kay's life was saved by a stainless-steel Sub-Zero refrigerator.

The kitchen was connected to the dining room and the refrigerator was at the far end of the kitchen. She opened the refrigerator door, then ducked down and stuck her head inside the refrigerator to look for the beer. She didn't hear or feel the bomb go off. She must have been unconscious for a brief period, and when she came to she was lying against one of the kitchen counters. She could see flames in the dining room—the room where Ara and her father had been sitting. She couldn't hear anything— it was like she'd stuck her head into a conch shell and all she could hear was this muffled, roaring sound; her head felt as if somebody had driven a nail through her skull. Blood was running down from her forehead and into her right eye, and she could see what appeared to be a long piece of jagged glass—maybe glass from the dining room table—piercing her right thigh. She tried to move and placed her left hand on the floor to push herself up, but when she pushed, the pain shot through her arm and she screamed. Something in her left arm was broken.

But she had to get up. She had to get to Ara before Ara burned to death.

That was the last thought she had.

18

It was complete chaos in the compound following the explosion. Sahid Khan's bodyguards started screaming in Pashto, pointing at Sterling's men, and Sterling was afraid that his guys might get into a firefight with Khan's security people. One of Sterling's men who had been trained as a medic rushed toward the burning house before Sterling could stop him. He came back five minutes later holding Kay Hamilton in his arms, followed by Eli Dolan, who had blood on the front of his shirt.

Dolan immediately took charge. He told Sterling, "You're going to have to stay here to deal with the locals. I'm taking Hamilton and a couple of your guys back to Kabul. I want to get out of here before the Afghan cops or military show up."

Before Sterling could object, the medic placed Hamilton in the backseat of one of the SUVs, got in the backseat with her, and began tending to her wounds. Dolan selected another of Sterling's guys at random, and he joined the medic in the vehicle, his AK-47 at the ready. Dolan got behind the wheel—and when he did, one of

Khan's security people pointed his weapon at him and started screaming in Pashto, probably saying that Dolan couldn't leave. Sterling was certain Khan's man was about to spray the SUV with his machine gun.

Sterling shouted, "They're taking the woman to a hospital. Don't shoot! They're taking her to a hospital!" Khan's guard seemed to understand what Sterling was saying—he probably recognized the word "hospital"—and although he still looked angry and like he wanted to shoot, he pointed his weapon away from Dolan.

Dolan pressed down on the gas pedal and the SUV went roaring through the gates and out of the compound, tires spinning on the hard-packed dirt.

Kay came to in a room that looked like a child's bedroom in a small house or apartment building. There was an IV stand next to the bed, dripping clear liquid into her right arm.

Her left arm was lying on top of the sheets and her upper arm was encased in a soft cast. Her head hurt, and it hurt when she breathed. She moved her right hand slowly so as not to dislodge the IV, and touched her forehead. There was a small bandage near her hairline; she didn't feel any stitches. She lifted up the sheet. She was wearing only panties and a bra. White elastic bands were wrapped around her torso and a large white pad was taped to her right thigh. She tried wiggling her toes and was relieved to see them move.

She must have fallen asleep again, because when she awoke a second time, Eli was sitting next to her bed in a chair, sleeping. He was unshaven, but it didn't look like more than a day's worth of beard. He was wearing the same clothes he'd worn at the meeting, except the front of his shirt was spotted brown with dried blood.

"Eli." Her voice came out in a croak not much louder than a whisper. Her throat was horribly dry, as if she hadn't had a drink of water in days. When he didn't wake up immediately, she again said, "Eli!"

This time he woke up and looked at her through bloodshot eyes. He stood and came next to the bed and took her right hand in his.

"You're going to be okay," he said. "You've got a broken bone in your left arm, four of your ribs are cracked, and you've got a wound in your thigh where you were hit by a piece of debris. The thigh wound isn't a big deal unless it gets infected. The biggest problem is you have one hell of a concussion. You need to lie as still as possible and not move your head a lot."

Kay didn't remember a doctor examining her or applying the bandages. Pointing at his shirt, she asked, "Were you hurt?"

"No. That's your blood. I'm fine."

"What happened?" she asked.

"Never mind that for now. We're going to take you out of here in about an hour and . . ."

"Where are we?"

"A house in Kabul."

She didn't remember that either: the trip from Ghazni back to Kabul. She wondered if she'd been unconscious the whole way or if she'd been given painkillers that knocked her out.

"We're going to transport you to the airport in an ambulance, and we have a charter flight headed out of here for Ramstein Air Base in Germany. That's where they take American military personnel who are severely wounded in Afghanistan and Iraq. The doc who patched you up here in Kabul is a good guy, trained in the U.S., but we'll have American doctors check you over again in Germany."

"Ara?" Kay said.

"We'll talk later, Kay. Right now you need to rest and we need to get out of this damn country."

Alpha's phone rang. It was Bravo. Why in the hell was he calling?

"What are we going to do about Hamilton?" Bravo said.

"What do you mean?" Alpha said.

"I mean, she survived, and I don't like that. She actually saw me come out of the meeting room after I planted the bomb. So I don't know what she knows or if she suspects me."

"She doesn't know anything, except for what I want her to know. She's not a problem."

"You don't know that for sure. You need to look for

an opportunity to take her out before she gets back to the States. I'm stuck here in Ghazni."

"There won't be an opportunity," Alpha said. "She's in a doctor's house, and he and his family and a nurse are nearby. Then she'll be taken by ambulance to an airfield. Anyway . . ."

Bravo interrupted. "I'm telling you, we need to get rid of her. She wasn't supposed to have survived."

"Listen to me," Alpha said. "We're not going to do a damn thing to Hamilton. Do you understand? She doesn't know anything. And the fact that she witnessed the money being transferred is actually a good thing."

"I don't know about that," Bravo said.

"Well, I do, and I'm ordering you not to take any action against her."

"You're not *ordering* me to do anything. I'm your partner in this thing, not your employee. So fuck you and your order."

The flight to Germany was made in a private jet that had a bedroom in the back and half a dozen first-class seats in the front. Kay was put in the bed and a middle-aged woman she assumed was a nurse fussed over her the entire flight, to the point where she became annoying. She took Kay's temperature, blood pressure, and pulse a dozen times, examined her pupils repeatedly using a small flashlight, and fed her clear soup.

She asked to speak to Eli, but the nurse told her he was on the phone.

She suspected the nurse gave her a sedative after that, because she slept most of the flight. When the plane landed, guys dressed like hospital orderlies in white coats and pants loaded her onto a gurney and placed her in the back of an ambulance. Eli stepped into the ambulance and said, "I'm heading back to the U.S. to talk to Callahan, but Anna Mercer will be waiting for you at the hospital."

"Goddamnit," Kay said, "I want some answers. Is Ara alive? What about her father?"

"They're dead, Kay. So is the Glardon engineer and the Afghan lawyer who came to the meeting with the Khans. They're all dead."

"But what happened?"

"It looks like a bomb was planted inside the credenza near the dining room table. We don't know any more at this point, and we couldn't stick around because Callahan wanted us out of Ghazni. He didn't want to give the local authorities a chance to grill us.

"If anyone asks about your injuries, tell them you were in a car accident and you don't remember anything because of the blow to your head. We'll get you back to D.C. as soon as the doctors in Germany say you're okay to travel."

All Kay could think about on the way to the hospital was the way Ara Khan had looked, not the last time she saw her in Ghazni but in New York: a beautiful, stylish, brilliant young woman drinking blue martinis with Kay and laughing about the guys hitting on them. That was the memory of Ara she would retain.

As Eli had said, Anna Mercer was waiting at the hospital. She dealt with whatever admission procedures had to be dealt with and Kay was signed in as Ms. Smith and whisked off to an examining room in a wheelchair. She was never alone with Mercer, so she couldn't ask her what she'd learned about what had happened in Ghazni Province. Before she was taken away, Mercer whispered into her ear, saying the same thing Eli had said: "You were in a traffic accident and don't remember anything because of the blow to your head."

Actually, that was one thing that surprised Kay: Her memory hadn't been significantly affected. She remembered everything that happened in Ghazni Province until the time she stuck her head into the Sub-Zero and reached for a beer for Sahid Khan. What she couldn't remember was what happened in the house after the bomb went off; she remembered nothing else that happened until she woke up in the doctor's house.

They kept her in Germany for three days. Her primary physician was a young army captain, and under different circumstances Kay would have found him appealing. The first thing he did after a general exam and a few X-rays was fix her broken arm. The humerus had broken above the elbow, and a surgeon put in a little metal plate and a couple of pins. For guys used to dealing with arms and legs blown off by roadside bombs, fixing a broken arm must have been a walk in the park.

As for the wound in her thigh, she was told that the Afghan doc had done a good job and all her American doctor did was rebandage it. He also wrapped clean bandages around her torso, which was all he could do for her ribs. They kept her in the hospital for two more days after her arm was repaired, the doc saying he just wanted to keep her under observation for a short time because of her concussion. She figured a typical American HMO would have booted her out the door the same day her arm was fixed.

For two days, Kay lay in bed and took short walks around the hospital, unable to think of anything other than what had happened in Afghanistan. The longer she waited to be released, the madder she got. It pissed her off that no one was telling her anything about what had happened.

She had already called her daughter and said she'd be home in a couple of days, and Jessica knew better than to ask where she was and what she was doing. She didn't tell Jessica that she'd been hurt; she didn't want to worry the girl. She also tried to call Thomas Callahan, Eli Dolan, and Anna Mercer. None of them returned her calls. She was particularly pissed at Dolan, a man she thought would have shown a bit more concern for her health as he'd been sleeping with her.

On the day she was to be discharged, Henry—the large Callahan Group receptionist with the prosthetic leg—showed up at the hospital. He was there to escort her back to Washington and to provide security for her during the trip. She doubted she needed security at this point; if she did, she hoped Henry would be able to do a better job than Nathan Sterling's men had done in Ghazni.

She flew back to D.C. in the same jet that had taken her out of Afghanistan. She and Henry were the only passengers, and Henry claimed not to know anything about anything.

19

When Jessica walked into the apartment, Kay was sitting on the sofa, wearing a T-shirt and shorts, her bad leg up on the coffee table with an ice pack on her thigh.

Jessica stopped, dropped her book bag on the floor, and her eyes grew wide. She took in the cast on Kay's arm, the bandage wrapped around her thigh, the small bandage on her bruised forehead. Fortunately, she couldn't see the elastic bands around Kay's rib cage.

"My God, what happened to you?" Jessica said.

"A stupid car accident," Kay lied. She'd told Jessica the company was sending her out of town for training, never mentioning that by *out of town* she meant Afghanistan. "I was in a van with some other people attending this class, and some idiot playing on his cell phone crossed the centerline. The guy driving the van overreacted and we went off the shoulder and the van rolled. Fortunately, everybody was wearing seat belts and no one was badly hurt."

"Why didn't you call me?"

"I didn't want to worry you. Really, I'm all right. Got a broken arm that's healing fine, a couple cracked ribs, and a little cut on my leg."

"You could have been killed," Jessica said, and then her eyes welled up with tears.

Kay suddenly felt horrible. She'd always thought of her daughter as being self-sufficient and independent, and it had never occurred to her that Jessica would react this way. But she could see now that her daughter wasn't just concerned for her; Jessica was *scared*. She had already lost two people she loved—her adoptive parents—and the thought of losing Kay, too, had hit her hard—harder than Kay would have ever expected. Jessica may have been intellectually capable of taking care of herself if she had to, but her daughter was still a kid—a kid who didn't want to be completely on her own and wanted someone in her life who cared for her. Kay felt like kicking herself for being so insensitive.

Making it appear easier than it really was, Kay got to her feet and said, "See, I'm fine. And I've got an appointment with the doc tomorrow for a checkup."

When Jessica just stood there—she was actually trembling a bit—Kay limped forward and took her in her arms. "Hey. Everything's all right. It's going to take more than a dumb car accident for you to get rid of me. Now, tell me what you've been up to while I was gone."

* * *

The day after returning to D.C., Kay limped into Callahan's office, her left arm in a soft cast above the elbow. All her injuries appeared to be healing okay, but her leg ached due to muscle damage caused by the shrapnel.

Callahan looked as he always did—rumpled, tired, bloodshot eyes—but he also looked as if he'd aged ten years since the last time Kay had seen him. She wondered if any of his other operations had gone as badly as the one in Afghanistan. Before he could say anything, Kay said, "I want to know what the hell happened, and so far you and Mercer have blown me off. You wouldn't even return my calls."

"Aw, calm down," Callahan said. "And sit down. You wanna cup of coffee?"

"No. I want answers." Kay swept the newspapers off the brown couch in front of Callahan's desk onto the floor and sat.

"Okay," Callahan said. "Here's what we know. Ara Khan, her father, the Glardon engineer, and that Afghan professor, lawyer, whoever the hell he was, were killed by a bomb placed in a credenza in the dining room where the meeting was held. The type of explosive used and the design of the bomb were similar to other Taliban bombs we've encountered over there, and a cell phone was most likely used to detonate the bomb."

"How do you know all this?"

"Because I have connections over there, and because Sterling is still there and has been talking to the Afghan cops investigating the bombing."

"Sterling?" Kay said. "You're getting information from him?"

"Yeah."

"Where's Cannon?"

"He's back in the U.S. Anyway, the bomb in the credenza was detonated right after the power in the house went off, and the reason the power went off was because a transformer at a substation five miles away exploded. At first folks thought lightning struck the transformer, but it was later determined that the transformer was destroyed by another cell phone bomb. In addition to the casualties from the bomb, an old man who was some sort of servant was found inside the house with his throat cut."

"Ah, jeez. They killed that little old man?" Kay said.

"Yeah. So here's what I think happened," Callahan said. "There are a lot of people who would have wanted to stop us from making a deal with Sahid Khan. The Taliban, because they oppose every fucking thing. Politicians in Kabul who may have wanted to cut their own deal over the mining operation. The Chinese, the Russians, and anybody else who wants the lithium."

Callahan lit a cigarette and blew smoke at the ceiling before he continued. "I think somebody found out about the meeting. The Khans probably talked to the wrong person, like the professor they brought with them. Or whoever did this had a spy in Khan's administration. Or the owner of the house where the meeting was held told somebody else about the meeting. Whatever the case, somebody found out the Khans were making a deal with us and decided to stop it."

Kay started shaking her head, but Callahan ignored the gesture.

"Then what they did," Callahan said, "was turn one of Khan's bodyguards, one of the guys he took with him to the meeting, and *this* was the guy who detonated the bomb. I also think they paid or forced the old man to plant the bomb; he had unlimited access to the house and was the best person to hide the bomb in the credenza before the meeting. The other thing is, Sterling and his guys were watching Khan's security people and Sterling said that none of Khan's people ever went inside the house. So the old man planted the bomb. Maybe they threatened his family, or maybe they just paid him. Whatever the case, he was the one who planted the bomb, and the other reason I think this, besides his access to the house, is *because* they killed him."

"Callahan, I don't believe for one minute . . ."

But Callahan kept talking. "After the meeting started, somebody working for whoever wanted the Khans gone, blew up the transformer. That was the signal to detonate the bomb in the house, because now the compound is in total darkness, making it easy for one of Khan's bodyguards to sneak into the house and cut the old man's throat."

"But why kill the old man?" Kay asked.

"So he wouldn't be able to give up whoever forced him to plant the bomb."

Kay didn't say anything for a long moment. She finally broke the silence, saying, "Callahan, I'm trying to figure out if you really believe all that bullshit you just told me or if you just expect me to believe it."

"What the hell does that mean?"

"Callahan, Ara Khan and her father lived in a world where you had to be able to keep a secret if you wanted to live. I don't believe for one damn minute that she or her dad told anyone about the meeting other than the professor who came with them, and they wouldn't have told him unless they trusted him completely. They didn't want anyone in Afghanistan to know they were about to come into fifty million bucks and cutting a deal to give away a good chunk of Afghanistan's natural resources. Hell, half the meeting was about how to keep the mining operation a secret for as long as possible."

"What are you saying? That you think somebody working for me did this?"

"Yeah, that's exactly what I'm saying." Kay paused a beat, then said, "And I think it was Eli Dolan. And I think Sterling could be involved, too."

"That's absurd," Callahan said.

"Listen to me, Callahan. Whoever detonated the bomb had to know that everybody was going to be sitting at the table, in front of the credenza, when the bomb went off. Somebody outside the house wouldn't have known if we'd decided to take a break or if Sahid or Ara had to use the bathroom or stepped out of the room to make a call. And none of Sahid Khan's security guys came near the meeting room when the meeting was going on, which is the same thing Sterling told you."

Now it was Kay's turn to plow ahead before Callahan could interrupt her. "Dolan obviously didn't do this by himself. Somebody blew up the transformer, and I don't think Dolan would have known how to make a cell phone bomb. But Cannon and Sterling's ex-soldiers would know how to make a bomb. So I think this is what happened: Dolan—it could only have been Dolan—sent a text to somebody—I don't know who—telling a guy to blow the transformer. What I'm saying is, Dolan put his hand in his pocket and pressed a button on his phone and nobody saw him send the text. When the power went off, that gave Dolan an excuse to leave the room, knowing everyone was sitting at the table and not walking around a blacked-out house."

"Eli said the reason he left the room was that Sterling called him and told him to find the old man because they couldn't start the generator."

"I was there, Callahan," Kay said. "Somebody called Dolan after the power went off, but I don't know who called for sure or what was said. All I know is that Dolan *said* Sterling called him and told him to go find the old man. But did that really happen? I don't know and neither do you. I only heard Dolan's side of the conversation. What I do know is that Dolan left the room and one minute later the bomb went off. And like I already told you, Sterling could have been in on this thing."

"Yeah, well, you also left the room before the bomb went off."

"Are you joking, Callahan? I have a broken arm, four cracked ribs, a concussion, and a piece of glass like a stiletto was driven halfway through my leg. Do you think I decided to hide behind a fucking refrigerator knowing a bomb big enough to flatten a house was going to explode?"

"So you miscalculated."

Kay couldn't tell if Callahan was serious or not, and before she could ask him, he said, "If your theory is correct, why would Dolan kill the old man or have him killed? For that matter, why blow up the transformer? Dolan could have just made up an excuse for leaving the room at any time during the meeting and detonated the bomb."

"They cut the power to cause confusion. With the power out, it would have been easy to get rid of the phone they used to detonate the bomb, but the main reason for cutting the power was to kill the old man. What I'm saying is, they killed the old man to make people believe, like *you* seem to believe, that the old man was the one who planted the bomb. In other words, killing the old man was *misdirection*, part of a charade to make people believe it was one of Khan's rivals who killed the old man and not Dolan or Sterling or one of Sterling's people."

"Hamilton, can you even imagine Eli Dolan cutting a man's throat? He's a banker, not an assassin."

"No, I can't imagine him doing that, but you have to at least consider the possibility that Dolan was involved."

This was a conclusion Kay had come to with great reluctance and only after a lot of thought. Her natural inclination had been to dismiss Dolan as a suspect, not only because of her feelings toward him but also because of the kind of person he appeared to be: He didn't seem capable of mass murder. But Kay was an ex-cop and there was one thing all cops learned quickly: You can't determine if a person is a criminal based on the way he looks or how he normally acts or whatever character witnesses might say about him. The serial killer was *always* the guy the neighbors never suspected, because he seemed so nice and normal; the con man who bilked grandmothers out of their life savings was the most likable fellow you ever met. Kay had known drug dealers who gave to charities and were kind to children, dogs, and old ladies—and who wouldn't hesitate for an instant to kill a snitch or a rival.

So Kay forced herself to ignore her feelings toward Dolan and based her decision on the traditional triad: means, motive, and opportunity. Dolan certainly had the opportunity to commit the crime: He could have placed the bomb while she'd been napping, then killed the old man after the power went out. All he would have needed was a knife he filched from the kitchen—and he was certainly strong enough to overpower an eighty-year-old man. Or, as she'd told Callahan, he conspired with one or more of Sterling's men, or Sterling himself, and one of them killed the old man. But she also remembered the blood on Dolan's shirt; he'd said it was her blood, but it could have been the old man's.

As for means, one of Sterling's mercenaries could have constructed the bombs; then all it would have taken was a cell phone to communicate with the substation bomber and detonate the bombs. But her main reasons for suspecting Dolan were the ones she'd given Callahan: He was the only one who knew when everybody would be in the dining room, sitting at the table, and he was the only one at the meeting—except for her—who survived the explosion.

Motive was a problem, however. Would a rich guy like Dolan kill five people for money? And the fifty million given to the Khans couldn't have been the motive, since Kay—and Ara Khan—had witnessed Dolan transfer the money to Sahid Khan's bank. Kay supposed the motive could be something political or ideological, but she doubted this was the case. What political motive could Dolan have? No, this had to be about money, because ninety percent of the time when a crime is committed—and it isn't a spontaneous act of passion—money is the motive. And in a case involving billions of dollars' worth of lithium, there was a whole lot of potential motive.

Almost as if he knew what she was thinking, Callahan said, "But *why* would Dolan do this?"

"For money. That's the only reason I can think of. We need to . . ."

"Dolan's richer than Midas," Callahan said. "He wouldn't have killed five people for money."

"How do you know he's rich?" Kay countered. "Everybody assumes he's rich because he's got a fancy place in Manhattan and worked in investment banking, but you don't know for sure. He could be up to his neck in debt. He could have lost all his money during the meltdown. And if he's working with somebody else to go after the lithium—some corporation or foreign government—we're talking about billions of dollars, and a few billion dollars is enough motive for anyone."

"I'm telling you, you're wrong about Eli."

"And I'm telling you that you need to start thinking like a cop instead of a spy."

Kay could tell that Callahan wasn't going to concede that she was right about Dolan, so she changed the subject. "What are the Afghans doing about all this?"

Callahan barked out a humorless laugh. "They're going nuts, of course. One of their governors was just assassinated, and two of the people at the meeting—you and Eli—boogied out of the country before anyone could question you. They've been pestering the State Department for answers, and the State Department is telling them they have no idea why two private companies, the Callahan Group and Glardon Mining, were meeting with Sahid Khan.

"This is why the Callahan Group exists, Hamilton.

The U.S. government can honestly state that it was not involved in anything we were doing over there. A guy who works for the Afghan ambassador here in Washington called me and I told him we were just having some preliminary discussions with the Khans over a private business venture with a Swiss company. I told him that's what the Callahan Group *does*: We facilitate overseas business ventures. I told him to look at our Web site. I said it's no different than if Starbucks went over there to set up a franchise, except my people just happened to be in the wrong place when a bomb went off, which happens about eight times a day in that fucking country. I also told the ambassador's guy the reason you and Eli left the country is you were injured and I was afraid my employees had been targeted for assassination, and I'm not about to send you back there to talk to the Afghan cops." Callahan sighed. "A lot of people aren't very happy with me right now, and the least of my worries are the Afghans."

"What's Sterling telling them?"

"Nothing. He doesn't know anything. His company was asked to provide security—which they obviously didn't do very well—but he has no idea what the meeting was about. He's also telling them the same thing I've been telling you: that the old man probably planted the bomb and Khan's guards most likely assassinated their boss."

"What about the money? The fifty million? I know the money was transferred before the bomb exploded, because I saw Dolan and Ara make the transfer."

"Ah, now that's a problem," Callahan said, rubbing a hand over his pale face.

"What do you mean?"

"I mean the money is in a Swiss bank and I'm guessing the only people authorized to take money from the account are Sahid Khan and his daughter. So unless I can devise a way to rob a Swiss bank, that money may sit there until the end of time—or until the end of money, whichever comes first."

Kay didn't really care about the fifty million. That was Callahan's problem. The only thing she cared about was tracking down the people who had killed Ara Khan. "So what are you going to do about Dolan?" she said.

"I don't know that I'm going to do anything about him. I'm not convinced he did anything wrong."

Kay stood up. "I'm going to get to the bottom of this."

"*You're* going to get to the bottom of it?" Callahan said.

"Yes. Somebody tried to kill me and they killed Ara Khan. I liked Ara. I liked her a lot. And I think, just like you said, she could have been one of the future female leaders of the Muslim world, but some son of a bitch blew her to pieces. I'm going to find out who it was."

"And how exactly do you plan to conduct your own investigation if you're not employed by me?"

"Are you saying you're firing me?"

"Not yet." Pointing a blunt finger at her face, he

added, "But if you don't start acting and talking like my employee, that'll happen pretty fuckin' quick."

Three hours later, Callahan found himself back in the apartment/safe house near Mount Vernon Square waiting for Smee. Smee was the one who'd called the meeting, and having a pretty good idea why Smee wanted to meet, this time Callahan didn't keep him waiting.

When Smee entered the apartment, Callahan was drinking a beer, watching Notre Dame get its ass kicked by Penn State in basketball. Had he been a contributing alumnus, he would have stopped contributing. Smee just stood there looking at him until Callahan muted the sound of the game.

"Mr. Lincoln wants to meet tonight at seven p.m. Are you ready to write down the address?"

"Smee, couldn't you have just written it down for me?"

Smee didn't respond.

"Well, shit," Callahan said. "Now I'm gonna have to find a pen and some paper."

Smee handed Callahan a fountain pen—typical of Smee to use a fountain pen—then carefully tore a piece of paper out of a small leather-bound notebook.

"Ready," Smee said, and then rattled off an address in Davidsonville, Maryland, including its nine-digit zip code. Although Callahan had never been to the address before, he knew it would be in an isolated setting with clear lines of sight for at least half a mile so anyone following him could be easily seen.

"Anything else?" Callahan said.

"My pen, please," Smee said.

Callahan handed it to him, and Smee turned to leave the apartment. As he opened the door, Callahan said, "Hey, come on, Smee. Have a beer and watch the game with me."

Smee left without responding.

Callahan knew that what he was now supposed to do was memorize the address and burn the piece of paper, but as he didn't have Smee's memory, he had no intention of doing that. He put the paper in his shirt pocket and turned up the sound on the game, although he wasn't really watching the game. He was thinking about what Kay Hamilton had said—and he'd come to the conclusion that Hamilton was probably right: The Khans hadn't told anybody about the meeting, which meant that somebody working for him had most likely killed the Khans. He still didn't believe it was Dolan but he couldn't ignore Hamilton's logic.

He turned off the television when Notre Dame was twenty points behind, wondering why in the hell they had a point guard who was only five foot nine.

20

After she left Callahan's office, Kay limped over to a restaurant on L Street and had lunch: a pastrami sandwich, a fat pickle, and iced tea. As she sat there, she thought again—for maybe the hundredth time—about the sequence of events prior to the bomb exploding.

They arrived at the compound outside Ghazni about ten a.m. Sterling's men swept the house, making sure nobody was inside, but as far as Kay knew, they didn't use any sort of bomb-detection equipment. Soon after they arrived, the old man, Yasir, prepared a lunch for her, Dolan, the Glardon mining engineer, and Nathan Sterling. The lunch was traditional Afghan fare, consisting of naan bread, steamed rice with carrots and raisins, and slivers of meat of an uncertain origin, possibly goat. They ate in the same dining room that was later used for the meeting. Sterling's people ate whatever rations they brought with them from Kabul and stayed at their posts outside the house.

After lunch she took a nap, so for two hours she had no idea who was doing what. In particular, she had no idea what Dolan and Sterling had been up to while she was sleeping. After her nap, she saw Sterling as she was coming down the stairs. He'd been coming from the direction of the kitchen, which was adjacent to the meeting room. She remembered thinking that he'd been surprised to see her and he said he'd been checking on the old man—and maybe he had been. On the other hand, maybe he was the one who'd planted the bomb.

She spent the next two hours talking with Eli and watching *The Godfather*. She recalled how Eli had seemed unusually tense. And while she was watching the movie, she again had no idea if Sterling or any of his men entered the house.

For dinner, the old man served a lamb stew and more naan, and a pot and bowls were taken outside for Sterling's men. After dinner, the old man disappeared and he didn't come near the kitchen or the dining room, where the meeting was being held. He apparently went to some other part of the large house, most likely the room where he slept.

As it was getting dark outside, Ara Khan and her father arrived with their security people. And, as far as Kay knew, none of Khan's people entered the house; for sure, none of them came near the meeting room—she would have seen them if they had—and she imagined that Sterling's people would have watched Khan's bodyguards closely, treating them as potential hostiles, not allies.

The meeting started, and a couple hours later, Dolan transferred the money to Sahid Khan's bank. A moment after that the power failed, and Dolan supposedly received a call from Sterling asking him to go find the old man, because Sterling's guys couldn't start the generator. A few seconds after Dolan left the room the bomb went off. And as she'd told Callahan, the only person who could have known that the Khans would be in the room, sitting in front of the credenza, when the bomb exploded was Dolan—the one person who'd survived the explosion unharmed.

But there was something Kay didn't understand, and she hadn't told this to Callahan: *Why did Dolan wait until after the money was transferred before he killed the Khans?* That was the one thing that didn't make sense to her. Dolan could have stepped from the meeting any time he wanted, knowing the Khans were sitting at the table, and then he could have detonated the bomb. On the other hand, if there was a reason he'd waited until after the money was transferred, then Dolan again became her prime suspect. He was the only one who wasn't killed—other than her—who knew when the transfer had been completed. But *why* did he wait? She didn't know and she didn't know how to find out. She also didn't know how to look into Dolan's finances to see if he was as rich as everyone thought he was.

So now what? What should she do next? Callahan had a valid point: How could she investigate Ara Khan's death without some sort of organization to assist her?

Then it occurred to her that there was an organization that could assist her.

Kay didn't know whether anyone was following her or listening to her phone calls. Most likely no one was, but she couldn't take the chance. As the Prussian military theorist von Clausewitz once said: *You have to plan for war based on your enemy's capabilities, not his intentions.* Or at least that's what one of Kay's old bosses at the DEA had once told her. Callahan may not have suspected her, but he certainly had the capability to follow her and monitor her phones.

Kay left the restaurant on L Street, then zipped in and out of buildings, made a brief trip on the Metro, then went in and out of a couple more buildings. Finally satisfied that she'd lost anyone tailing her—or would never lose them—she made a call from a pay phone. All the running around had made her leg ache even more.

"I need to see you tonight," Kay said. "The organization I'm currently working for may have just killed five people and almost killed me. In other words, it's a big fucking deal."

There was a long pause. "I assume you're calling from a secure phone."

"You assume wrong. I'm calling from a pay phone and nobody knows I'm using this particular phone. I hope nobody is listening in on your phone."

"Nobody is."

"Good. Meet me tonight at eight at St. Margaret's Episcopal Church on Connecticut, and make sure you're not followed."

Another long pause. "Okay."

21

Callahan arrived at the address in Davidsonville at seven thirty p.m.; he was supposed to be there at seven. He hadn't intended to be late, as he knew that would just piss them off, but traffic leaving Washington was heavier than he'd expected. The damn rush hour was twenty hours long these days. As he *had* expected, the meeting place was a farmhouse sitting on four or five fallow acres; it looked as if it had been built back when they still used mules to plow.

He knocked, and Prescott answered the door. Prescott was as tall as he was—five foot ten—skinny and with a chest as flat as an ironing board. Her hair was short and wavy and dyed platinum blond, which he'd always found incongruent with Prescott's personality. He'd never thought of her caring in any way about the way she looked; she certainly didn't dress as if she cared. She was wearing a drab brown skirt, white stockings with penny loafers, and a white cardigan sweater that should have been placed in a Goodwill bin a decade ago. But for some reason she dyed and styled her hair like a 1920s flapper, and she'd even applied a film of red lipstick over lips so thin it was hard to think of them as lips.

Prescott led him into an old farmhouse kitchen. There were Mason jars filled with pickled vegetables sitting on shelves, a big, battered wooden table made from six-inch-wide planks, and a gas oven that looked three decades old. The oven could prove useful if Lincoln and his two pals ordered him to stick his head inside it as his penalty for fucking up.

Lincoln was sitting at the head of the table, a mug of coffee in his right hand. He was a big man, six foot four, and probably weighed two hundred fifty pounds. He was big enough to have played football in college, but Callahan knew Lincoln had never played sports, unless you considered chess a sport. He had short gray hair and a big-nosed, craggy face, like it had been chipped out of granite by an incompetent sculptor. Not a handsome man, but an impressive-and intimidating-looking one. He was wearing a black suit and almost certainly had come straight from work. Lincoln rarely left his office before eight or nine p.m. On his meaty left hand was a wedding ring; Callahan had never met Lincoln's wife, but he couldn't imagine anyone being married to him.

Sitting to Lincoln's right was Grayson. Like Prescott, Grayson was tall and lanky. His hair was white and softer than goose down, and he wore wire-rimmed aviator classes. He was the only one of the three that looked as if he might actually possess a sense of humor, although Callahan had never heard him say anything the least bit funny. He favored tweed suits, and he reminded Callahan of a history professor he'd had at Notre Dame, but Callahan knew that three decades ago Grayson had been a Delta Force soldier and had literally cut a few people's throats. Grayson was still cutting throats, but now he didn't do it personally. The rumor was that Grayson was gay.

Prescott took the chair on Lincoln's left, and Lincoln gestured for Callahan to take the seat at the opposite end of the table from him. If Callahan took that seat it would have the appearance of the three of them sitting at one end of the table like a tribunal, with Callahan at the other end, like a guy applying for a job—or like a guy about to get his ass chewed out by his bosses for the job he'd just done.

"Hey, sorry I'm late," Callahan said, making no attempt to sound sincere, then he walked over to the stove, where there was a blue metal percolator-type coffeepot. In a cupboard he found a chipped cup with a picture of an Irish setter on it, and he took a seat at the table on the same side as Grayson, a seat away from Grayson. He wasn't going to sit at the end of the goddamned table.

"What the fuck happened over there?" Prescott said. Of the three of them, she was definitely the most vulgar, and Callahan actually liked her for that. He couldn't remember Lincoln ever swearing; Lincoln looked scary enough that he didn't need to swear.

"I don't know," Callahan said. "But I have the awful

feeling that one of my own people was involved." He didn't bother to tell them that it was Kay Hamilton who led him to this conclusion. One of the privileges of being the boss was taking credit for your employees' ideas.

"Jesus!" Prescott said. "My God," Grayson moaned. Lincoln didn't bother to invoke the name of a deity. He just closed his eyes.

"Explain," Lincoln said, and Callahan did. He basically told them what Hamilton had told him. "I've obviously got a lot of work to do to prove this, and I'm going to need your help resource-wise."

The resources Lincoln, Grayson, and Prescott had at their disposal in terms of equipment, money, and personnel were vast, and the personnel were extremely competent. And were it not for the money they controlled, the Callahan Group would not have existed.

"Do you think there's any other way we can get there first with regard to the lithium?" Lincoln asked.

"I doubt it," Callahan said. "Without Sahid Khan in Ghazni and us having some kind of special relationship with him, it's just going to be the usual scramble. We'll have to get the lithium the same way we've done it in the past for other precious metals."

No one said anything for a long, uncomfortable moment as they all stared glumly at Callahan. And there was a lot to be glum about: Their plan to control the lithium mining, place the man they wanted in the presidential palace in Kabul, and eventually get an enlightened female in a position of power was all gone. Gone, too, was fifty million U.S. dollars. They'd all known from the beginning that their scheme had been ambitious—maybe overly ambitious—and fraught with potential problems, but they'd believed it was possible. Now nothing they'd envisioned was possible.

"What I'm really disappointed about," Grayson said, "is losing that young woman. I really believed she could have made a difference in that part of the world."

Callahan didn't say anything. He wasn't going to keep saying he was sorry. The milk had been spilt, the water had passed under the bridge, the die had been cast; it was time to move on. It was time for revenge.

"What do you plan to do next?" Prescott asked, and Callahan told them. He noted, as usual, that they didn't have any useful suggestions. It was all on him.

"I want status reports on this once a week," Lincoln said. Then he added, unnecessarily, "Via Mr. Meece, of course."

"No," Callahan said. "I'm not going to waste my time doing that. When I've got something to report, I'll let Smee know."

Prescott slammed one of her bony hands down on the table. "Hey! You've already fucked this up beyond belief. Don't you go forgetting who the hell's in charge here."

"Nobody's in charge here," Callahan said, looking directly into her dead-fish eyes. "I do the things you don't want your own agencies doing, so all the risk will be on my head. But I don't work for you—I work *with* you. Any time you want to start doing your own dirty work, all you have to do is cut off the money and I'll go find another job." Callahan had made this speech before, but it needed to be said every once in a while to make sure they understood. "Now I have to get back to Washington to clean up the mess in my own house."

Callahan rose and started to leave the room, but before he reached the door, Lincoln said, "Callahan, can you do me a favor?"

"What's that?"

"Stop calling Mr. Meece Smee. He keeps complaining to me about it."

22

At seven p.m., an hour before her meeting at St. Margaret's, Kay stuck her head into Jessica's room. She'd expected to find her daughter hunched over a book, doing her homework, but she wasn't. She was lying on her bed, talking to someone on her cell phone, and Kay heard her say, "Oh, that's just bullshit." There was a brief pause, and Jessica let out a high-pitched laugh and said, "Now I *know* you're a lying bitch! She'd never do that."

Kay thought—for maybe two seconds—about giving her daughter a lecture on the unattractiveness of young women speaking in such a vulgar fashion, but knew she wouldn't be able to manage the hypocrisy necessary for such a discussion.

Kay had met with Tanaka, Jessica's guidance counselor, a handsome guy with spiky dark hair that gave him a bit of a rock-star vibe. He told her pretty much the same thing Jessica had said: He'd taken a special interest in Jessica and four other students who all had the test scores, the brains and, most important, the stamina and long-distance drive to become doctors.

"It's a waste of time for kids like your daughter to

spend another year in high school," Tanaka had said. "As it is, she'll almost be your age by the time she's allowed to practice if she elects a specialty like internal medicine or neurosurgery."

Jesus. Neurosurgery. "And you think you can get her into Duke?" Kay had said.

"Yeah, my family has some pull with the school. Actually, we have a lot of pull."

"I'm curious," Kay had said. "Why are you teaching in a high school if you have those kind of connections?"

"Because I like my job. I like being around bright kids like Jessica. Frankly, and I'm embarrassed to say this, but I don't have the dedication to teach in some inner-city school where half the kids can't read and they have metal detectors at every entrance. But a school like this, with the kind of students they admit . . . Well, it's fun and it gives me hope for this country. But I won't be teaching much longer. My dad's getting old and he expects me to come home and run the business."

"What business is that?" Kay asked.

"You ever heard of TanTech? It's the largest privately owned medical research firm in the country. Which reminds me: If Duke becomes a financial hardship, give me a call. The family has a foundation that can help."

Which made Kay immediately wonder, being the cynic she was, if what Tanaka was actually doing was recruiting her daughter for his daddy's company. Nah, he didn't seem like that kind of guy. But now here was the future neurosurgeon lying on her bed, gossiping like a typical goofy teenager.

"Excuse me," Kay said. "I have to go out for a couple of hours. Set the security system after I leave."

Her daughter gave her a distracted good-bye wave, and then said to whomever she was talking to: "No! She didn't! In the chem lab? You gotta be—"

"And don't stay up too late," Kay said. *There. That sounded pretty mom-like.*

St. Margaret's was a twenty-minute walk from Kay's apartment, but it took her forty-five minutes to get there because she wanted to make sure she wasn't being followed. When she left the apartment, she was wearing a white sweater, her hair was down, and she was carrying a large purse. She reversed directions abruptly several times to see who was behind her and to see if any of those people changed directions when she did. Half an hour after leaving her apartment, she went into a bar, and in the restroom she pinned up her hair, put on a baseball cap, and put on a dark nylon Windbreaker. She then left the purse she'd been carrying in the restroom waste container and exited the bar looking completely different from the person who entered it. After almost an hour of evasive tactics, she was sure she wasn't being followed but for some reason had a feeling she was being watched—which she knew was absurd. TV

192 | M. A. LAWSON

movies aside, you can't feel someone following you, and she chalked up her apprehension to paranoia. She arrived at St. Margaret's at exactly eight p.m.

She thought the main doors to the church might be locked, but they weren't. If they had been, she would have met her person on the steps. Lucky for her, the Episcopalians apparently had a 24/7 rule when it came to allowing folks to talk to God—or more likely, being an urban church, they locked the church up later so it didn't become a hostel for the homeless.

Kay had never been religious, but one of the things she'd always liked about churches and chapels was how peaceful they were when they were empty; she felt calmer as soon as she entered the place. It was dimly lit but bright enough to see, and there were a couple of small spotlights that illuminated a stained-glass window behind the altar and a gold-colored cross on the altar. That is, she assumed the cross wasn't really gold—even Episcopalians couldn't be that trusting.

She took a seat in a pew in the last row, close to the door. Ten minutes passed and she thought to herself: *Shit. She's decided not to come. She doesn't want to get tangled up in this mess or she doesn't want to tangle with the Callahan Group.* Thirty seconds later, Barb Reynolds, her old mentor from the DEA, sat down next to her.

Barb reminded Kay a lot of Anna Mercer. Like Mercer she had short dark hair, and like Mercer she dressed well and looked incredible for her age. She was almost fifty but could have passed for a woman a decade younger, thanks to exercise, diet, and a wee bit of help from Botox. Her eyes were green, but a different shade of green from Ara Khan's.

"I was afraid you weren't going to come," Kay said.

"I got here half an hour ago. I was waiting outside to see if anyone was following you. I think you're clean."

"Okay. Let me tell you what's going on. But I'd like to know something first. After you fired me in San Diego, you hooked me up with the Callahan Group. I'd like to know how you even knew about the Group."

"I knew about it because Thomas Callahan offered me a job a few years ago."

"Why didn't you take it?"

"For one thing, I like the job I have, and at the time I had over twenty years vested in a civil service pension and I wasn't willing to give that up. I also turned him down because I was just a tiny bit leery about some off-the-books organization that does sneaky things for the president. I didn't want to end up being Thomas Callahan's codefendant. I also suspected that Callahan's story about working for the president might be a lie, which made me even more leery."

"But you apparently didn't care if I ended up being Callahan's codefendant."

"Hey! Don't take that tone with me. You were unemployed and I thought I was doing you a favor. Nobody twisted your arm to make you take the job."

"Sorry," Kay said, although she wasn't feeling all that contrite. "But how did you meet Callahan in the first place?"

Barb shook her head impatiently, meaning: *What difference does it make?* "We've both worked in this town a long time," she said, "and our paths just crossed at some point."

Hmmm, Kay thought. That sounded so deliberately vague that she wondered if Barb had ever had a fling with Callahan. Callahan couldn't have always looked the way he did now.

But as there was no point pressing Barb on a question she didn't intend to answer, Kay said, "Okay, here's what's going on"—and she proceeded to tell Barb about the lithium in Ghazni Province and how Callahan's grand plan fell apart when someone detonated the bomb that killed Ara and her father.

"My God!" Barb said when Kay told her how she was alive only due to dumb luck and a substantial appliance. "I noticed you were limping when you walked into the church, but I had no idea."

"My arm and ribs are healing fine, I've stopped having headaches, but my damn leg is taking longer to mend. Anyway, I'm okay."

"So what do you need from me?" Barb asked.

The reason Kay had called Barb was that there was one thing her ex-employer did very well: They could follow a money trail even when people were trying to hide the trail.

There are basically three parts to narcotics trafficking: Making the dope is part one and selling it is part two. Part three is trying to figure out what to do with tremendous amounts of illegal cash that starts off as a crumpled bill in some junkie's trembling hand and ends up as one of millions of similar bills all banded together and placed in cardboard boxes and safes. All this cash then has to be accounted for in some seemingly legitimate fashion—meaning it has to be laundered clean— so people don't go to jail for income-tax evasion or have to explain to federal agents where all the money came from. After the money is laundered, it can then be placed in various institutions and invested in things that make more money. It was either launder the money or leave all that cash sitting in boxes moldering in a warehouse.

What the DEA had learned to do was follow the money. They were very good at tracing it to various off-shore banks and battering down the paper walls of phony businesses that were empty shells erected solely for the purpose of hiding the loot. Kay, however, had never been involved in that side of the DEA's operation; she'd been a gun-packing field agent, not a CPA.

"I figure," Kay told Barb, "that if somebody killed the Khans, they were most likely paid to do so. I mean, maybe the Taliban killed them for some wacky, political, religious reason. Or maybe some politician in Kabul did it so he could be the one to negotiate the mining rights. But I don't think that's the case. I don't think anyone in Afghanistan knew what Ara and her father were doing.

I think someone connected to the Callahan Group sold them out."

"Sold them out to who?" Barb asked.

"I don't know. To whoever can make money off lithium. There's a fairly rare metal in the ground over there worth billions and somebody wants it. And since we're talking billions, I think whoever killed Ara and stopped the deal from going through would pay whoever helped them millions. Nobody would do something like this for a few thousand bucks.

"So what I'd like you to do, Barb, is look into the finances of everybody that I know of who was part of this. That includes half a dozen people at the Callahan Group, including Callahan. I also want you to check out Cannon and Sterling and the men they brought with them to Afghanistan. I don't have the names of all of Cannon and Sterling's people, but I know they were all on the same flight from Dulles, traveling as a group, and they probably billed the flight to the same credit card. So I'm guessing you can get their names."

"Okay," Barb said, "but I can tell you right now that Thomas Callahan wouldn't have killed Ara Khan for money. Callahan is a conniving, wife-cheating alcoholic, but he's a patriot and not a murderer."

"People change," Kay said.

"Not Callahan," Barb said.

"Well, I need proof, or as close to proof as you can get me. The guy I'm most suspicious of is Eli Dolan. The problem with Dolan is that he's supposedly richer than God and it's hard to imagine he would have done this for money. What I need to know is if Dolan's as rich as everyone thinks he is."

"What exactly am I supposed to tell my finance guys when they ask me why I'm investigating these people?"

"That's easy. The Callahan Group and C and S Logistics are international outfits who do business in places like Afghanistan. You know, Barb, a place where they grow poppies and terrorists. You just tell your people that somebody whispered something into your ear about these companies and opium, and you want to see if anyone's richer than they should be."

"Yeah, okay. Is there anything else?"

Kay noticed that Barb didn't ask her how she was supposed to get any warrants she might need. Barb had ways to deal with those pesky legal impediments, and the Patriot Act made her job even easier; the Patriot Act was actually used more often to investigate the finances of drug dealers than terrorists.

In answer to Barb's question, Kay said, "Yeah, there's one other thing. I want to know if the fifty million really ended up in Sahid Khan's Swiss bank account. I'm assuming it's there, because I saw Ara type in the account number and I watched Dolan hit the SEND button. But I'm bothered that the bombing occurred immediately after the transfer. I can't understand why they waited until the money was transferred when they could have killed the Khans any time after the meeting started."

"Do you have the account number?"

"No, just the name of the bank. Bonhôte and Cie in Neuchâtel, Switzerland. I heard Dolan say the name."

"It may be a little difficult to find out if there's fifty million in a Swiss bank without an account number. For that matter, even if I had the account number, I'm still not sure I can find out what's in the account. There's a reason people put their money in Swiss banks, and it's not the interest rates."

"Hey, just do what you can. That's all I'm asking."

"Anything else? Please tell me no."

"No, there's nothing else. I thought about asking you to check the phone records of all these people, to see if anyone made any calls to suspicious characters in Afghanistan or to somebody who might want the lithium, but these are people who would know better than to make calls that can be traced. So no, there's nothing else. Just look into the money."

"Okay," Barb said, not sounding thrilled.

Kay handed her the list of people she wanted investigated and Barb started to rise from the pew, but Kay put a hand on her arm. "What did you mean when you said that Callahan's story about working for the president might be a lie?"

Barb shrugged. "The story just doesn't ring true to me. It never did. But that's not based on anything I know for sure, just instinct and being around Washington for thirty years."

"But somebody in the government must be helping

him," Kay said. "Callahan is getting classified information and large amounts of money from somewhere."

"Yeah, but probably not the president. I never thought Bush was the brightest guy in the world, but I always thought he was honest. I don't think he would have done what Callahan said he did. As for Obama, the Republicans are just looking for a reason to impeach him, and I think the last thing he'd do is get mixed up with some rogue group like Callahan's.

"The other thing that always sounded phony to me was *the president's guy*, as Callahan calls him. He said one worked for Bush and another guy took his place when Obama took office. Well, I don't know if you've ever noticed, but turnover on the White House senior staff is higher than at your average McDonald's. Hardly anyone ever sticks around for an entire term. I mean, Obama had *five* chiefs of staff in his first six years, so I can't imagine the kind of guy Callahan said he met lasting four years on Bush's staff, and another guy just like him sticking with Obama for six years. Plus, you don't usually see the sort of continuity between two different administrations that Callahan is saying happened.

"The last thing is the White House is incapable of keeping a secret; the place leaks like a sinking ship, and half the time things get leaked because somebody wants to stab somebody else in the back. If people in the White House knew that Callahan existed, I think that would have come out years ago."

"So if the president isn't running Callahan, then who is?" Kay asked.

"My guess is some group in the intelligence community. Those sneaky bastards know how to keep a secret and they've been playing games like this for years."

"Which agency?" Kay asked.

"It could be any of them, or more than one. There are sixteen organizations in this country tasked with intelligence acquisition, and half of those are engaged in covert ops. So it could be the CIA, the DIA, the NSA, the NRO, even the FBI. Pick three letters from the alphabet. And it wouldn't be the people at the very top of these agencies. Those folks get changed out every time there's a new guy in the Oval Office. So it's probably some old-timers, people who've been around forever and are able to control the money their agencies are given. Anyway, my gut tells me that the president has no idea the Callahan Group exists but somebody in the government does. Which means that Callahan's not telling you the complete truth, which also isn't surprising, knowing Thomas Callahan."

Barb rose from the pew and patted Kay on the shoulder. "Maybe you should stick around after I leave, and light a candle. Say a prayer to the patron saint of lost causes."

23

Kay knew it was going to take Barb several days to pry into the financial lives of all the people she was interested in, and all she could do was wait. In the meantime, she'd continue to be a faithful employee of the Callahan Group.

Callahan had told her he wanted her back in the training program. "I want you back in the Farsi class," Callahan said. "You can never tell when we might have to jump into Iran."

Kay didn't know if he meant jump into Iran literally— like out of an airplane—or if that was just an expression for doing something related to Iran, most likely with their nuclear weapons program. She also wondered if Callahan wanted her back in training just to keep her busy. But if he thought she was going to be a good soldier and follow orders blindly and give up on finding who'd killed Ara and why . . . Well, he obviously didn't know her at all.

As for Dolan, she had only talked to him once since the last time she saw him, which was on the flight from Afghanistan to the military hospital in Ramstein, Germany.

He called her the day after she got back to the States and asked her how she was doing insofar as recovering from her injuries. He'd sounded genuinely concerned for her—which meant nothing.

"I'm fine," Kay said—and that's all she said. She could have pretended that nothing had changed between them, but she wasn't able to do that.

Sensing her coldness, Dolan said, "I've heard from Callahan that you have doubts about me." Now, that *really* pissed her off, that Callahan would tell the most logical suspect that she thought he might be guilty. Dolan paused long enough to give her an opportunity to deny that she thought he might be a murderer, and when she didn't, he said, "All I can tell you, Kay, is that I didn't have anything to do with Ara's death, and I'm hurt—very hurt—that you'd even think so."

Kay rolled her eyes—a gesture Dolan couldn't see over the phone.

"Then what do you think happened, Eli? I mean, if we put aside the lucky coincidence of you leaving the room right before the bomb went off, how do you explain what happened?"

"It wasn't a lucky coincidence, goddamnit! The power went off and Sterling asked me to find the old man. If Sterling hadn't called, I would have been sitting there when the bomb exploded."

"You didn't answer my question, Eli. What do you think happened?"

"I think somebody over in Afghanistan found out

about the meeting. Callahan told you the CIA had a spy in Khan's government, and I think it's pretty damn likely that the Taliban or somebody else had spies, too. Whatever the case, somebody told the Taliban or some corrupt son of a bitch in Kabul about the meeting, and that's why the Khans were killed. That makes a hell of a lot more sense than me pulling some kind of double cross on Callahan and trying to kill you."

"And I'm saying that theory is bullshit, which is the same thing I told Callahan. Ara Khan and her father were too damn smart to have leaked the meeting. They lived in that godforsaken country and they knew how dangerous it was."

Dolan didn't say anything for a moment, then said, "I don't know what else to tell you, Kay. I really like you—I think I was falling in love with you—but if you can't trust me . . ."

"Yeah, right," Kay said, and hung up.

It occurred to her later that maybe she shouldn't have been so honest about considering him a suspect in Ara's death. That was like waving a red flag at a bull that had already gored a few people, and Dolan was a very smart bull.

Callahan called a couple nights later while Kay was sitting there with an ice pack on her bad leg, watching a rerun of a show called *Boss* where Kelsey Grammer, the guy who used to play in the sitcom *Frasier*, was this nasty, evil, corrupt mayor of Chicago. Kay was surprised Grammer was so good in the role, and she was enjoying the show, and wished Callahan had picked another time to call.

"Eli just resigned."

Kay didn't know what to say or what she thought about that.

"I need him, Hamilton. He's the one guy working for me who's just about irreplaceable."

"Why did he resign?" Kay asked.

"Well, I may have screwed up. I asked him to take a polygraph test and he was offended."

"Offended?"

"Yeah. He said he couldn't work with people who didn't trust him and who would even think he'd killed Ara."

"Did it ever occur to you, Callahan, that what he's really doing by quitting is making it harder to prove he's guilty? You're not going to be able to polygraph him if he's not an employee."

"You're wrong about Eli. I only asked him to take the polygraph so you'd quit thinking he was guilty. But he didn't buy that explanation."

"Why did you call me, Callahan?" Kay said. "Just to share the news?"

"No, I want you to go up to Manhattan and talk to him. I know you were close to him and he likes you."

What the hell did *that* mean? That Callahan knew she was sleeping with Dolan?

"I want you to apologize for suspecting him and convince him to come back to work for me. Like I said, I really need him for the financial stuff."

"I'm not going to do that," Kay said. "I'm not convinced he wasn't involved, and I don't think you're digging hard enough to prove he's guilty."

"You're going to do what I tell you," Callahan said.

"No, I'm not. Not when it comes to Dolan. And I gotta go now. I smell something burning in the kitchen."

Actually, the microwave had just dinged, signaling the popcorn was done. And screw Callahan. She wasn't going to beg a guy she didn't trust to come back to work with her, and she sure as hell wasn't apologizing to anyone.

She turned off the television, pissed that Callahan had made her miss a good chunk of the show. As she sat there, something else occurred to her: Assuming Eli Dolan hadn't conspired to kill Ara Khan, Kay could actually see him quitting because he was offended or his feelings were hurt.

Throughout his life, people may have been jealous of Dolan because of his wealth and his success, but he was a man who'd probably never been really disliked by anyone—his ex-wife maybe being the only exception. He was good-looking and charming and fun to be with. He wasn't an arrogant asshole who lorded his money or his intelligence over others. Kay could imagine that no one had ever accused him of being dishonest or doing something illegal; certainly, no one had ever asked him to take a polygraph test to prove his innocence. So she could see that he indeed may have been hurt very badly by the way Callahan—and particularly Kay—had treated him.

This, however, said something about his character, and what it said wasn't good.

When Kay worked for the DEA, she'd had bosses chew her up one side and down the other for being insubordinate. Male coworkers had treated her like crap because she was a woman. She'd stood toe-to-toe with guys, screaming curses at them as they screamed back at her. But she took her lumps without whining—and she never even thought of quitting because someone was *mean* to her.

If it hadn't been for what happened in Afghanistan, Kay probably would have continued to see Dolan. Maybe she might have married him. But she didn't want to be married to a guy who . . . who what? Who bruises so easily?

Four days after their meeting at St. Margaret's, Barb called Kay.

"Hey, sweetie," Barb said. "I was just wondering how you and Jessica were doing. I haven't seen you in months. Anyway, ol' Bob's out of town and I figure we're due for a girls' night out."

"That sounds great," Kay said. She figured Barb was

talking this way in case someone was monitoring Kay's phone.

"When and where?" Kay asked.

"How 'bout tonight? Say eight. You remember where we went the last time we met?"

"Yeah. You want to go there again?" Kay figured Barb meant St. Margaret's.

"Nah, I didn't think the food was that great. But there's a little place just a block south of there. I can't remember the name. It's bad enough my ass has dropped down to my knees, and now my memory's going, too."

That was a lie. Barb had a butt like a thirty-year-old's.

"Anyway, it's just a block south of the place we met last time, on the same street. It's the only place on the block that has a piano bar."

"I'll find it," Kay said.

The restaurant was called the Russia House. It was about a block south of St. Margaret's on Connecticut Avenue, but it wasn't the only restaurant on the block. It was, however, the only one that had a piano bar. Kay found it on her way home from work and then left her house at seven to make sure she could shake a tail if she had one. She still had that feeling that somebody was watching her.

Barb, as she had done last time, arrived late.

"Why did you want to meet here?" Kay asked.

"Because I'd prefer to have this discussion over a drink rather than sitting in a pew. Considering the life I've led, I never feel comfortable in churches. And this place makes a great martini."

Kay wasn't sure what Barb meant, about the life she'd led. She did know that Barb hadn't always been faithful to ol' Bob.

After their drinks arrived, Kay said, "So. What did you find out?"

"A number of interesting things. Number one on my list is that the fifty million never made it into Sahid Khan's bank account."

"What?" Kay said. "Where did it go?"

"I have no idea. I just know it didn't end up in Khan's bank. It appears that somebody either stole it or that it was never sent to Khan's account."

"I saw Ara put in the account number, and Dolan transferred the money with Ara watching him," Kay said.

"I don't know what to tell you about what you saw or what Dolan and Ara did. All I know is that the money isn't in the bank."

"How did you find this out?" Kay asked. "I mean, since I didn't have the account number."

Barb laughed. "I went to my money wizard and asked him, 'Can you find out if fifty million was deposited into a certain Swiss bank if I don't have an account number?' You know what he said?"

"No."

"He said: it depends on the bank. And I said, 'What does that mean? You can hack into some banks and not others?' And he said . . ."

Kay could tell Barb was enjoying telling the story but just wished she'd get to the point.

". . . and he said, everything's not about hacking and computers and all that high-tech stuff. He said, I have a relationship with certain bankers and I'll just call the banker and ask if money was placed in this guy's account on a certain date, and he'll tell me."

"That must mean that you've threatened or bribed a few bankers at some of the banks the narco traffickers use."

"Maybe," Barb said. "I didn't ask for the details. Anyway, a banker at Khan's bank was the one who said fifty million was never deposited into Khan's account."

Kay thought for a moment, then said, "I wonder if Dolan could have put a program on his computer that made it *look* like the money was going to Khan's bank but really sent it somewhere else?"

"I don't know," Barb said, "but let me tell you what I learned about Eli Dolan. By the standards of normal people, he's rich. His net worth is about twenty million, which includes his ten-million-dollar loft in Manhattan with a view of the East River and his two-million-dollar town house in Georgetown. The houses are both paid off and he has no significant debt. However, right now Dolan only has about seven million in liquid assets. Back in 2007, before he quit investment banking, his net worth was about sixty million, but he lost a shitload during the meltdown and was a partner in a company that lost a big lawsuit. Sometimes even the smartest guys in the room do dumb things. The question, of course, is would a man with a net worth of twenty million kill several people to increase his net worth?"

"Maybe," Kay said. "If you or I owned twelve million bucks' worth of expensive real estate and had seven million in the bank, we'd think we were in heaven. But Eli Dolan isn't like you and me. He's part of the whole Wall Street–Bernie Madoff enough-is-never-enough crowd. He might think he's one step from the breadline with only seven mil in the bank."

When Kay's drink was only one-third gone, Barb signaled the bartender for another martini. Kay never tried to keep up with Barb when they drank together.

"The thing is," Kay said, "Dolan had the opportunity. Like I said, it was his computer. So maybe he stuck a program on it to make it look like the money was going to Khan's bank when it was really going someplace else."

"I suppose that could have happened," Barb said. "But Dolan isn't a programmer; he's not a computer guy. I mean he's smart, but what he's smart at is understanding banking systems and how the government accounts for its money and moves it around. He'd need help, I think, to develop the kind of program you're talking about."

"Did you find a heavy-duty computer guy connected to Dolan?"

"No, but I wasn't looking for one."

"What else did you find out?"

"Thomas Callahan, as I expected, is practically broke. He lives in a crummy apartment and has about fourteen cents in a savings account. His problem is all his ex-wives; they live in the houses he used to own and took what savings he once had. When he retires, he's going to have a pension that's comparable to a postal worker's because one of his ex-wives will get half his pension. But my guys found no evidence that he's suddenly wealthy, and I'm not surprised. Thomas Callahan would never have killed Ara Khan."

"Yeah, maybe," Kay said, but she was thinking there was no point in debating the issue with Barb. She was obviously biased when it came to Callahan.

"Sylvia Sorenson is in about the same financial shape as Callahan, but for a different reason. Her problem is her mother's medical condition. Sorenson has never been married, lives in an apartment with her mother, and pays nurse's aides to stay with her mom when she's at work or has to go out of town. One of the two dozen medications her mother takes costs twelve hundred bucks a month, and naturally it's not covered by insurance. So Sorenson basically has nothing to show after working her whole life, and unless she's a saint, she's probably just waiting for her mom to die."

Kay had never seriously considered Sylvia Sorenson as a suspect; Sylvia wouldn't have the balls to do something like this. At least, Kay didn't think so.

"Mercer is in slightly better financial shape than Callahan and Sorenson," Barb said. "Her net worth is around half a million, most of that being the equity in her house. She's got about a hundred and fifty grand in an IRA, and when you think about it, that's not very much considering she's been steadily employed for over twenty years. Mercer's problem is she spends money on herself and her house almost as fast as she makes it, and she's taken out loans a couple of times to remodel her house."

The way Mercer dressed, Kay wasn't surprised to hear this.

"So in terms of their finances, I guess you could say that Callahan, Sorenson, and Mercer all have a money motive. Callahan's broke because of his ex-wives, Sorenson's practically broke because of her mother, and Mercer, although she's not broke, certainly isn't rich, because she's a spender and not a saver. On the other hand, these people's finances have been this way for a long time, so I don't know why any of them would suddenly decide to kill a bunch of folks to get rich."

"What about Cannon and Sterling?" Kay asked.

"After Cannon and Sterling retired from the army, they found a couple of angel investors to help them start up their security company. And at the time, it probably didn't seem like a bad investment when we were involved in simultaneous wars in Afghanistan and Iraq and a bunch of undeclared wars in places like Somalia and the Philippines. But then the wars died down and the contracts started going to the big, connected outfits like Blackwater and Halliburton's pals. Right now, C and S Logistics has a gig in Yemen protecting a few oil wells, and another job in South Africa guarding a guy who's probably a diamond smuggler. But that's it. The company did pretty well its first five years, but right now it's barely solvent.

"But Sterling is in a lot worse shape than Cannon. Cannon's carrying some debt and he invested a lot of his own money in the company, but he lives conservatively and his wife has a good job. Sterling, on the other hand, went a little crazy after they started up the company. He not only invested his savings, he went through an expensive divorce, then bought a McMansion in West Virginia he can no longer afford. So Cannon and Sterling really needed the contract for protecting the mining operation in Afghanistan, but Sterling needed it more than Cannon."

"Then I don't understand," Kay said. "If their company really needed the contract, then neither of them would have any motive for killing the Khans."

"Wrong," Barb said. "Based on what you told me, the mining operation was never a sure thing. Khan could have taken the fifty million and done nothing, in which case there'd be no security contract for C and S Logistics. Or the guys in Kabul could have screwed everything up and stopped Khan from allowing Glardon to mine the lithium. Or, because of the politics in Afghanistan, it could have taken forever for the mining operation to start, in which case the company would have no money coming in for a long time. So maybe Sterling, or Cannon—or both of them—figured the best way to get rich and get out of debt was to steal fifty million and retire from the security business."

"But are they the kind of men who would do something like this? I didn't like Cannon or Sterling when I met them, but just because they seemed like assholes, that doesn't mean they're killers." Kay was playing devil's advocate—particularly when it came to Sterling—but she wanted to hear what Barb thought.

"I called a guy I know at the Pentagon, because I wondered the same thing," Barb said. "Cannon wasn't made a general mainly because he didn't have the charisma or the political savvy to operate at the one- or two-star level, so he just retired. Sterling, however, was forced to retire. They threw his ass out."

"Why?" Kay asked.

"You remember the deck of cards in Iraq? You know, Saddam was the ace of spades, Chemical Ali was the king of spades?"

"Yeah."

"Sterling found out that one of the cards—the jack of diamonds or some damn thing—was hiding out in an apartment building in Basra and he sent in some troops to kill him. Well, it not only turned out that the guy wasn't there, but Sterling's men killed about a dozen civilians, including a couple of women and kids. Collateral damage is one thing, but a complete disregard for the civilian population is a different story. Sterling wasn't court-martialed, because the army didn't want the publicity, but they bounced his ass out of the service as fast as they could. Now, does that mean that he'd be willing to kill Ara Khan? I don't know, but to me he's a better candidate than Cannon both in terms of his personality and his finances. Plus, didn't you tell me that Cannon wasn't at the house where the meeting took place?"

"Yeah, he was supposedly checking out the dry salt lakes. But I still can't eliminate him, because everything was done with cell phones. Cannon could have blown up the transformer and then called Sterling or somebody back at the house to detonate the other bomb and kill the old man." Kay paused for a moment, then said, "I assume you didn't find a large amount of money sitting in either Sterling's or Cannon's account."

"I did not," Barb said. "We're still checking out the men they brought with them to Afghanistan, and I'll let you know if we find something. Now, that's enough business. Let's have another martini and you can tell me about Jessica and your love life. Bob really is out of town."

Kay didn't bother to tell Barb that her love life blew up the same day Ara Khan was killed.

"I don't know," Kay said. "I really should get back home. I hardly ever see my daughter."

"You will *not* be a party pooper. I will not stand for it."

*   *   *

The morning after spending the evening drinking with Barb Reynolds, her head aching like the Rose Bowl Parade had walked over it, Kay dutifully showed up at her Farsi class. She'd just taken her seat and put on her headphones when her phone beeped the signal for a text message. She looked at the screen. The message was from Barb and it said: GOTTA MEET. ASAP. MY OFFICE.

Kay didn't know what was going on, but the fact that Barb wanted to meet right away and was no longer concerned about keeping her meetings with Kay secret, probably meant that something bad had happened.

Kay left the campus and took the Metro to the Pentagon City stop and walked over to the DEA's headquarters. She told the guard at the security checkpoint that she was there to see Barb and handed over the Glock she'd been packing ever since returning from Afghanistan.

As soon as she was in Barb's office, Barb shut the door and said, "There was a trip wire on the accounts we looked at and somebody pinged us."

"What the hell does that mean?" Kay asked.

"It means that when we looked at the financial records of people connected to Thomas Callahan, somebody had set an alarm, an alert, a trap, a trip wire, whatever you want to call it. The alarm was designed to tell whoever set it that some unauthorized person was looking at those accounts. The second thing the security system did was trace it back to us—and by *us* I mean the DEA." Barb paused before she said, "Kay, anyone with half a brain will know that only one person working for Callahan has a DEA connection."

"Aw, shit," Kay said.

"We don't know who set the trip wires. For all I know, Callahan could have set them. By that I mean, maybe Callahan had one of his nerds set up a system so he would know if anyone was prying into the private lives of his employees. The other possibility is somebody involved in this mess in Afghanistan set the trip wires so he would know if someone was poking around, and he placed trip wires on everybody's accounts, including his own, so it wouldn't be obvious that he was trying to protect himself."

"So what do you think I should do?"

"Talk to Callahan. You have to trust somebody, Kay. Have you told Callahan that the fifty million never made it to Khan's bank?"

"No. He's not in Washington," Kay said. "I don't know where he went, I was just told he was out of the country. But even if he was here, I'm still not sure I'd tell him. I don't trust him. Plus, if he knew I was digging into this on my own and got you involved, he'd fire me."

"Kay, listen to me. You can trust Callahan. He doesn't give a shit about money. You've seen the way he dresses, and I know college students who live in nicer apartments. Callahan cares about power. He cares about political intrigue. He genuinely cares about this country, and he loves what he does. He has no desire whatsoever to be a multimillionaire living in the lap of luxury. The laps of various females is a different story. Anyway, you need to tell him what you've learned."

Kay shook her head. "I don't know. I'll think about it."

"Kay, the other thing you need to understand is that you may be in danger. Somebody out there knows you're mucking around in their financial affairs and trying to find out what really happened in Afghanistan."

"That means you're in danger, too."

"Not like you. I belong to a large, very lethal government organization. I have assets I can deploy to protect me, and I will. And even if somebody knows that you and I are friends, my personal computer wasn't used to investigate the bank accounts. The computer involved sits in a room where a dozen people work. What this means is that whoever traced this back to the DEA knows that other people know what I know.

"But you're in danger because you're on your own and working outside the Callahan Group. If you weren't flying solo, you wouldn't have come to the DEA for help. The other thing is, you were there when the bomb went off, and someone might think that you know more than you really do and more than what I've passed on to you."

"Yeah, all right. I'll talk to Callahan when he gets back."

"No! Call him today! I've heard there's this marvel-

ous new invention called the cell phone. Even a Lud-
dite like Callahan has one."

Kay wasn't going to call Callahan. She had to do this
face-to-face. She had to look into Callahan's bloodshot
eyes to see if he was telling the truth.

"Okay, I will," she lied to Barb.

24

"We've got a problem," Alpha said.

"What's that?" Bravo said.

"Hamilton. She's conducting her own investigation and she's talking to people outside the Callahan Group to get information."

"Goddamnit, I knew something like this was going to happen. And remember, you're the one who said to leave her alone."

Alpha ignored Bravo's I-told-you-so complaint.

"Who's she been talking to?" Bravo asked.

"Her old friends at the DEA. She's got them looking at the finances of everyone involved in Afghanistan."

"Son of a bitch! How do you know this?"

"Because I do. And you don't need to know how." Alpha wasn't going to tell him how Finley had set up the trip wires on people's bank accounts."

"Does she know the money never made it to Khan's account?"

"I don't know," Alpha said. "All I know is that she's looking at our bank accounts, probably to see if anybody's richer than they should be. She won't find anything since none of the money was transferred to our existing accounts, but what I want you to do is put somebody on her. I want to know where she goes and who she talks to."

"What we should do is get rid of her before she has a chance to fuck things up."

"No. Killing her could make matters worse, not better."

"How could killing her make things worse?"

"Because her death will be investigated by professionals, and you can never tell where the investigation will lead. We're not in Afghanistan, where law enforcement barely functions. If she's killed, Callahan will get a forensics team involved, and I don't know what else he might do."

"She has a daughter. Maybe we can control her through her daughter if she becomes a problem."

"Do you know what happened to the last person who tried to use Hamilton's daughter to control her?"

"No."

"Hamilton blew the guy's head off. I mean, she *literally* blew it off."

"I can handle Hamilton."

"You just do what I tell you and watch her."

"Maybe. We'll see."

"Goddamnit, I'm telling you not to take any action against her. Don't cross me on this."

"Oh, yeah? What are you going to do if I do?"

25

He didn't like this. He didn't like having to do a job when he hadn't been given adequate time to plan. The military way—the professional way—was to do extensive recon, take photos, then sit in a room, analyze the situation, and plan the op down to the last detail—including contingency plans if something went wrong. But the boss said there was no time for that.

He'd gotten inside the building by holding the door open for a tenant whose arms were filled with grocery bags, then found Hamilton's apartment. He immediately saw he had two problems to deal with: The door had a good lock and there was an ADT security sticker on the door, meaning the apartment had an alarm system. It usually took the cops fifteen or twenty minutes to respond to an alarm, and fifteen minutes should be enough time to do what he needed to do, provided he could pick the lock, which he wasn't sure he could. He was a guy who normally bashed down doors without trying to unlock them.

Before he left the apartment building, he went to one of the side doors and blocked it open so he'd be able to get back inside the building quickly, then went back to his car to think. In the short briefing he'd been given, he was told Hamilton had a kid and the kid went to school, which meant the kid should get home before Hamilton. When he went to school, classes usually let out at three or four, and he doubted that Hamilton got home before six.

He had a picture of the kid—he didn't know how the boss had gotten it, Facebook probably—and he knew what Hamilton looked like so he didn't need a picture of her. If he saw the kid go into the apartment building, he'd go back inside the building and just knock on Hamilton's door. He'd tell the kid he was a maintenance guy or a gas company guy or some fucking thing—how hard could it be to con a kid?—and when the kid opened the door, he'd be in. Then he'd take care of the kid—the boss said he didn't care what happened to her—then wait for Hamilton to come home.

Kay called Callahan's office and was informed that he still wasn't back from wherever he'd gone to. She wondered where the hell he was. Not knowing who else to call, she called Anna Mercer and asked if she knew when Callahan might return.

"Why do you want to know?" Mercer asked.

"Because I need to talk to him about something."

"About what?"

"Something personal. So can you tell me when he's getting back?"

"No. You don't have need to know."

What a bitch.

She went to her Farsi class after talking to Mercer, which was good, because the language was enough of a challenge that it forced her to concentrate on the words being force-fed into her brain through the headset—as opposed to thinking about Eli Dolan and what she was going to tell Callahan. After class, she usually went to the gym for a workout. Her arm and her ribs were fine, but she was still feeling some pain in her leg. The leg was really beginning to annoy her. She was a person who needed to exercise—she felt fat and sluggish when she didn't—and the leg was keeping her from going all out like she usually did. She figured, for the sake of her leg, it would be best to skip the workout and go home. She looked at her watch; if she hurried, she could be home before Jessica and be the one who made dinner for a change.

There she was—at least, he thought it was her: a short blond girl with a knapsack, wearing jeans and a hooded sweatshirt. He glanced at the photo again. Yeah, it was the kid. He wondered how old she was.

He'd give her ten minutes, enough time for her to pick up the mail, disable the alarm, and relax a little. While he waited, he stuck the Beretta in his waistband and zipped up his jacket so it wasn't visible. Then he stepped out of the car and put his wallet and cell phone inside the trunk, in the well where the spare tire was. He could just see his wallet falling out or his phone coming off his belt while he was taking care of business. Wouldn't that be a bitch?

He was just starting across the street when he saw Hamilton coming down the block. He'd recognize that body and the long blond hair anywhere. Shit! What the hell was she doing home from work so early? He turned around and went back to his car; now he needed to come up with a different plan.

W hen Kay got home, she was surprised to find that Jessica, instead of studying that night, was going to do something that normal kids do: It was Friday night and she was going out for a pizza with some of her girlfriends, then to a Dave Matthews concert at the Verizon Center. An hour later, Jessica left—still dressed as she'd been for school—in jeans and a sweatshirt. The girl had no sense of fashion.

Since Jessica was going out for pizza, there was no need to fix a nice dinner for the two of them, as she'd planned. Instead she had a beer, watched the news, and had a Lean Cuisine. Then she had a second Lean Cuisine.

She checked out the drivel on the tube and rejected the offerings; she picked up a novel that Jessica had recommended, then put it back down because she knew she'd never finish it. The damn book was almost five hundred pages long! She spent five minutes looking over her shoulder into the bathroom mirror and concluded her ass was expanding even though she knew she hadn't gained a pound.

She decided to go for a run. She needed to move. As she changed into sweatpants and a long-sleeved jersey, she told herself that she'd take it easy and wouldn't push the leg too hard. She grabbed her keys and opened the door, then stopped.

Don't be a dummy.

She went back into the bedroom and opened the gun safe in the closet. Inside the safe was her Glock—Kay's weapon of choice and the type she'd carried when she worked at the DEA—and a little short-barreled .32 that fit in an ankle holster. She'd purchased both guns in Virginia and had bought the .32 only because it was on sale and would fit easily in her purse—and because she thought it was cool.

When Jessica had first moved in with her in San Diego, she'd kept the gun safe locked. After her daughter was kidnapped—and after she realized Jessica was ten times smarter than she'd ever be—she decided to leave the safe unlocked so Jessica could get to a weapon quickly if she ever needed one. She wasn't concerned about Jessica accidentally shooting herself or anyone else. When they moved to D.C., she forced Jessica to go with her to a range one day to shoot the guns. Her daughter—being the pinko, liberal communist she was—accompanied her reluctantly, but insisted she'd never use the guns, no matter what. She said if she ever found herself in a situation where she needed a weapon, she'd call a cop—and Kay almost gave her another NRA bumper sticker quote: *A gun in your hand is better than a cop on the phone.* Then she figured why bother to have another gun-control argument with a teenager who would start quoting Gandhi.

Kay Velcroed the .32's holster to her right ankle, which she realized wasn't the smartest thing to do because her right leg was the one that had been wounded and the gun just added extra weight. On the other hand, she didn't want to strap it to her left ankle since she was right-handed. She reminded herself again that she was going to take it slow.

He saw the car park in the loading zone in front of the apartment building, and a moment later the kid came out and got into the car. Shit. If the kid had come outside alone and hadn't jumped into a car, he might have been able to snatch her and then use her as a hostage to force Hamilton to open her apartment door. But that wasn't going to happen now.

So what should he do? He reached for a cigarette in his shirt pocket—then laughed. He'd stopped smoking over a year before and was glad he had; it was a nasty, disgusting habit. But at a time like this, when he needed to think, a cigarette would have been good.

Maybe what he should do was wait until the kid returned and see if he could grab her before she went back inside. Or better yet, go into the building now and hide out near the elevator, and when the kid returned, no matter when that was, get her going into the elevator and then use her to force Hamilton to open the door.

Wait a minute! Hamilton had just opened the door to the apartment building. She was dressed like she was going for a run. Yeah, now she was stretching. He hated to keep changing the plan, but maybe this was a good thing. Maybe he could make this work.

I t was dark outside, but Kay could see okay; there were streetlights, not to mention passing cars. She stretched for a few minutes, then picked a direction: up Connecticut, toward the National Zoo.

She jogged more slowly than she usually did, just enjoying the night air and the feel of the blood moving through her body. As she jogged, she thought idly about what she'd do if Callahan fired her—and she wasn't all that sure she'd care. She was making a decent salary, but aside from what had happened in Afghanistan, she'd spent too much time in classrooms and hadn't seen the kind of action she wanted. Worse was Barb saying that Callahan had probably lied to her about who he really worked for.

She figured that if Callahan really worked for the president like he'd said, and if he got in trouble one day with Congress, she was too far down the ladder to get in trouble herself. But if Callahan had lied to her about whom he worked for, then she didn't know how precarious her position was legally. There had to be some way she could find out if . . .

Hamilton was headed up Connecticut, toward the zoo, and he figured she'd stay on Connecticut because it was fairly well lit. He hit the gas and passed her, looking to his left for the right kind of spot. Then he saw it: a little alley that provided access to a loading dock on one side of a big apartment building. If he stood in the alley, close to the sidewalk, she wouldn't be able to see him until she passed the alley—and when she did, he'd grab her.

He liked his other plan better—the one that involved using the kid to gain access to Hamilton's apartment and killing her inside the apartment—but this would do.

He took the knife out of the glove compartment and put it in his belt at the back of his pants. For what he wanted to do, a knife would be better than the Beretta. He jogged over to the alley entrance and got a nice surprise: There was a Dumpster just a couple yards into the alley. When Hamilton jogged past the alley, he'd grab her and pull her behind the Dumpster. A passing car might see him take her, but he'd snatch her out of sight in less than three seconds. He'd take the risk.

He looked back up Connecticut. Hamilton was a block away, coming toward him at a steady pace. He put on a ski mask and stepped into the alley.

* * *

Kay was thinking about Eli Dolan as she passed the mouth of an alley—and she was completely unprepared when the man came at her from behind and wrapped his forearm across her throat. Keeping the pressure on her throat—he had her in a choke hold and was cutting off her wind—he dragged her into an alley, stopping when they were behind a Dumpster overloaded with trash.

"You fight me and I'll slice your face up," he hissed into her ear.

When he stopped dragging her, Kay was finally able to get her feet set. She had to do something before she passed out, which she assumed was his plan: choke her until she was unconscious, drop her behind the Dumpster so he couldn't be seen from the street, rip off her sweatpants, and rape her—and then maybe kill her.

The guy wasn't as big as Bowman—the monster who had beaten the hell out of her in the hand-to-hand combat course—but he was big. He outweighed her by maybe fifty pounds and was about six feet tall. She could tell by the muscular forearm across her throat and the way he felt pressed up against her back that he was in good shape.

Then Kay did all those things that she'd been taught.

She snapped her head back hard and hit him in the nose, slammed her right foot down as hard as she could on his instep, then swung her right fist back, hoping to hit him in the balls. She missed his balls and hit him in the thigh, but the guy had been unprepared for her to fight back, maybe thinking she had to be on the verge of passing out. Or maybe thinking she'd be too scared to fight. He obviously didn't know her.

Thanks mostly to the head snap, she was able to break the grip he had on her throat, and she spun about to confront him—and he hit her in the face with his right fist, knocking her to the ground. Fortunately, he didn't knock her out.

As Kay sat there, trying to recover from the blow to her face, he reached behind his back and pulled out a knife that had a six-inch serrated blade. "You broke my nose, you bitch. I'm going to . . ."

Kay was on her butt, her legs sprawled out in front of her, about six feet from him. While he was still talking— telling her how he was going to make her suffer—she reached down to her ankle, pulled out the .32, and shot him twice in the chest. She never even thought about telling him to drop the knife.

She sat there for a moment, pointing the gun at him, waiting to see if he was going to get up—and waiting for her pulse rate to drop below a hundred. She finally rose to her feet and walked over and looked down at him. He didn't seem to be alive. She knelt down next to him and, while pressing the muzzle of the gun against his head, checked *his* pulse rate. It was zero. Good.

She pulled the ski mask off his head. She knew she should have left it in place so the cops could see what he'd looked like before she shot him, but she wanted to see who he was. Her first impression was that he looked familiar, but she didn't recognize him. His head was knobby and shaved, he had a couple days' worth of beard, and there was a bump on the bridge of his nose that had been there before she broke it. Her overall impression was that if you put his picture in a photo array and asked people to pick out the guy most likely to own a pit bull and get drunk and beat his wife, they'd pick this guy's picture. But maybe she was prejudiced.

26

Kay needed to call the cops but didn't have her phone with her. She walked to the mouth of the alley—she was limping again; she'd hurt her leg when she'd stomped on the damn guy's foot—and looked up and down Connecticut. The block was all apartment buildings, but not the type to have doormen sitting in the lobby. Naturally, there wasn't a pay phone in sight.

Two guys stepped out of one of the buildings and began walking toward her. They were holding hands. She walked toward them, and when she was about twenty yards away, she said, "I need you to call the cops."

They stopped, and she kept walking toward them. "I need you to call the cops," she repeated. "A guy just tried to rape me and I shot him."

One of the men looked down and saw she was holding the .32 in her hand; she'd actually forgotten she was holding it. He took a step backward and half raised his hands in a surrender gesture.

"No, no," Kay said. "I'm not going to hurt you. Now, please. Call the cops. I'm going to wait for them back by the body."

The D.C. Metro Police showed up in less than five minutes—about the expected response time when they get a call saying a woman's walking around with a gun in her hand and had just admitted that she'd killed someone. When they arrived, Kay was standing at the mouth of the alley, and she raised both hands to show she was unarmed. The two cops—one white, one black, both young—exited their patrol car holding guns.

"Where's your weapon?" one of them said, pointing his gun at her chest.

Kay pointed down at her feet. "Right there."

"Step away from it. Now," the cop said.

"Okay, guys, but I'm the victim here. So settle down."

Kay had thought it would be pretty straightforward: She'd show them the bruise on her face where the rapist had hit her, the ski mask lying next to his head, the knife lying on the ground next to his hand, and they'd say, "Thank you, ma'am, for ridding the city of this menace." She should have known better.

From the cops' perspective it wasn't all that clear-cut. How did they know she hadn't planted the knife? For that matter, how did they know she hadn't attacked the man and he drew a knife to defend himself? And what was she doing jogging at night, packing a sneaky little .32 in an ankle holster? And how was it that she was able to overcome a man bigger than her, whom she claimed had her in a choke hold? It was also pretty amazing how she'd been able to put two bullets into his chest in a circle the size of a fifty-cent piece while scared and scuttling along on her butt, trying to back away from the guy.

They read her the Miranda statement and took her to the station.

At the station they put her into an interrogation room, made her wait for an hour, and then a detective came in and asked her all the questions she'd already been asked. The one thing that stumped her was when the detective asked if she'd ever seen the man before. She said, "I'm not sure. He looked familiar, but I can't place him. Who is he?"

Instead of answering her question, the cop said, "Okay, let's take this one more time from the top. You claim you were jogging down Connecticut and . . ."

It was the *you claim* that did it. "All right. I've had enough of this bullshit. I'm ex-DEA, I know my rights, and I want to make a phone call right now. So you either let me make a call or you get your dumb ass out of here and get a public defender in here."

There were two people she could call: Barb Reynolds and Anna Mercer. She assumed Callahan was still out of the country. She figured that Barb had done her enough favors lately and didn't deserve to get dragged into this mess.

"This is Hamilton," she said when Mercer answered her phone, "and this call is probably being monitored.

I'm down at the police station on Indiana Avenue. I just killed a man who tried to rape me, and the cops are being assholes about the whole thing and treating me like a suspect."

"My God," Mercer said. "Are you all right?"

"Yeah, I'm fine, but can you get someone down here to spring me from this place?"

Twenty minutes later, Sylvia Sorenson opened the door to the interrogation room. She was wearing a black raincoat over jeans and a dark blue T-shirt that looked two sizes too large. Judging by her tousled hair, Mercer must have roused Sylvia from her bed and she'd probably been sleeping in the T-shirt. "You're free to go," she said to Kay.

As they walked down the hall, the detective who'd questioned Kay came up to her and said, "I apologize, ma'am, for—"

"Hey!" Sylvia snapped. "Don't talk to my client, and you just remember what I told you."

"Yes, ma'am," the detective said.

"What did you do to get me sprung?" Kay asked as she and Sylvia were leaving the building.

Sylvia smiled—this small, cruel slice of a smile—and when she did, Kay thought she looked a bit feral and she remembered Mercer's comment about Sylvia the wolverine.

"I had a little discussion with that cop regarding the law," Sylvia said. "I also pointed out to him that fucking around with a decorated ex–DEA agent currently employed by a former member of the National Security Council was not a good career move."

Kay wished she'd seen that: Sylvia dressing down the detective.

"Do you need a ride home?" Sylvia asked.

Kay looked in the bathroom mirror. Her face had a reddish lump near her right cheekbone where the guy had hit her, and it would probably turn purple tomorrow. She also had a headache, and her leg was throbbing. What she was really worried about was that the punch in the face might have affected the concussion she'd had. She'd go see the doctor tomorrow. She didn't want to end up like some punch-drunk NFL lineman from repeated blows to the head.

She was really getting tired of being injured.

She called Anna Mercer again. "I'm back home. Thanks for siccing Sylvia on the cops."

"Yeah, Sylvia can be pretty formidable when she sets her mind to it."

"I'd like to get the name of the guy who attacked me. He looked familiar."

"What are you saying? You think this was more than a random attack?"

"I don't know. He just looked familiar, and I'd like to know his name."

"I'll have Sylvia get his name tomorrow," Mercer said. "I'm just glad you're okay."

* * *

When Jessica got home from the Dave Matthews concert and saw Kate holding an ice pack to her face, she shrieked, "Oh my God! What happened to you now?"

"Aw, I did something stupid. I went for a jog and I guess my leg wasn't quite ready for it, and I stumbled and landed on my face. Does it look that bad?"

"It looks like somebody punched you. You look like a battered wife."

That was too close to the mark, and Kay wondered if she should tell her daughter the truth, that somebody had tried to rape her. Maybe she should; maybe it was a mistake to hide what had happened from her. But Kay didn't want to scare her again. Jessica's reaction to Kay's lie that she'd been in a car accident had been bad enough, and she didn't want the girl dwelling on how vulnerable people were and how capricious life could be. On the other hand, not telling her could be a disservice to her. Jessica knew, at least intellectually, that rape was a possibility, but she probably didn't really think that it could happen to her or anyone close to her. Shielding her daughter from the harsh realities of life might be worse in the long run than giving her another scare. The other thing Kay realized was that what she'd done could become public knowledge. The police didn't typically release the names of rape victims to the media, but since a man had been killed, it was hard to predict what information might become public. She could just see some cop knocking on the door and saying to Jessica, "Hi, I'm here to talk to your mom about the rapist she killed the other night."

She started to say *Okay, I'm not telling you the truth, here's what really happened,* and then another thought occurred to her. It still bothered her that the man she'd killed had looked familiar, and she wondered if what had happened tonight might have some connection to the Callahan Group or Afghanistan. Tomorrow she'd get the guy's name and also see if the cops had any intention of pursuing the issue. And if the attack on her had any connection to Callahan, then she really couldn't talk to Jessica about it. She'd decide tomorrow.

27

Alpha was furious. If Bravo had been in the room, Alpha would have killed him.

Alpha called one of the prepaid cell phones they used to communicate.

"You stupid son of a bitch! I told you to just watch her. Why did you try to kill her?"

He didn't answer. He was probably trying to figure out how Alpha knew that he'd sent someone to kill Hamilton. Before he could say anything, Alpha said, "Well, Hamilton killed the guy you sent, genius."

"Aw, shit," he said.

"*Aw, shit*? That's all you have to say? The only good news is the cops don't know who he is yet. Fortunately, he didn't have any ID on him. But in a couple of hours they'll run his prints, and since I'm guessing he's ex-military, his prints will be on file. I need his name, and I need it before Callahan learns who he is. It still might be possible to recover from the dumbass thing you've done."

"How?"

"Never mind *how*. What's his name?"

"Eric Nelson. He was one of the men I used in Afghanistan. He was Charlie."

"Text me his DOB and SS number." Then Alpha couldn't help it. "Why in the hell did you do it? Goddamnit, tell me why."

"Because she saw me in the house right after I planted the bomb and then . . ."

"She didn't see you actually plant the bomb, and you gave her a reason for why you were in the house."

"But then she goes and looks at my finances and finds out the same thing you did—that I'm broke. So now she has a motive. Then she gets the DEA involved. What if she has the DEA start monitoring my banking transactions and the first time I remove money from that account your boy set up, they find the five million. If that happens—"

"You're getting paranoid. I'm telling you they'll never find the money that Finley hid for you. Finley's a genius. You just follow the procedures he put in place to—"

"Yeah, so you say. But maybe they got a couple geniuses working for the DEA, and with Hamilton pushing them . . . I figured if Nelson raped her before he killed her, nobody would connect us to her death or to what happened in Afghanistan. I mean, you have about ten rapes a day in that goddamn city."

"Listen to me," Alpha said. "I don't have any more time to talk right now, but I swear to God, you arrogant prick, if you do one more thing without clearing it with me first, I'll kill you."

"Yeah, well, good luck with that," he said, and hung up.

Now Alpha had to really scramble and hope that Finley could do what was necessary. Alpha called him—he was awake, of course, because the freak slept only about three hours a night—and told him what he needed to do before daylight: He had to move a quarter million dollars into an offshore bank and make it look like the money came from Pakistan.

"The money has to be traceable," Alpha said, "but it can't be too easy to trace. Do you understand, Finley? I want Callahan to have to dig hard to find the money. If it's too easy, he'll get suspicious."

28

Callahan was back, and he summoned Kay to his office. Judging by the way he looked, he'd taken the red-eye from wherever he'd been. But then, he always looked like that. Seeing the bruise on Kay's face, he asked, "What did the doctor say?"

Kay figured that Sylvia or Anna had told him what had happened to her. "He said to take a couple ibuprofen when my head hurts. I'm okay. Am I going to have a problem with the cops about the guy I killed?"

"No. They've been told to drop the whole thing and call it self-defense."

"Who told them?"

"People with enough weight to crush careers. When I found out who attacked you, I had to nip things in the bud. As far as the cops are concerned, you're just a fair-haired girl with powerful connections and a scary lawyer, but they don't have any real reason to think you murdered the guy."

"So who was he?"

"We'll get to that later. Right now, I want to know what the hell you've been up to. And don't lie to me. I know you've been digging into the whole Afghanistan fiasco."

"That's why I came here today, to tell you what I've been doing and what I found out."

Callahan made a so-get-on-with-it gesture.

"The biggest thing I learned," Kay said, "is that the fifty million that was supposedly sent to Sahid Khan's bank never made it into his account. The money disappeared. Somebody stole it."

Kay waited for Callahan to say: *Oh, my God! How did you discover this?* But he didn't. Instead he said, "I already know that, Hamilton. Didn't it ever occur to you that I would look into the money? What the hell do you think I've been doing since the last time I talked to you?"

Before Kay could answer, Callahan said, "I was told before I hired you that you would disobey orders if you thought you were right—and that you *always* think you're right—and that you lied to your bosses at the DEA and federal judges and anybody else you thought didn't need to know the truth. It looks like I should have listened to the people who told me those things." Pointing a thick finger at her face, he said, "I gave you a direct order not to screw around with what happened in Afghanistan."

"I didn't think you were going to do anything," Kay said.

"How the *hell* could you possibly think that?" Callahan shouted. "An operation I was in charge of blew up in my face."

"All I knew was that you didn't take me seriously when I told you Dolan might have been involved."

"I took you seriously, goddamnit! I just didn't agree with you."

Callahan's face was beet red; she hoped he didn't have a stroke.

"Do you want me to tell you what else I learned," Kay said, "or do you just want to keep gnawing on my ass?"

Callahan almost smiled. "Yeah. Tell me what else you learned."

"I learned that Dolan isn't as rich everyone thinks he is."

"I found that out, too," Callahan said. "But I still don't believe he was involved in Ara's death."

"I also learned that C and S Logistics is barely making it and Sterling, in particular, is up to his neck in debt. He really needed that security contract in Afghanistan, but since the contract wasn't a sure thing, maybe he decided the smart thing to do was steal fifty million and retire."

Callahan nodded as if he'd come to the same conclusion. "Did you look at my finances, too?" he asked.

"Yeah. You're practically broke, but you've always been practically broke."

"Who else did you check out?"

"Mercer, Sorenson, Cannon, and everybody that Sterling and Cannon took with them to Afghanistan."

"Did you check out Harris?"

"No. Who's Harris?"

"A guy who worked with Eli."

"I didn't know about him."

"That's right, you didn't. You see, Hamilton, you're not as smart as you think you are. And who did the financial checks for you? You're not smart enough to have done those, either."

He was just going to keep punching her in the face with how smart she *wasn't.* "Barb Reynolds," she said.

"Aw, goddamnit," Callahan muttered. "And I suppose you told Barb everything."

"I had to. I needed her help, and I couldn't trust anybody working for the Group. Including you."

Callahan laughed. "So why are you trusting me now?

She almost said: *Because I don't have a choice.* Instead she said, "Because Barb convinced me I should. And there's something else. Barb said there was something called a trip wire on the accounts of the people she investigated. This means that someone was able to see that the DEA was investigating and was able to trace the investigation back to the DEA. I need to know if you're the one who put the trip wires in place."

"No," Callahan said. "I learned the same thing you did. I used a couple of guys over at . . . Never mind who I used. Anyway, they told me the same thing, that somebody wanted to know if they were being investigated and by who, but whoever set the trip wires was able to hide his identity."

"I still think it could be Dolan."

"Well, I don't," Callahan said.

"Hiding money is what he does for a living."

"Dolan doesn't have the computer skills to snatch money out of thin air on its way to a Swiss bank."

"It was *his* computer," Kay countered. "He put a program on it so he could steal the money, and if he didn't do it personally, then he got somebody to help him."

"Not necessarily," Callahan said. "People I talked to told me it's possible that an exceptional hacker could have gotten past the security systems on Dolan's machine and downloaded a program he wouldn't have known about."

"You gotta look harder at Dolan," Kay said.

"Goddamnit, quit saying that! That's another thing I was told about you: You get tunnel vision when you think you're right. And there's something else you don't know, Miss Smarty Pants."

Kay couldn't help but smile. Her mother used to call her Miss Smarty Pants when she was little. After she got knocked up at age fifteen, her mother didn't call her that anymore. "What else don't I know?" Kay asked.

"The guy you killed last night worked for Cannon and Sterling. His name is Nelson, and he was with you in Afghanistan."

"I thought I recognized him," Kay said. "When we were in Afghanistan, all the security guys had beards and were wearing hats and turbans and shit to blend in with the locals, and I never really got a good look at any of them. Did you ask Cannon or Sterling about him?"

"Yeah. Sterling said he had no idea what Nelson was

doing in D.C. or why he attacked you. He said Nelson quit after he got back from Afghanistan, said that he'd had enough of traveling to shitholes and getting shot at. He was ex-army, two tours in Iraq, and had worked for Sterling for three years, but there wasn't anything special about him. What I'm saying is, he was bright enough to work for Sterling but not bright enough to plan what happened in Afghanistan.

"The other thing Sterling said—and Nelson's military file confirmed this—is that Nelson got in trouble in Iraq for sexually harassing a female soldier. But if you read between the lines, Nelson might have actually raped the woman. Sterling said that maybe when Nelson saw you in Afghanistan, he got fixated on you. Sexually. And that's why he attacked you."

"I wouldn't trust Sterling," Kay said.

"I don't trust him. I'm just telling you what he said."

"Did Nelson know how to build a bomb?" she asked.

"Yeah. All Cannon and Sterling people have demolitions training. Plus, Nelson had firsthand experience with IEDs in Iraq."

"So maybe he was the one who built the bombs."

"Yeah, maybe, but there's something else. I had a guy take another look at Nelson's finances this morning. He had two hundred and fifty thousand in an offshore account, and we were able to trace the money back to a mosque in Pakistan that's financed the Taliban in the past."

"What?" Kay said. "Are you saying you think this

really was a Taliban operation? That the Taliban paid Nelson to kill Ara, and they're the ones who stole the money? I mean, I can't believe . . ."

"No, I don't think that," Callahan said. "What I think is that somebody else thinks I'm as stupid as you seem to think I am."

"I don't think you're—"

"It was hard to find the money in Nelson's account—maybe that's why Barb's people didn't find it—and it was really hard to trace it back to the mosque. But it wasn't *that* hard. What I'm saying is, everything else associated with this op computer-wise was done by a genius. We can't figure out who set the trip wires on everybody's bank accounts. We can't figure out how the fifty million disappeared. But in the case of tracing Nelson's money, this genius hacker-programmer freak made things easy enough that some guy who's *almost* as smart as him could trace the money."

Callahan lit a cigarette and exhaled the smoke through his nose, making Kay think of a weary, white-faced dragon. "I think somebody set this up so that if I started poking around, I'd find Nelson's Taliban connection. But I don't believe the Taliban had anything to do with this. In other words, I actually agree with you, Hamilton. Ara Khan and her father would never have told anyone about that meeting. This was an inside job."

"So what are we going to do?"

"*We?* We're a *we* now?"

"What are we going to do?" Kay repeated.

29

Callahan wanted breakfast, so he and Kay walked over to a restaurant on L Street where all the waitresses knew Callahan. One busty old-timer called him "Honey" and pressed her broad hip against his shoulder as she took his order.

"There were nine people, including you and me, who played a significant role in the operation, and two of those people worked together to kill the Khans," Callahan said. "I'm going to exclude you and me. I'm excluding me because I know I'm innocent. I kind of like that: Callahan the Innocent. Makes me sound like a pope." When Kay didn't crack a smile, he said, "I'm excluding you because you were almost killed over there and because Sterling's guy tried to kill you here."

"Well, that's damn big of you," Kay said.

"So we have seven suspects: Eli Dolan, Anna Mercer, Sylvia Sorenson, Paul Harris, Ernst Glardon, Steven Cannon, and Nathan Sterling."

"Who's Harris?" Kay asked. "You just said he was working with Eli."

"He's an engineer and he once worked for Sociedad

Química y Minera, a company in Chile involved in lithium mining in South America. Eli trusted him and needed his expertise, so we had him sign a nondisclosure agreement and brought him in. Harris is a suspect only because he knew that we were planning to go after the lithium, but not a strong one, and the main reason why is he never knew about the money we were planning to give Sahid Khan."

"Unless Dolan told him about the money," Kay said.

Callahan ignored Kay's comment and continued. "I know Ernst Glardon didn't do it, because he didn't know about the money we were giving to Khan either, and the mining operation would have benefited his company. Plus, Ernst is an idiot. If he wasn't one, Eli wouldn't have been able to assume control of his company.

"I'm also going to eliminate Cannon as a serious suspect. He wasn't at the house when the bombs went off and—"

"How do you know he wasn't on the other side of the wall that surrounded the house and detonated the bomb from there?" Kay said. "Or how do you know he wasn't the guy who blew the transformer? Everything was done with cell phones, and just because he said he was going to the dry lakes doesn't mean he really went there."

"He *did* go to the lakes," Callahan said. "I took a trip to Switzerland since the last time we met. That's when I found out the money never made it to Khan's bank. While I was there, I talked to the Glardon engineer who went with Cannon to look at the lakes. At the time the bombs went off, Cannon was with the engineer and miles away from the house and the substation." Callahan laughed. "That engineer never slept the whole time he was with Cannon. They were out in the middle of nowhere in an area where the Taliban roam, and the guy was scared shitless. Anyway, I suppose the engineer could be in on this, too, and he lied to me, but that's unlikely. I also realize that Cannon could have planned this thing so he didn't have to be at the house, but I think that would be too complicated.

"So for now I'm crossing Cannon, Harris, and Ernst Glardon off my list, and we're down to Nathan Sterling and somebody working for me who knew how much money I was giving Sahid Khan. Which means Anna, Sylvia, and your favorite suspect, Eli Dolan."

The busty waitress brought Callahan's breakfast: an omelet that looked like it took six eggs to make and with enough hash browns to choke a horse. Callahan started eating, talking as he did so.

"I have no doubt that Sterling was involved. I mean, once you accept that the Taliban and Sahid Khan's security people had nothing to do with what happened, he's the only one left who was in a position to control things at the house where the meeting was held. And it was his guy, Nelson, who tried to kill you."

"But you can't be sure that Sterling was personally involved," Kay said. "Whoever planned this could have worked with some of Sterling's people, like Nelson. I don't necessarily believe that. I'm just saying, hypothetically, that—"

Callahan shook his head. "Let's say you were the person who planned this. How would you know which of Cannon and Sterling's people they'd be taking with them to Afghanistan? And how could you be certain that Cannon or Sterling would just let the guys you picked run around on their own and do things like build a couple bombs and plant one at the substation? And how would you know which of their people would be willing to do this? But Sterling was in a position to pick his people and control what they were doing in Afghanistan, so I'm positive he was involved."

"But you don't have any proof," Kay said.

Poking his fork at her face for emphasis, Callahan said, "You need to understand something, Hamilton. I don't *need* proof. I just need to be convinced I'm right. I'm not going to have anybody arrested. I'm not going to take anyone to court, and I'm not trying to build a legal case that eliminates reasonable doubt. I just have to know I'm right."

Before Kay could ask what he planned to do once he knew he was right, Callahan continued. "But like I said, there was a *brain* behind all this, somebody who knew we were giving Khan the money. Sterling wouldn't have known about the money I was planning to give to Sahid Khan, either—not unless somebody working for me told him. And since I didn't tell him, and since I'm guessing you didn't either, I think either Anna or Sylvia told him."

"How do you know it wasn't Dolan?"

"I'll tell you how I know. Because Sterling called Dolan to get him out of the meeting room." Kay started to object, but Callahan held up a hand, stopping her. "Listen to me. First, Sterling's cell phone records showed he called Dolan's phone, so Dolan wasn't lying about who called him. But the big thing is, whoever planned this wanted Dolan to live so he'd be a suspect."

"What?"

"The first time I met with you after you got back from Afghanistan, I told you I thought that maybe the Khans had told somebody about the meeting and whoever they told turned one of Khan's bodyguards to kill the Khans. And that's what the person who planned this *wanted* me to think. But then you convinced me that Ara and her dad wouldn't have told anyone. Which made me wonder: Why did they wait until the money was transferred before they blew the bomb?"

"Yeah, I wondered the same thing."

"Then I found out, just like you did, that the money was stolen. I think whoever planned this was hoping that I'd never find out the money was stolen, but in case I did, she wanted to give me a suspect. And *that's* why they saved Eli, because he'd be the logical suspect."

Kay had to admit that he had a point. But Callahan wasn't finished.

"And you can't ignore the fact that Eli had no motive,"

Callahan said. "The money sure as hell wouldn't have been a motive for him. The only reason he's allowed his net worth to dwindle to a mere twenty million is he's been too busy working for me. With his smarts and connections, he could go back to Goldman Sachs anytime he wanted. And I can't think of any political reason why he'd want to kill the Khans or destroy an operation that he'd been working on for a year."

"Yeah, maybe you're right," Kay said. "Although . . ."

"You just can't admit you might be wrong, can you?" Callahan said.

Kay decided to ignore that. "So if it wasn't Eli, who was it? Sylvia or Anna? Personally, I have a hard time seeing Sylvia as the person behind this."

"A lot of people have made the mistake of underestimating Sylvia. They didn't make her a commander in the United States Navy for being a wallflower, and I hired her because I was aware of the work she did when she was at the Pentagon. When it comes to doing her job, Sylvia can be as tricky and cutthroat as any lawyer you've ever known."

"Yeah, but is she capable of cold-blooded murder?"

"I wouldn't have thought so," Callahan said. "But then, I can't imagine Anna being a killer, either."

Callahan raised a hand to get the check and the blond waitress brought it to him. She placed a hand on the back of his thick neck, ruffled the hair hanging over his collar, and asked if he'd enjoyed his breakfast. Callahan left a tip that Kay figured was fifty percent of the bill. It was no wonder the waitresses all loved him; nor was it any wonder that he was almost broke.

As they were walking back to the office, Kay said, "We need proof, Callahan. We need evidence. Maybe not enough to take to court, but we need something. And although you might be right about Eli—and I'll admit you could be—we need something more."

"We're not going to get any evidence from the crime scene, because the crime scene's in Afghanistan," Callahan said. "We're not going to get evidence off Eli's computer, because it was destroyed when the bomb went off. There's no money in anybody's bank account we can find, which also means I can't prove anyone's richer than they should be."

"Have you looked at phone calls?"

"No, and I'm not going to waste time doing that. All the people involved are smart enough not leave a communication trail."

"Then polygraph them," Kay said. "Polygraph them all: Eli, Anna, and Sylvia."

Callahan laughed. "I can't polygraph Eli, because he quit. Sylvia gets so nervous when she's hooked up to the machine that it looks like she's lying when she's asked if her name is Sylvia Sorenson. As for Anna, she had training when she was at the CIA to beat a polygraph test, and she's good at it. If I test her, the results won't mean anything."

Kay didn't say anything for a moment as she walked along beside Callahan. She noticed he was breathing way too heavily for the short distance they'd walked. He needed to lose weight and stop smoking.

"If you're right about Eli," Kay said, "then there's another player involved in this. I mean, if Eli didn't program his own computer to steal the money, then somebody else did. So unless you think that Anna or Sylvia have the computer skills . . ."

"They don't," Callahan said. "Someplace out there is a computer guy who helped with all this."

"Or computer gal, Callahan. I mean, if you think it was a woman who betrayed you, you shouldn't be such a sexist."

Callahan laughed.

"How would Sylvia or Anna have found the computer person to help them?" Kay said. "Do you have people on retainer?"

"Now, that's actually a damn good question. We don't have people on retainer, but I have access to some of the best computer people in this country, including some five-star hackers, but I'm the *only* one that has access to them. Sylvia and Anna would have to find somebody, and they sure as hell didn't place an ad in the Help Wanted pages." Callahan smiled at Kay and said, "I'm going to do the same thing one of them did to find a guy who could snatch money out of thin air."

"Which is?"

"Don't worry about that. I want you to go home and

rest up. If I can get a lead on the computer guy, I'm going to have you run him down and deal with him."

"Deal with him how?" Kay said.

Instead of answering her question, Callahan said, "And watch your back, Kay. Somebody's tried to kill you twice now. They could try again."

That was the first time she remembered him calling her Kay.

30

Callahan left a message for Smee, telling the weasel he needed to talk to him. An hour later, he met with Smee in an office near Dupont Circle that had a FOR LEASE sign in the window. He told Smee what he wanted. He'd used Prescott's people to do the financial reviews and to answer the computer questions, but now he wanted Grayson's folks to help him find the computer guy. Grayson was in the right organization to do that.

Callahan returned to his office, poured a cup of coffee, then tipped a little bourbon into the cup.

Sylvia or Anna? Which one had killed the Khans?

Sylvia was the person who had the most motive, a lot more motive than either Eli or Anna. Callahan didn't know anyone personally who lived in more miserable circumstances. She'd been caring for her sick mother seemingly forever—and Callahan knew her mother was a sharp-tongued, complaining, ungrateful hag. She didn't have a husband, because what man would want to marry into a situation where he would become a full-time nursing partner? She made over two hundred grand a year as his top lawyer, but lived in a shitty apartment, drove a shitty car, and dressed in shitty clothes because her mother's medical expenses had bled her dry. When she took vacation time, she did so when her mother was hospitalized for one reason or another. If Callahan had been in Sylvia's situation, he would have smothered the old bat with a pillow years ago.

So did Sylvia do it? Had she finally been pushed over the edge? Had she finally decided it was time to live not just a normal life but a better-than-normal life to make up for all the years she'd sacrificed? Callahan had no doubt she had the brains to steal the money and plan the operation. And if she had the money she could escape from her mother and assuage her conscience by putting the old woman in the finest medical facility in the country. But kill five people? Would Sylvia do that?

No. She wouldn't do that. And the reason he knew this was the sacrifices she'd made for her mother.

It was Anna who had betrayed him and killed Ara Khan—and admitting this just broke Callahan's heart.

For some time, Callahan had sensed Mercer's growing bitterness—which really wasn't at all unusual for people like her when they reached middle age. People who have spent their entire careers serving the U.S. government—the people at the top, the admirals and generals, the intelligence people who protect the nation, presidential appointees responsible for billions of dollars managing federal programs—rarely made more than two hundred grand a year. So it wasn't unusual at all for these senior people to grouse about the fact that Wall Street bankers, who had nowhere near their level of responsibility, made multimillion-dollar salaries. All senior civil servants, at some point in their lives, can't help but think how much more they could have made had they taken their ideas and ambition to the private sector.

Some of these people, however, could at least take solace in the fact that the citizens they served knew who they were and what they did, and admired them. When a man said he'd been the chairman of the Joint Chiefs of Staff, director of the CIA, secretary of defense or state— people knew that he'd been somebody who mattered. And these people, because of their fame and their past positions, were usually able to get lucrative private-sector jobs after they retired. Most civil servants, however, including Thomas Callahan and Anna Mercer, had no claim to fame. Nobody could tell you who had been the deputy director of some agency or the undersecretary at another. From the standpoint of public recognition, they were nobodies.

Callahan could see that all this began to grate on Mercer. Not only didn't she make the kind of money she could have made if she'd taken her talents to Exxon or Pfizer or Morgan Stanley, the worst part was, she'd always been a second banana. She'd always been somebody's deputy—as she was now Callahan's. Moreover, because she worked for the Callahan Group, she wasn't even allowed to tell folks what she'd accomplished; there'd be no book deals for Anna Mercer.

Callahan figured that sometime in the past year, Mercer decided that if she was going to be an invisible servant to an ungrateful nation, at least she was going to be a rich one. She was not going to settle for a time-share in Fort Lauderdale that she visited two weeks a year. She wasn't going to drive a car until it had two hundred thousand miles on the odometer. She was *not* going to fly fucking coach.

Instead, she decided to steal fifty million dollars the government could never report as having been stolen. She wouldn't get all the money, however—she'd have to share part of it with her cohorts—but Callahan was betting that she'd kept the lion's share for herself. If she only kept thirty of the fifty million. . . Well, thirty million wasn't chicken feed.

If all she'd done was steal the money, that would have bothered Callahan, of course, but she'd done more than that. What really bothered him was the reason she killed Ara Khan. She didn't need to kill Ara to steal the money—she killed Ara because Ara's death was all part of the smoke screen that Anna had to create to hide her involvement and make him think that the Taliban or someone in Kabul had planted the bomb.

Like he'd told Hamilton, Anna had been hoping that no one would be able to penetrate the secrecy and security of a Swiss bank and discover that the fifty million never made it into Sahid Khan's account. She had to kill the

Khans, because if they called their banker the day after the meeting, then they—and Callahan—would know the money had been stolen. So in case Callahan did learn that she'd stolen the money, she'd arranged things so Eli Dolan became the primary suspect. He felt bad now that he'd ever suspected Eli; he imagined Hamilton did, too.

So he knew it was Anna—but he didn't *really* know. Like Hamilton had said, he needed proof, at least a little. But until he had some proof, he had to make sure that Anna didn't run. As smart as she was, if she ran he might not ever find her.

Callahan's thoughts were interrupted by an e-mail ding from his laptop. The e-mail was from Amazon; he'd bought one book from them two years ago and now he got six e-mails a day from a company that was trying to take over the world. The e-mail said his order would be shipped at six p.m., which meant that he would meet again with Smee at six to get the information he'd asked for.

He pondered what he was about to do next for a couple of minutes, then picked up the phone and asked Mercer to come to his office.

31

Mercer wondered what Callahan wanted. She hadn't seen him since he'd returned from Switzerland. He was on the phone when she entered his office, and all she heard him say was "That sounds good, honey. I'll see you at seven."

She wondered who he was talking to. She hoped *honey* wasn't a future Mrs. Callahan, which would make her Mrs. Callahan Number 5. The last thing Callahan needed was one more ex-wife.

"You look terrible, Thomas," Mercer said. "You really should go home and get some sleep."

"Aw, I'm all right. I took a little nap on the couch. Anyway, I wanted to see how the Liberia thing was going. I hope it's going okay, because I need to be able to give the president's guy a little good news after what I told him yesterday."

"What do you mean?" Mercer asked.

"Yesterday I had to tell him that fifty million U.S. dollars is now sitting in a dead man's bank account and we're not going to be able to get the money back—and that was the *best* news I had for him. I told him that with Sahid Khan dead there's going to be a political dogfight in Ghazni Province to replace Khan, that we have no idea who his replacement might be, and our best chance to acquire the mining rights was blown up with the bomb that killed the Khans. He also wasn't happy to hear that our best hope for placing an enlightened female in a ruling position in Afghanistan is gone."

"Do you have any idea who planted the bomb yet?" Mercer asked.

"No. I mean, I'm pretty sure the old man whose throat was cut planted the bomb, but I don't know who he was working for. The bomb could also have been planted by one of Cannon and Sterling's people."

"One of Sterling's people?" Mercer said.

"Yeah. You know that guy who tried to rape Hamilton? I found out his name was Eric Nelson, and when I ran a background check on him, I found out he worked for Cannon and Sterling."

"You're kidding! Why would someone who worked for them try to kill Hamilton or be involved in the bombing?"

"Maybe because Nelson had a quarter of a million in a bank account that came from a mosque in Pakistan, a mosque that funds the Taliban."

"I'm totally confused, Thomas. Are you saying one of Sterling's people was working for the Taliban?"

"I don't know, but it looks that way. Sterling told me the guy quit right after he came back from Afghanistan. So what all this could mean is that somebody over in

Afghanistan found out about the meeting, found out that Sterling was providing security, and paid Nelson to plant or detonate the bomb."

"I don't know," Mercer said, sounding skeptical. "I can't imagine someone in the Taliban being able to turn one of Sterling's people. How would they even contact the guy? And even if what you're saying is correct, why kill Hamilton?"

Callahan made an unattractive snorting sound. "Because Hamilton—and I'm thinking about firing her ass for this—went to her old boss at the DEA and had her start looking at everybody's bank accounts, including mine and yours. Hamilton figured that if somebody killed the Khans they did it for money, and she was checking out everybody's finances, including Cannon and Sterling and all the people who worked for them. Somehow, whoever set this up found out she was poking around and sent Nelson to take care of her."

"Could Sterling or Cannon be personally involved?" Mercer asked.

"I suppose," Callahan said, "but they were looking at a contract that was going to make their company a ton of money. Why would they want to screw that up by killing the Khans?"

Callahan rubbed his face, as if he was trying to scrub away the fatigue. "So right now I don't have a fucking clue who's behind this, and I'm so tired I can't think straight. All I know is the only evidence I have is pointing to one of Sterling's mercenaries and it looks like he was working for somebody connected to a mosque in Pakistan."

"I don't know what to say, Thomas. I need to go think about all this. But why did you go to Switzerland?"

"To talk to Ernst Glardon. I wanted to see if he could have engineered this whole thing, and I wanted to look him in the eye while I was talking to him. I concluded he's clean and he really didn't have a motive for killing the Khans. Just like with Sterling, his company would have benefited from the mining operation. The other thing I did over there was try to verify that the fifty million really made it into Khan's account, but I couldn't get the bank to give me the time of day, even after somebody at the White House leaned on them. But the money *has* to be in the account. Eli told me he sent it and Hamilton verified that he did, so where else could it be?

"Anyway," Callahan said, "the reason I wanted to see you was Liberia. Like I said, I'd like to give the president's guy some good news for a change."

The Liberia operation, which Mercer was handling mostly on her own, was relatively simple compared to the lithium op. The current president of Liberia, who happened to be female, had been elected by the narrowest of margins, but she was doing a good job of pulling together all the squabbling tribes. The woman also appeared to be incorruptible—and an incorruptible African politician was a truly rare bird.

The problem was the woman's vice president, a man named Joseph Nyenabo. Nyenabo, who was more corrupt than past mayors of Chicago, was doing everything he could to undermine his president and was constantly bad-mouthing her in the press. As bad as that was, the American ambassador to Liberia had learned that Nyenabo had been in a number of backroom meetings with a couple of colonels and was now contemplating his own little coup. The president's guy—or so Callahan had said—suggested it would be good if the Liberian vice president no longer occupied the office.

Mercer initially considered implicating Nyenabo in a crime, such as dumping a chunk of money into his bank account as evidence that he'd taken a bribe or embezzled. She ultimately rejected that idea, however. Trials in places like Liberia were always messy and drawn out, would distract the president for months, and when all was said and done, Nyenabo would still be around to cause mischief.

"I think I'll have the situation resolved this week," Mercer said.

"That's good to hear. What's the plan?"

"I've had people watching Mr. Nyenabo, and two weeks ago we discovered that he's become infatuated with the fifteen-year-old wife of one of his bodyguards. I don't know if the girl is equally smitten with him, or if she's just afraid to spurn his advances. In any case, three times in the last two weeks, Mr. Nyenabo has given his faithful bodyguard some task to occupy him so Nyenabo could spend a couple of hours with the man's young wife. The bodyguard, by the way, is known for his volatile temper, drinks on the job, takes drugs that don't bode well for self-control, and is always armed.

"The next time Mr. Nyenabo visits his new mistress, we're going to call the bodyguard and tell him what's going on in his own bedroom. My hope is that he will burst in on his boss and his wife, and shoot his boss. I hope he doesn't shoot his wife. If Mr. Nyenabo survives the encounter I'll regroup, but if my plan works and if Mr. Nyenabo is killed, his death will be attributed to a simple act of passion and have no political overtones."

"Good," Callahan said. "I like it. And thanks for minding the store while I've been so preoccupied with the Khan thing. I don't know what I'd do without you."

A fter Mercer left his office, Callahan wondered if she'd swallowed all the bullshit he'd just fed her—and he decided that he couldn't take the chance that she hadn't.

He heaved himself out of his chair and ambled slowly down the hall to the reception area, where Henry was seated—standing guard over an enterprise that was in shambles.

"I want a twenty-four/seven net around Anna Mercer," Callahan said. "Pull in anybody you need. Trainees, instructors, whoever is here in D.C."

Henry raised an eyebrow in surprise, but the only thing he said was: "Yes, sir."

32

Anna Mercer returned to her office, picked up Scarlett, and holding the fluffy white cat in her arms, began to pace—although she could only take about seven strides before she had to turn. That was another thing that had always pissed her off: an office the size of a prison cell, and windowless to boot.

"What should I do, Scarlett?" she whispered to the cat.

What she wanted to do was kill Nathan Sterling.

It had been a perfect plan until Sterling fucked everything up by trying to kill Hamilton. She'd found Finley and he developed the program to steal the money. She'd subtly steered the security contract toward Sterling's company, knowing he was financially desperate, and then convinced him to help her. When Sterling reconnoitered the meeting place in Afghanistan, he acquired the materials to manufacture the bombs and one of his men constructed them. Sterling planted the bomb in the meeting room himself when Hamilton and Dolan were elsewhere in the house.

When Dolan hit the SEND button to transfer the fifty million to Sahid Khan's account, Finley knew because of the program he'd installed to capture the money. Finley texted Anna, she texted Sterling, and Sterling texted the man who blew up the transformer. Sterling then called Dolan to get him out of the meeting room, and Sterling detonated the bomb. When the power was disrupted, Nelson snuck into the house and dispatched the old man. And while all these events in Afghanistan were taking place, Finley hid the money they'd stolen in accounts that would never be identified.

It had been a *beautiful* plan, an absolutely perfect plan, but then that idiot Sterling . . .

Enough. She needed to make a decision; she needed to decide if she should run or not.

If Callahan really believed, as he'd said, that the money was in Sahid Khan's bank and that the Taliban had killed the Khans, there was no need to run. She'd wait at least a year, long enough to put the whole lithium operation in Callahan's rearview mirror, then tell him she'd had enough of Washington and resign. After that, she'd move to someplace sunny—most likely Southern California—start up a small business and launder the money she'd stolen through the business; then she'd just sit back and enjoy her life.

The sixty-four-thousand-dollar question—actually, the fifty-*million*-dollar question—was this: Had Callahan lied to her so that she'd think she'd gotten away with what she'd done?

"Did he lie to me, Scarlett? Did that bad man lie?" Scarlett didn't answer.

She thought back on everything Callahan had said in his office and finally decided. Callahan had lied; Callahan had overplayed his hand. And the reason she knew this was that he'd acted defeated and as if he didn't know what to do next. Callahan always had a plan, and he'd never admit to defeat.

She felt Scarlett's claws rake the back of her right hand and she let out a yelp of surprise and pain. She dropped Scarlett to the ground and the cat immediately ran and hid under her desk. It was her fault Scarlett had scratched her: She'd been squeezing the poor thing too hard as she thought about Callahan's deception. She'd almost cracked Scarlett's tiny ribs.

And now she was going to have to do what Scarlett had done: run for her life and hide.

The good news was that she'd planned for this possibility.

Mercer looked at her watch. It was one p.m. She wanted to catch a train to New York that left at five. She picked up the phone, made a call, and a woman answered.

"Hello," the woman said in heavily accented English. She'd been born in Ukraine.

"This is Anna Mercer. Where are you?"

"Tysons Corner."

"Good. That means you can be at my house in less

than an hour. I want you there before two. Do you understand?"

"I'm meeting a client in fifteen minutes."

"I told you when I retained you that you might have to drop whatever you were doing. And I'm sure I'm paying you a lot more than your client. So call him, tell him to put his dick back in his pants, and that you're not going to make it."

The woman didn't respond.

"If you don't do what I want, I'm going to find someone else and you're going to be out five grand," Mercer said.

"All right. I'll be there by two."

"*Before* two," Mercer said. "The key is on the back deck, under the red flowerpot. The code to the security alarm is S-C-A-R-L-E-T-T. Write that down. And once you're inside my house, just take a seat, and don't touch anything and don't drink anything. Do you understand?"

"Yes."

M ercer waited an hour, wondering what that bastard, Callahan, was doing.

At two, she left her office carrying Scarlett and stopped at Henry's desk in the reception area.

"Henry, can you tell Callahan that Scarlett and I have to go see my sister? She's gone off her meds again. I'll call later and let you know how soon I can be back."

"Ah, jeez," Henry said, sounding genuinely concerned for her. "Family. What can you do?"

Mercer's sister was a schizophrenic who lived in Wilmington, North Carolina. Mercer had always been terrified she might inherit the disease. Half a dozen times during all the years she'd worked for Callahan, her sister had stopped taking her meds, gone berserk, and ended up in jail or a psych ward. Since Mercer's mother was dead and her father had abandoned the family years before, Mercer usually dealt with her sibling's situation by calling an aunt who lived in Raleigh and forcing her aunt to go deal with the crazy bitch. Fortunately, however, there had been times when she'd gone to Wilmington herself to take care of the psycho.

As Mercer drove to her place in Arlington, she tried to see if anyone was following her. She couldn't see anyone, but she was sure—if Callahan suspected her— that someone was tailing her. She entered her house and saw the Ukrainian sitting on the couch. The woman was wearing four-inch stiletto heels, and the hem of her skirt was about six inches above her knees. She had on so much makeup that she reminded Mercer of Liz Taylor playing Cleopatra.

"Go scrub all that shit off your face," Mercer said. "Just put on some lipstick."

Five minutes later, when the woman returned from the bathroom, Mercer handed her an envelope containing five thousand dollars and the keys to her Mercedes.

* * *

After the Ukrainian drove off, Mercer walked about her house, touching various pieces of furniture: the dining room table, a love seat in the living room, a vase she'd bought at an estate sale that was worth ten times more than she'd paid for it.

She loved her home—and she was saying good-bye to it.

She bought the place for four hundred and fifty thousand ten years ago. It wasn't that big, only three bedrooms and two bathrooms, but property was expensive in Arlington—and she bought it before the bottom fell out of the real estate market. Then she spent ten years making it perfect: remodeling the kitchen, installing tile and gorgeous hardwood floors, selecting each painting and piece of furniture only after considerable thought. For a decade she went to estate sales and visited furniture showrooms and antiques stores, and consulted with interior designers whom she discovered were no better than she was when it came to decorating. She knew she was never going to see her lovely home again, and she started crying. She just couldn't help it.

Five minutes later, she dried her tears, walked into her bedroom, and pulled her disappearing-forever suitcase out of the closet. Inside the suitcase—actually, a roll-on bag that could be stored in the overhead compartment of an airplane—were a couple of changes of clothes and a passport.

The passport was made out to a British citizen named Amy Murdock, and the picture in the passport matched Mercer's simple Amy Murdock disguise: a blond wig to cover her short dark hair, a couple of molded chunks of rubber to make her face look fatter, a bridge that fit over her teeth to give her an unattractive overbite—everyone knew how bad British dentistry was—and glasses with hideous red frames.

The passport and accompanying credit cards were, of course, flawless. One of the benefits of being in the businesses she'd been in most of her life was that she knew people who could make the documents she needed.

The final item in her disappearing-forever suitcase was the Heckler & Koch P30. It was the same weapon she'd taken with her the day she met Sterling at Devil's Backbone in Virginia.

She tossed some clothes onto her bed and a few things on the floor near the closet, making it appear as if she'd packed in a hurry; then she dropped a cell phone onto the floor and kicked it under the bed.

She found Scarlett sitting in a sunbeam on a window ledge in her living room and picked her up. She'd had a cat since she was eleven, and Scarlett was the fourth one she'd owned. All her cats had been named Scarlett. As she walked toward the bathroom, she said, "Oh, Scarlett, I promise you that one day Nathan Sterling will pay for what he did."

She called a cab and tried not to cry as she waited for it, but as she was closing her front door she looked at a painting hanging in her foyer. She'd found it in a tiny shop in Middleburg, and it showed an old man wearing a red beret, sitting on a chair, and he seemed to be contemplating the life he'd led, a life that was almost over. She'd always loved that painting—and she started crying again as she walked down the sidewalk to meet the cab.

33

The *honey* Callahan had been speaking to when Anna Mercer entered his office was Kay Hamilton. As promised, he met her at seven p.m. in the bar of a hotel called One Washington Circle in Foggy Bottom. The bar was so dark that Callahan could barely see the olives in his martini; it just *looked* like a place where people in Washington would meet to hatch conspiracies.

Hamilton arrived right on time, dressed in a T-shirt, tight jeans, running shoes, and a brown leather bomber jacket. He was certain the jacket concealed a weapon. As she walked across the room toward his table, hips swaying, Callahan was impressed, as always, with how damn good-looking she was and he couldn't help but regret that he was old and fat.

When the waitress asked what Hamilton wanted, Callahan said, "No booze for you, Missy. I want you to go see the computer guy tonight."

"You know who he is?"

"Well, I'm not positive, but I'm pretty sure." Callahan sipped his drink. "There are only about a thousand people on this planet who could have downloaded the program onto Dolan's computer that was used to snatch the money. About half of these people live overseas in places like China, Russia, Israel, and Iran. We don't know a lot of these foreigners by name, but we know they exist because of shit they've pulled hacking into American systems. But I don't think Anna or Sylvia— and I'm about ninety-nine percent sure it's Anna— would have worked with some hacker in Russia or China. So I think the guy is here in the U.S.

"I've also eliminated anyone that's not within a fairly easy commute of Washington, because she'd want this person close enough to be able to talk face-to-face. Anyway, I've got half a dozen names that for one reason or another fit the bill. Like this one guy up at MIT who has to be the world's oldest grad student. He hacked JPMorgan Chase one time just to prove he could steal their money if he really wanted to, and then called Jamie Dimon's unlisted number to let him know what he did just to rattle Jamie.

"There's another guy at Princeton who's basically trying to extort the New York Stock Exchange into buying a security upgrade from him. He says he's found a flaw in one of their programs and could make the Dow drop three thousand points anytime he wants to, and he's good enough that they believe him. There's also a whack job in Baltimore who the NSA says is the most brilliant guy they ever hired when it came to cracking encrypted messages, but they fired him when he insisted on publishing a paper to show how smart he is. He didn't like the fact that everything he worked on was classified.

"Anyway, I found half a dozen people who fit the bill, all of them on the East Coast, but the guy I really like has a connection to Eli."

"I thought you thought Dolan was clean," Kay said.

"I do think he's clean. But I also think that Mercer wants me to think that he *isn't* clean, and if she could, she'd find somebody that has some link to him, somebody he went to school with or worked with in the past."

"Who is he?"

"His name is Rodger Finley. He was a quant at Goldman Sachs the same time Eli worked there, but Goldman fired him a couple of years ago because he's a fruitcake. Since Goldman fired him, as near as anybody can tell, Finley's been sitting in his apartment in New York playing video games and screwing around with math problems that nobody can solve. He's a fucking nut. He's also almost broke, because he hasn't drawn a paycheck in two years. So I think he might be the guy."

"How would Anna or Sylvia have found him?"

"The same way I did. The NSA, Homeland, the FBI, and the Pentagon all have files on dangerous hackers. They have the files, of course, because they're worried about these people screwing up all kinds of things— defense networks, power grids, financial systems—and Mercer would have talked with her contacts in these agencies. You gotta remember, Anna Mercer has been around this town for a long time, almost as long as me, and she's ex-CIA. Anyway, I found out that the Pentagon had a file on Finley."

"The Pentagon? Sylvia was the one who worked at the Pentagon."

"Yeah, well, maybe I'm giving Mercer too much credit for being devious, but I think that's another reason she picked Finley. What I'm saying is if she'd picked someone in a CIA database, the evidence would—"

"We have no evidence."

"—the evidence would have pointed at her. I think she picked someone off a Pentagon database because that would point to Sylvia."

All the wheels-within-wheels shit was too much for Kay. She wanted something concrete, something more than Callahan's guesses. "What do you want me to do?" she said.

Callahan drained his martini glass, then raised it to signal the waitress he was ready for another.

"Don't you think you've had enough to drink? You look like the walking dead."

Callahan laughed. "I'm Irish, Hamilton. There's no such thing as enough."

"What do you want me to do?" she said again, not in the mood for humor.

"I want you to go to New York and confront Finley. I want you to scare the shit out of him and see if you can get him to admit he was working for Mercer. In other words, do what you used to do when you were a cop. Tell him you *know* he's guilty and if he doesn't want to spend the rest of his life in a cement room in a super-max, he'd better give up Mercer. If he tries to contact Mercer after you talk to him, I'll know."

"How will you know?"

"Because a certain agency will be monitoring any calls or e-mails he sends."

"Which agency?"

"Never mind which agency."

"What if Finley's not the one?"

"Then you move on to the next-best guy on my list, the guy at MIT."

Hamilton shook her head, not enamored with his plan.

"Hey, if you got a better idea," Callahan said, "I'm all ears."

Kay called Jessica and told her she had to take a trip out of town and had to leave immediately. "I'm not sure when I'll be back. And, hey! You and Brian behave yourselves. And make sure you set the alarm when you're in the apartment and, well, you know, be careful."

"Have a nice trip, Kay," her daughter said. "And *you* be careful. You're the one who keeps coming home with black-and-blue marks on your face."

34

At 7:45 p.m., Anna Mercer stepped off the Amtrak train in Penn Station. She had no idea that Kay Hamilton was in a jet on her way to New York.

She went to the restroom, stepped into one of the stalls, and removed the Heckler & Koch P30 from her suitcase. She screwed on the silencer and placed the pistol in the right-hand pocket of her trench coat. Twenty minutes later, a cab dropped her off in front of Finley's apartment building in Brooklyn.

Finley was surprised to see her, of course.

"What are you doing here?" he shrieked. "Once I moved the money, you said we were finished. You said you'd never contact me again. Go away."

"I need to talk to you, Rodger. It's important. And I promise that after tonight you'll never see me again."

"Fine. Come in. But make it quick. I'm busy."

Mercer sat down in the red recliner where Finley sat when he played his video games. Finley looked annoyed that she'd sat there. The recliner was *his* chair. He pulled over one of the armless rolling chairs near all his computers, took a seat, then raised his hands in a dramatic *So what are we doing here?* gesture.

"I need to know something, Rodger. I need to know if there's anything in this apartment—in any of your machines, on a flash drive, on a disc—that can be tied to the money we took. I need to know if there's even a *fragment* of the program you downloaded onto Dolan's computer."

"That's why you came here? That's why you're wasting my time? I've told you about six times that I got rid of everything. There's nothing here."

As if she hadn't heard him, she said, "The most important thing, Rodger, is I need to be one hundred percent certain that no one can trace any part of the money to *my* account."

"No! No one can! And it pisses me off that you keep asking this. There's nobody on this planet that will be able to follow the money, and there's nothing in this room that will lead them to it. Why are you asking me this again?"

"I just need to be sure, Rodger." She studied his face as he glared at her, trying to tell if he was lying, knowing it was hopeless. "Okay," she said. "I believe you, Rodger. And I want to thank you again for everything you've done for me."

Then she took the silenced P30 from the pocket of her trench coat and shot Finley in the heart, and then shot him a second time in the forehead as he sat there in the rolling chair. She didn't know why he didn't fall off the chair, but he didn't. That was odd.

It had been mandatory to kill Finley; she had no choice. Finley was the one person who, if he talked, could ruin everything, because he would tell Callahan, under duress, where her money was. And the only way Callahan would be able to find her after she disappeared would be to follow the money to her hideaway.

She was going to take care of Nathan Sterling, too, but Sterling didn't concern her as much as Rodger Finley. Sterling had no idea where her money was.

She picked up the shell casings ejected when she shot Finley. Her plan was to walk a couple of blocks before she caught a cab to the airport, and drop the gun and the casings into a sewer drain or a trash can someplace along the way.

She took one last look around Finley's smelly loft.

Finley, to her amazement, was still sitting upright in his chair. That was *so* weird.

35

Had Kay arrived at Rodger Finley's apartment building nineteen minutes earlier, she would have run into Anna Mercer, stepping out of the elevator, pulling her roll-along suitcase behind her. But she didn't.

Kay didn't bother to buzz Finley's apartment; she let herself in. She put on thin leather gloves and picked the lock on the front door of Finley's building with an electric lock picker that made as much noise as ice being crushed in a blender. Not a tool she would have chosen had she been a cat burglar. She walked up the stairs to Finley's third-floor apartment and knocked softly on the door. When no one answered, she knocked louder.

Before she left D.C., Callahan had given her a file on Finley. The most salient fact in the file, as it related to Kay's current mission, was that Finley rarely left his apartment. The file said he spent an inordinate amount of time playing a fantasy role-playing game that only geniuses played. The other thing Finley had been doing the last three months was arguing with a mathematician in China.

The Chinaman and Finley, according to the file, disagreed about something related to string theory. Kay had no idea what string theory was, but the file informed her that it was a theory attempting to reconcile quantum mechanics and Einstein's theory of general relativity, and the only people who understood what that meant were physicists and mathematicians and other folk with oversized brains. The funny thing was—or at least Kay thought it was funny—was that Finley and the China-man had no common language and they were "argu-ing" by exchanging mathematical formulas. At any rate, Finley should have been at home, playing games, playing with numbers, playing with himself.

Kay tried Finley's doorknob and the door was locked, so she used the noisy lock picker to open the door. She then pulled out her Glock and pushed open the door with her foot. All the lights were on in the apartment, and she could see Finley from the doorway, sitting up-right in a chair. He had blood running down the front of his shirt and a red-black hole in the center of his fore-head. She walked over to him, and although she knew she was wasting her time, she touched his throat to feel for a pulse—and Finley fell out of the chair.

Kay woke up Callahan in D.C. She didn't know if he'd just gone to bed early or passed out from all the booze he'd consumed. "Finley's dead," she said.

"Goddamnit," Callahan muttered.

"He was shot. His body is still warm, so this didn't happen very long ago. What do you want me to do?"

"Give me a minute," Callahan said. "I gotta wake up." She heard Callahan set the phone down, then heard disgusting noises as he hawked up whatever was in his throat. The next thing she thought she heard was water running as Callahan most likely splashed water on his face.

Callahan picked up the phone again, and she heard a cigarette lighter click. "Do you see a computer in the place?"

"Are you kidding me?" Kay said. "There are a dozen computers, and I have no idea what some of the other electronic shit in here does."

"Okay. I'm going to get some guys over there and have them box up all the machines. They'll take them someplace and see if they can find anything useful, although I doubt they'll find anything. While you're waiting for the computer guys to get there, play detective. You know, look around and see if you can find a fuckin' clue, anything that ties Finley to Mercer or Sterling or the op in Afghanistan. I don't think you'll find anything, but we gotta look. While you're doing that, I'm going to have the guys I have following Mercer pick her up."

"Where is she right now?" Kay asked. Kay knew that Mercer had claimed her sister was having some sort of mental health problem and she was on her way to see her in Wilmington, North Carolina. When she saw Finley's body, her first thought had been that Mercer was creating an alibi.

In answer to Kay's question, Callahan said, "She's about

fifty miles south of Raleigh. She's been driving like an old lady. I told the guys following her to stick with her and to see if she's really going to visit her schizoid sister like she said, but now I'm going to have them pull her over." Callahan paused and said, "I have this horrible feeling that Mercer's not going to be in the car they're following. I'll call you back."

Ten minutes later, Callahan called Kay back. "She wasn't in the car. A Russian hooker who works for an escort service was driving. Mercer contacted her a month ago. She found her on the Internet and she looks a lot like Mercer, same height, same short hair, and Mercer paid her five grand to drive to North Carolina. The guys I had following Mercer said they saw Mercer's Mercedes pull out of her garage about three, and since it was Mercer's car and somebody who looked like Mercer was driving, they assumed it was her. I spoke to Mercer in my office about one this afternoon, and she stayed in her office until two. What she must have done was call the hooker and told her to go to her house, and as soon as Mercer got home, she had the gal get in her car and head south.

"I've got people headed to Mercer's place right now, but I know she won't be there. I think while my guys were following the hooker, Mercer took a plane or a train to New York and killed Finley so we wouldn't be able to question him. And now she's going to disappear and it's going to be almost impossible to find her."

"Callahan, can you think of anything to say—just

one single thing—that might sound the tiniest bit optimistic?"

"No. I think we're fucked."

Kay didn't say anything for a moment, thinking about the possibility of Anna Mercer getting away with what she'd done. "Are you sure Dolan is clean?"

"Yeah. How many times do I have to tell you?" Callahan said.

"Well, if you're sure, then call him and tell him to get his ass over here. He can help me search. He knows a lot more about the Afghan operation than I do."

"I told you, he quit."

"Well, *un*quit him. Tell him to stop acting like a spoiled rich kid."

Callahan hesitated. "All right."

"What do I do about Finley?"

"I don't know. I gotta think about that," Callahan said.

Kay, still wearing gloves, wandered through Finley's apartment, poking into those places she used to poke into when she was working for the DEA and looking for drugs. She probed the dark corners of closets, checked the pockets of coats and jackets, looked inside toilet bowl tanks, under mattresses, and inside the freezer for anything that wasn't food. She tried not to make too much of a mess, because she knew at some point the NYPD was going to show up and do their own search. That is, the NYPD would show up if Callahan wanted Finley's body to be discovered.

She found very little paper in the place: no bills, no checkbook, no tax returns, no books, no newspapers. Finley apparently was one of those people who truly believed in a paperless world and did everything online. She assumed his iPad contained his library and his personal files were in one of his many computers—and she wasn't about to touch any of the electronics. She could imagine steam hissing out of the computers if she touched a keyboard. She did find his passport, and as near as she could tell, Finley hadn't left the country in five years. He made one trip to London when he was working for Goldman Sachs. She was thinking about removing the covers on the electrical outlets, when someone rapped softly on the door. She looked through the peephole. It was Eli Dolan.

He was dressed similar to her—in jeans, a T-shirt, and a lightweight jacket. On his feet were battered Top-Siders, probably what he wore when he went yachting with his rich friends. He looked good, she had to admit, although he needed a shave. In fact, he looked fantastic, and she could feel the heat being generated someplace south of her heart.

He looked over at Finley's body, then looked at her, a grim set to his mouth.

"Look, I'm—"

Kay had been about to say she was sorry for having doubted him, but before she could get the words out of her mouth, Dolan said, "So I guess you finally decided

I'm innocent." Before she could respond, he continued. "You can't even *imagine* how angry I was that you and Callahan suspected me of killing Ara Khan. I've worked for Callahan for years, and as for you . . . I thought we meant something to each other."

Then she couldn't help herself, probably because he was acting so pissy and petulant. "Oh, grow up," she said. "Fifty million bucks was stolen and five—"

"What do you mean fifty million was stolen?"

Judging by the look on his face, he apparently, genuinely, didn't know the fifty million never made it to Khan's account. Kay wondered what Callahan had told him. She continued.

"—and five people were killed. You were a viable suspect and we treated you like one. What else could we do?"

"You could have trusted me," Dolan said.

"We don't have time for this right now. Callahan is convinced Anna Mercer is the one who orchestrated the Khans' deaths and stole the money." Seeing again that he was confused, she quickly explained everything to him: how the money never made it to Sahid Khan's bank account, Callahan's logic for concluding Mercer and Sterling were the guilty parties, and how Callahan had locked in on Finley as Mercer's helper.

When she finished, he said, "I can't believe Anna would do this."

"Well, Callahan's sure she did, but he'd still like some proof. Some guys are going to be here soon to pick up all the computer equipment, but I thought, since you knew

Finley and were intimately involved in the Afghan op, that maybe you'd be able to spot something searching the place."

"I didn't know Finley," Dolan said, and she could see him tightening up, thinking he was being accused of something else. God, he was sensitive.

"He worked at Goldman Sachs the same time you were there," Kay said. "He was a quant."

"Goldman employed more than thirty thousand people, worldwide, when I was there. I didn't work with all of them."

"He was in the New York office," Kay said.

"I didn't know him," Dolan said with an edge to his voice.

"Okay. Fine. I believe you," Kay said. "But Callahan thinks that one of the reasons Mercer picked Finley to help her was because there was a connection between you and him—namely, that you both had the same employer. That wouldn't be proof that you worked with Finley to steal the money, but it would be another brick in the wall."

"All right," Dolan said, but Kay wasn't sure what that meant: *All right, all is forgiven* or *All right, I'll work with you for now.*

They searched together for another thirty minutes but had no more luck than Kay did searching alone. They were interrupted by a knock on the door, and Kay was praying it was the computer movers and not the police. It was.

Two burly guys and one not-so-burly guy entered the loft carrying stacks of collapsed cardboard boxes. The not-so-burly one acted as if Kay and Dolan weren't even in the room and started unhooking the cables and power cords from all the machines; when he was finished, his teammates loaded the boxes. After all the big items were loaded, he walked around picking up smaller things: flash drives, stand-alone hard drives, and discs. When those were collected, he did a lap around the apartment holding a black box in his hand.

"What's that?" Kay asked.

"I'm looking for electronic noise signatures to see if there's something not in plain sight." Two minutes later, he said, "There's nothing else. You're to call Callahan when we're gone."

Kay did. "We're done here," she told Callahan. "Dolan and I didn't find anything, and all the machines are gone. What's next?"

"I don't know," Callahan said.

"Did Mercer split like you thought?"

"Yeah. She's gone. She wasn't at her house, and we can't find her via the GPS chip in her cell phone, which means she's ditched the phone. And there's something else we found in her house, and I gotta tell you, this really freaked me out. We found Scarlett."

"I don't understand," Kay said. "So what if she left the cat?"

"She didn't *leave* it, she killed it. Mercer gave her an injection of pentobarbital, the same thing vets use to euthanize pets. I mean, talk about cold-blooded. I always thought she loved that animal. I guess she figured it would be too much of a hassle to take it with her if she was on the run, but instead of letting it go . . ."

Kay had to admit she was shocked by what Mercer had done, but she didn't have time to think about Scarlett. She wanted to get out of Finley's apartment. "What do we do about Finley?" she asked.

"Call the cops. An anonymous call. Do it on the way to the airport. I want you and Eli back here in D.C. I need you to help me figure out how to find Anna."

"What if he won't come?"

"Just ask him, Hamilton. If he says no, then tell him thanks for his help and come back by yourself. I'm not expecting you to kidnap the guy."

Earlier that evening—while Kay Hamilton and Eli Dolan were searching Rodger Finley's apartment—a chubby-faced blond woman wearing red-framed glasses and sturdy shoes boarded an Air Canada flight to Geneva.

She took a seat in first class, and as they were waiting for the lemmings in coach to board, a flight attendant asked, "Would you care for a glass of champagne, Ms. Murdock?"

In an upper-class British accent, Ms. Murdock replied, "Yes, that would be lovely, dear."

36

Kay and Eli didn't speak during the cab ride to the charter jet terminal at JFK. They sat in the backseat, as far away from each other as they could get. She didn't know what Eli was thinking about—and she didn't feel like asking him. She figured he was sulking because she still hadn't apologized for suspecting him. When she'd asked him to accompany her to D.C. to help Callahan, all he'd said was "Yeah, okay."

Kay didn't know what to do about him. She was still attracted to him. And now that she was sure that he hadn't killed Ara Khan, she knew if she wanted to rekindle what they once had she was going to have to apologize for ever having doubted him. And maybe a simple apology wouldn't be enough. But right now wasn't the right time to decide anything. They didn't speak on the short flight on the chartered jet to D.C., either. Kay was asleep before the jet taxied out onto the runway.

Callahan was waiting for them in his office. He wasn't dressed in one of his wrinkled gray suits, but instead wore baggy blue jeans and a Notre Dame sweatshirt so faded from repeated washings you could barely read the name of the school. He was, however, wearing the same battered loafers he usually wore with his suits, this time sans socks. His ankles were the color of skim milk and looked like they might be swollen.

"Well, we really fucked this up" were his first words to Eli and Kay after they took a seat on the brown couch in front of his desk.

Kay almost said: *What do you mean* we, *white man*— but didn't see the point.

"I now have all the proof I need that Anna and Nathan Sterling conspired to kill the Khans, so now it's just a matter of finding Anna and taking care of Sterling."

"What proof do you have?" Kay said. "All we found in New York was Finley's corpse, and we didn't find any connection to Mercer."

Callahan lit a cigarette, ignoring the look of displeasure on Hamilton's face. "Mercer ditching her surveillance team was all the proof I needed. The fact that Finley, one of the few people who could have helped her pull this off, is killed at the same time she disappears . . . Well, I don't need anything else. I told you before that I wasn't looking for evidence that would stand up in court."

"But we don't know that she personally killed Finley," Kay said. "Maybe she has someone helping her."

"I don't think so. Anna wouldn't have wanted any more partners, and she was in New York tonight."

"How do you know that?"

"Because I've been busy while you were in New York not finding anything. I had Homeland check flights to see if she flew to New York, and also asked them to check surveillance cameras in Penn Station in case she took the train."

"How did you get Homeland to do that for you?" Kay asked.

"Don't ask me questions like that, Hamilton. Anyway, Mercer took the five o'clock Amtrak to New York and arrived there at seven forty-five. She didn't buy the ticket under her own name, so I don't know what name she's using, but the cameras in Penn Station saw her getting off the train. Which means she was in New York before you found Finley's body."

"Do you have any idea where she might be right now?" Kay asked.

"No. I had Homeland check passenger manifests for flights leaving New York, and she wasn't on any of them— at least, not using her own name. The problem is, she could easily get a fake ID. TSA has her photo and is looking at surveillance footage in the New York airports, but it's probably going to be hours before I hear back from them. And for all I know, she didn't take a plane out of New York. Maybe she rented a car and drove into Canada. She could be anywhere."

"And the proof that she was working with Sterling?" Kay said.

"Like I told you, after Mercer's surveillance team

discovered they were following the wrong woman, I sent guys over to her house. One of the first things they found, in addition to Scarlett's corpse—I still can't believe she did that—was a burner cell phone under her bed. Now, her bedroom was a mess, clothes strewn all over the place, like she went home and rushed around like crazy, packing as fast as she could to get away, and while she was doing all this rushing around, the phone fell out of a pocket or something and got kicked under the bed.

"But I know that's bullshit. I know she didn't panic. She sat in her office for an hour after I last talked to her, and she made the arrangement with the hooker to drive her car south a month ago. I think she left the phone there on purpose."

"So what's the significance of the phone?" Kay asked.

"There was only one number in the contacts list, and according to the cell phone provider, that phone is currently in Fairmount, West Virginia, where Sterling lives. That's good enough for me."

"The phone could belong to someone working for Sterling," Kay said. "You know, someone else who lives in Fairmount." She was starting to sound like a defense lawyer, which wasn't a role she normally assumed.

"It's Sterling's," Callahan said.

"Well, you could prove that by calling the phone number. If Sterling answers, you say you dialed the wrong number. But that way you'll know for sure it's Sterling."

"I don't want to do that," Callahan said. "If Sterling gets a wrong-number call to a number that only Mercer had, he'll get suspicious. I don't want to give him any advance notice that I'm coming after him."

"Why do you think Mercer left the phone where you could find it?" Kay asked.

Callahan shrugged. "I don't know for sure, but my guess is that Anna was *giving* me Sterling. I think she just wants him gone so he can't cause her any problems in the future. She knows I'm not going to take anyone to court, and she also knows what will happen to Sterling if I'm convinced he was involved."

"Won't she be worried that Sterling will confess?"

"No. She knows I don't need a confession from Sterling to know she's guilty. And she won't be worried at all about Sterling knowing where she is, because I'm positive she never told him where she was going. I think she just views Sterling as a loose end, and she wants me to snip it off for her."

"So what do you intend to do to Sterling?" Kay asked.

"What the hell do you think I'm going to do?" Callahan said. There was no twinkle in his eyes.

"How are we going to find Anna?" Dolan asked, switching the discussion away from Callahan's plans for Nathan Sterling.

"I don't know," Callahan said. "What I do know is that she's got some sort of bulletproof ID and we're not going to find her using credit-card purchases or passenger manifests or cell phones or anything simple like that."

"How much money do you think she has?" Dolan asked.

"My guess is at least half of the fifty million," Callahan said. "She would have been forced to share some with Sterling and Finley, but no way would she have given them more than half. So let's assume twenty-five to thirty million. That amount isn't enough for her to make the Forbes 400 list, but it's enough for her to lead a very comfortable life."

"But what would she do?" Kay said. "Raise Arabian stallions? Collect Fabergé eggs?"

Callahan stubbed out the cigarette he'd been smoking. "That's actually a good question," he said, "and probably the way we're going to find her. And the answer is: She'll shop and pamper herself."

"Shop?" Kay said.

"Yeah. I don't know if you ever noticed, but Anna dresses very well. Then there's her house; you need to go look at her house. It's not that big, but it's magnificent, and as far as I know, it was the only hobby she ever had. After she bought the place, she had it completely remodeled and she didn't scrimp. Granite countertops, hardwood floors, fancy rugs, good artwork, top-of-the-line appliances. She *loved* that house, and when she wasn't working, she used to go to estate sales to find bargains."

"Besides clothes and her home, is there anything else?" Kay asked. "Expensive cars? Jewelry? Will she contact her family or a boyfriend?"

"Not cars," Callahan said. "Anna drove a used Mercedes, and with twenty-five million she'll buy a new car, most likely another Mercedes or something similar. But she's never really cared about cars; she'll get something respectable, but not a Ferrari. As for her family, the only family she has is her sister and an aunt in Raleigh, and she's never been close to either of them. When Anna told Henry she was going to see her wacky sister in Wilmington, I should have stopped her right then.

"I also know she doesn't have a boyfriend. Every once in a while, I get a massage. I don't do it very often, but sometimes I feel like having someone pummel my muscles and rub my back, and every five or six months I'll get one. That's Anna and sex. Every once in a while, she gets the urge and has sex with someone, but she doesn't do it frequently and she has no interest whatsoever in having a sloppy man clutter up her beautiful home. Companionship is not a priority for her."

"How would you know about her sex life?" Kay asked.

Now the twinkle was back in Callahan's eyes. "We used to talk about our love lives sometimes, mostly bitching that neither one of us really had one. Although, come to think of it, in the last year Anna hasn't been all that forthcoming about who she's been screwing.

"Anyway, to get back to how we'll find her, it won't be because she contacts her sister or tries to hook up with an old lover. As for jewelry, she likes jewelry, just like she likes clothes, but she can't afford to be a regular customer at Harry Winston's with only twenty-five or thirty mil in the bank. She'll buy nice earrings and other doodads, but nothing so outrageous that one of her purchases will make the news.

"But we may find her because she likes to be pampered. At least once a month, she'd go to a place here in D.C. to get spa treatments. You know, massages, facials, the whole package. She's been doing that the last five years, maybe thinking after she turned forty she needed the facials. I think she'll spend a lot of time at spas."

Callahan reached into a drawer on the lower right-hand side of his desk and pulled out a bottle of Courvoisier. "Anyone want a drink?" he asked. Dolan and Kay both shook their heads. Callahan filled half a coffee cup with the brandy.

"So here's what I think she's going to do," Callahan said. "She's going to settle in some foreign country, buy a nice house, and spend a lot of time remodeling it and filling it with nice things. She'll buy expensive clothes, spend time in spas, and take vacations to sunny spots when she has the urge."

"Why are you so sure she'll pick a foreign country?" Kay asked.

"Because that will make it harder for me to find her. Here in the U.S., I have a lot of pull with federal law-enforcement agencies. I don't have that kind of pull overseas."

"Then where do you think she'll move to?" Kay

asked. "Someplace where we don't have an extradition treaty?"

"No. She knows I'm not going to try to extradite her, and most places where we don't have extradition treaties aren't really all that nice. Plus, you usually end up paying some government bagman to leave you alone. Then there's the language problem. She speaks passable French, but she isn't really fluent in the language. She's not like you when it comes to languages. I think she'll pick someplace in Europe, England or Ireland, maybe Switzerland. She won't go to the Orient, because she'd be afraid she might stand out as a rich white woman. And because she's a bit of a bigot. She won't pick Australia because it's too remote, and Canada is too close to the U.S. So I'm guessing an English-speaking country in Europe so she'll be able to take shopping trips to Paris or Berlin and go to the Costa del Sol when she wants to sit on the beach.

"And one other thing," Callahan said. "I think she's going to get plastic surgery to change her appearance. She's not going to spend the rest of her life hiding inside a house like bin Laden. She'll want to be free to move about and not worry about her face being spotted on some surveillance camera."

"Maybe we can find her that way," Kay said. "You know, distribute pictures of her current face to likely doctors."

"I doubt that will work," Eli said. "I mean, we could

mail her picture to every plastic surgeon in the world, but those people tend to treat patient confidentiality rather seriously. The other thing is, unless Anna's dumber than I think she is, she won't pick a plastic surgeon in the country where she's living or using her bottom-line ID."

"We could offer a reward," Kay said. "A million bucks to the doctor who'll give her up."

"Yeah, maybe," Eli said, "but I doubt that will work if she picks a reputable doctor, and she will. She's not going to have her face cut on by a second-rate surgeon, and a first-rate surgeon probably makes more than a million a year."

"Not to mention," Callahan said, "that I've already pissed away fifty million dollars and I don't feel like pissing away any more."

Callahan rubbed a hand over his doughy, pale face and said, "Look. I'm beat. I've been up all night and so have you guys. Go home and get some sleep, and we'll meet back here at three p.m."

"I'm not sure I'll be coming back," Dolan said.

"Aw, come on, Eli," Callahan said. "I'm sorry I doubted you. Okay? What do I have to do to get you to forgive me? Get down on my knees? Plus, Mercer tried to set you up. Don't you want some payback?"

"I haven't decided," Dolan said, and walked out of Callahan's office.

"He'll come around," Callahan said to Kay.

Kay didn't say anything, but now she was thinking

306 | M. A. LAWSON

that maybe she didn't care if he came back. What did it take for the guy to get over a little mistake? Well, maybe not a *little* mistake, but still a mistake. Like Callahan had said, did they have to get down on their knees and beg? Well, she wasn't getting down on her knees for anyone.

37

By the time Kay got home, Jessica had left for school. Two ships passing in the night—except one ship had left a message for the other, a Post-it note on the refrigerator door: "If you have time, it would be nice if you could pick up a few things from the store." This guilt-inducing sentence was followed by a list of all the healthy foods her daughter wanted her to purchase.

Kay went into her bedroom, set the alarm for noon, stripped off her jeans, and fell into bed. When the alarm went off a couple of hours later, she felt like her head was stuffed with cotton as a result of sleep deprivation. She took a quick shower, put on clean jeans and a T-shirt, and went to the store and purchased everything on Jessica's list plus a couple of other items her daughter wouldn't approve of, like Oreo cookies and beer nuts.

After she restocked the shelves and the freezer, it was time to leave for K Street. She put a note where her daughter's note had been. "May have to work late. Call you later." She hesitated, then added, "Love you. Kay."

* * *

Kay walked into Callahan's office at exactly three p.m. She had many faults, but tardiness was not one of them. Callahan was once more dressed in a suit and looking as if he hadn't slept any more than she had, but he seemed alert and cheerful. Eli wasn't there.

"Are we going to wait for Eli?" she asked.

"Let's give him a few minutes," Callahan said. "You want some coffee?"

"Sure."

Callahan poured them coffee, adding cream and about six pounds of sugar to his cup. He was just handing Kay her cup when Eli walked into the office.

"You want some coffee?" Callahan asked, not saying that he was glad that Eli had decided to join them.

"No, I'm fine," Eli said. He opened his mouth to say something else—and Kay thought that he might have planned a little speech about why he had decided to return—but then he changed his mind and didn't say anything more.

Callahan dropped into the chair behind his cluttered desk and said, "Okay. Here's what we're going to do unless you two have a better idea. First, Anna Mercer. Homeland is going to be encouraged to look very hard for her."

There it was again, Kay thought: Callahan's special connection to Homeland. "What reason will you give Homeland to encourage them?" she asked.

"Finley," Callahan said, "was a dangerous hacker who had a record for busting into a Pentagon database. Mercer is ex-CIA. Homeland will be told that Finley and Mercer were connected, and it's imperative we find out what they were doing. The fact that Finley's dead and she's disappeared off the face of the earth shows she's up to something.

"Then we're going to assume she's living in the United Kingdom. That may be a bad assumption, but we have to start somewhere. Homeland, working with Scotland Yard and MI6 and whoever else they work with over there, will be asked to look for single women, approximately forty years of age, who've bought a house in the one-to-two-million-dollar range."

"You gotta be kidding!" Kay said. "That list is going to be tremendously long. I mean, a million-dollar house isn't *that* big a deal. I'll bet there will be thousands of women buying million-dollar homes in the U.K. in the next two or three months. And you're talking England, Wales, Scotland, and I guess Ireland. I mean . . ."

"I realize all that, Hamilton," Callahan said, "but we have to start somewhere. And if they find a single woman buying an expensive house, they'll be able to do background checks, and if the woman is somebody real, she'll have a history. There will be marriage records, property records of previous homes she's owned, tax records, scholastic records. There's no way Mercer will have been able to build a background that will be deep enough for her to have a completely documented history. So that's the plan: find single gals in their forties buying expensive homes, and then start pulling the string to see if the woman is real."

"But—" Kay started to say.

"The other thing is, I had someone inventory the furniture in Mercer's house in Arlington, and I'm guessing that when she furnishes her home, she'll buy some of the same brands of furniture she's bought in the past. And also maybe a cat. She's always had a cat."

Kay groaned. "But what if she's not living in the U.K.? What if she decides to rent for a year or two instead of buying property? What if she gets somebody to buy the property for her so it's not in her name? And a fucking cat? You gotta be shittin' me. Half the single women on the planet own a cat."

Callahan's response to all her objections was one he'd used before: "Hey, if you got a better idea, I'm all ears."

When Kay just shook her head, Callahan said, "Okay. Then that's it for now. We'll just have to wait for a while to see what Homeland and the Brits come up with, and in the meantime, we've got other irons in the fire. For one thing, Mercer was working an op in Liberia that she didn't finish before she split and—"

"Wait a minute!" Kay said. "What about Sterling?"

"Don't worry about Sterling. I'll take care of him."

"You mean, you're going to kill him."

Somebody had to say the word *kill* and quit pretending they were discussing some other, more benign, solution.

"Hamilton, listen to me," Callahan said. "Sterling is never going to go to jail or pay in any other way for what he did. For one thing, we can't prove he killed Ara Khan. We can't investigate a murder that occurred in Afghanistan. And if we connect Sterling to the stolen fifty million, I can't take him to court. I can't talk about what we were trying to do in Ghazni Province, and I sure as hell can't talk about where the money came from. I'm also going to ask Sterling where he put his share of the money. I know he won't know where Anna is and where she put her money, but maybe I can find out where he stashed his."

"And you're going to do this personally?" Kay said.

"Yes. I can't ask somebody working for me to kill and torture a U.S. citizen, particularly when the man's death has nothing to do with national security. This isn't about national security, not at this point. It's about payback. It's about revenge."

Kay shook her head. "Callahan, look at yourself. You couldn't run fifty yards without collapsing. Maybe twenty or thirty years ago you were a real badass, but you're in no condition to take on a guy like Sterling. He's not only in better physical shape than you, he also runs a company that employs people who were trained to kill by the U.S. military."

Callahan opened his mouth to protest, but before he could, Kay said, "I'll take care of Sterling. You've been training me for this sort of thing, and although I don't know this for a fact, I'm willing to bet that I've killed more people than you have."

Kay was referring to four drug dealers she'd killed in Miami and two more in Mexico.

"She's right, Thomas," Dolan said. "And I'll help her."

"No, you won't," Kay said. "You need to help Callahan find Anna Mercer. If I need any kind of equipment or personnel support, I'll let Callahan know, but I'm doing this on my own."

Callahan, the stubborn bastard, shook his head.

"Callahan," Kay said, "this is the kind of thing you hired me for, and we both know it. Let me do my job."

PART III

38

Anna Mercer's head hurt as if a blacksmith were pounding on it with a ball-peen hammer. It hurt so bad she couldn't even localize the pain and was unable to tell if it was coming from her chin, her cheeks, or her nose. She reached for the button to call the nurse and ask for more medication, but stopped before she pressed it. No, she'd endure the pain, at least a while longer. She was terrified of becoming addicted to pain medication; she'd just heard too many stories of people becoming addicts and their lives falling apart after surgery. But maybe it had been a mistake to have all the surgeries performed at once.

After she arrived in Geneva from New York, she immediately took a cab to the clinic she'd chosen on the outskirts of the city. It was a lovely place: ivy-covered brick walls, a breathtaking view of Lake Léman, large wooded areas with walking trails, and a spa that offered every amenity. It was surrounded by a high stone wall so the patients wouldn't be concerned about outsiders seeing them walking around with bandages on their noses and purple and yellow bruises all over their faces.

She'd selected the clinic when she was developing her disappear-forever plan. It was horrendously expensive and she could have had the surgeries performed in any number of places that were cheaper, but she'd selected it because of its reputation for protecting the privacy of its clients, many of whom were celebrities. When it came to the surgeries, privacy was much more important to her than money.

She met with her primary doctor the day after her arrival and spent three days deciding what sort of face she wanted to live with for the rest of her life. She'd always thought that her chin was a bit small and her nose too sharp, so those flaws would be remedied. Her cheekbones were good but could be enhanced a bit, and then, of course, it would be necessary to do the work around the eyes and under the chin to minimize the signs of forty-five years of living. The final result—at least in the three-dimensional pictures she was shown—was marvelous. Not only would she be better- and younger-looking, but the most important thing was that she wouldn't look like Anna Mercer.

She wouldn't know, however, if the actual finished product would match the pictures for almost a month; it would take that long for the swelling to go down and for wounds from the surgery to heal. She needed to be completely healed before she left the secluded grounds of the clinic because she was planning to go straight to Luxembourg to have her final identity documents prepared— passport, driver's license, credit cards, et cetera—and she wanted the pictures on the documents to match her new face. The cost to begin a new life—the surgeries, staying at the clinic for a month, preparation of flawless identity documents—was going to be close to eight hundred thousand dollars, and worth every penny to keep Thomas Callahan from finding her.

She didn't really feel bad about what she'd done—maybe she should, but she didn't. Did that make her a sociopath? She didn't think so—but the truth was, the only thing she really felt bad about was Scarlett. She certainly didn't feel bad about the Khans. When Callahan had devised his grand plan to go after the lithium in Afghanistan, the first thought she'd had was not whether Callahan's plan would work. No. The first thought she'd had was: The Khans were going to get rich! Why should a corrupt, opium-growing politician and his daughter benefit and not her? The only thing she had to show after serving her country for a quarter century was her little house in Arlington, and yet instead of Callahan rewarding her, he was going to make a couple of foreigners multimillionaires.

She wasn't going to agonize over what she'd done. While she was healing, she would find a new home—if she could just get past the pain and concentrate. She had decided she wanted to live within driving distance of London, and she wanted waterfront property; she'd never been able to afford waterfront property in the past. She didn't need a home with five or six bedrooms and a large family room—she had no family and no intention of starting one. What she wanted was a place that had large, open rooms—high ceilings, lots of windows—hardwood floors, a modern kitchen, an enormous master bedroom, roomy bathrooms, a huge walk-in closet, fireplaces in both the bedroom and the great room, and a cute room for an office. She could see the place clearly in her mind's eye—and she could hardly wait to begin decorating it.

She'd write down her criteria, find a reputable real estate agent, and have the agent begin the hunt. In a month, she wanted to step off a plane at Heathrow and drive immediately to the home she planned to purchase. What she was *not* going to do was worry about Callahan finding her. She was not going to second-guess herself, worrying that she may have made some sort of mistake. She'd done everything she could to avoid being found, and she would trust that what she'd done was sufficient. Yes, she'd focus on finding a lovely new place to live.

She opened her laptop and found a U.K. real estate site, but then closed her eyes as another wave of pain washed over her. Maybe she should call the nurse. As she lay with her eyes closed, she wondered if Nathan Sterling was feeling any pain yet. She certainly hoped so; it was really Sterling's fault that Scarlett was dead.

39

Kay watched from her car as Nathan Sterling stopped his Cadillac Escalade at the main gate of his company's corporate headquarters. He showed the guard his ID, something that Kay was sure was totally unnecessary, as the guard certainly recognized one of the big bosses—but Sterling was probably following procedures that he had mandated for all people entering the facility.

C&S Logistics had three hundred acres in Marion County, West Virginia, the land purchased with money obtained from their investors—investors who, at this point, were probably disappointed with the company's lackluster financial performance. A chain-link fence surrounded the property and trees along the perimeter had been left standing to block the view of folks driving past. Kay could see surveillance cameras mounted on fence posts, and she imagined the cameras were monitored from the guardhouse near the main gate.

Aerial photographs provided by Callahan—she had no idea how Callahan had obtained the photos—showed that behind the fence were training areas, including obstacle courses and firing ranges, a barrack, a mess hall, and a two-story office complex with antennae and satellite dishes sprouting from the roof. There were large metal sheds for vehicles, a helicopter pad, and a number of small concrete buildings that she guessed were arsenals for weapons and contained fuel and explosives. She didn't really care what was in the buildings, however, as she had no intention of attempting to breach Sterling's headquarters.

She'd been in West Virginia for three days watching Sterling, and the only reason she'd followed him from his home to his headquarters this morning was to confirm that he was sticking to his routine. Each of the three days she'd been watching him, he left his house at six a.m. and didn't return to his home until about seven thirty or eight p.m., as he stopped each night at one of the local restaurants for dinner.

Considering the nature of his business, Kay was worried that he could leave at any time, take a trip to D.C. to round up more clients or go someplace overseas where his people were working.

After Sterling passed through the company's main gate, Kay started up her car and headed toward Fairmount, West Virginia, where she was meeting a man. The route to Fairmount took her right by Sterling's house. The house was in a new development that had huge brick Colonial-style homes—none less than five thousand square feet—each home sitting on its own three-to-five-acre lot. It would take a man half a day on a sit-down lawn mower to cut the grass at some of the places. The other thing about the homes in the development was that each one sat on a small hill, giving the houses the appearance of medieval castles overlooking their fiefdoms. Kay wondered if the hills where the houses were situated were natural or if they'd been created. Whatever the case, Kay had no idea why Sterling, who lived alone, would want to own such a large house.

According to the dossier provided by Callahan, Sterling had divorced his wife of twenty-five years soon after he was forced to retire from the army. Apparently, the wife had been something nice to have hanging on his arm when he thought he still had a shot at being a general, but he shed himself of her four months after he left the service. He was also estranged from his two grown children, a boy and a girl. Phone records showed that until two months earlier he'd frequently called a forty-year-old divorcée who lived in nearby Clarksburg, West Virginia, but was no longer calling her.

The impression Kay had of Sterling when she met him in Afghanistan and they argued over whether she'd be permitted to have a gun was that he was an arrogant prick with a low opinion of women. She wouldn't be surprised if this contributed to his breaking up with the lady from Clarksburg. Maybe she was reading too much into a single encounter—but she didn't think so.

She had no intention of misjudging Sterling, however. He may have been almost sixty, about Callahan's age, but unlike Callahan, he was in excellent shape. He trained with his mercenaries, jogged and lifted weights almost every day, and he looked as if he weighed the same as he did when he graduated from West Point. His scholastic records also showed that he wasn't a dummy—he graduated in the top ten percent of his class—and, like most high-ranking military officers, he'd gone on to receive postgraduate training. Lastly, he was an excellent shot with both a rifle and a pistol, and he always went about armed.

She would not underestimate Nathan Sterling.

K ay drove into the parking lot of a supermarket called Shop 'n Save in Fairmount. She was driving a long-body, white panel van, the type painters and plumbers tend to use. On the roof of the van was an extension ladder, but it was just for show. Kay had no intention of using the ladder. She checked her watch. It was seven thirty. She was right on time.

At seven forty-five, a vintage 1984 Cadillac Coupe de Ville, maroon in color with a massive chrome grille, parked next to Kay's van. A serious-looking little guy in his sixties with a face like a prune—sour and wrinkled—stepped from the Cadillac. He was wearing a black trilby hat and black-framed glasses, the type with lenses that change color depending on the light. In his right hand was a small gym bag.

He opened the passenger-side door of Kay's van; his legs were so short it took some effort for him to get up into the passenger seat. Probably because of his size and the hat, Kay thought he looked like a onetime jockey, although she was pretty sure his primary occupation had never been riding the ponies.

"You Betty?" he asked Kay.

"Yeah," she said.

"I'm Archie."

Yeah, right, Kay thought. We're both a couple of comic book characters.

"You got the two grand?" Archie asked.

She pulled a roll from the front pocket of her jeans and handed it to him.

"Okay. Let's go," Archie said, for some reason thinking he was in charge.

Kay drove back to Sterling's place and stopped in front of a black, wrought-iron gate that barred the entrance to a long driveway that ran from the main road to Sterling's home. On a post near the gate was a box that contained a doorbell button, a mesh screen like you see on intercom systems, and a keypad. If visitors came, they could push the doorbell button and tell Sterling they were there, and Sterling would open the gate from inside his house. A second option was he could give trusted visitors the code to the keypad to open the gate. The way Sterling opened the gate, however, was with a remote control he kept in his car, and Kay was betting—

or hoping—that the same remote opened the door to his three-car garage.

Archie told Kay to turn the van around so the rear of the van was pointed at the gate; then he and Kay crawled between the front seats and into the back of the van. Archie then opened the van's double doors and from his gym bag he took out a device that looked like a TV remote, except it was about twice the width of TV remotes that Kay had used. He jacked a cable into one end of the remote and then jacked the other end of the cable into a black box about the size of a smartphone. He pointed the remote at Sterling's gate and Kay saw red lights start to run across the screen on the smartphone-sized box. Thirty seconds later, maybe less, Sterling's gate started to open. Kay knew from watching Sterling that the gate would automatically close in ninety seconds.

Archie closed the van's back doors, disconnected the cable from the remote, and handed it to Kay. He dumped the cable and the other device into his gym bag. Mission accomplished.

They drove back to the Shop 'n Save parking lot in silence and Archie stepped out of the van. Before he closed the door, Kay said something that probably didn't need to be said, as Callahan had vouched for the little guy, but she said it anyway: "You know what will happen if you talk to anybody about this."

Archie sneered at her, slammed the door shut, and strutted back to his Cadillac.

Kay couldn't help but smile.

* * *

Kay drove back to Sterling's house, pointed the remote at the gate, the gate opened, and she drove through it. She figured the best thing to do at this point was to be both quick and direct—there was no point in sneaking around.

Sterling had two neighbors, one to the north, one to the south, but because all the homes sat on such large lots, the neighbors' houses were at least half a mile away. If a neighbor happened to look out, he or she would see Kay driving through the gate in the type of vehicle a contractor might use. Hopefully, the neighbor would then think that Sterling had given the contractor the access code to open the gate. Most likely, however, nobody would even see her open the gate and go up the driveway.

When she reached the top of the driveway, she pointed the remote at Sterling's garage and smiled when the garage door opened. She had a backup plan if the remote hadn't worked on the garage door, but now she wouldn't need to use it. Next, she just sat in her car and waited to see if an alarm would sound. None did, which is what she'd expected.

The same security company provided security for all the houses in Sterling's development. In the basic security plan, which it appeared Sterling had based on the size of his monthly bill, all the exterior doors were alarmed, including the door that permitted entry to the house from the attached garage. The roll-up garage door, however, was not alarmed. In addition to alarms on the doors, the windows on the first floor of the house were alarmed, and inside the house there were weight-sensitive detectors located beneath the floor in strategic places. The concept was that if an intruder was able to get into the house by crawling through a window on one of the upper floors, and if the intruder weighed more than a house cat, he would set off one of the floor alarms.

If the alarm system was set, or "armed," the owner had sixty seconds to disarm the system after he entered the house by punching a six-digit code into a keypad. If the system wasn't disarmed in sixty seconds, then a Klaxon would go off, making a god-awful racket, and a signal would be sent to the security company. The Klaxon would sound for ten minutes; with luck, the noise alone would scare off any intruders and alert the neighbors. At the same time, the security company would call the house to see if the owner had accidentally set off the alarm; if no one answered the landline in the house, the security company would call the owner on his cell phone and simultaneously call the cops. It usually took the cops about fifteen or twenty minutes to show up, and when they did, they'd walk around outside the house looking for signs that someone had broken in.

Kay wasn't concerned, however, about the Klaxon going off or the cops coming, because she had no intention of entering the house and attempting to disarm the security system. What Kay was worried about were cameras. If the homeowner wanted to pay the price, the basic security package could be upgraded to include cameras installed both inside and outside the house. If an alarm sounded, the security company would look at the cameras to see if there was an intruder in the house, and the cameras would have a record of everything they'd videoed in the last twenty-four hours. The security cameras could also be monitored by the homeowner via the homeowner's smartphone or laptop.

But based on the size of Sterling's security bill, Kay was pretty sure he only had the basic package and didn't have cameras installed. She hoped. She put on a baseball cap and sunglasses and then, like an old-time bandit, tied a bandanna around her head to obscure the lower part of her face. She stepped from the van and walked along the front of the house checking for cameras. She didn't see any, and she would have, because cameras installed by a security company were usually very obvious; the company *wanted* potential intruders to see the cameras.

Kay had one final task before she left. She walked into the garage, and the first thing she did was check for cameras, and again she didn't see any. The center bay of the garage was where Sterling parked his Escalade, and it was empty. In the bay closest to the house was a BMW Z3 sports car, the top down, a set of golf clubs in the abbreviated backseat. The third bay of the garage contained a Harley-Davidson motorcycle, a snowblower, storage lockers, a workbench, and a rolling cabinet containing a bunch of tools.

What Kay didn't see was a great place to hide.

Kay left the garage, got back into the van, and used the remote to close the garage door. Her reconnaissance of Sterling's place was complete; she was now ready to kill the man. She started the van and drove back toward the main gate, which opened automatically as she approached it, and turned in the direction of the motel where she was staying. She could have taken care of Sterling that night but decided not to, for one simple reason: the meteorologists were predicting rain tomorrow and rain would be good; she just hoped the weather bozos were right for once.

B ack at her motel, she called Callahan and gave him an update. When she finished, he said, "Are you sure you're going to be able to do this, Hamilton?" Kay hung up without answering.

It was too early for dinner and she was feeling restless, so she changed and went for a three-mile run. As she was running, it began to rain. Good. She took a shower, dried her hair, and changed back into jeans, a simple white pullover sweater, and her running shoes—practically formal attire for dining in rural West Virginia. She opted for a chain restaurant that was within walking distance of her motel. Before leaving her room, she put on a baseball cap and a lightweight jacket because the rain had picked up, which again was good as far as she was concerned.

She ordered a predinner martini; she wasn't exactly celebrating—it was too early to celebrate—but she was feeling pretty good about the way things were going. She was nervous, of course, because something could always go wrong, but she wasn't afraid. She had confidence in her skills.

What she *was* worried about was the question Callahan had asked her: Would she be able to kill Nathan Sterling when the time came? When she'd killed the drug dealer Marco Alvarez and three of Marco's men in Miami, it had been an act of self-defense: They were shooting at her, but she shot them first. They started the fight; she just finished it. She'd never been in a situation, however, where she'd *executed* someone.

It wasn't a moral issue for her, not really. Nathan Sterling deserved to die for killing Ara Khan, and she knew, as Callahan had said, that there was no court of law that was ever going to find him guilty and sentence him to death. But would she be able to pull the trigger when the time came? The problem was, she couldn't *see* herself doing it. She could see Nathan Sterling kneeling on the ground, her holding a gun to the back of his head, him begging for his life—but she couldn't see herself pulling the trigger.

What should she do? Call up Callahan and tell him that she didn't know if she could do it? No. That wasn't right. That was just passing the buck. If she backed out,

Callahan would find someone else to do a job she knew needed to be done but that she didn't have the courage to do herself. So. It was decided: She'd do what she'd agreed to do and she'd live with whatever the consequences might be. Which made her wonder: Was this the reason she'd been hired in the first place, because Callahan knew—even if she didn't—that she had the necessary coldness to be an assassin? Whatever the case, it was time to stop agonizing. She needed to keep this simple for herself, because if she had doubts she was liable to fail. Doubts led to hesitation, and hesitation could be fatal.

Nathan Sterling had killed Ara Khan and he had to pay for what he'd done. End of discussion.

She had a steak for dinner, sautéed mushrooms, and a baked potato slathered with butter and sour cream. Because of the baked potato, she exerted a little willpower and passed on the apple pie à la mode for dessert. As she was leaving the restaurant, she passed through the bar and by two guys who'd been giving her the eye the whole time she'd been eating. One of them called out, "Hey! Don't leave yet. Come on over and have a drink with us." The guy who spoke was actually kind of a stud—tall, well built, wavy dark hair, and a smile brighter than the grille on Archie's vintage Cadillac—but she wasn't in the mood. "Sorry, guys. I can't tonight."

She wondered what Eli Dolan was doing tonight. She wondered who Eli Dolan was with tonight.

* * *

Back at the motel, she called the landline in the condo but Jessica didn't answer. Ever since Afghanistan, she'd tried to be more diligent about checking in on her daughter and letting her know that everything was all right. But where the hell was she? The little nerd was usually hunched over her textbooks at this time of night. She called Jessica's cell phone and her daughter answered, speaking softly, "Hey, Kay. What's up?"

"Where are you?" Kay asked. Why was Jessica whispering?

"At the Library of Congress, if you can believe it. You know, with the Internet, I can't remember the last time I was in a library, but I had to come here to find what I was looking for."

Kay didn't care why she was at the library. "How did you get there?" she asked, already knowing the answer.

"I took the Metro, of course."

Ah, jeez. The closest Metro stop to the Library of Congress was the Capitol South Metro station, which meant that after her daughter left the library she'd be walking around Capitol Hill in the dark. Kay now wished that she'd told Jessica about the attempted rape so she'd be more cautious.

"Did you go by yourself?" Kay asked.

"No. Brian came with me," Jessica said.

"That's good," Kay said, genuinely relieved, but she

was also thinking that Jessica's gangly boyfriend was not her idea of a bodyguard. "But I want you and Brian to take a cab home, Jessica. Okay?"

"Oh, we'll be fine."

"Jessica, take a cab. Please."

"Yeah, yeah, all right."

"And when you get home, send Brian home. I mean it, Jessica." Kay had this unwanted image of Brian and her daughter grappling on the couch in the apartment; Brian may not have been bodyguard material, but that didn't mean he didn't have hormones. Kay also knew she was being somewhat unfair when it came to Brian: She assumed he was the aggressor and not her daughter, which she knew wasn't necessarily the case.

To change the subject, Jessica said, "When are you going to be home?"

"I'm hoping tomorrow night, but it'll probably be sometime after midnight."

"Well, you be careful," her daughter said. Jessica didn't know what she was doing in West Virginia, but after Kay had come home twice with injuries, Jessica probably figured that "be careful" was sound advice.

"I'll see you tomorrow," Kay said.

After she hung up, Kay lay on the motel bed thinking: What if things went south tomorrow? What would happen to Jessica if she were killed? She knew her daughter would be devastated for a while and frightened, but she'd recover, and as smart and self-sufficient as Jessica was, she'd be all right. Kay had an up-to-date will, but the other thing she'd done after she saw how scared Jessica had been after the supposed car accident was talk to Barb Reynolds. She got Barb to agree that if anything happened to her, Barb would become Jessica's guardian. So Jessica would be okay if Kay was killed working for Callahan. Kay had a sizable life insurance policy, so money wouldn't be an issue, and with Barb's guidance, Jessica would deal with whatever problems came her way. The saddest thing would be that Kay wouldn't be around to see her grow up, become a doctor and someone who could make a difference in this world—unlike her mother.

Well, that's enough of that depressing shit.

Kay turned on the television. On HBO was an episode of *Boardwalk Empire*, a show where Steve Buscemi was a deadly, charismatic Prohibition-era gangster. She had seen the show before and she loved it, and she figured watching actors slaughter each other on TV with Thompson machine guns had to be better than brooding about leaving her daughter motherless.

The next morning, Kay again followed Nathan Sterling from his house to his company's headquarters. All she could do now was hope that Sterling would stick to his routine, which meant he should be returning to his house about seven thirty p.m. If he did something that kept him from returning home at the time he normally did, that would be all right. What would not be all right was if he brought someone home with him. Kay was not going to kill an innocent person, and she'd have to find a way to deal with anyone who might happen to be with Sterling. In the four days she'd been following him, each night he had returned home and stayed there. The man must have some sort of social life, but so far she'd seen no evidence of one. Whatever the case, all she could do at this point was hope that he stuck to his routine and came home alone.

Kay sat parked outside Sterling's headquarters for three hours to see if Sterling would leave, and when he didn't, she drove back to her motel. It was raining so hard now that she had to set the wipers on their maximum speed. She had a late breakfast at the same place she'd dined the night before and read the local paper and the *New York Times.* After breakfast, she returned to her hotel room and packed. Since all the clothes she'd brought with her could fit into a knapsack, it took her three minutes. She then spent half an hour cleaning her Glock, not because the Glock needed cleaning but to give herself something to do. While she was cleaning the weapon, she mentally rehearsed what she was going to do at Sterling's place.

At noon, she opened the door to leave her motel. It was still raining, and suddenly something occurred to her, something she should have thought of earlier. She went into the motel bathroom and stole two towels.

Getting to Sterling's place was a bit of a problem. She couldn't drive there and leave the van parked in front of his house; it wouldn't do for Sterling to come home and see a strange vehicle parked anywhere near his place. She drove the van to a small public park that was about four miles from Sterling's house and dropped the keys on the floor, beneath the driver's seat. She was pretty sure the van would be okay, and the way it was raining, it was unlikely anyone would be picnicking in the park today.

She got out of the van, shrugged into her knapsack, and began walking toward Sterling's. While she was walking, she called a number Callahan had given her and told the man who answered—she had no idea who he was—where the van was parked. He would pick it up that night and return it to the rental place the following morning.

Kay was wearing her baseball cap and a jacket that was supposed to be waterproof, but she knew she'd be soaked by the time she arrived at Sterling's place. An hour and twenty minutes later, she pushed the button on the super-duper remote that her dour friend Archie had programmed and Sterling's gate swung open. She checked as she was walking up the driveway to make sure the gate closed automatically as it was supposed to. It wouldn't do for Sterling to come home and see his gate open.

As she walked up the driveway, she glanced over at Sterling's neighbors' houses and could barely see them because it was raining so hard—which was why she'd waited for rain. She figured if Sterling's neighbors

336 | M. A. LAWSON

happened to look out their windows, it would be hard for them to see her walking up Sterling's driveway from half a mile away, and even harder with the rain pouring down.

She used the remote again and the garage door opened. She entered the garage, found the garage door button by the door allowing entry to the house, and closed the garage door. She then walked over and dropped her knapsack down in front of the BMW Z3, still parked with its top down and the golf bag in the backseat. She took off her running shoes, pulled the towels she'd stolen from the motel out of her knapsack, and used the towels to wipe away the wet footprints leading from the garage door to her hiding place.

She now had four or five hours to wait before Sterling came home—she had wanted to be at his place early in case he came home early—so she had plenty of time to dry out.

She knew from watching Sterling that when he came home, he would drive his Escalade up to the garage, open the garage door with his remote, and park the Escalade in the middle bay. He would then walk to the door leading from the garage into his house, push the button to close the garage door, enter the house, and disarm the security system. She would stay on the floor in front of the BMW convertible, and he wouldn't see her unless for some reason he decided to walk to the front of the BMW, which seemed unlikely. And if he did, that would be okay because she'd be ready for him.

She preferred, however, to wait until he was inside the house and had disarmed the security system; then she would enter the house and get the drop on him. She wouldn't kill him immediately unless he forced her to by reaching for a weapon. She wanted to ask him a few questions first.

She put her shoes back on and took off her rain-soaked jacket—she didn't want anything to inhibit her ability to move her arms—and removed the baseball cap. She stuffed both items into her knapsack along with the towels she'd used to dry the floor, and took a seat on the floor in front of the BMW. As it was going to be quite a while before Sterling came home, she needed to be careful her legs didn't cramp up on her. She was completely surprised when the garage door opened only forty minutes after she'd entered the garage.

That is, she was surprised but not displeased. Sterling must have decided to leave work early for some reason—and this was good. She could finish the job and be on her way.

For some reason, however, Sterling didn't drive his Escalade into the garage. She sat there crouched behind the front bumper of the BMW, the Glock in her hand, waiting. What was he doing? Why didn't he drive the SUV into the garage? Then she found out.

"Whoever you are, throw out any weapons you have and stand up. I know you're behind the Z3."

Goddamnit. *How* did he know?

"I'm not going to give you another warning. There

are two of us, and if you don't throw out your weapon and stand up in the next three seconds, we're going to start shooting under the car, skipping bullets off the concrete."

Kay looked quickly under the BMW. She could see two pairs of shoes. She figured in a couple of seconds, Sterling would do just what he said and start shooting under the BMW, and the guy with him would try to flank her and start shooting at her from her left-hand side. She could fire under the car and hope to hit one of them in the foot or leg, but that was going to be a tough shot, and she was pretty sure if she started a gunfight with a combat-experienced ex-soldier, she was going to lose. On the other hand, if she gave up her weapon, Sterling was going to kill her for sure—unless she could bullshit her way out of this.

"One," Sterling said. "Two."

"All right," Kay said. "I'm coming out."

Kay put the Glock on the floor and gave it a hard shove, and the pistol slid on the concrete, coming to rest in the bay where the Escalade was normally parked. She stood up, her hands in the air.

"Jesus, it's you! What the hell are you doing here?" Sterling said.

"Callahan sent me to talk to you, and Callahan knows I'm here."

"If you wanted to talk to me, why didn't you come to my office?"

"Callahan figured it would be better if we talked privately."

Sterling laughed. "Bullshit. I think you came here to kill me, but I can't believe Callahan would send a woman."

With Sterling was a tough-looking, dark-complex-ioned guy with a shaved head and a couple days' worth of beard. He had a tattoo on the right side of his neck that looked like a blue spiderweb. He was wearing a tight-fitting, olive-drab T-shirt, camo pants, and tan desert combat boots. He was shorter than Kay, maybe five foot six, but well built. He reminded her of her hand-to-hand combat instructor, Simmons. He was holding a .45 in a two-handed grip and the weapon was pointed at her chest.

Sterling was dressed in a white shirt and tie. He'd probably left his suit jacket in the Escalade. He was as she'd remembered him from Afghanistan: tall and rangy, short gray hair—and reeking of arrogance. He, too, was holding a .45 and his weapon was also pointed at her chest—which made Kay wonder why she hadn't been smart enough to wear a bulletproof vest.

Sterling waggled his gun at her. "Move to your left so you're not behind the car."

Kay did as instructed and took two steps to her left—Simon Says—her hands still in the air.

"How did you know I was here?" she said. She *really* wanted the answer to that question before she died. She wanted to know if she'd been betrayed or if she'd just fucked up.

Sterling smiled. "A short time ago, I had a problem with a former employee and I decided to beef up the security here at my home."

Kay was pretty sure the "former employee" was that guy, Nelson, who tried to rape and kill her and failed. After she killed Nelson, Sterling probably began to worry that Callahan didn't buy his story that Nelson had quit and that Sterling had nothing to do with the attack on Kay—and that's when he'd beefed up his security.

"One of the things I did," Sterling said, "was install a few cameras outside and inside my house. The cameras are connected to motion detectors and they send a signal to my smartphone when they're activated. So I saw you yesterday, scoping out my place, and I saw you walk into the garage. I didn't know it was you because of that bandanna you were wearing, and then you took off yesterday before I could get here. But today, I made it on time. I saw you go into the garage. I knew you didn't go into the house or you would have tripped a camera in there. So I knew you were in the garage, and the only place you could be was hiding behind the Z3."

This meant that the cameras he'd installed were so damn small or so well camouflaged that Kay hadn't seen them yesterday when she'd toured the outside of Sterling's house looking for cameras. The good news, based on everything he'd just said, was that he didn't have a camera in the garage. If he'd had one there, he would have gotten a clear image of her face when she'd wiped up her wet footprints from the garage floor. But he hadn't known it was her. He'd said *Jesus, it's you!* when he saw her. This also meant that the cameras outside the house, with the rain pouring down and her wearing a hat, hadn't captured a clear image of her, either. At least, she hoped not. She also hoped that the pictures taken by the outside cameras had gone only to Sterling's smartphone, like he'd said, and not to some other computer's hard drive.

Sterling concluded his diatribe by saying: "I mean, for Christ's sake, Hamilton, I run a security company. Did you really think it was going to be this easy? I knew you were an arrogant bitch the moment I met you."

Talk about the pot calling the kettle black, but he had a point about her assuming it would be so easy. It was also nice to know that she hadn't been betrayed; it was not so nice to know she'd been a fool.

Kay was about to tell him once again that Callahan knew she was there and if he killed her, Callahan would send in a team to take him out. Before Kay could say anything, however, Sterling said, "Frisk her, Ramirez. Make sure she's not carrying any other weapons, and if she has a phone, get it. For that matter, remove everything she has in her pockets."

"Yes, sir," Ramirez said—and then he did something really stupid.

He shoved the .45 he was carrying into the front of

his pants and he didn't put the safety on. He walked toward Kay, and Kay, trying to look like she was scared, said, "Please. Don't hurt me." This made Ramirez smile and it also put him more at ease, thinking Kay was frightened.

When Ramirez reached her, he said, "Turn around and grab the wall," and then he reached up with his right hand to touch her left shoulder to spin her around, and when he did this he was standing between her and Sterling. Instead of turning, Kay reached out with her left hand, grabbed Ramirez's T-shirt and jerked him toward her, and at the same time she reached down with her right hand, grabbed Ramirez's gun—and pulled the trigger without removing the gun from his pants.

She didn't know if she'd just blown Ramirez's dick off or if the bullet had ended up in one of his legs, but whatever the case, he screamed in pain and his eyes bulged with shock. Kay didn't let him drop to the ground, however. She quickly pulled the gun out of his pants and, still clutching Ramirez to her, using him as a shield, she fired at Sterling. And missed.

Sterling fired back immediately. His first bullet went whizzing past her left ear. Since she and Ramirez were almost the same height, and because she was holding Ramirez in front of her, Sterling then did the only thing he could do: He fired directly at Ramirez's back, hoping the bullet would pass through Ramirez and hit her.

After that it was a gunfight that lasted less than three

seconds. She just kept pulling the trigger as fast as she could, hoping to hit Sterling, and Sterling did the same thing: He kept shooting at her, hoping to hit her in the face, half his bullets hitting Ramirez in the back. She had no idea how many bullets they both fired—at least a dozen was her guess—and one of her bullets hit Sterling in the chest.

She knew she wasn't better than Sterling—she was just luckier. She was lucky she hit him, firing without really aiming, and while holding Ramirez upright. But where she really got lucky was that none of the bullets Sterling had fired passed through Ramirez's body, which meant that Sterling was probably using frangible ammo—dumdums—the type air marshals used. Why Sterling had loaded his gun with that type of bullet she didn't know, but she thanked God that he had.

Kay dropped Ramirez to the ground, and she couldn't believe it when she heard him moan. He'd been hit so many times she knew he'd be dead very soon, and she was astounded he was still alive. He was a tough little motherfucker. She ignored Ramirez, however, and focused on Sterling. He was lying on the ground, but she could tell he was still alive, too, and his gun was in his hand. She pointed her weapon at Sterling, intending to shoot him again if necessary, but it wasn't necessary. Sterling was too weak to lift his weapon and aim it at her.

She started to approach Sterling but then looked down at Ramirez. His eyes were closed and blood was seeping from his mouth. She wondered how long it was going to take him to die.

She thought about it for less than a second and shot him in the head. There was no point in letting him suffer.

She walked over to Sterling and kicked the gun out of his hand, then knelt down next to him. He had a classic, bubbling chest wound, meaning her bullet had pierced a lung and air was escaping through the hole. Had she wanted to save him, she would have put a piece of plastic, like Saran Wrap, over the wound to seal it and then wrapped bandages around his chest to keep the plastic in place—but she didn't want to save him.

"If you tell me where Anna Mercer is, I'll call the medics," she said to Sterling.

Without opening his eyes, he said, "I don't know where she is."

Kay believed him.

"How much did she pay you to help her?"

Sterling's lips were moving, but he couldn't—or wouldn't—speak.

"Tell me how much she paid you and I'll call the medics," Kay said. She wasn't going to call anyone.

"Five."

"Five million?"

"Yeah."

That's all she really needed to know. If her plan had worked out and she'd been able to question him, she would have tried to make him tell her where the money was and force him to transfer it back to one of Callahan's accounts. That wasn't going to happen now, however, because Sterling died a few heartbeats later.

The garage door was still open, so Kay closed it. She then searched the storage lockers in the garage and found some plastic garbage bags, rags, and a gallon of a liquid chemical for removing oil stains from concrete. The label on the bottle said the product contained bleach, which was good, as bleach made it harder to get DNA results.

She used the rags and the chemical cleaning agent to wipe up all the blood she could see, then placed the rags, Sterling and his buddy's guns, and all the shell casings she could find in the garbage bag. She couldn't be sure that she found all the casings, but she couldn't search any longer.

She took one final look around the garage; a hotshot CSI team like you see on TV would certainly find evidence that a shoot-out had taken place in the garage and blood had been spilled, but to a casual observer, everything looked fine. One other bit of luck: None of Sterling's bullets had hit a window, and where they'd hit the back wall of the garage they'd fragmented and the wall was just dinged up in a couple of places. All the bullets she'd fired at Sterling, except for the one that hit him, had flown out the open garage door.

She found the keys to the Escalade in one of Sterling's

pockets, put on her baseball cap, and tied her bandanna around her face to make sure Sterling's invisible surveillance cameras didn't record her. She then opened the garage door, drove Sterling's Escalade into the garage, and closed the garage door again.

It took her about ten minutes to load Sterling, Ramirez, the garbage bag with the bloody rags, and her knapsack into the Escalade. She searched the garage storage lockers again, found a paint-splattered tarp, and tossed it over the bodies. She opened the garage door, hopped into the Escalade, and began to back it out of the garage—when she suddenly slammed on the brakes.

What the hell was wrong with her? She'd forgotten to get Sterling's smartphone, the one that had images of her walking up the driveway and entering the garage. She'd better get her head on straight. She pulled the tarp off Sterling and retrieved the phone.

Kay called Callahan. She was driving Sterling's Escalade very carefully, making sure she stayed below the speed limit. The last thing she needed was to get stopped by a cop with two corpses in the car.

"I have two items to be disposed of, plus the vehicle I'm driving, plus the contents of a garbage bag inside the vehicle."

"*Two* items?" Callahan said.

"Yeah. There was a complication."

"Okay. Is the drop-off point still the same?" Callahan asked.

"Yeah. I'll be there in an hour."

"You'll find a blue Camry at the drop-off point, keys on the left rear tire. A couple of guys will be there to take care of the disposal in exactly an hour and a half, so you need to be gone before they get there."

"Copy that," Kay said.

"Come to the office as soon as you're back in D.C. I want to hear what happened."

"No. I'm going home to my daughter. I'll talk to you tomorrow."

She hung up before Callahan could remind her that he was the boss.

40

Nathan Sterling wasn't reported missing for five days, two of those days falling on a weekend.

Sterling's partner, Cannon, was out of town the first day Sterling was absent from work, which happened to be a Friday. Cannon and his wife had decided to take a long weekend at Nag's Head. The administrative assistant that Cannon and Sterling shared was surprised when Sterling didn't call her and tell her he wouldn't be coming in, but he was a rude, inconsiderate man and she didn't think too much of it. She was annoyed by his absence but certainly wasn't alarmed or concerned.

When he didn't show up on Monday, Cannon and the admin assistant both called Sterling several times but he didn't return their calls. Again, the admin assistant wasn't concerned—but Cannon was. He'd grown to dislike Sterling during the years they'd worked together, but Sterling had always been reliable. On Tuesday, when Sterling still hadn't returned his calls, Cannon called the cops. He told them that Sterling lived alone and maybe he'd had an accident or a heart attack, though a heart attack seemed unlikely given Sterling's physical condition.

The police entered Sterling's house—they had to call the security company to disarm the security system—and looked around, but saw no signs of foul play. They just glanced into the garage and saw it was empty except for the Z3. The cops checked flight records but could find no evidence that Sterling had taken a plane anywhere. They checked his credit cards, but he didn't appear to be using them, nor could they locate him via his phone. The cops informed Cannon that they'd keep their eyes open for his partner, but there wasn't much else they planned to do, particularly as there was no evidence that Sterling had been harmed or that he'd committed a crime and fled.

Cannon immediately had a CPA come in and audit the C&S books. Cannon knew Sterling was in bad financial shape, and he wondered if he'd embezzled from their failing company. The CPA said no money was missing—not that there'd been a lot of cash there to begin with—and maybe Cannon ought to think about filing for bankruptcy if business didn't pick up.

No one at C&S Logistics noticed or cared that Ramirez was absent from work the same days Sterling was missing. Ramirez lived alone, had few friends at the company, and had a drinking problem. Maybe Ramirez was on a bender. Or maybe, since Ramirez had just gotten back from Afghanistan, he'd taken a few days off. Or maybe, Ramirez being the asshole he was, he just quit and didn't bother to give notice.

Ramirez was like the line from that Dixie Chicks song

"Goodbye Earl": He was a missing person whom nobody missed at all.

There was nothing new with regard to Anna Mercer: The damn woman was just gone. The Brits were searching databases for home purchases made by single women in their forties, looking for people who had no apparent history, but so far no one who might be Mercer had been found. To complicate matters, a lot of the women who purchased homes in the U.K. weren't U.K. citizens, divorced women often used their maiden names, and property records for home purchases weren't updated in a timely manner.

"Jesus," Kay complained one day to Callahan, "there must be something else we can do. The worst thing is, we don't even know if she's in the U.K. She could be in fucking Timbuktu for all you know."

"Hamilton, will you relax," Callahan told her. "It's only been three weeks. I know you don't want to hear this, but it may take us years."

41

Five weeks after Anna Mercer disappeared, Callahan pulled Kay out of the training program to take part in an operation.

The pre-op briefing was held in Callahan's conference room. In addition to Kay and Callahan, three other people were present: a good-looking young couple in their twenties named Rick and Sharon—no last names—and a no-nonsense guy in his forties who had short gray hair, was tall and slender, and wore wire-rimmed glasses. The man was introduced as Morgan, and Callahan said Morgan was the one who would be in charge of the operation. Kay never found out if Morgan was his first name, his last name, or an alias.

Morgan began by showing photographs of a hotel in Geneva, Switzerland, one exterior shot followed by several pictures of the hotel lobby, the elevators, and a hallway on the sixth floor. He then showed pictures of four Korean men who all looked tough enough to bite the heads off alligators.

"These four men are the subject's security detail, and two are always guarding him," Morgan said. "You need to memorize their faces, as we don't know who will be on duty tomorrow night. One will be in the hotel lobby and the other will be stationed outside the subject's room, and they relieve each other every two hours. We've only had one day to observe them, but last night the guards switched positions at seven, nine, eleven, et cetera. Odd hours, in other words.

"The operation will start at exactly eight p.m. Hamilton, your job will be to watch the guard in the lobby, whoever he is. If he leaves the lobby and gets in the elevator *before* eight p.m., you'll call me, I'll abort the op, and we'll regroup. But if he leaves the lobby and gets in the elevator between eight and eight ten p.m., then you'll get in the elevator with him. If he punches the button for the sixth floor, you will make sure he doesn't get off the elevator. You'll be given a gun that fires a tranquilizer dart to incapacitate him. The reason you were selected for this op is we think he'll be less on guard if a woman gets into the elevator with him."

"What if there are other people in the elevator?" Kay asked. "What do I do with him after I shoot him?"

Irritated by the interruption, Morgan said, "We'll get to all that. Right now I'm just giving you an overview of the plan, and like I said, your job will be to make sure the lobby guard doesn't get off the elevator on the sixth floor."

Before Kay could ask another question, Morgan said to the young couple, "As I said, on the sixth floor will be another guard, standing in front of the door to room 618. You two will be the distraction. You'll get off the elevator at exactly eight p.m. and you'll pretend to be a couple of young drunks in love. You'll stagger down the hallway, laughing, playing grab ass, making a bunch of noise. Before you reach room 618, and when you're four or five feet from the guard, you," Morgan said, pointing at Sharon, "will fall to the ground like you've had too much to drink. As you fall, you'll let out a shriek which I'll hear, and while the guard is looking at the two of you, I'll open the door to room 619, which is directly across the hall from the guard, and I'll tranq him."

To the young man, Morgan said, "You will also be carrying a weapon that fires a tranquilizer dart, and if necessary, you'll be able to shoot the guard as well as help me overpower him if he doesn't go down immediately. The guard, by the way, will be armed with a gun that fires real bullets, and he will not hesitate to kill you. Once the guard is out, I'll knock on the door to room 618, a man will exit, and you'll drag the guard into the room. Then all three of you will leave the hotel. Okay? Everybody clear on the big picture?"

The young couple nodded. Kay didn't nod—she looked over at Callahan. Had Callahan been a more sensitive type, he would have known that Kay was not happy with what she was hearing.

"Now," Morgan said, "I'm going to cover contingency plans, communications, transportation, escape routes, and what to do if things go wrong."

And that's what they did for the next hour.

When they were finished, Morgan said, "We're leaving

for Geneva in two hours, and I want everybody at Dulles with half an hour to spare. That should give you enough time to go home and pack a bag. Assume you'll be gone two or three days. When we're on the plane, we'll go over everything half a dozen more times."

Callahan said, "I'm sorry, guys, but I got very little notice for this job and the only window we have is for tomorrow night. Okay, get moving and be at the airport on time."

The young couple rose to leave, but Kay said to Callahan, "I want to speak with you privately."

"If it concerns this mission, I want to hear what you have to say," Morgan said.

"What part of *privately* didn't you understand?" Kay said.

Before Morgan could blow a gasket, Callahan made a calm-down gesture with his hands and said, "It's okay, Morgan. Let me talk to her."

Morgan left the conference room, and Callahan said, "What's the problem?"

"I'm not going to work like this."

"Like what?"

"I am not going to be part of an operation where I don't know the reason for the operation."

"Hamilton, this is the way covert ops work. Everything's strictly need to know. Things are compartmentalized. And the reason we do it this way is so if you're caught and interrogated, we can possibly limit the damage *because* you don't know everything. The other reason, quite frankly, is the less people know, the less chance there is of someone leaking information, intentionally or unintentionally. That's the whole principle behind need to know."

"Fuck need to know, Callahan," Kay said. "I am not going to shoot a man with a horse tranquilizer without knowing why. I am not going to risk going to jail or getting killed without knowing why. And if I don't agree, uh, morally with the reason you're doing something, then I might not participate."

Morally wasn't exactly the right word. What she meant was that she had principles, and although it might be hard for her to articulate exactly what those principles were, there were things she wasn't willing to do.

Callahan looked at her for a moment, his lips set in a firm line. "Okay. If that's the way you're going to be, then I'm going to have to let you go. Good luck finding a job. I'll have somebody contact you in the next couple of days with regard to severance pay, that sort of thing, and to go over the nondisclosure agreement with you again."

"Fine," Kay said, and rose from her chair. She had her hand on the doorknob when Callahan said, "Oh, goddamnit, sit down."

She sat back down, and Callahan stared at her for another few seconds, trying not to smile. "I don't know what I'm going to do with you, Hamilton. I imagine that one of these days I am going to have to fire you, but for now, you've won." He paused, then said, "I just hate it when somebody calls my bluff."

"So who's the man in room 618?" Kay asked.

"He's a North Korean physicist and he's in Geneva because he's attending a convention hosted by CERN."

"Cern?" Kay said.

"Yeah. CERN stands for the Conseil Européen pour la Recherche Nucléaire," Callahan said in surprisingly good French, "which translates into the European Council for Nuclear Research, and just outside Geneva, on the French–Swiss border, is where one end of the Hadron Collider is located. The Korean's there to attend a convention and hear about the latest stuff going on with the collider. It's an egghead convention."

Kay found out later that the Hadron Collider was the world's largest particle accelerator, which still didn't mean anything to her.

"Anyway, this guy is one of their top guys, and two days ago he passed a note to an American scientist saying he wanted to defect, and the scientist passed the note on to the U.S. Consulate in Geneva. We obviously want the guy, because we want to know where certain North Korean programs stand, like their ability to actually hit California with a nuclear missile."

"So why doesn't the CIA help him? Why us?"

"The CIA would be happy to escort the guy to the embassy in Bern for asylum, but they are not going to help him escape if that means overpowering his bodyguards. If this operation is successful, in a week or two the North Korean scientist will hold a press conference saying he hired a private security company to help him defect and the U.S. government had nothing to do with it. Nobody will believe him, but that doesn't matter. What does matter is, if you or anyone else on Morgan's team gets caught or killed, the U.S. government will be able to honestly say that you're not government agents, and nobody will be able to prove otherwise."

"And what happens after Morgan takes out the guard in the hotel?"

"Morgan will take the scientist to another room in the hotel and just sit there with him for a few days until the North Korean delegation goes home, then walk him over to the consulate. Now, are you *morally* okay with this operation, Hamilton? Would you like to help your country better understand North Korea's ability to start a nuclear war?"

"Yeah, I'm okay with this," she said.

"Well, whoop-de-fuckin'-doo. I'll let the president know."

The operation went flawlessly, and all Kay did was sit in the lobby and watch the lobby guard for half an hour. When Morgan called her at ten minutes after eight, saying he had the Korean scientist in custody, she left the hotel and drove back to the safe house in Geneva.

I n the first week of March, two months after Anna Mercer had disappeared, Callahan sent Kay down to Fort Benning to take the survival course. Kay wondered if one of his reasons for doing this was to get her out of D.C.

and give her something to do so she'd quit bugging him about the lack of progress in locating Mercer. She bugged him about Mercer at least once a week. And actually she was glad to go; she was tired of attending language classes and was looking forward to something physical.

There were twenty other people in the class; three were women, including her. Half the attendees were military; the remainder were civilians from unnamed government agencies. Kay was registered under the name Karen Hart, and she assumed other folks in the class might also be using cover names. The objective of the class was to teach them how to survive if they ended up behind enemy lines in some spot without food, water, or a cell phone. They taught her how to make snowshoes out of branches, how to snare wee animals for lunch, and how to identify those plants that were edible and those that would poison her. Every day there was a five-mile run to make sure everyone stayed in shape.

For the final exam, a helicopter dropped her off in a remote section of the Blue Ridge Mountains and she was told to make her way to a small town a hundred and fifty miles away in four days. She was given a warm ski jacket to wear, a hunting knife, waterproof matches, a compass, a topographical map, and a GPS device so they could locate her if she got lost. The GPS device also had a button she could push to summon help. Pushing the button, of course, was an automatic failure.

The first day, she dutifully trudged through the

woods. She wasn't worried about water, as the map indicated she'd be crossing streams, but food was problematic. She wasn't going to find a bush laden with blueberries at this time of year. On the other hand, it wasn't like she was going to starve in three days; she had no intention of having squirrel for dinner.

The second morning she came upon a small shack in the woods and her nose—trained by the DEA—told her that she'd stumbled onto some yokel's meth lab. She started to go around the shack, but then noticed two Kawasaki quads—four-wheel-drive, all-terrain vehicles.

She snuck down to look at the quads. She figured the guys inside the cabin would be too busy cooking their meth to notice her. At least she hoped that was the case, because she also figured that they'd be armed. The ignition keys were in both vehicles—which wasn't surprising, considering the remoteness of the location—and there was a knapsack strapped onto the rack behind the seat of one of the vehicles. She pulled the keys from one of the quads and tossed them into the woods, then started up the second machine—the one with the knapsack—and took off.

She wondered how far the meth cookers would have to walk; she doubted that they'd had survival training.

She arrived at her destination point well fed and well rested. The backpack had contained a six-pack of beer and four ham sandwiches. Her instructor praised her for making such good time, and she modestly accepted his praise. She didn't tell him that she'd driven most of the way, nor did she consider that she'd cheated: It was a survival course, after all, and she just did what she needed to do to survive.

After she returned from Georgia, she asked Callahan for a week off—she hadn't had any time off since she'd hired on with him—and he told her to take two if she wanted, sounding like he'd be glad to have her out of his hair for a while.

One of the things she did during her vacation was drive to Durham so Jessica could check out Duke University, where it appeared she'd be headed next year. Kay had decided she was okay with Jessica skipping her senior year in high school and heading off to college. And Jessica was definitely okay with the decision and looking forward to college life.

Kay was still somewhat leery about Tanaka—son of the founder of TanTech Research—helping her daughter get into Duke. Being an ex-cop, she couldn't help but look gift horses in the mouth. She used an old pal in the DEA down in Miami to check Tanaka out—to make sure he wasn't some sort of sexual deviate who preyed on teenage girls—but her pal said Tanaka was clean. In fact, he appeared to be more than clean: The guy had even spent a couple years in Africa when he got out of college, helping out over there.

They took a long walk around the campus, looking at the dorms and cafeterias and the labs in the science buildings. Kay thought the campus was gorgeous, with its grassy quads and ponds and flower-lined paths, and she was excited her daughter might be attending school there. Jessica, who had read about the place and liked to show off, informed Kay that the architecture was neo-Gothic, whatever that meant.

"Did you know that Richard Nixon went to law school here?" Jessica said.

"It looks like he should have paid more attention," Kay said. "And no, I didn't know that. The only name I know associated with Duke is Mike Krzyzewski."

"Who's he?" Jessica asked.

"You gotta be kidding me, Jessica! He's the guy who coached the Blue Devils to like a dozen basketball Final Fours. You know, the NCCA championship?"

"Whatever" was Jessica's response. Basketball was not high on the list of things she cared about.

Kay also liked the town of Durham, particularly the Bull City area. Bull City used to be home to the tobacco industry, but now the buildings and warehouses were occupied by restaurants, shops, and bars. She liked the Southern cooking, not bothered a bit that everything was fried. Kay wondered if Jessica and her boyfriend would split up when she left for college.

As they were driving back to D.C., Kay thought about Eli Dolan. Though she'd only seen him once since the hunt for Anna Mercer had begun, she thought about him all the time. He'd been spending most of his time in New York, and when she'd asked Callahan what he was doing, all Mr. Need-To-Know Callahan would tell her was that Eli was looking into something involving the World Bank and an unnamed third-world country—and that's all he'd say.

One time, she ran into Eli in the reception area. It didn't help that Henry was at his desk and able to hear what they were saying. It was an awkward encounter, both of them seemingly tongue-tied. She wanted to tell him how good he looked and how she missed him, but all that came out was "How have you been?" He said "Fine," then mumbled that he was late for a meeting and left before she could say anything else.

She could tell he was still attracted to her, but she figured that he'd moved on with his life. He was probably dating some supermodel in New York—or maybe three supermodels simultaneously. As for her, even though she missed him, she was beginning to think that maybe separating was for the best. She told herself again that it wasn't smart to date a coworker and that his preferring to live in New York made things too complicated.

And it wasn't like the damn guy was perfect. He was obviously stubborn, overly sensitive, and he hadn't shown much interest in Jessica. And Kay still hadn't forgotten what he'd said about divorcing his first wife: how he became bored with her after five years of marriage. How long would it take before he became bored with her? So maybe it was for the best—but she missed him.

When Kay returned to work the day after her vacation was over, the first thing she did was call Callahan and ask how the search for Anna Mercer was proceeding. In answer to her question, Callahan said, "Goddamnit, quit hounding me."

42

Kay entered Callahan's conference room to find Morgan and Callahan already there, and she had the feeling that they'd been talking about her—which she didn't like. She hadn't seen Morgan since Geneva, and he didn't say, "Hey, great to see you! Glad to be working with you again!" He just nodded and said, "Hamilton."

A moment later, two more men entered the room. One of them was Bowman, the big bastard Kay had kicked in the nuts during the hand-to-hand combat course. He stared at Kay for a moment, then smiled and said, "Stay away from me, Hamilton. I might want kids someday." Maybe Bowman was all right.

The other man was almost as big as Bowman, maybe six-two, and built like a serious weight lifter. Like Bowman, his hair was cut military short. Callahan didn't bother to introduce the man; Kay later found out his name was Dotson.

Callahan started off by saying, "The CIA has its big tit caught in the wringer, and half an hour ago I was asked to help them out.

"In 2005, they faked the death of a guy named

Leonid Viktoryvich Titov and snuck him out of Russia. It was a brilliant operation and, of course, you've never heard about it because it was a roaring success. The reason we wanted Titov was because of the kind of job he had. He was a weapons inspector and he had extensive knowledge about where the Russians store nuclear materials, the kind that can be sold to terrorists to make suitcase bombs. The CIA got him back to Langley and spent two years bleeding him dry. He identified storage locations, how well they were secured, points of vulnerability, that sort of thing. He also identified the people who basically had the keys to the facilities. In other words, people who, if they got desperate enough or greedy enough, could make a deal with al-Qaeda or Hezbollah or whatever group of nuts might want to build a dirty bomb.

"In 2007, the agency figured they'd gotten all they were going to get out of Titov, gave him a new identity and a nice severance package. He bought a bookstore in Middleburg, Virginia, and then, in 2010, got himself a Russian mail-order bride. I guess he was lonely and wanted to hear his native tongue again. His wife is a gorgeous bimbo named Natalya who's twenty-five years younger than him, and when the CIA vetted her they found out she'd been a hooker in St. Petersburg—but Titov didn't care. He saw her picture and fell in love. The story should have ended with *They lived happily ever after*—but it didn't.

"Natalya has been kidnapped. By Chechens. We

don't know how many or their identities. They snatched her out of Titov's house while he was at work, then called him and said they wanted information related to a specific nuclear facility in southern Russia. The CIA doesn't know why they selected that particular place other than it's close to Chechnya, but what the Chechens wanted was basically the same information the CIA wanted when they debriefed Titov. They wanted to know the type of security systems installed, where cameras are located, how many guards were normally on each shift, people who had access codes, et cetera. Titov was told to draw a detailed map of the facility and write down the information they needed. They also said they wanted two hundred and fifty grand in cash, which is almost exactly how much money Titov has in his bank account."

"How did they know how much money he had?" Morgan asked.

Callahan shrugged. "I don't know. They probably forced the information out of his wife. Or maybe they had some way to access his accounts. I don't know. Anyway, to make sure Titov had an incentive to cooperate they e-mailed him a photo of Natalya, sitting naked in a chair, wearing an explosive vest. Titov could see dynamite sticks attached to the vest. They told him if he didn't give them what they wanted, the lovely Natalya would be blown to bits, and likewise if anyone tried to free her. They gave him three hours—two and a half hours from now—to get the money together and write down everything they wanted. He convinced them he'd need the time to get the money.

"So. Our job is to make sure the Chechens don't get the information. Or if they do get it, to make sure it doesn't leave the country. I hate to say this, but we don't really care about Titov or his wife. We'd prefer not to see them killed, of course, but Titov has no more value as an intelligence asset and his wife never had any. Everybody understand?"

Everybody nodded—except Kay.

"Right now, Titov's wife is located in a house outside of Middleburg and—"

"How do you know that?" Kay asked.

"Natalya Titov is severely allergic to practically everything on the planet. She's allergic to shellfish, peanuts, eggs. A bee sting will kill her. She wears a medic alert device, one with a button she can push to call the medics, and the device has a GPS chip so she can be located. Because Natalya didn't want to wear a big clunky device like you see on grandmas at nursing homes, her device is contained in a heart-shaped locket she wears. The guys who kidnapped her might not have even noticed the locket, and she was still wearing it in the picture they e-mailed to Titov. And these guys probably aren't all that worried about Titov getting the cops or the FBI involved. They know he wouldn't put his hot young wife in jeopardy, not with a bomb strapped to her."

When Callahan mentioned Natalya's medic alert

button, Kay had a fleeting thought about Anna Mercer—something Mercer had once said—but she didn't have time to think about Mercer now because Callahan was still talking.

"The problem," Callahan said, "is we don't know where Titov is or where he's going to meet the Chechens to pass on the information. And the reason we don't know is because Titov doesn't want us to know. Titov's not a dummy. He knows all the CIA would have to do is grab him so he couldn't pass anything on to the Chechens, and he isn't going to allow that. He wants us to try to free his wife, and if we can't do that, then he's going to give the Chechens what they want."

"Wait a minute," Kay said. "Back up. How do we know any of this stuff? And why isn't the CIA or the FBI dealing with this?"

"I don't have time—"

"Yeah, you do," Kay said. "Just give us the condensed version."

It looked like Callahan was going to refuse, then probably figured it would take less time to tell her than to argue with her. "When Titov was told his wife had been kidnapped, he contacted his handler at the CIA, who was the main guy he worked with when the agency was debriefing him. He told his handler about his wife's medic alert device, gave him the data, and the CIA located Natalya. Or, I should say, they located the device. I'm just assuming she's still wearing it."

"So why doesn't the CIA go get her?" Kay asked. "Why us?"

"Two reasons," Callahan said. "First, as I'm sure you already know, the CIA isn't allowed to operate in this country. They're not a law-enforcement agency."

"Yeah, right," Kay said, "like that would ever stop them."

"The second reason is the CIA doesn't know how the Chechens found Titov. There are maybe a dozen people at Langley who knew he was living in Middleburg, and Titov's handler is afraid one of those people might have sold Titov to the Chechens. The CIA will eventually find out if they have a traitor in their ranks, but for now, Titov's handler doesn't want to use anybody at Langley because he doesn't know who he can trust."

"That still doesn't explain why they're not using the FBI," Kay said.

"They're not using the FBI because the CIA doesn't want to end up with egg all over its face. They know if the FBI frees Titov's wife and captures the Chechens, it'll be all over the news. I mean, have you ever seen an FBI hostage operation, Hamilton? They'd have fifty agents involved, communication vans, personnel carriers, guys dressed in body armor, and five minutes after the operation started, ten news helicopters would be circling overhead. The end result would be the CIA having to deal with the embarrassment of having a turncoat in their own house, not to mention the Russians finding out that we slipped Titov out of Russia under their noses and know a whole lot more about their nuclear facilities than they probably want us to know. Okay? Can we stop with the questions now? We're running out of time."

Kay nodded, but she knew Callahan was keeping something from her. How would the CIA know to contact Callahan, since he supposedly worked directly for the president?

"The reason you four were picked," Callahan said, "is simply because you were all here in Washington and can get down to Middleburg in a hurry. The reason you were picked, Hamilton, is because you're a woman. If these guys raped Titov's wife—and they may have, judging by the naked picture they sent to Titov—I figured it would be nice if there was a woman along to comfort her. Or whatever. While we've been talking, Henry's packed a couple of bags containing what I think you'll need. Bowman, your rifle is in the bag."

Kay figured that meant Bowman's personal sniper rifle.

Callahan looked at his watch. "You now have two hours and fifteen minutes to get to Middleburg, scope out the house where she's being kept, and figure a way to get her out of there."

T he house where Natalya Titov was being held captive was on an unpaved road twenty miles west of Middleburg. It was a small, unkempt place with paint flaking off the siding and a cedar shake roof covered with moss. There were no other houses within sight. Callahan had called to say that the house was a rental property owned by an elderly woman in nearby Front Royal, and the current tenant was a man named Malik Zakayev.

Morgan drove the Ford SUV they were using past the house and stopped in a place where it couldn't be seen from the house. Everyone was wearing earbuds and throat mikes so they could communicate. Dotson—the man Kay had never met before—got out of the SUV and belly-crawled through weeds and shrubs until he had an unobstructed view of the house. He pointed a thermal imaging camera at the house, and a moment later Kay heard him say: "There are only two people in the house. They both appear to be sitting down in a room that's just to the left of the front door. All the curtains are closed, so I can't see them visually."

"We could approach the house from the back," Morgan said, "and as long as whoever's with Titov's wife stays where he is, we can enter through the back door. The problem is, if the guy with Natalya is really hardcore, he might detonate the bomb as soon as he sees us."

As Bowman was saying this, a UPS truck drove by.

"How good are you with that rifle, Bowman?" Kay asked.

"Very good."

"If somebody drives down the driveway, the guy with Natalya will pull back one of the curtains to take a look."

"So?" Morgan says.

"So if Bowman's as good as he thinks he is, Bowman can shoot him in the head. But he has to turn the guy's lights off instantaneously. His brain can't have time to send a signal to a finger with a button on a detonator. Can you do that, Bowman?"

"Yeah. The ammo I'm using will turn the guy's brain to mush so fast he won't even know he's been shot." Bowman paused. "I know this. I've been in a situation like this before." Kay figured that before Bowman came to work for Callahan he was probably a military sniper or maybe a cop used in hostage situations. But there wasn't time to review Bowman's résumé.

"But how would we approach the front door without alarming the guy?" Morgan asked. "If he sees someone coming down the driveway, he might think he's being attacked and detonate the bomb as soon as he sees someone coming."

"That UPS truck that just drove by," Kay said. "Let's go get it. One of us will swap places with the driver and drive it down the driveway. The guy with Natalya will pull back the curtains, and relax when he sees the truck and the driver wearing his little UPS uniform. Then, while he's thinking about what to do, whether he should open the door for the UPS guy or pretend no one's home, Bowman shoots him. If Bowman misses, we're fucked, of course."

"I won't miss," Bowman said.

"Then let's go kidnap a UPS driver," Kay said. She couldn't help it, but she was actually enjoying herself.

They all put on ski masks and left Dotson watching the house with the thermal imaging camera. They caught up with the UPS truck two miles down the road. Morgan swerved in front of the truck and hit the brakes, forcing the UPS driver to stop. Bowman and Kay jumped out of the SUV and pointed their guns at the driver's face. The driver, who turned out to be a woman, immediately screamed when she saw two masked people pointing weapons at her face.

Kay said, "Shut the hell up before I shoot you."

Kay told the driver to get out of the truck and walked her around the side of the truck not visible from the road. They were lucky they were out in the sticks and traffic was sparse. "Take off your uniform," Kay told the woman. Kay had assumed the UPS driver would be a man and that Morgan or one of the other guys would have to impersonate the driver. So much for assumptions.

The driver was about two inches shorter than Kay and thirty pounds heavier. She was wearing a standard UPS uniform: brown short-sleeved shirt, brown shorts that came down to her chunky knees, and a brown baseball cap with the UPS logo. She appeared to be about forty, had short dark hair and brown eyes that were currently about the size of hard-boiled eggs. She was so scared she was almost hyperventilating.

"Take a deep breath and calm down," Kay said. "We're not going to hurt you. We just want your truck and your uniform. We're not even going to steal the packages from your truck. So get undressed."

When the woman just stood there, Kay yelled, "Move!"

The woman started to unbutton her blouse. Kay was wearing a T-shirt and jeans and low-topped boots. She stripped off the jeans, wishing she'd chosen a pair of panties that morning that weren't quite so revealing. Bowman was getting an eyeful. She put the UPS uniform shirt on over her T-shirt, and when the driver had her shorts off, Kay put on the shorts. To keep the shorts from falling off her hips, she had to cinch the UPS driver's belt as tight as it would go. She plucked the driver's ball cap off her head but didn't put it on, because she was still wearing the ski mask.

The pudgy driver was now wearing only her bra, panties, and her boots. She looked embarrassed in addition to looking scared. "Please don't hurt me," she said. "I've got two kids."

Kay said, "I told you, we're not going to hurt you."

"What do we do with her?" Bowman said.

"Where's your ID, your driver's license?" Kay said to the driver.

"In the back pocket of my shorts," she said.

Sure enough, the woman's wallet was in the back

pocket of the shorts Kay was wearing. She took out the wallet and looked at the woman's driver's license. Her name was Carol Walker. In the wallet was also a picture of two plump teenage girls who looked just like their mother.

"Okay, Carol," Kay said. "You're going to walk down this road and not talk to anybody for two hours. Go find a place to sit or whatever. In two hours, you can find a pay phone and call somebody to pick you up. But don't call the cops. I'm going to keep your driver's license, since it's got your address on it, and if the cops show up and interfere with what we're doing, then somebody's going to kill your kids. Do you understand?"

"Yes."

"Good. Start walking."

"But I can't go walking around like this," she said, meaning wearing only a bra and panties.

"Give her your Windbreaker," Kay said to Bowman.

Bowman made a face, then shrugged out of his Windbreaker and handed it to the driver. Bowman was so damn big that the Windbreaker reached almost to her knees.

"Okay, Carol, start walking," Kay said. "We'll leave your truck someplace where it'll be found. I promise. But I'm also promising that if you call anybody in less than two hours, you'll regret it. Do you believe me?"

"Yes."

"Remember, we know who you are and where you live."

Carol started walking down the road, and Kay got into the UPS truck. She made a U-turn and headed back to the house where Natalya Titov was being held captive. Morgan and Bowman followed in the SUV. When they arrived back at the house, Dotson confirmed that the two people in the house were still sitting in the room. Kay wondered if they could be watching television, Natalya still tied to a chair, wearing the bomb vest.

"Okay," Morgan said. "Bowman, get into position next to Dotson. As soon as you say you're ready, Hamilton will drive down the driveway in the UPS truck. When the guy shows his head in the window, take him out. Hamilton, you wait a minute before you go into the house after Bowman shoots the guy. You know, long enough in case the bomb goes off after he's hit."

Kay was thinking *this* was the real reason the CIA had involved the Callahan Group. No way would the FBI shoot a guy just because a GPS device showed he was in a room with Natalya, not knowing if Natalya was still there or who the guy even was. The FBI would have spent ten hours trying to talk Natalya's captor out of the house, and while that was going on, Titov would have handed over the information to the Chechens.

Kay got into the UPS truck, took off her ski mask, and put on the UPS ball cap. Two minutes later, she heard Bowman in her earpiece: "I'm in position."

You better not miss, Bowman.

Kay drove down the driveway and stopped thirty feet from the front door. She gunned the engine, hoping the guy inside the house would hear it. But he didn't; nobody pulled back a curtain to look out the window. If Natalya and her captor were watching TV like Kay thought, maybe they couldn't hear the truck. Shit.

Kay hesitated for a moment, then picked up a small package from the area behind the driver's seat. She got out of the truck, walked up to the front door, and pushed the doorbell button. "UPS!" she called out. She was thinking that if the bomb strapped to Natalya was as big as the one in Afghanistan, she could be dead in the next couple of minutes.

A moment later, she saw a man's hand pull aside a curtain and a man's face appeared—a young guy with a beard—and then the man's head exploded like a watermelon hit with a sledgehammer. Kay heard a woman scream inside the house but didn't go in. She threw herself to the ground in case the guy still had the motor skills to detonate the bomb. After a moment, when the only thing she could hear was the woman inside the house still screaming, she got up. She turned the doorknob, which was locked, then stepped back and kicked the door as hard as she could and it flew open.

The first thing Kay looked for was the man Bowman had shot, to make sure he was dead and not holding anything that looked like a detonator in his hand. He was lying under the front window, dressed in jeans and a white T-shirt. He was holding a pistol in his dead right hand—but nothing that looked like a detonator.

Natalya Titov was standing in front of a couch wearing

tight white jeans and a sleeveless blue blouse. She was barefoot. Kay's mind registered that the television set was on, tuned to *The Ellen DeGeneres Show*. Natalya's face and blouse were splattered with blood; the guy's head had just *disintegrated* and there was blood all over the room.

Natalya stopped screaming when she saw Kay and the Glock Kay was holding in her hand. She had her hands up to her mouth and was saying something over and over again in Russian, probably something like "Oh, my God. Oh, my God." Kay could see a gold, heart-shaped pendant hanging from a chain around her neck. The medic alert device. Once again, Kay had a fleeting thought of Anna Mercer, but she pushed it away to focus on Natalya.

"You're all right," Kay said. "You're safe."

Natalya Titov was a dark-haired beauty, maybe twenty-five years old, and with the body she had, Kay could imagine that she'd probably been in demand as a hooker in St. Petersburg. She could also understand why Leonid Titov had fallen in love with her.

"Where's the dynamite vest?" Kay asked. She could hear the vehicle containing Morgan, Bowman, and Dotson coming down the driveway and skidding to a stop in front of the house.

Natalya pointed to her left at a small dining room table, and Kay could see a canvas vest with what looked like sticks of dynamite attached to it. She took a breath and walked over to it—and saw the sticks weren't dynamite. They were road flares wrapped in a reddish-brown paper. There were a bunch of red, blue, and white wires Scotch-taped to the road flairs, the wires going to nothing electronic. There was no cell phone or receiver or blasting cap attached to the wires. The bomb vest was a fake, but it had looked like the real thing in the e-mail picture that had been sent to Natalya's husband.

Natalya was sobbing now, sitting on the couch. Kay sat down next to her and put an arm around her shoulder. "Hey, you're okay," she said. "And we're going to get your husband out of this mess. But did they hurt you? We're you raped?"

"No, I'm okay," Natalya said in heavily accented English. She paused a beat, then added, "Thank you. How did you find me?"

"Your locket," Kay said. "The medic alert device."

Natalya closed her eyes when Kay said this, probably saying a silent prayer of thanks.

Morgan, Bowman, and Dotson rushed into the house. Morgan looked at Natalya and the dead man and called Callahan. "We got the wife. Get us Titov's location."

Morgan hung up and said to Kay, "Is she all right?"

"Yeah," Kay said. "She's just shook up from seeing that guy's head blown apart."

Morgan pointed at the corpse and asked Dotson, "See if he has ID on him. And get his cell phone."

Dotson opened the dead man's wallet and said, "His name's Malik Zakayev. The guy the house is rented to."

Morgan asked Natalya, "How many men were with Malik?"

Natalya didn't answer, still in shock. Morgan repeated the question.

"I only saw one," she said. "Him and another man who took me from my house."

"Where is he?"

"I don't know. He left an hour ago."

"Did you hear the other man's name?"

"No."

"What did he look like?" Morgan asked.

Natalya shrugged. "Like him," she said, pointing at Malik. "Young, with a beard, but not so tall."

Morgan's cell phone rang. Kay heard him say, "How far is that from here?"

Morgan hung up and said, "Callahan talked to Titov. He's . . ."

"How was Callahan able to contact him?" Kay asked.

"I don't know," Morgan said. "Titov must have devised some method for communicating with him that wouldn't reveal his location. Anyway, he's in a motel called the Little River Inn, room 110, about fifteen miles from here; he knows his wife is safe. The kidnappers are supposed to call him in half an hour and tell him where to bring the information in exchange for his wife."

Morgan thought for a moment and said, "The guy working with Malik will probably come back here. He'll want to pick up Malik and Natalya for the exchange. I suppose there's a possibility he won't pick up Malik and will meet with Titov alone, but I doubt it.

"Hamilton, I want you to take Natalya to her husband. I want her out of here. Dotson, Bowman, and I will wait here. When the other Chechen comes back here, we'll take him. If the guy doesn't come back and arranges a place for Titov to meet him, we'll go to the meeting place and take him there."

Kay didn't like being cut out of the action, but decided not to argue about it. Morgan was right that Natalya shouldn't be exposed to any more danger, nor did Natalya need to see Morgan kill the other kidnapper if it came to that.

"You need to get the UPS truck out of sight," Kay said.

"Yeah," Morgan said. "We'll take care of it. Just get her out of here."

Kay took off the UPS uniform and put her jeans back on. She would take Natalya with her in the SUV Morgan had been driving. If Morgan and company needed transportation, they would have to use the UPS truck. When Kay had changed, she said to Natalya, who was still sitting on the couch, "Let's go."

"I need to wash the blood off my face," Natalya said. "And I have to take this blouse off. It's wet with his blood. I can feel it. It's making me sick. Let me see if I can find a shirt or a jacket to put on."

"Okay, do it quick," Kay said.

Natalya was gone a couple minutes, longer than Kay would have liked. The other Chechen could come back at any moment. When Natalya returned, her face had been scrubbed clean and she was wearing a man's long-sleeved plaid shirt, which had probably belonged to Malik. The tails of the shirt were not tucked in.

As they were leaving, Kay heard Morgan tell Bow-man to move the UPS truck, then take a position outside the house. Morgan and Dotson would remain inside to wait for the other Chechen.

Kay focused on driving, moving fast, to get to the motel where Titov was waiting. She wasn't really paying any attention to Natalya—and was completely surprised when Natalya pulled a stubby .25 automatic out from under the tails of the long shirt she was wearing. They were only a couple miles from the house where Natalya had been held captive.

"Pull over to the side of the road and stop. Now!" Natalya said.

Aw, shit.

"I didn't think about the damn locket," Natalya said. "I've been wearing it for three years and . . . Give me your cell phone. If you try anything, I will shoot you in the face the way you shot Malik."

"Okay," Kay said. "Just relax. I gotta unbuckle my seat belt to reach my phone." Kay unclipped the seat belt so she could reach into the back pocket of her jeans for her phone. She was thinking that when Natalya di-aled whomever she was about to call, she'd be distracted long enough for Kay to smash a fist into her pretty face and take the .25 away from her. She held the phone out to Natalya—but Natalya wasn't a complete idiot.

"No," she said. "Dial this number: 703-555-1492. Hurry!"

Kay dialed the number, and Natalya said, "Now give me the phone." The gun was steady in Natalya's hand, still pointed at Kay's face. A moment later, Natalya said, "It's me. Where are you?" A pause. "You can't go back to the house. Some men killed Malik." A pause. "Shut up! There's no time for that. Listen to me. You can't go back to the house. Three men are waiting there. They'll kill you. Meet me at the Little River Inn. You remember where it is? Titov is there, waiting for me. He'll have the money with him and the information." A pause. "There's no time right now. I'll explain everything later. I'll be at the motel in about fifteen minutes."

Natalya disconnected the call and looked at Kay. The gun was still pointed at Kay's face. Then Natalya's eyes narrowed and her full lips compressed—and Kay thought: *Oh, God*.

Natalya pulled the trigger on the little .25—but the gun didn't fire. In her rush to get a weapon from Malik's house, she never checked to see if the safety was on. Kay screamed, "You cunt!" and lunged at her—thankful that her seat belt was undone—and then just beat the shit out of Natalya Titov. By the time Kay was finished, she was holding the .25 and Natalya had a broken nose.

Kay found her cell phone, which had fallen to the floor during the brief fight. She was still shaken from almost being killed—she felt like punching Natalya in the nose again—and had to take a couple deep breaths before she called Morgan. "The other Chechen's not coming back to the house," she said. "He's headed toward the motel where Titov is. I don't have time to explain, but Natalya was in on this thing. I'm just a couple miles down the road, east of the house. Drive the UPS truck east until you see me, then we'll all go in the SUV to the motel, and on the way we'll figure out a way to take the other guy—who I'm guessing is Natalya's boyfriend."

43

Kay was waiting for Callahan to get off the phone so she could talk to him about the idea she had that might help them catch Mercer.

It had turned out that Kay had been right about Natalya: While Leonid Titov was busy each day in his little bookstore, his good-looking young wife met a handsome guy named Danilbek, but who called himself Danny. She discovered that he and his older brother—Malik—had been born in Chechnya but raised in America. Natalya and Danilbek fell in love, and during the course of the following year they hatched their plan.

Natalya knew about her husband's background, and her lover, who wasn't the least bit radical, knew a couple of truly radical Chechens in D.C. They came up with the idea of faking Natalya's kidnapping, getting the money Titov had in savings and some information Danilbek could sell to the hard-core guys in D.C. to make more money. After which, *they* would live happily ever after.

Morgan had no problem capturing Danilbek at the motel in Middleburg where he'd been sitting in his car waiting for Natalya to show up. Kay had no idea what happened to Leonid Titov, Natalya, and Danilbek after that. According to Callahan, the CIA was dealing with them and the Group's services were no longer required.

Callahan finally got off the phone.

"Did you look at Anna Mercer's medical records?" Kay asked.

"No," Callahan said. "I didn't see any reason to. Anna was as healthy as a horse. She never missed work for anything more serious than the flu."

"You need to check her medical records. Natalya's medic alert device made me remember something Mercer said to me the first time I met her. When she told me I had to take a physical before coming to work for you, I told her that I'd had a physical that year. Well, Mercer said, 'A lot can happen in a year. I should know.'"

"Huh," Callahan said.

"So I have no idea what she meant," Kay said, "but maybe she's got something wrong with her that we can use to locate her, like if she takes some exotic drug or needs kidney dialysis or something like that."

Kay was back in Callahan's office six hours later.

"Three years ago," Callahan said, "during a routine physical, Anna had some blood work done and they found her hemoglobin and hematocrit levels were high. This led to the diagnosis of a fairly rare but not really too serious blood disease called polycythemia vera. It's a condition where your body makes too many red blood cells. If it isn't treated, it can lead to heart attacks and strokes."

"When you say the disease is *fairly rare*, exactly how rare is it?" Kay asked.

"Well, it's not *super* rare," Callahan said. "About one person in a hundred thousand has it."

"How's it treated?"

"Ah, now, that's the thing," Callahan said. "The way this disease is treated, if it's not too bad, is by taking blood from the patient."

"Taking blood?" Kay said.

"That's right. You just take a pint of blood from the patient every few weeks, and sometimes that's enough to keep the disease under control. In case you're interested, the fancy name for bleeding someone like they used to do in the Middle Ages is *phlebotomy*. So what Mercer has been doing for the last three years, unbeknownst to me, is going to a blood donor clinic and they drain some blood out of her. In order to do this, of course, her doctor had to give the clinic a note saying she had polycythemia vera and phlebotomy was required. Like I said, this disease isn't that big a deal at the stage she's at. If it gets worse, she'll have to increase the phlebotomy treatments, and there are a couple of drugs she'll have to take." Callahan moved papers around on his desk until he found what he was looking for. "One of the drugs is called hydroxyurea—I think that's how you pronounce it—and the other is interferon-alpha, whatever the hell that is.

"So this could help, Hamilton. In addition to looking for single women buying one-million-dollar-plus homes and who go to fancy spas and like certain brands of furniture, we'll look for ladies who are being treated for polycythemia vera. And because the British have a national health care system, I figure we'll have a leg up on accessing medical records. Keep your fingers crossed."

PART IV

44

"I think we've found her," Callahan said. "Got her with the blood thing."

"Well, it's about damn time," Kay said.

"Hey, they hunted for bin Laden for a decade; I'd call four months pretty damn good. I was really surprised at how many rich, single women in their forties are buying expensive homes in England. I'm willing to bet that most of them got their money when they divorced their husbands because they were fooling around with younger women."

Kay just made a face in response to that piggish remark.

"Anyway," Callahan said, "a woman who is supposedly forty, according to her passport—which would make her five years younger than Anna—gave blood at a clinic in London for the purpose of controlling polycythemia vera. There's no record of this woman ever giving blood before. This same woman purchased a waterfront home two months ago for one point two million pounds, which is almost two million U.S. dollars. The place is near a picturesque spot called Viking Bay, which is near

Margate, about eighty miles east of London, and not too far from the famous White Cliffs of Dover. She also bought a dining room table identical to the one Mercer had in her home in Arlington."

"I thought you said Mercer had her blood drawn every month or so."

"She used to," Callahan said, "but her disease isn't that severe, she's not on medication, and she may have been willing to take the risk to have it drawn less frequently. Plus, like I said, she went to a clinic in London, about an hour and a half from where she lives. All I know is, I think this woman could be Anna Mercer."

Callahan reached across his desk—the effort made harder by the size of his gut—and handed Kay a picture of a woman with short blond hair who Kay thought looked about thirty-five, only four years older than her.

"This woman doesn't look anything like Mercer," Kay said.

"I know that," Callahan said. "But it's like I told you, I was almost positive she'd get plastic surgery to change her appearance. Her weight and height match Mercer's, and I had a couple of surgeons here in D.C. compare this picture to Mercer's old face and they said a good surgeon could make her look exactly like the woman in the picture."

"What do we need to do to confirm it's her?"

"DNA or fingerprints. We got Mercer's DNA when we searched her house, and we obviously have her fingerprints."

"Okay," Kay said, getting to her feet. "I'm heading over there tomorrow."

"You don't need to go. There are people in England I can use to follow her and get fingerprints off of something she touches."

"I'm going. I don't want to wait around forever for somebody to prove it's not her, and if it is her, I need to come up with a plan for dealing with her."

Before Callahan could object, she left the room. Because her back was to him, she couldn't see the smile on Callahan's pale face as she walked through the door. She would have hated that smile, because it meant she was predictable.

K ay walked along the beach in front of a house belonging to a woman named Abigail Merchant. There was no sign of spring in the air here on Viking Bay; it was a gray gloomy day, the wind blowing at about twenty knots, the rain slashing her face. Kay was wearing yellow rain gear, the hood covering her head.

The house Merchant had purchased wasn't all that impressive from the outside; that is, it didn't look to Kay like a two-million-dollar home, but it was seaside property with a magnificent view. Kay knew that the inside of the place, however, would look like something featured in one of those glossy magazines that showcased the homes of people with money and good taste. Kay had seen Abigail Merchant's credit-card statements, and they showed that in a two-month period Merchant had replaced hardwood floors, knocked down walls to expand the great room and the master bedroom, and replaced every appliance and fixture in the bathrooms and kitchen. She must have used a bullwhip on the contractors to get so much work done in such a short period of time.

Kay had yet to see Merchant, because after Merchant completed the remodeling job, she decided to take a vacation. Merchant was staying in a five-star hotel in Majorca, enjoying the sun and getting a treatment at a spa every day that cost about four hundred bucks. She spent three hundred dollars on one meal and she dined alone. She had a flight to return to the U.K. the day after tomorrow.

Kay had considered breaking into Merchant's home, where she was sure she would be able to find something with Merchant's fingerprints on it, but in the end decided not to. Merchant had a good security system that included cameras, and although Callahan had assured her that he had a guy who could get Kay into the house without setting off the alarms, Kay wanted to confirm that Merchant was Mercer before she broke the law and invaded the woman's home. Again, according to her credit cards, Merchant dined out practically every day even when she was at home, and Kay was confident she'd be able to acquire a glass or a knife or something with Merchant's prints on it.

Kay left the beach and walked between the home of

Merchant and her neighbor to the north. The houses in the neighborhood were all about a hundred and fifty feet apart but not enclosed by fences. Technically, Kay was trespassing, but she knew Merchant wasn't home to challenge her, and if Merchant's elderly neighbor—a woman who used a walker—came out to shoo her away, she'd apologize and be on her way. She'd say she was just trying to get up from the beach to the road that passed in front of Merchant's house and didn't want to walk all the way back to the place that allowed the unwashed masses access to the beach.

All Kay was doing on this visit was a general recon. She wanted to see the house, the beach, and the neighborhood. As she passed between the two houses, she kept her head down and the raincoat hood pulled tight around her face; she knew there was a security camera on the front of Merchant's home, over the garage, facing the street, and a second camera on the back of the house, facing the beach. She didn't want one of the cameras capturing a clear image of her face.

She walked up to the road that passed in front of Merchant's house. She knew that at night the road wasn't heavily traveled, and she could see there weren't any nearby streetlights. Merchant did, however, have a light near her garage door. She stood a little longer on the road looking at the garage—and a plan began to form. She walked back to her rental car, tossed the wet raincoat onto the backseat, and climbed behind the wheel, thankful to be out of the wind and rain. She couldn't help but think that if she had stolen fifty million bucks she sure as hell wouldn't have relocated to rainy old England.

She took out her phone and called Callahan's man, the one who had briefed her on Merchant's home security system. "Are you sure the garage isn't alarmed?" she said.

"Yes, dear. The door between the house and the garage *is* alarmed, but the garage roll-up doors aren't, and there are no cameras or motion detectors in the garage."

Just like Nathan Sterling's garage, Kay thought.

"But," the man said, "do you see the floodlight that's about halfway between the center of the garage door and the door to the house?"

"Yeah," Kay said.

"That's a complicated light. It contains a motion detector that turns on a camera installed in the base of the light. The motion detector also turns on the light. So if someone approaches the front door, the motion detector activates the camera and the floodlight, and the camera videotapes whatever set off the detector. But there's a flaw in the system, or at least I think it's a flaw. You see . . ."

"Tell me about the flaw later, but start thinking about how I can get into the garage," Kay said, and hung up.

There was no point spending too much time worrying about how to get past Merchant's home security system until she confirmed that Abigail Merchant was indeed Anna Mercer.

Merchant was back from Majorca, and at seven a.m. the morning after she returned, Kay was parked down the road from Merchant's house in a Toyota sedan. Kay didn't expect Merchant to leave her house at such an early hour, particularly as she'd just gotten home from a trip, but if she did, Kay would follow her and try to obtain her fingerprints.

Sitting with Kay in the Toyota were a man and a woman. They were all drinking coffee purchased from Starbucks; Starbucks had spread across the planet faster than any virus. The woman was in her sixties, dowdy, plump, and matronly. Her name was Blanche, or so she said. The man called himself Robert, was in his twenties, had longish hair, glasses, and looked rather wimpy. Both Blanche and Robert were dressed casually, but well enough to enter upscale restaurants and retail stores.

Callahan had provided Blanche and Robert when Kay told him what personnel she needed. Kay knew that they weren't employees of the Callahan group; they were, instead, people Callahan had on retainer and used when he needed them. Kay didn't like the fact that she was working with two strangers, and all she could do was hope that Callahan had vetted them properly. Kay also didn't like that these two had seen her face, and she intended to talk to Callahan later to understand what he was doing to make sure they didn't someday give her up to the English bobbies. Unfortunately, she had no choice but to use them, as she couldn't allow Merchant to see her face.

Kay was surprised when Merchant's garage door rolled up at eight a.m. and Merchant's black E-Class Mercedes-Benz, this year's model, backed out. Kay started her car and followed the Mercedes.

Merchant drove to Broadstairs, an oceanside town a short distance from Margate, and parked near a gym called Elite Fitness Studios on Thanet Road. Kay could see the exercise machines inside the place through its front windows. Merchant got out of her car carrying a large gym bag. She was wearing a beautiful leather trench coat over a robin's egg blue jogging suit. Her short blond hair was a bit mussed, as if she hadn't combed it before she left her house, and she didn't appear to be wearing any makeup. Kay watched Merchant walk to the entrance of the gym, and she arrived at the door at the same time another woman did. Merchant and the woman chatted briefly, then Merchant graciously held the door for the other woman.

Even though she'd spent hours with Mercer, sat numerous times no more than two feet away from her, Kay couldn't tell if the woman was Mercer. She'd been sure that if Merchant was Mercer, something would give her away: the way she walked, the way she held her head, maybe a gesture when she talked. There wasn't anything she'd seen so far, however, that allowed her to draw a conclusion; it appeared that she just hadn't paid enough attention to those sorts of details when she'd been with Mercer.

Well, there was one superficial indicator that the woman could be Mercer: The leather trench coat she was wearing had to have cost over a grand. Merchant definitely had Anna Mercer's taste for expensive clothes.

"We're just going to have to sit here and wait until she finishes her workout," Kay said to Blanche and Robert. "Why don't you two go get breakfast? I'm buying. Oh, and take a leak, because I don't know when you'll get another chance. Be back in half an hour." Actually, Kay just wanted them out of the car; Blanche was a talker, and Kay wasn't in the mood for listening.

Three hours later—while Blanche was going on and on about something one of her grandchildren had done and when Kay was about to strangle the woman if she didn't shut up—Merchant stepped out of the gym. Kay doubted she'd been exercising for three hours, and wondered if she'd had a massage or taken some steam. Whatever the case, she looked marvelous: hair perfectly combed, makeup perfectly applied, glowing with good health. She was still wearing the leather trench coat, but not the jogging suit. Instead, she had on a burgundy-colored skirt, a white sweater, and gorgeous knee-high leather boots that matched the trench coat.

Kay followed as Merchant drove to Margate and parked near the Ambrette Restaurant on King Street and sauntered inside.

Perfect.

"Okay, guys, you know what to do," Kay said to Robert and Blanche.

"Righto," Blanche responded, and she and Robert left the car. Blanche entered the restaurant first and Robert followed her in five minutes later.

Kay had already discussed with them what they should do if Merchant went to a restaurant: Blanche would try to get a table as close to Merchant's as she could, and as soon as Merchant paid her bill and left the table, and before a busboy could scoop up a glass or cup Merchant had used, Robert would knock the dishes off his table or blunder into someone else's table, making as much of a commotion as he could, and when everyone in the restaurant was looking at him, Blanche would snatch the item.

An hour later, Merchant left the restaurant and Blanche came out five minutes after her.

"Well?" Kay said as soon as Blanche got into the car.

Blanche handed Kay a wineglass wrapped in a cloth napkin.

Two hours later, Callahan informed Kay that Abigail Merchant was Anna Mercer.

"Do you have a plan?" Callahan asked, and Kay heard the sound a cigarette lighter makes. Kay could see him sitting at his desk in Washington, his pale, heavy face, his battered loafers on his desk, blowing smoke at the ceiling as he waited for her to respond.

"I'm not going to kill her," Kay said. Before Callahan could object or ask her why not, she said, "I want her to suffer. A bullet in the head just isn't good enough, at least not for me."

What she had just said to Callahan wasn't the whole truth: She did want Anna Mercer to suffer—she wanted her to suffer greatly—but that wasn't the only reason she wasn't willing to kill her.

Kay had done a lot of thinking since she'd killed Nathan Sterling. She'd never found out if she could be a cold-blooded executioner; Sterling eliminated her dilemma when he tried to kill her. She was now in the same position with Anna Mercer—trying to visualize herself dispassionately executing the woman—but this time she knew the answer: She couldn't kill someone that way; it just wasn't in her nature. If Callahan asked her to assassinate someone who was an imminent threat to the United States, then she could do it—but Mercer was not an imminent threat to national security; she was a murderer and a thief and she'd betrayed her country, but she didn't meet Kay Hamilton's personal criteria for assassination. There was a difference, in Kay's mind, between executing someone for a crime they'd committed and assassinating someone to prevent a crime—but she wasn't going to try to explain this to Callahan. She could barely explain it to herself.

She heard Callahan sigh into his phone. It was one of those *Please, Lord, grant me patience* sighs. "So what *do* you want to do?" Callahan asked.

"I don't know yet. Give me a couple of days."

Kay called Jessica after talking to Callahan, asked how things were going, and got the response she'd expected: Everything was going fine—but Jessica sounded a little down. Kay wondered if she'd had a fight with her boyfriend, or maybe she was just feeling lonely. God, she was a lousy mother.

"Are you sure everything's all right?" she asked. "Nothing's bothering you?"

"Nah, everything's cool here," Jessica said. "How's everything going with you?"

After she hung up, she sat for a moment, still holding the phone in her hand, then called Barb Reynolds. "I'm outta town and not sure when I'll be back. How about doing me a favor and take my daughter out to dinner or something. She sounded kind of low when I talked to her a couple minutes ago. Use your mommy antennae, and make sure everything's okay with her."

Kay said this knowing that although Barb had raised two boys she wasn't any more maternal than she was. But she couldn't think of anyone else to ask.

"Sure," Barb said. "I like your daughter. And when she gets her medical degree and I'm old and feeble, I want to be able to call her up and get free advice."

After Kay spoke to everyone she wanted to speak with on the other side of the Atlantic, she went for a run and took a shower. While she was drying her hair, she thought that after she'd had some dinner, she'd go spy on Anna Mercer some more. She was hoping that by watching the woman, some idea would occur to her insofar as avenging Ara Khan's death without killing Mercer.

As she was getting dressed, she turned on the television in her hotel room in time to hear a newscaster talk about how two thugs had been arrested less than an hour after they had robbed and beaten a merchant in London. It seemed that CCTV cameras had tracked them almost continually from the merchant's store, to the subway, while in the subway, and practically to the doorstep of the building where they lived. The announcer then said something to the effect that you'd think these idiots would know that the British population was being constantly monitored by cameras all over the country's capital city.

And it was like a little cartoon lightbulb clicked on over Kay Hamilton's head.

45

Kay called Callahan and told him what she needed: the security expert who'd researched Merchant's home security system, a man and a woman with a special skill set, and information that Callahan would have to obtain from the British cops, although the information was most likely not classified. Callahan was not happy to hear any of this.

"Aw, come on, Hamilton," he said, "gimme a fuckin' break. Why can't you just take care of her the easy way? This is too complicated, involves too many people, and there are too many things that can go wrong."

"Callahan, if we don't do this my way, then you've just wasted a lot of time and money training me."

Callahan didn't respond immediately. She knew he was pleased with how she'd handled Nathan Sterling and the bogus Chechen kidnapping of Titov's wife, but she also knew she wasn't irreplaceable. Furthermore, she was pissing him off by continually refusing to bend to his will. She wondered if he was about to tell her that he would, regretfully, accept her resignation.

He didn't.

* * *

The man and woman Kay needed for the operation arrived two days later. Judging by their accents they were Irish, and if they spoke fast, Kay couldn't understand what the hell they were saying. They were in their early thirties; the woman was about five foot six, the man a couple inches taller. They were both slender and had short, dark hair, the woman's hair not much longer than the man's; they looked so much alike that they could have been twins. They said their names were Jack and Jackie—Kay assumed the names were false but wasn't sure—and they took a single room in the same hotel where Kay was staying. Kay didn't know if she was abetting incest or not; she didn't care what they did in their hotel room as long as they could do the job.

Kay met with the security system expert at a coffee shop the following day. He was a tall, stout, grandfatherly-looking man with glasses and bright blue eyes that reminded her of Callahan's eyes. He was bald except for a white horseshoe of hair that circled his skull just above his big ears, and he wore a bright red vest under his gray tweed sport coat. He was a handsome man until he smiled and exposed stubby, crooked teeth. He introduced himself as Geoffrey, and Kay thought he looked like a Geoffrey.

Kay explained to Geoffrey half her plan—the half he needed to know—and asked if it could be done.

"Easily," he said. "You see, the house actually has two

separate security systems, and as I mentioned the other day, one of those systems is somewhat flawed. The primary system is the alarms she has on her doors and windows and the motion detectors inside the house. The idea of the primary system is that if a thief opens a door or a window or steps in the wrong place, a hideously loud alarm will sound and the security company will be notified and dispatch the coppers. There's a standard keypad, of course, for arming and disarming the alarm system.

"The pertinent thing that you need to know about the primary system is that it has a backup power supply. That is, if power to the house is interrupted because a power line is cut, the alarm system will still be functional. Are you with me, dear?"

"Yes," Kay said. For some reason, it didn't bother her that he called her *dear*.

"The secondary system is the cameras, floodlights, and motion detectors outside the house. They're basically designed to scare someone off. If a thief approaches the house at night, the motion detectors will sense him, the light will go on—hopefully scaring the bugger away—and the camera will take a picture. A video, actually. The secondary system does not send a signal to the security company, as it can be set off by any passing cat.

"Now, as you know, there are two floodlight cameras installed: one at the front of the house to detect someone approaching the front door, and one at the back of the house, facing the beach. The homeowner is probably most concerned about people approaching the house from the beach at night and breaking in through the sliding door that opens onto the deck facing the water.

"But herein lies the problem," Geoffrey said, flashing the briefest of smiles. Kay could imagine him as a young man trying to smile without exposing his teeth or covering his mouth when he laughed. "The camera-floodlight system is separate from the house alarm system and the floodlights are wired into the house's normal electrical system. What this means is that there is no backup power supply for the floodlights, motion detectors, and cameras. If power to the house is disrupted, then the cameras won't work until power is restored. The other problem with the secondary system is that if you know where the motion detectors are and how they work, you can evade them."

A fter meeting with Geoffrey, Kay waited until it was dark outside, then drove around the Thanet area of England. The Thanet area is located in the county of Kent and includes the towns of Margate, Broadstairs, and Ramsgate, all within a short distance of Mercer's home near Viking Bay. Kay was looking at CCTV cameras.

There are almost a hundred CCTV security cameras in the Thanet District—it says so right on the Thanet Council's Web site—and Callahan had obtained for Kay the location of a dozen cameras that seemed best suited for what she had in mind. Kay drove to each location, studied the cameras, the streets they were on, the general lighting in the area, the amount of traffic on the streets, and nearby homes and businesses. She finally selected the one that best suited her purpose.

The following day, Kay met with Jack and Jackie and told them what she wanted them to do. She also directed them to rent a car and reconnoiter the selected CCTV camera location so they could see for themselves what they'd be up against.

It was driving her crazy not knowing if they were perverted siblings or simply a couple who had identical names and looked like twins.

T he next day, at eight a.m., Kay parked her car near Mercer's home in a location where she'd be able to see Mercer backing her car out of the garage. Geoffrey was with her. In a separate car, parked on the same street, were Jack and Jackie. She didn't want Geoffrey and the odd couple to see each other.

Unfortunately, Mercer didn't leave her home at all that day. Kay could see smoke coming out of one of the chimneys and figured Mercer had elected to sit in front of a cheery fire and read a good book on a blustery, overcast day. Weather-wise, this time of year the coast of England sucked. At four p.m., when Kay was about ready to go crazy after sitting in a car for eight hours, she told her team that they were done for the day and dropped Geoffrey off at a pub before she returned to her hotel.

The next morning, her team took up their positions again. To Kay's relief, at nine a.m., Mercer left in her Mercedes, and Jack and Jackie followed Mercer in their car. Surveillance wasn't their area of expertise, but Kay figured they'd be able to do what was needed. Kay noticed the first time she followed Mercer that Mercer didn't seem to do anything to detect or shake a tail, and Kay figured that after still being free four months after fleeing the United States, Mercer was now confident that Callahan would never find her.

Kay and Geoffrey continued to sit in Kay's car after Mercer drove away. She was waiting to hear from Jack and Jackie regarding Mercer's destination. Half an hour later, Jackie called and said that Mercer was on the M2 and appeared to be headed to London. This was good news, but Kay decided to wait a bit longer.

An hour later, Jackie called again and said Mercer had checked into the Mayfair Hotel. This was consistent with a pattern that Kay had noticed in Abigail Merchant's credit-card records: She'd periodically make the trip to London, check into a good hotel, and spend a couple of days shopping and dining. Kay figured that Mercer wouldn't return home for at least twenty-four hours, which would give her and Geoffrey plenty of time to invade Mercer's home.

The only problem with breaking into Mercer's house was her neighbor to the north, the lady who used a walker. The neighbor to the south couldn't see Mercer's home clearly, because the view was blocked by shrubs and trees. There was no fence or greenery, however, to prevent the old lady with the walker from seeing people approach Mercer's front door. Kay decided that she and Geoffrey would just have to take the risk.

They entered Mercer's property by walking quickly along the southern edge of Mercer's front yard, as far as possible from the home of the old lady to the north. When they reached the southern front corner of Mercer's house, they sidled along the front of the house, staying close to the house and under the eaves. They did this because the motion detector in the floodlight camera was mounted on the edge of the roof, and although it pointed downward, it also pointed outward, as it was designed to catch people approaching Mercer's front door. The motion detector wouldn't detect them if they stayed under the eaves—or so Geoffrey said. Geoffrey used a set of lock picks to quickly open the front door—it took him all of twenty seconds—and Mercer's home security system immediately started beeping. Geoffrey walked calmly over to the keypad and entered an eight-digit security code.

When Kay had asked him how he was going to obtain the code to Mercer's security system, she'd expected some sort of high-tech answer, like maybe he would hack into the security company's computers to obtain the code. Or maybe he would bring with him one of those gadgets you see in caper movies and he would disassemble the keypad, snap alligator clips onto wires, and the gadget would determine the code—numbers flashing by on a screen as the clock ticked down, he and Kay sweating dramatically—and just before the time expired, the code would be solved.

Geoffrey's answer to her question, however, was neither high-tech nor dramatic. "The security company has a master code they can use in case of an emergency or if they have to troubleshoot a homeowner's system. Rather like a master key for hotel rooms. I paid a lady at the security company to give me the master."

"Oh" had been Kay's response.

After the security system had been disarmed, Geoffrey—who couldn't have been any calmer if he'd been standing in his own home—said, "I'd suggest we watch the street for about ten minutes to see if one of the neighbors called the coppers. If one of them did, I'm afraid we'll have to scamper out the back door and hope they didn't send young lads that are able to catch us. Or, more likely, catch *me*, as you look as if you might be able to outrun the local bobbies." So they waited ten minutes.

"Okay," Geoffrey said. "While you skulk about, I'm going to locate the breaker box."

What Geoffrey was going to do was attach an electronic "switch" on the wire going to the floodlight camera on the front of Mercer's house. The switch, which you can buy for about twenty bucks on eBay, was operated by a small remote control with a range of five hundred feet. In other words, a person standing outside Mercer's home could push a button on the remote and disrupt power going to the floodlight, disabling the camera and motion detector, and then turn the power back on remotely whenever desired. As the switch would only be on the wire going to the floodlight camera over Mercer's garage, power throughout the rest of the house would not be affected.

While Geoffrey was doing his job, Kay walked around the house and saw it was just as fabulous as she'd imagined: glossy hardwood floors, Oriental rugs, stunning pictures perfectly framed, furniture made from exotic woods. All the countertops were granite, or maybe marble. The only thing missing were photographs of people. There were no pictures of Mercer's family or anyone else she'd been close to, and the absence of photographs made Kay wonder if Mercer ever got lonely. She suspected not.

She located the room Mercer used for an office, and in the top center drawer of a gorgeous desk with inlaid woods made by an American company called Parnian, Kay found what she was looking for: a spare ignition key to Mercer's Mercedes and a fob attached to the key for locking and unlocking the doors.

There was a time when she could have made a wax impression of the key and taken the impression to a shady locksmith and have a key made. Those days were long gone. These days, ignition keys for automobiles were high-tech devices that had a transponder that electronically communicated with the vehicle to prevent theft, and the car wouldn't start if the key wasn't programmed to match the vehicle. Kay knew this because when she lost her car key once, it cost her about two hundred bucks to get a new one.

She wrote down all the identification numbers on the key and the fob, then searched Mercer's desk until she found a file that contained Mercer's automobile insurance policy. In that file, she found the make and model of Mercer's Mercedes and the VIN number for the car.

She then made a cursory effort to find information related to where Mercer had parked her share of the fifty million, but as she expected, she didn't find anything. There were no convenient paper statements from some bank tallying up how much Mercer was making in interest. She turned on the laptop computer on Mercer's desk, saw it was password protected, and powered it down. Mercer would not use her birthday as a password.

She could hear Geoffrey whistling, and a moment later he walked into the office where Kay was standing. "What a lovely home," he said. "This woman has exquisite taste."

"All done?" Kay asked him.

"Indeed," he said. "It was quite simple, as there was a single exposed wire in the garage going from one of the receptacles to the floodlight. I didn't even have to cut the power, so we won't have to run around resetting the clocks. Here you go." He handed her two small red remotes. Each remote was about the size of a disposable cigarette lighter and there was a black button in the center. Push the black button once and power to the floodlight camera mounted over the garage was disrupted; push the button a second time and power was restored.

"I also need an ignition key for a Mercedes." She handed Geoffrey the slip of paper that contained the information she'd written down. He looked at the paper and said, "Not a problem. I can have it for you tomorrow."

"Okay," Kay said, "let's take care of the garage door."

They walked into Mercer's single-car garage, which was practically bare. There were, of course, no yard tools or any other kind of equipment normal people would use to maintain a home, since Mercer hired people to do whatever work she needed done. There was a mountain bike propped against one wall that looked as if it had never been ridden; the tires on the bike were as clean as the seat.

Geoffrey then did exactly what that little man, Archie, had done in West Virginia. He took a black device that looked like a television remote, connected it with a USB cable to a small electronic box, and programmed the black remote to open Mercer's garage door.

So Kay now had two identical small red remotes that would disrupt power to the floodlight camera mounted near Mercer's front door and one large black remote for opening Mercer's garage door. As Geoffrey handed her the garage door remote, he said, "Like Bob's your uncle"—a British expression that made no sense to Kay.

"I want to do one other thing," Kay said. "I'm going to go into her office and I want you to shut the door leading from the garage into the house, and when I yell, I want you to open the garage door all the way up. I want to see if I can hear it opening when I'm in her office."

"Okeydokey," Geoffrey said. Kay couldn't believe how relaxed the damn guy was. She was expecting at any moment to hear a voice on a bullhorn saying: *You inside the house. Come out with your hands up.*

Kay walked into Mercer's office and called out to Geoffrey. She couldn't hear the garage door opening. It probably helped that Mercer's office was at the far end of the house, a long way from the garage.

Before she and Geoffrey left, she took a moment to look again at Mercer's magnificent living room. She could imagine the hours Mercer must have spent picking out each piece of furniture. She could imagine the pleasure Mercer must take each time she sat in the room.

She could also imagine the pain it would cause Mercer when she took it all away from her.

Geoffrey rearmed the security system and he and Kay left the house—taking the same path they took before, along the front of the house and under the eaves—and five minutes later were driving away.

"What say we go for a pint," Geoffrey said. "Ethel's not expecting me home until half past five."

"Sounds good to me," Kay said. After the nerve-rattling experience of breaking into Mercer's place, she could definitely use a drink.

* * *

Kay woke at seven the following morning with a slight hangover from drinking with Geoffrey. The Guinness she'd swilled had looked—and tasted, initially—like something drained from an engine crankcase, but after a couple of pints she'd gotten used to it. She bought a cup of coffee from the hotel restaurant and proceeded to the business center, where she typed out every action that Jack and Jackie would take that night. She printed out three copies, and at nine a.m. she went to the lobby where the couple was waiting. They looked bright eyed and cheerful—like they had just enjoyed delightful wake-up sex—and they were dressed almost identically in blue jeans, white T-shirts, and black leather jackets. She found it bizarre that they would dress the same way—but then, they *were* bizarre.

They had breakfast together in the hotel restaurant, and while they were waiting for their food to arrive, Kay gave them a copy of the plan. Jack looked at it and said, "Ah, the script."

Fortunately, they were quite bright; they didn't have any trouble understanding what they were supposed to do and they asked good questions. The only problem was that when they spoke in their god-awful Irish accents, Kay had to continually ask them to slow down and repeat what they'd just said. She wished it were like TV, with little white captions running along the bottom of the screen.

After breakfast, they drove to Mercer's house and Kay pointed out a few salient features, then they drove to the spot where the CCTV camera was located and Kay walked them through the plan again.

"So. Are you guys okay with this?" she asked.

She thought Jack said *It'll be a walk in the park*, but she wasn't sure.

46

Kay parked on the street in front of Anna Mercer's house at eight thirty p.m. She used one of the small red remotes provided by Geoffrey to disrupt power to the floodlight camera system so she wouldn't be captured on film, then walked up to Mercer's front door and rang the doorbell.

The porch light next to Mercer's front door came on and the peephole door opened, and Kay watched as Anna Mercer's eyes widened in shock when she saw it was Kay standing on her front porch.

Mercer recovered quickly, however. "Who are you and what do you want at this time of night?" She said this in a passable British accent.

Kay shook her head. "It's over, Anna. Let me in."

"I have no idea what you're talking about, and my name isn't Anna. Now, leave immediately or I'll call the police."

"Anna, it's over. We found you. The other day when you went to that restaurant in Margate, we took a wineglass you used and matched your fingerprints. Now, let me in so we can talk. If Callahan wanted you dead, we could have killed you any time after you got back from Majorca."

Kay kept saying "we," as she wanted Mercer to picture a squad of heavily armed men standing by, waiting for Kay to give the command to attack.

Mercer's eyes closed—a gesture of either surrender or resignation—and she said, "Just a minute." She dropped the Limey accent when she said this. She closed the peephole door and, about thirty seconds later, she opened the front door, and when she did, she was holding a pistol in her hand. It was pointed at Kay's chest.

Kay ignored the gun and stepped past Mercer and into the house, and with her back to Mercer, she pretended to take in the decor. "Wow," she said. "This place is fabulous, Anna." Turning to face Mercer, she said, "And you're fabulous, too. You'll have to give me the name of the surgeon you used." Then, being just a bit catty, she added, "When I get to be your age, I might make an appointment with him."

"What do you want?" Mercer said. The despair in her voice was evident; it looked as if she was struggling not to cry.

"Let's sit down," Kay said. "And put the gun down. It's really not in your best interest to shoot me."

Kay could imagine Mercer killing her, then killing herself. That wouldn't be good.

They took seats in Mercer's living room, Kay on a love seat, pretending to be completely relaxed, Mercer facing her, sitting in an overstuffed chair near the fireplace, ready to spring up at any moment. She was still holding the pistol, but now it was lying in her lap and not pointed at Kay.

"You know Nathan Sterling's dead, don't you?" Kay said.

"I read on the Internet that he'd disappeared," Mercer said.

"He's dead. I killed him. And thanks for leaving that cell phone lying under your bed back in Arlington. It was all the proof Callahan needed to convince himself Sterling had worked with you."

Mercer didn't care about Nathan Sterling. "How did you find me?"

"God! I can't believe how good you look," Kay said. "You don't have a single wrinkle on your face. It's amazing."

"Damn it! Tell me how you found me!"

"Your blood," Kay said, and explained how they searched for single women her age with polycythemia vera buying expensive homes. "When you gave blood in London a couple weeks ago, we thought it might be you and then confirmed it through fingerprints."

"But how did you even know I had the disease? I never told Callahan. I never told anyone. And I figured with a new face and the ID I was using, I'd still be safe, even if Callahan discovered it."

Kay didn't bother to say that she was the one who figured out Mercer's medical secret, not Callahan.

"I tried to take my own blood when I first got here,"

Mercer said, "but I couldn't do it. I just couldn't jam that big needle into a vein."

Kay didn't know what that meant: Was Mercer saying she was too squeamish to push a needle into her arm—she certainly didn't have a problem pushing a needle into Scarlett—or did she have the kind of veins that were hard to put a needle into? She didn't care.

"I even contacted a private nursing outfit to have them come here and take my blood, but they wouldn't do it because they said they weren't equipped to dispose of the blood, like it was toxic or something."

"Anna," Kay finally said, interrupting her monologue, "I really don't give a shit."

"So why haven't you killed me?" Mercer asked.

"Because Callahan won't let me. In spite of what you did to Ara Khan, he's decided to let you live. I don't know why. I guess he must still feel something for you. All I know is, he's giving you a break." She paused before she said, "But he wants the money back. All of it."

Mercer didn't say anything, but Kay could imagine what was going through her head: relief that Callahan was allowing her to live, but, at the same time, wondering *how* she would live if she was broke.

"I don't have all of it," she said.

"I know that," Kay said. "Sterling got five, and I don't know what you paid Finley or the two guys that helped Sterling, but my guess is that you have close to forty million left after you bought this house. Callahan wants it, and he wants it tonight.

"We know you have the money in some bank where you can transfer it quickly to another bank if you have to run, and you're going to transfer it to one of Callahan's accounts. If you don't, then the people waiting outside *will* kill you. And don't even think about running again. Now that we know where you are and what you look like, we won't lose you a second time."

Mercer started to cry, big tears streaming down her marvelous, unlined face. "The reason I did it . . ."

She stopped, not knowing what to say next, or maybe she was wondering how honest she should be. She started over: "I spent all those years working for Callahan and . . ."

"I don't want to hear it," Kay said. "You killed a young woman who could have made a real difference in this world, and there's nothing you can say to rationalize what you did. Now, let's go transfer the money. I'm assuming we can do that from your laptop. And this time, the money will go where it's supposed to since Finley's no longer alive to make it disappear."

"How do I know you won't kill me after I transfer the money?"

"Well, for one thing, I'm not armed and you have a gun. But I can assure you, somebody will kill you if you don't transfer the money."

Kay stood up and said, "Let's get this over with."

As Kay was following Mercer back to her home office, she speed-dialed a number on her phone.

* * *

Jackie felt her phone vibrate twice, then stop.

Jackie had driven with Kay in Kay's rental car. She left the car and walked directly down Mercer's driveway. She wasn't concerned about being captured on video by the floodlight camera, as Kay had disrupted power to the camera before she entered Mercer's home.

Jackie used the garage door remote that Geoffrey had programmed to open Mercer's garage door. Kay had told her that if Mercer was in her office, Mercer wouldn't hear the door opening. Jackie climbed into Mercer's Mercedes and, using the ignition key that Geoffrey had made for Kay, she started the car. She then pressed the button on the second red remote Geoffrey had provided and restored power to the floodlight camera.

The floodlight camera videoed the Mercedes backing out of Mercer's garage and recorded the time.

Fifteen minutes later, Jackie entered a romantically lighted—meaning *dimly* lighted—bar in Margate and ordered the first of what would be several martinis. Jackie was wearing a blond wig that matched Mercer's hairstyle and a shade of lipstick Mercer favored. And although Jackie was about the same height and weight as Mercer, she didn't look like Mercer—no one would have a problem telling them apart if they were standing side by side in a lineup—but Jackie had no remarkable facial features, such as an overlong nose or rabbity teeth, and in the poorly lighted bar it was hard to see her face clearly.

Jackie was also wearing a leather trench coat identical to the one Kay had seen Mercer wearing the day they took Mercer's fingerprints; the damn coat had cost the Callahan Group fifteen hundred dollars.

I t took an hour to transfer the money. The bulk of it was in a Luxembourg account, and when the transfer was complete, Kay called Callahan to verify the money was in the Callahan Group's account. "Are we done now?" Mercer said after Kay spoke to Callahan.

"No," Kay said. "You have over a million in a Barclays money market fund and thirty-eight thousand in your checking account. We want it all."

"What am I supposed to live on?" Mercer said.

"Not my problem," Kay said, "but I suppose you'll have to sell this place. Do they have yard sales in England? We were thinking about making you transfer the title on the house to us, but figured that would be just too much of a hassle."

Kay knew what Mercer was now thinking: Since she had no pension, Mercer was going to have to live the rest of her life on the proceeds from selling her house and furniture, and might end up with about two million bucks to live on for the rest of her life. She was going to have a hard time finding anything but low-paying jobs; she certainly wasn't going to be able to put down on a résumé what she'd done for Uncle Sam. And two million isn't really all that much money when you're only forty-five years old and might live another forty years.

But Kay didn't intend to leave Mercer anywhere near two million. She wasn't going to tell her that, however. She wanted to leave her with just a glimmer of hope regarding her future so Kay's revenge would be even more terrible. As she'd told Callahan, she wanted Mercer to suffer.

Mercer finished transferring the money she had in British banks, then just sat there in front of her gorgeous Parnian desk with her eyes closed and her head bent as if she were about to be beheaded. Kay was still standing behind her. She'd been standing behind her the whole time she was making the money transfers so she could see what Mercer was doing on the laptop.

Kay reached into the right-hand pocket of her bomber jacket and took out a small ampule. She slipped the plastic sheath off the needle attached to the ampule.

"I have to know something, Anna. Why did you kill Scarlett?"

"I just . . . I couldn't bear the thought of her in one of those disgusting animal shelters, surrounded by homeless cats. I thought she'd be better off dead than to be put in a place that was no better than a prison."

"Well," Kay said, "I guess you're going to find out if being dead is better than prison," and she slammed the needle into Mercer's arm.

Mercer's eyes popped open; she looked terrified. She

was probably thinking that Kay had poisoned her the way she'd poisoned poor Scarlett. "What did you do?" she said.

Five seconds later, Mercer's head fell onto the desk and Kay pulled her out of the chair and laid her on the floor. The drug Kay had just administered would keep Mercer unconscious for about two hours.

Kay walked to the front door of Mercer's house and, using one of the small red remotes, disrupted power again to the floodlight camera. She walked up the road in front of Mercer's house—out of range of the camera—and punched the button on the remote a second time, restoring power to the camera.

Kay got into her rental car, checked the time, then called Jackie. "Have one more martini, then meet me in front of the bar."

Jackie, as Kay instructed, ordered another martini— her third—and slowly poured the alcohol onto the rug under her table as she had done with the other two drinks she'd ordered. She then paid the bill with a Visa card that had the same numbers as Abigail Merchant's Visa card, and walked outside the bar to find Kay waiting for her.

"Where's the Mercedes?" Kay asked.

Jackie pointed; it was right across the street.

Jackie and Kay walked over to the Mercedes. Jackie got behind the wheel and Kay into the passenger seat. Jackie was wearing thin black leather driving gloves.

Kay called Jack. "We're on our way," she said.

Jackie drove for approximately ten minutes and stopped. Kay called Jack again. "Call me when it's clear."

"It's clear now," Jack said. "There's not a fookin' soul around." At least, that's what Kay thought he said.

To Jackie, Kay said, "Don't blow this. We've only got one shot."

Jackie didn't respond—her lips just twitched in a brief smile—but Kay could see that she was excited.

Kay stepped out of the car; Jack was waiting a block away. He was wearing a long-billed, much-abused baseball cap that partly obscured his unshaven face, a filthy ski jacket that had once been white, and dirty beige-colored khakis. He looked like he might be homeless. Kay wished she could get closer to where Jack was standing so she'd be able to see better, but couldn't because she didn't want to be captured by the CCTV camera at the intersection. She rapped twice on the roof of the Mercedes with her palm, and Jackie revved the engine like Danica Patrick on the starting line at the Daytona 500.

Jackie stomped on the gas pedal and then—traveling at approximately forty miles an hour—hit Jack crossing the intersection monitored by the CCTV camera.

Jack was flung high into the air and landed in the gutter like a broken doll. Jackie hit the brakes after the collision, got out of her car, and, walking a bit unsteadily, went over to Jack. She had her hands over her mouth—like a woman who couldn't believe what she'd just done—and the gesture helped obscure her face. Her hairstyle was completely visible, as was the trench coat she was wearing.

Keeping her head down, Jackie touched Jack's throat, looking for a pulse, then stood up, her back to the camera. She then appeared to look up and down the street, as if to see if anyone was nearby watching her. When she did this, she allowed the camera only the barest glimpse of her profile from the rear.

Jackie dragged Jack over to the rear of the Mercedes, popped the trunk, lifted him into the trunk with some effort, and drove away.

Jackie circled the block and drove back to where Kay was waiting. She popped the trunk again, and Jack hopped out and flashed a grin at Kay.

"You okay?" Kay asked Jack.

"Right as rain," Jack said.

"My Jack, he's a genius, he is," Jackie said. "He made it look like I broke him in two."

Kay wondered where they got their training—Hollywood or the BBC. Probably Hollywood. *Masterpiece Theatre* was all *Downton Abbey* and Jane Austen remakes, and the stunts involved horses and buggies more often than vehicular homicide.

There was a metal trash can on the curb near where Kay was standing. She picked it up, relieved that it didn't weigh very much, and said to Jackie, "Which side of the car hit him?"

"The passenger side," she responded.

Kay smashed the trash can into the front headlight on the passenger side, breaking the headlight.

Kay pulled a jackknife with a four-inch blade from a pocket, flipped out the blade, and handed it to Jack. "I need some blood," she said.

"Aw, man, do I have to do that?" Jack said.

"Yes," Kay said, "you're the only one here with male blood. Get on with it."

Jack winced when he cut his left palm.

"Cut deeper, you wimp," Kay said. "I need more blood."

"Aw, Christ," Jack said, like he was about to ampu-tate his own hand, but he drew the knife across his palm again. When his blood was flowing freely, Kay had him dribble a bit over the area of the broken headlight, dribble a bit more onto the expensive leather trench coat Jackie was wearing, then had him deposit a tablespoon of blood in the trunk of the Mercedes.

"Okay, that's good," Kay said. To Jackie she said, "Drive the Mercedes back to Mercer's place and wait for me in the garage. The garage door's open. I'll follow you in my car."

To Jack she said, "You can head back to the hotel." Jack had come in the car he and Jackie had rented. "Good work," she added.

"Jaysus, this hurts," Jack said, pressing a handkerchief against his self-inflicted wound. Kay just shook her head: Getting tossed into the air by a vehicle moving at forty miles an hour and weighing almost a ton didn't bother him, but he was whining like a little girl about a small cut on his palm.

Kay followed Jackie back to Mercer's, stopping her car about half a block from Mercer's house. Jackie drove directly into the garage—and the floodlight camera videoed her driving the Mercedes into the garage and recorded the time.

Kay used one of the red remotes to disrupt power to the floodlight camera and joined Jackie in the garage.

"Give me the trench coat," she said, and Jackie handed her the coat, now smeared with Jack's blood.

Kay entered the house and walked back to Mercer's office to make sure Mercer was still unconscious. She was. Kay picked up Mercer's laptop; she planned to take it with her when she left. She was concerned that the laptop would have a record of the time when Mercer had transferred the money. Kay knew that Mercer couldn't tell anybody about the money, but she didn't want the laptop to provide her any sort of alibi. Next she looked into the closet near the front door, found

Mercer's leather trench coat, and replaced it with the one Jackie had been wearing.

The end result of everything that had transpired in the last two hours was that there was a video record of Mercer's car leaving Mercer's garage at approximately nine p.m. and returning to the garage at approximately eleven p.m. Those times coincided with the time Jackie was swilling martinis paid for using Mercer's credit-card number. There was also now a trench coat in Mercer's closet smeared with Jack's blood and matching the blood in the trunk of Mercer's car—the same trench coat that would have been captured by the CCTV camera as Jackie was placing Jack in the trunk of Mercer's Mercedes-Benz.

Photographs, credit-card numbers, and blood analysis were much, much better, in Kay's opinion, than human eyewitnesses.

On the way back to their hotel, Kay left Jackie in the car and used a public phone to call the police. Adopting a Jamaican accent, she said she'd been walking, coming home from work, and saw a woman hit a man with her car but the woman didn't call the police. Instead, she placed the man's body in the boot of her car. The police operator asked for the address where the accident had occurred and Kay gave it to her. When she asked for Kay's name and address, Kay said that because of her immigration status she preferred not to provide that information.

When the operator asked how long ago the incident happened, Kay gave the exact time, and when asked why she'd waited so long to call, she said she couldn't find a public phone. Kay knew the call was being recorded, and she concluded by saying, "I'm sure she killed that poor man. If she'd been taking him to hospital, she wouldn't have put him in the boot."

When they reached the hotel, Kay couldn't help herself. "How long have you and Jack been married?" she asked Jackie.

Jackie laughed and said, "We're not married. We're livin' in sin."

But that's all she said, the bitch, and Kay still had no idea if they were brother and sister or just a twisted couple who looked like twins.

47

Anna Mercer—known to the police as Abigail Merchant based on her driver's license, passport, and credit cards—was arrested six hours after Kay called the police. Hoping to get her to confess and plead guilty, and thus save the Crown the expense of a trial, the cops laid out their case: CCTV camera footage of her hitting a man with her car and dumping the body into the trunk; a clear image of the license plate on a car registered to Merchant; credit-card statements supported by statements from a waitress that Merchant had had three large, dry vodka martinis in a two-hour period; blood on the damaged right front fender and in the trunk of Merchant's car; a video recording obtained from Merchant's own security system showing her leaving and returning to her home consistent with the time she'd spent in the bar and when the man had been run over.

The fact that Merchant refused to reveal what she had done with the body added another dimension to the case. For one thing, the poor man couldn't be identified and his next of kin notified, and her refusal to say where the body was showed just how cold and calculating Merchant was. That wouldn't go over at all well at her trial.

Merchant's only response to these charges was to say she was being framed. She couldn't say by whom, but she claimed it was obvious that that's what had occurred. She screamed that she couldn't tell them where the damn body was because there was no body.

At her first appearance in court, a bewigged judge clucked his tongue at her brazen lies—but he did grant her bail. When the police received a phone call a day later, her bail was revoked.

K ay called Callahan and asked: "Did you take care of the fingerprints?"

"Yeah, that turned out to be pretty easy, because the only time she was fingerprinted was when she first signed on at the State Department. She never got a DUI or worked for anybody else who required fingerprints, so her prints weren't on file in a bunch of other places, like criminal databases."

"Good," Kay said.

"When are you coming back?" Callahan said.

"Soon. I just have a couple more things to do."

F ollowing the anonymous call from the woman with the Jamaican accent, the police dug a bit deeper into Abigail Merchant's background—and discovered she

had no background. Merchant had appeared out of nowhere approximately three months before, and although she claimed to be a British citizen she had no
employment, tax, or scholastic history in the U.K. They
took her fingerprints, but she had no fingerprints on
file, not in the U.K, or with Interpol, or in the United
States. This brought British intelligence into the case,
wondering if Merchant was some sort of undercover-
sleeper agent working for a foreign government. The
Cold War was supposedly over, but this was the sort of
thing the damn Russians would do.

When the police confronted Merchant with the fact
that she was not whom she appeared to be, she didn't
say anything. She couldn't point the finger at Callahan,
because Callahan would have her killed for sure. She
obviously couldn't say she'd obtained false documents
to flee the U.S. after killing Ara Khan and stealing fifty
million dollars.

Mercer was informed that her bail was being revoked
until she cooperated and told them who she really was,
or until such time as they could figure out who she was.
They took her passport, clamped a GPS bracelet onto
her right ankle so they could keep track of her, and gave
her a week to put her affairs in order.

Mercer hired a lawyer in London who had a good
reputation, but when the man asked for a twenty-five-
thousand-pound retainer, she said that was going to be a
problem. She explained that she had only ten thousand
dollars in cash and she needed some of that to live on.

(Hamilton had forced her to transfer all the money she had in British banks but hadn't known about a box in her attic that contained her rainy-day cash.) However, Mercer told the lawyer, she was putting her home on the market immediately, expected to clear at least a million and a half dollars, and as soon as the sale was complete she'd be able to pay his fees. The lawyer wasn't a bad guy: He took five thousand for his initial retainer and agreed to trust her for the remainder of his fee provided he could confirm she was making a genuine effort to sell the house and, when it was sold, the money would be put into an escrow account.

Mercer contacted a real estate agent and, crying the whole time she was talking to the man, told him to put her house on the market and to sell all the furniture for the best price he could get. She said things were going to be a bit complicated as she would be in jail, awaiting trial. The agent wasn't a bad guy: He raised his commission by only one percentage point to compensate for the hassle.

One day while Mercer was meeting with her lawyer—and two days before she would be remanded to jail to await trial—Kay punctured two of the tires on Mercer's Mercedes to give herself some extra time, then she picked up three hooligans that the old thief Geoffrey had recommended. The hooligans had shaved heads, multiple piercings, and numerous tattoos. In other words, they looked like the guys who started riots at British soccer games, and at ten in the morning they all smelled of beer.

Kay drove to Mercer's house and, using her magic remotes, killed power to the floodlight camera over Mercer's garage, opened Mercer's garage door, and drove her car into the garage. The hooligans then unloaded Kay's rental car, taking from the trunk sledgehammers, crowbars, gallon-sized cans of purple paint, and two chain saws. Kay and her three companions entered Mercer's house via the door in the garage that permitted entry to the house and, using the code previously obtained by Geoffrey, disarmed the security system.

Then the hooligans destroyed Anna Mercer's fabulous home.

They smashed toilets and marble countertops with the sledgehammers. They plugged all the sinks and turned on the water to flood the floors. They splashed purple paint about until the paint cans were empty. They punched holes in walls, ripped out electrical wiring, and used the chain saws to cut enormous, jagged holes in the hardwood floors. Almost every piece of furniture in the house was demolished, including the beautiful love seat that Kay had sat on when she'd visited Mercer. After they finished with everything in the living sections of the house, Kay directed two of the hooligans into the attic, where they cheerfully chain-sawed through a number of joists necessary for structural support, and cut a four-by-four-foot hole in the roof.

Mercer's homeowner's insurance would—eventually—pay for the damage and, being an insurance company, they wouldn't give her anywhere near enough to cover all the repairs or to replace what had been destroyed. It would take months to repair the damage—the structural damage to the roof was going to be a bitch to fix—and there'd be no one available to really supervise the repairs. If Mercer sold the house in the condition it was in, she'd be lucky to get one-tenth the price she'd paid for it.

Mercer would have been much better off if Kay had simply burned down the house—which was why she didn't burn it down.

Mercer was supposed to turn herself in a week after the judge had revoked her bail—but she didn't. When the police arrived at her house, they found her sitting on the back deck, facing Viking Bay. She was soaked to the skin from a gentle rain, and there was one empty vodka bottle on the deck and one half-full bottle on a table next to the Adirondack chair in which she was sitting. On the same table was the pistol she'd pointed at Kay Hamilton.

The police assumed that she'd been sitting there contemplating suicide—and they were correct. She seemed almost catatonic as they led her away.

* * *

As near as Kay could figure, based on a Google search, the maximum penalty in the U.K. for a hit-and-run death was fourteen years—and she was confident Mercer would spend at least that much time behind bars in view of the disappearance of the victim's body, Mercer's refusal to cooperate, and her questionable identity. She'd spend fourteen years in jail thinking about everything she'd lost and knowing that when she got out, she'd be sixty years old, totally broke, a felon with a record, and unemployable.

Kay thought all that was better than shooting a bullet into Mercer's head and putting her out of her misery.

She had only one thing left to do with regard to Mercer.

Kay called Jessica and said, "Hey, do you think it would be okay if you missed a couple days of school?"

"Yeah, I guess. Why?"

"I was thinking that you should fly over to Merry Old England and meet me. We'll go see the place where Henry the Eighth chopped the heads off all his wives."

"Well, actually, he only executed two of them. Anne Boleyn and—"

"Whatever," Kay said, rolling her eyes. "You wanna come?"

"Yeah! That would be great!"

"So get a ticket to fly over here on Thursday and we'll fly back home together next Tuesday. And Jessica, pack a few things so we can go out to dinner someplace nice."

She meant: Bring something besides jeans and sweat-shirts.

"One other thing. Fly first class. Mommy's getting a bonus."

She hadn't spoken to Callahan about a bonus, but she would. She figured she deserved one.

The morning of the day she was supposed to pick up Jessica at Heathrow Airport, Kay stopped at the jail where Anna Mercer was being held pending her trial.

When Mercer was led into the visitors' room, she didn't really look all that bad except for the fact that her hair was plastered to her head as if she hadn't showered in days and her dark roots were beginning to show. She moved like she was shell-shocked, and a guard had to lead her over to the table where Kay was waiting.

"I want to show you something, Anna," Kay said.

Mercer didn't respond—and Kay wasn't sure that Mercer had understood what she'd said. The lights were on, but nobody was home.

Kay took out an eight-by-ten color photo and placed it facedown on the table. Mercer didn't react.

"I have it on good authority," Kay said, "that you're

going to be incarcerated in Bronzefield Prison in Surrey. Bronzefield is a Category A prison for females, meaning it's a maximum-security pen for really bad apples. You're a designated bad apple not only because you killed a guy and hid the body, but because nobody knows who you are."

Kay flipped the picture over so Mercer could see it— but Mercer didn't look at it.

"Look at the picture, Anna," Kay said. When Mercer still didn't look, Kay barked, "Anna!"

Mercer finally looked down at the picture, but she didn't react.

The picture showed a woman with a face that would terrify children—or grown men, for that matter. She was of mixed race, dark complexioned, her head was large, her eyes were small, and her nose appeared to have been squashed flat. Her hair sprang out from her head in all directions.

"That's Margaret Chase—Big Maggie to her friends," Kay said. "She's currently serving twenty-five years without the possibility of parole in Bronzefield. She's six feet three inches tall and weighs two hundred and forty pounds. She's in Bronzefield for killing her husband, his girlfriend, and her husband's Yorkie terrier, and you know how the British feel about dogs. She beat them all to death with a cast-iron frying pan.

"Anyway, the Callahan Group has placed Ms. Chase on retainer. She came quite cheap: six cartons of cigarettes, two dozen chocolate bars, and twenty-five pounds will be mailed to her every other month by a lady named Blanche, one of our associates in the U.K.

"The reason I'm telling you about Margaret Chase, Anna, is if we hear you're talking to anyone about the Callahan Group, Maggie is going to pay you a visit. Do you understand, Anna?"

Mercer didn't respond; she just continued to stare down at the picture. But Kay couldn't tell if she was really seeing it.

Kay stood up. "Well, I sure as hell hope you understand, because everything I just told you was true." Kay picked up the picture of Margaret Chase and walked away, leaving Mercer sitting at the table staring down at the place where the picture had been.

Jessica was beaming when Kay met her at baggage claim at Heathrow. She was so excited she couldn't stand still, and she reminded Kay of a little kid who'd just heard the ice-cream truck coming down the street.

Jessica held up a book that was over four hundred pages long: Fodor's travel guide to London. "I read this on the flight and made up a list of the places we have to go see. Did you know that right where this airport is, that in 1564 . . ."

Kay knew she was going to be bored stiff looking at museums and art galleries and ancient castles for the next four days—but if it made her daughter happy, that was all that mattered. She was going to make more of an effort in the future to enjoy Jessica's company before she grew up and became a hotshot doctor too busy to spend time with her mom.

48

On the flight back to D.C. from London, Kay tried to sleep but couldn't. She was exhausted from her and Jessica's whirlwind, seemingly nonstop tour of London, but she couldn't get her brain to stop spinning.

Jessica, on the other hand, was having no problem sleeping, and she had a small smile on her face like she was dreaming about something pleasant. Kay thought she looked so incredibly young, and she couldn't imagine the road that lay ahead of her, the years of studying, the exams, the constant pressure of life-and-death decisions. But if anyone could do it, she knew Jessica could. They'd had a great time in London, and she felt closer to the girl than she ever had.

Kay had also reached a decision about Jessica and Brian and sex. Although she still thought sixteen was too young for sex, she knew she couldn't stop Jessica—any more than her mother had been able to stop her when she was fifteen. Next year the girl would be seventeen and in college, and she'd have almost no control over her daughter's life at that point. The best thing she could do was make sure that Jessica understood that she'd always be there for her, no matter what. And she would be.

The reason she couldn't sleep had nothing to do with Jessica, however. It was because she had two decisions to make—and one of those involved Eli Dolan. She wanted him back—and if she was going to get him back, she needed to make the first move, because it was obvious by now that he wasn't going to. She still hadn't apologized to him for suspecting him—and she still didn't really feel that she owed him an apology. He may not have been guilty, but suspecting him had been logical.

No, that was not the right way to approach him, talking about how she'd acted *logically*. That wasn't going to fly. She was going to have to say that she was sorry; she wasn't going to grovel—but she'd say she was sorry. She'd say that she should have listened to her heart instead of her brain, and in the future, she'd be more trusting and less cynical and not jump to conclusions so quickly and . . .

Yeah, right. Anyway, when she got back she'd fly up to New York and talk to Eli.

The bigger decision she had to make, even greater than the one involving Eli, was did she want to keep working for Thomas Callahan? She liked being involved in covert ops—that's where the action was. And what she'd done recently with the North Korean scientist in Geneva, the Chechen kidnappers, Nathan Sterling, and Anna Mercer—she was good at those kinds of jobs. The problem was, she had no way to know if Callahan was telling her the truth. For example, she'd asked him once—this was a few weeks after the Afghanistan operation had fallen apart—if the lithium had really been intended for peaceful energy production. He'd acted surprised and said, "Yeah, of course, why wouldn't you think so?"

She'd responded by saying, "Because DARPA works on military applications, and I'm wondering if they were really planning to use the lithium to build a big, better, more powerful bomb." She didn't tell him that it was Jessica who had led her to ask the question.

"Hell, we don't need any more nuclear bombs," Callahan had said. "And why would I lie about something like that?" Before Kay could respond to what Callahan clearly considered a rhetorical question, he said, "Although I was talking to a guy the other night—just a guy, not the president's guy—and he was telling me how there are these asteroids out in space, zooming around, and a few of them have come pretty close to hitting the earth. Close being like a hundred thousand miles. Anyway, he was saying one day we might have to send a spaceship up with a great big bomb and explode it on an asteroid to knock it off course. Like that Bruce Willis movie."

Kay had thought, *Bruce Willis, my ass,* but she couldn't tell if he was lying. And the answer to Callahan's rhetorical question *Why would I lie?* was that he might think lying was in the country's best interest and that a person at Kay's level shouldn't be told the truth because the truth needed to be carefully guarded. Which led to another issue: Exactly who was it who was deciding who needed to know the truth?

Kay had come to the conclusion, like Barb Reynolds had said, that Callahan didn't really work for the president. He had all these spidery connections to places like the CIA, the Pentagon, and Homeland Security. He had people who gave him computer advice and were able to monitor phone calls, which could mean the NSA, and he was able to get these agencies to do his bidding. Kay had never liked the checks and balances imposed on federal agencies by a virtually useless organization like Congress, but logic told her that *someone* had to do some checking or things could get totally out of control. Callahan—and whomever the hell he worked for or with—certainly thought they were doing the right thing when it came to protecting the country, but they were the *only* ones deciding what was right . . . and that could be dangerous.

So what should she do? The smart thing would be to quit. Just walk away while she could, before she was indicted as Callahan's codefendant or before she got killed. But then who would employ her and how would she support herself and her daughter?

Oh, hell, she'd decide later, the next time she talked to Callahan. She had made up her mind about one thing: When she got back to D.C. she was going to *make* Callahan tell her whom he really worked for, and if he wouldn't . . . Well, she'd cross that bridge when she came to it, and maybe tell Callahan where he could shove that nondisclosure agreement she'd signed.

49

This time Callahan met his partners—who still thought they were his bosses—at a horse ranch in northern Virginia, a lovely place with rolling green pastures that were enclosed by white wooden fences. There was a FOR SALE sign hanging on the gate that led to the house.

Prescott met him at the door—her platinum-blond flapper's hair contrasting absurdly with her sixty-year-old, perpetually frowning, wrinkled face.

She greeted him with: "Why in the hell can't you ever get to these meetings on time?"

"I had to go to the emergency room," Callahan said. "I thought I was having a heart attack."

"Oh, bullshit," Prescott said.

Callahan just shrugged in response to her comment, but he was telling the truth. He actually had thought he was having a heart attack, and he drove himself to a hospital, where a doctor told him it was indigestion, not a heart attack, and for God's sake, lose some weight and stop smoking.

Once again they gathered in the kitchen, where there was a table large enough for them to all sit together.

Callahan wondered why they couldn't sit in the living room and, by the way, have a drink while they chatted.

The kitchen table was round, so Lincoln couldn't sit at the head of it, although he probably figured that wherever he sat was the head. Prescott took a seat to Lincoln's right. Grayson was already seated on Lincoln's left-hand side; Grayson was wearing his usual tweed sport jacket, this one with patches on the elbows, but he had a tan, making Callahan wonder where he'd been. None of these people ever took vacations.

"We're not happy, Callahan," Lincoln said. "We're not happy at all that you disobeyed our order to terminate Anna Mercer."

When Hamilton had refused to kill Mercer, Callahan had no choice but to tell Lincoln that it had been *his* decision. He told Lincoln the same thing that Hamilton had said to him: that he wanted Mercer to suffer for what she had done and that a bullet to the head was really too good for her.

"She's been taken care of and she's not going to talk," Callahan said. "So is that why you wanted to meet today, to argue some more about killing Mercer?"

"No," Lincoln said, "but we will hold you responsible if she ever does talk."

Callahan didn't know what *hold you responsible* meant—and he didn't give a shit. What did they think they were going to do? Put a letter of reprimand in his personnel file—like he actually *had* a personnel file?

"We're also not happy with this new operative of

yours, this Hamilton woman," Prescott said. "We've been told you can't control her."

Whoa!

"You've been *told*?" Callahan said. "Are you telling me that you've turned one of my own people and that person is reporting to you directly?"

Prescott twitched her almost nonexistent lips—a movement intended to resemble a smile. "The way things have gone the last few months, we feel the need to keep closer tabs on you, Callahan."

"Well, I'm going to find out who this person is," Callahan said decisively—he suspected it was Morgan—"and then I'm going to rip his nuts off."

Before any of them could comment on his turning Morgan into a gelding, he said, "And Hamilton's a great operative. She's a little hardheaded, but she gets the job done."

"We want her gone, Callahan," Lincoln said.

"I'll think about it," Callahan said—but he wouldn't. "Is there anything else?"

Before Prescott could erupt like a volcano and rain lava-like curses down upon his head, Grayson said, "Who's going to replace Anna Mercer?"

"I don't know," Callahan said, "and she's going to be tough to replace."

What Callahan meant was that he'd never been a detail guy. He was a big-picture thinker, and Mercer had always taken care of the details. And he couldn't replace Mercer with somebody like Hamilton; Hamilton had proved she could plan an operation, but she didn't know Washington, D.C., and how all the various agencies worked together— or, more accurately, how they *didn't* work together.

"We'll see if we can find you a replacement," Lincoln said, pretending he was being helpful. "We have a couple candidates in mind."

"The hell you will," Callahan said. "There's no way you're going to pick my staff."

They all just sat there staring at him for a couple of minutes as if their glowering faces would intimidate him. Finally, after a silence, Callahan said, "Well, if there's nothing else, I might as well get back to work."

"There is something else," Lincoln said. "Venezuela. That's the main reason we wanted to see you today. With Hugo Chávez gone, we see certain opportunities opening up for us down there."

Which made Callahan immediately think of Kay Hamilton, who spoke Spanish like a native.

"But Callahan," Lincoln said, "I'm telling you right now that things can't continue the way they've been. We're not going to tolerate your flippancy and your in-subordination any longer."

Callahan sighed. It was time for the speech. Again.

"Guys," he said, "anytime you don't like the way I work, all you have to do is start using your own agents to do the things you ask me to do. But until you grow the balls to do that"—he said this looking directly at Prescott—"people like me and Kay Hamilton are the best option you've got."

AUTHOR'S NOTE AND ACKNOWLEDGMENTS

The idea for *Viking Bay* came when I read an article about the 2007 U.S. Geological Survey that identified the large lithium deposits in Afghanistan. The funny part is that I had actually written the first draft of the novel when I came across James Risen's 2010 article in the *New York Times* where he wrote about the Chinese attempting to bribe the Afghan minister of mines with thirty million dollars to obtain copper mining rights. I had no idea, until I read Risen's article, that my fictional plot was so close to reality.

I want to thank John and Jenny Matterface, long-time fans of my DeMarco books who live within walking distance of Viking Bay. John and Jenny graciously read and helped with the scenes set in the Viking Bay area. Any errors with regard to the U.K. scenes are mine and mine alone.

I also want to thank Joe Lehnen of the Virginia Department of Forestry. Joe was kind enough to take the time to talk with me about the Devil's Backbone State Forest and send me some maps. I picked Devil's Backbone as the place where Anna Mercer and Nathan

Sterling met simply because I liked the name. I did make up the campsite where Sterling and Mercer met.

Last, I want to thank everyone at Blue Rider Press and penguin associated with this book and the previous Kay Hamilton book, *Rosarito Beach*. In particular, I want to thank Eliza Rosenberry, whom I failed to acknowledge in *Rosarito Beach,* and who worked so hard on the publicity and book tour associated with that book. I also want to thank, once again, my editor, David Rosenthal, for all his work on *Viking Bay*. The plot of *Viking Bay* was significantly improved because of his astute comments.

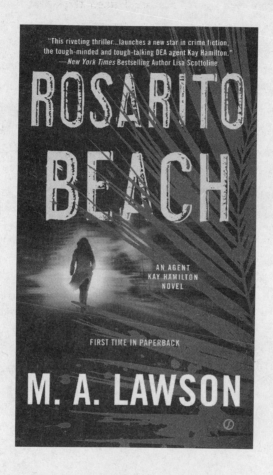